What people are saying about Rubble and the Wreckage

Can you trust a serial killer that has no remorse? That bathes in manipulation? I am not going to tell you if Christian trusts, believes, or falls for any of it but I will tell you it's a drug for those who crave a dark twist in their daily reads. It's hot between these two. It's also suspenseful and nerve wracking. Venture outside your comfort zone for this book. —*Diverse Reader*

A psychological thriller, this book was a page-turner from beginning to end. I highly recommend Rubble and Wreckage. —*Joyfully Jay Reviews*

This is a wonderful book for the person who likes stories that offer in depth character studies of flawed people. Both men are very complicated and probably equally fragmented except on opposite sides of the law. Rubble and the Wreckage is a sizzling read. Nothing is what it seems; nor is it so simplistic as a killer grooming a writer to be a patsy for murder like a predictable TV movie. —*Love Bytes Reviews*

Author Rodd Clark grabs your interest quickly in this book and never lets you go. (It) is a deep, well thought out, eloquent book. This book is definitely a must read if you like M/M romance, psychological thrillers. —*Rebels and Readers Books*

If you are looking for something sort of darkish with a non-traditional storyline that makes you think outside the box, you should check it out. —*Fangirl Moments and My Two Cents*

Rodd is an amazing narrator and manages to weave a thrilling and intriguing tale of Sex, Lust, Love, Mystery and Danger. —*Bayou Book Reviews*

RUBBLE AND THE WRECKAGE

The Gabriel Church Tales, Book One

Rodd Clark

A NineStar Press Publication

Published by NineStar Press
P.O. Box 91792,
Albuquerque, New Mexico, 87199 USA.
www.ninestarpress.com

Rubble and the Wreckage

Printed in the USA
First Edition
April, 2018

Print ISBN: 978-1-948608-58-9

Also available in eBook, ISBN: 978-1-948608-53-4

Warning: This book contains sexual content, which may only be suitable for mature readers, and scenes of graphic violence, suggestion of child sexual abuse, on-page child physical abuse, use of derogatory language, and homophobia.

Special thanks to
Richard for allowing me to have the courage to continue the plan.

The world is a kosmos;
to pray for a change in its arrangements is to pray for its destruction.
Creed and Deed—A Series of Disclosures by Felix Adler, 1880

"Everything crumbles..."
Gabriel Church

Introduction

"TELL ME YOUR story," Christian Maxwell began, wetting his lips and leaning in. He stared at the killer across the table and rested his forearms on the notepad before him, watching how those pale eyes were darting from side to side as he surveyed his surroundings. Even with his look of nonchalant detachment, it's clear he was a man who lived his life on a razor's edge and nothing escaped his observations.

Gabriel Church looked back at the writer. His eyes implored, practically begging for good and gory details. The man squinted a bit in excitement for that which was to follow, glassy-eyed in anticipation. His expression was wanting. Gabe had seen that look many times before.

Gabe was reminded of that old saying "Better the devil you know." Although he barely knew this guy, he might as well be making money off his story as anyone else. Just like the first time he thought of telling what happened, the memories came through as something indifferent and emotionless, and with more afterthought than close consideration.

"Ever been out to the Florida Keys?" Gabe asked. When he only received a nod from Maxwell to his question, he continued absently, "For me it was like driving to the Keys, a few miles over the speed limit on that old US Route 1—you know, the one they called *the Highway that Goes to Sea*—under fleecy clouds with the fresh coastal winds slapping you in your face, under a vast, unending blue on blue...it is rather freeing." His hands wrapped around the dusty old cover of the book he was holding, more as an effect than something to read.

With a faraway gaze in his eyes, Christian listened to him speaking. He pretended to jot notes down and concentrating more on that distant expression on Church's face. Christian let the words take him to Florida, where he imagined the wind slapping his hair, the sun beating down as he rode in the passenger seat of Church's mental trip along Highway 1. It was going to be a good book when he finished it.

He didn't want to interrupt the man but couldn't resist. "It didn't begin in Florida did it? I presumed it happened elsewhere."

The killer's posture changed as he replied. He sat up straight in the chair, his eyes narrowed. "If you think you know where it started then why are we sitting around hashing old news?" His voice was steady and cold and dampness grew under Christian's pits.

"Because no one has ever asked you for your side of it. Usually a serial murderer doesn't get a chance to explain why he murders. And I"—pointing to his chest—"want to give you that opportunity."

"Mighty big of you," Gabe said as he reclined backward in his chair and stared at him in knowing, mocking fashion. It was as if he was acquiescing solely because it represented an interesting way to spend his idle time... He rubbed his rough forefinger across the lip of the wine glass as a carnal abstraction as he watched Maxwell jot his notes, even though they hadn't even begun his tale. "Shouldn't you wait till I start to speak before you scribble down all those pretty words?"

Christian looked up and smiled sheepishly. "It's just mood stuff. You'll have to get used to that early on—meaning my process." He put his pen down and folded his hands neatly to hide his notes. "I'm a little fastidious or obsessive at times."

"No worries. The same has been said of me."

The bent smile of a killer reappeared and twisted Church's face into a mocking evil caricature, sending a shiver down Christian's spine. He smiled back and returned a look that seemed to place them on equal understanding. It was going to be tough yet totally worth it, he thought. At least after the book was complete. And so he picked up a pen and fell headlong into his task and flashed another imploring gaze in the direction of his sexy study subject then waited.

Gabe recognized the untidy anticipation and reluctantly continued, "Actually, it began in Texas, still we need to go back to where the...umm, desires, I guess is the word, first came into clear focus, don't we? I mean, you want the full picture, don't you?"

When Christian didn't even offer a conciliatory word, Gabe continued. "Before Florida, before Seattle, I had been somewhere else... It was a better place for me because it still held some type of promise. Nothing exactly carved into stone...if you'll pardon the pun." Church's head lolled back as if he were about to break into a hearty laugh.

He was a dangerous, sick man. Anyone could see that. His reference to the markers of his varied victims, as well as his nonchalant manner in describing his affinity to murder, was unsettling, even for someone as akin to pathology as he was. In college, Christian Maxwell was known for a dark sense of humor and an uncomfortably quiet nature. It was off-putting to many of his peers. His so-called friends would jokingly offer that it was going to be Christian who would be famous, more for the salvo of bullets that hit other students from his safe vantage in some random clock tower or rooftop.

The look on Maxwell's face, as he sat across from Gabe, was pensive as if he was about to interrupt again but questioned the insolence. The killer had nothing but time, and didn't like breaking his train of thought so early.

"You're looking like you want to derail the train, my boy. So what's your affliction, Adelaide? You have some thoughts you wanna share?"

Christian hung his head in shameful anticipation of the words that would follow. His efforts in getting the interview were substantial, and he didn't want to fuck up before he even got the first few chapters down on paper. He wanted it to linger, to drag out the tale and capture every subtle nuance. He thought the killer might become agitated with schoolboy innocence and enthusiasm.

In truth, Gabe was enjoying the salivating younger man hanging on his every word, like a lover anticipating their next stimulating, wet kisses.

"I'm sorry. I apologize, I do... I just wanted to ask you about the first time you killed?"

Gabe laid the book on the table at his side and crossed his arms. "Patience is a virtue, son. To know the story, we have to go back. Back to before I would gain fame with my exploits."

Café patrons brushed past their table on a regular basis. Each man and woman who walked by seemed absorbed in their own dreary lives; each one seemed conjoined to a cell phone that was fused to their ear. The killer took a sip of his wine and gestured to the throngs of people around him. "This is why it's so easy to become a killer," Gabe offered, waving a hand to indicate the self-absorbed masses at his left and right, "Because no one seems to be concerned with anything but their own mundane lives. None of these assholes have a life that warrants their constant connection to offices and friends. Nothing they have to offer is worthy of their inscrutable attentions. What did Ezra Pound say? 'Where the dead walked and the living were made of cardboard'?"

Christian looked up from his notes, catching the man staring intently at him.

"What? You think just because I'm a killer I can't be well-read?" Gabe asked, smiling. Leaning in closer, he rested his wine glass between them, grinning to show he understood that both men shared a common epiphany. He was quickly carving out how they would react to one another: him with nothing but a sardonic grin and Maxwell with a glint of understanding in his eyes.

"The secret to moving so unobtrusively through life without being caught as you commit such horrible crimes is to act like a moron. Just pretend your life is as important as the sacks of shit that surround you. It's hard to look pomposity directly in the eye. Given any other option, a person will choose to look away just to ignore it." Turning back to his wine, he said, "It's all the settling of dust and too many days. You wipe it, and it just gets dirty again. People think their lives mean a good goddamn, but they don't. If you know this certainty, you can move through the crowds as quietly as a mouse in a barn filled with cats."

Church's eyes shone like diamonds as he recalled his life. He was just as happy in telling the tale as Christian was to listen. He drained the last remnants of his wine and handed the empty glass across the table. "To keep talking, I need a drink," he said with some authority.

Christian took his cue, grabbing the glass and hurrying to the counter. He wouldn't wait for table service. This was just a high-end café, and a waitress wouldn't be handy. As he slunk off like a servant to do his bidding, leaving the killer alone at the table, he had forgotten to carry his notepad along. When Christian returned minutes later, he saw his companion scanning his notes, smiling. He was nervous about what Church would say after he had finally written the story out.

"You've already outlined some broad brushstrokes of my life," Church said as he tossed the pad back onto the table and whisked the glass of chardonnay out of Christian's hand.

"What is your religious stand?" Gabe asked. As Maxwell seemed dumbstruck by the random question, he continued, "Do you believe in God?"

"Err, well, I guess I was raised Protestant, but I haven't been inside a church since before college. Why do you ask?"

"A faith in God may be an intricate aspect of our time together, one never knows..." Gabe trailed off, distracted by the crash of other ideas racing in his head, waiting impatiently to escape.

"I wasn't always a killer as you know, and you may want to know what drives the beast before you hear about my first endeavor with murder."

Christian seized his chair and pulled the legal notepad closer. With a pen in hand, he looked at Gabe: the face of an infamous murderer. Maxwell appeared much like a begging waif; those words *"May I have another, sir?"* just waiting to fall from hungry lips.

For the next hour, Christian Maxwell wrote furiously as Gabriel Church told his story. The die had been cast in those sixty minutes or so. He was a killer who was regaling his student, all to the creation of a madman and the events of murder. As he spoke, even he saw the transposition from disciple to something more. The look in his eyes was proof—he was breathing in the contagion with every word the killer uttered.

Chapter One

WALKING THROUGH DREAMY memories might be a favored pastime of the old and the weary. For Gabriel Church it was a drain. He pocketed those recollections where they couldn't be easily found. But now he was sifting through the decay, retrieving them for his obsessive confidant. He enjoyed talking about his life, at least how it ended up during these last few years, and he enjoyed seeing the astonished look on the faces of his audience; however, having to dredge up the past was exhausting. But he understood it was good to begin a story from the beginning. How else might he explain his life, without explaining where he had escaped from? He knew his father was a big part of the equation of what was to become Gabriel Lee Church, so he began with him.

Bennett Church wasn't a kind man; specifically he wasn't kind to his children or his wife. His family was forced to receive the brunt of his emotional instability. They accepted their fate with every backhanded swing or disdainful look. The public saw a much different persona in Bennett, and when Gabe arrived at school with occasional blue bruises, black eyes, or tiny scratches, no one could have envisioned just how he got them. "Boys will be boys," they would say, but the secretive, shameful looks from the Church children should have been ample reason to question what lay before them, exposed, like an open nerve.

"You need to build up your character," his father would say as he set unreasonable tasks as punishments for the smallest of infractions in his daily routine. When Gabe had been six or seven years old, Bennett found him playing with his tools on the garage floor one Sunday afternoon and lit into him with a vengeance. A man of reason might see that as a potential bonding moment between a father and a son who was obviously emulating the man he admired. A sane man might laugh at the sight of such a small boy playing at the pretense of hero worship or developing strong masculine characteristics. But Bennett didn't see things the same way most fathers did; instead, he slapped the boy on the back of his neck watching the wrench the boy held go flying from his tiny hand.

Gripping the boy by the nape with a single arm, he yanked him quickly from the concrete floor, pulled the boy's pants down, and gave him a sound thrashing on his bare bottom. Nevertheless, that wasn't his only punishment. He forced Gabe to clean the gutters for the remainder of that once lazy Sunday, and the image of that diminutive lad dragging a ladder around that weighed nearly as much as he, and struggling to prop it against the house was saddening to watch. Gabe's mother had witnessed his punishment from her position at the kitchen window as she was washing dishes. Gabriel glimpsed her eyeing him as he stoically dragged the ladder from spot to spot, pulling gunk and dead and rotting leaves from the trough. His eyes seemed to beckon to her, while instead she chose to look down and focus her attentions on her soap-filled glasses and dirty dinner plates. It was about that time where the boy learned the first of many tragic lessons to come.

Little Gabriel Church may have cried that afternoon; he couldn't quite remember, but he had stared at a red Popsicle he had pulled from the fridge before he first found himself playing in the garage. He'd forgotten about it because of his whipping and subsequent punishment. He stared at the large red stain as it dissolved into a puddle on the driveway, melting in the oppressive Tennessee humidity. He couldn't seem to pull his gaze away. It was as if the pooling red had somehow fractured his mind, and he found comfort with that. It may have been but a single moment in time, but it was a moment that would have lasting effects.

Bennett never issued a decree, or commanded any punishment, without watching the outcome. The day of the gutters, he'd pulled out a lawn chair from the garage to observe his son's progress. But more importantly, to ensure the satisfactory completion of the task. Gabe remembered it well. It had been an aluminum chair with blue nylon webbing; the kind they first sold in the fifties and still sold to this day. Bennett sat drinking a beer and lounging in that familiar old blue lawn chair, and the boy could almost catch a sneer in a corner of each eye. He was too young to understand that look at the time. Yet given his later experiences, he might've recognized it later for what it truly was...sadism. There were twisted mechanics in Bennett's logic. Gabe and his sister, as well as his mother, had been the recipients of that logic, and the ensuing punishments for failure in adhering to Bennett's strict codes. Not all moments held Bennett's wrath, some days he was simply quiet and even-tempered. To Gabe, it was like watching a hungry dog that wouldn't eat... It was only then that you needed to worry.

Bennett would turn out to be a case study in psychosis; his son would study the man with an obsessive duality, equally afraid while utterly fascinated. Bennett's wife and daughter though never saw that keen understanding masking the man's true nature. They were fortuitously blind where Gabe's vision seemed more clearly defined. It would take years before Sissy Church found the strength, or courage, to finally leave her husband, and even then only from the sanctuary of her sister's place in upstate New York. It wasn't surprising to anyone who knew her though; the scars were plainly visible and the damage too ingrained in hers, and her children's psyches. An intangible fabric stretched too thin across the loom and borne from years of untold abuses too numerous to count. Sadly for Gabe and his younger sister, they would never truly learn whether there had lasting effects from their upbringing, because they had nothing to compare it against. It was all the normal they'd ever known. Yet for Sissy it was that persist reminder lingering continuous and unanswered through her mind... "What if I'd only left sooner?"

CHRISTIAN WAS AN educated man. He understood as Church recounted his childhood and the influences that had shaped him. It would never be a single item that made him a killer, and it couldn't be. There would be too many stimuli and far too many weighty pressures creating a sociopath like Church, but he'd taken notice of how the killer began his tale with the story of his father.

The downtown streets of Seattle began to bustle with evening crowds. The patrons at the Cherry Street Grinder were finishing their coffee and liquors, and the mood transformed from afternoon leisure to the excitement of Seattle nightlife. Church had finished three glasses of wine in the hour or so they sat at a table as Christian scribbled frantically on his notepad, desperate to capture every shade of the man he claimed as his subject. And it was only the beginning. He couldn't chain the man to a table and hold him prisoner. But there was going to be a great deal he needed to hear before even beginning his draft. Seeing the brooding irritation building in the killer meant he had to keep him entertained without overstepping his role.

"So...when will you be ready to discuss your first murder?" The words fell like stones from his lips. He could see Church was caught off guard—

apparently recalling painful memories pissed him off—because when he turned toward his spellbound audience, Christian caught the killer's expression and another shudder crept down his spine. Someone dropped a utensil somewhere off in the direction of the kitchen, and the sound shattered the indelicate moment. Christian was thankful for the noise, which startled the café dwellers and pulled focus from his question. He caught the lingering scent of freshly ground coffee, and noting the lateness of the day, he had to remember he was in Seattle. Caffeine-swilling, healthy-looking people—the type who thought wearing cargo shorts to a wedding was damned appropriate. But he loved it here. There didn't seem to be any other city that better suited his relaxed and laid-back attitude. What else could one expect in a town founded by whores and flannel-wearing loggers?

Church had settled back into his chair and crossed his arms again. His light-gray eyes sliced a countenance that Christian could not fathom—it was cold and unreadable. His look could have said a dozen different things, but their emotional void made any understanding a challenge. Watching him, Christian began to see what a powerful hold he might have exercised over more than a few of his many victims. Had he enticed his quarry with his strong features or white smile? Or was it something sinister he wondered; like stalking a wounded gazelle from the shadows he hid inside? There were questions that Christian needed answering, and he only hoped Gabriel Church would allow him another meeting under that great pretense of him writing the life story of a soon-to-be-famous serial killer.

It was as if Church had picked up on the writer's brooding contemplations and attempted to ease his concerns. "S'all good, little buddy..."

Christian's thoughts and any explanation for his arbitrary statement trailed off and became absorbed in the sounds of people brushing past in mid-conversation holding coffee cups and wine glasses, like the oblivious sheep they were.

"We can jump ahead if you're so inclined...but trust the Sherpa, and know we will be traveling back around to the beginning before it's all said and done." Church gazed off at some distant horizon and placed a finger on his lips in abstract reflection, as if remembering his first victim was something he had to pull from his memory. And actually he remembered it all too well. Christian sat mesmerized, hanging impatiently for every detail of the story to come.

"My first kill came when I was quite young. My temper was worse back then, and I stumbled around without focus or direction. I have gained a maturity and wisdom to the things I do now, but the first time had been rash and unplanned. I would say it ended badly, but every foal that'd ever fallen from its mama's womb had to struggle to stand. I guess I wasn't any different."

"I was twenty-one and feeling smug and certain back then. I'd been drinking a lot in those days, and my inexperience always led me down the wrong paths. I'd been headed to Fresno. A friend told me about a guy who was hiring, and I needed work. But the drive cross-country didn't really do me much good. It took longer than it should, and I became distracted along the way. Originally I had told my well-meaning friend I'd meet up with him in Fresno—he was gonna put in a good word for me with the owner. It was some shitty dispatch job at a freight company, but like I said, I was only twenty-one and didn't have a lot of appreciable skills...unlike now."

Church quickly grabbed his crotch, surprising Christian. "Ya see, I had a twenty-one-year-old cock and a love of beer. Who'd ever thought I would've made it across the country for some fucked up interview before I found trouble...and trouble I did find."

As Christian scrawled notes, the speed of his writing almost made the words indecipherable. The excitement had prickled the hairs on the back of his neck, and he mentally tried to race ahead during Church's tale, anticipating the outcome.

"I had stumbled into a bar at some midpoint in my journey. I was in some rundown city just out of Dallas. The drive left me tired and parched, and that shit hole was the first place I came to. I think my intention was to get a motel room, have a bite and shower, and rest up for another long day on the road, but that didn't work out as planned."

The younger man looked up from his writing. It dawned on him, at that moment, how deep and resonant the killer's voice was. He had an unmistakable timbre, which seemed pleasing to his ear, and even though the words were flat and without range, he never had that drone of a long-blowing horn. All in all, it was a pleasant sound. Church seemed to choose his words carefully, like he was practicing them in his mind before they escaped his tongue.

"I never made the motel, rather, choosing to stop in for a cold one at some rustic pool bar, and when I did I spied a group of men playing poker at one of the tables in the back. Musta been a regular game, 'cause they all seemed to know each other pretty well. Now, I'm not a great card player, and I don't know why, but I asked to join in, and they all agreed. Too heartily, I see that now, but I guess I had money in my pocket I was itchin' to lose, or it was the cold Budweiser hitting me fast, or that old familiar devil crooking his finger at me, imploring me to sit and play."

"And so you stayed," Christian offered as some lame crest to his story, and to illustrate just how enthralled he was.

"Yeah, I stayed, then after a few rounds of cards and beers one of them saw I was winning...and that by God was just sheer luck! 'Cause like I said, I wasn't good at cards. Then this asshole starts suggesting I was cheating. Looking back, I'm sure none of the guys at the table really thought I was cheating. I suppose it was just backslapping bullshit by drunk fuckers who were used to ribbing each other too much. Still, I was a stranger at their table and being cocky and twenty-one didn't take too kindly to the accusation. There were words, harsher I suppose than they shoulda been. Then I decided it was time to head out, but only after I raked in my winnings and pocketed the cash. Dammit, I didn't cheat anyone! I was just a lucky son of a bitch."

Church looked down at his empty glass and then up at Christian. There was a clear understanding that on the next lull in the conversation the writer was expected to scurry his ass up to the bar for more drinks. Gabe's look seemed to say "I'm not your sister, and I don't give it up for free!"

"Of course, I didn't do the wise thing and drive my beat-up Chevelle to the nearest motor lodge, leaving the distasteful incident behind. *No.* I sat outside the bar and waited for two more hours, just watching the door. When the big man who'd sullied my character walked out and got into his pickup and then drove down the highway—presumably headed home—he had someone following him." Church leaned closer to Christian and whispered so others might not hear his story.

"It didn't take much. It had been barren out there on those no-name rural roads. Running his truck off the road was just good driving on my part. Didn't give a shit what it mighta done to my car, I was too pissed to care. I tried one of those pit maneuvers the cops are so proud of. His truck barreled off the road and into a tree line, upending nearly a quarter mile of barbwire fence. I'm about as good at driving as I was at cards, just lucky, thoroughly lucky that night, but he was probably three sheets to the wind by then anyway. His head must've hit the steering wheel 'cause when I came up behind him, he seemed dazed. I slammed my own car into park and ran to his driver's side door and flung it open.

He was a big man, outweighed me real good. But he was either too drunk or too dazed to comprehend what was happening. I pulled him to the ground and kicked him square in the head. My boots had steel toes, and the blood splattered, like when we used to shoot up watermelons when I was a kid. I had already grabbed my hunting knife from the glove box and drove it all the way to the hilt, right there into the side of that fat fucker's neck. If the kick hadn't done it, the blade did. He wallowed like a sick cat in the grass and weeds on that dark, deserted stretch of road. Eventually he bled out, but not before he received a few choice kicks to the stomach and even one in his nuts."

Christian stopped writing long enough to look up. "Looking back now, after all that's gone down, do you regret killing him?"

"Regret's a powerful word, and I can't regret it because I hadn't any feelings either way at the time. I was just being stupid and rash. I mean I should've gotten caught on that one kill alone. As it stood, I didn't. And once I yanked the knife outta that guy's neck, I sped away contented to leave that shit-stain of a town behind. And I didn't stop until I was almost to Arizona. Fortunately for me, the county police were too stupid or lax to ever try and hunt me down. In fact, until now, no one else had even heard of that part of my tale."

Church smiled through sickly grin, as if they were somehow linked by some furtive secret of clandestine lovers who met under the cover of night. Christian only returned his stare unaffected, yet silently wondered about all the things that must be going through the other man's mind. He had become connected to a murder in some backwoods town in East Texas— one that might be recorded in some dusty banker's box, sitting forgotten on a metal rack and slapped with a big label, the words "cold case files" stamped on the side.

He felt an odd sensation sitting across the table from someone who freely admitted to murder, knowing that single homicide would start a chain of events that would remain miraculously unbroken by his arrest or conviction. It was equally strange carrying the knowledge that Church and he were the only living souls who knew what truly happened that night, and how that ill-fated poker player had actually died.

Christian would, at the first opportunity, research unsolved stabbings in cities near Dallas during those years when Church could have been in the vicinity. But he failed to reason what he would do if he found a case fitting Gabriel's details. Would he inform the police? There hadn't ever been anything more than a gentleman's understanding between the two men that Christian would record the life story of Gabriel Lee Church. The killer had not asked for his complicity in any crimes, nor had he ever asked for his silence.

This should have alarmed him, because there were always questions hovering in the ether between them: What was his endgame? Why did he want his story told? Did he have some nefarious plan for his biographer? And why had he granted him such unfettered access into his very personal horror movie?

Outside the Cherry Street Grinder, the typical mist of rain began to splatter on the sidewalks and windows. One thing Christian enjoyed about the city was how often it rained. Still, very few true-residents actually carried umbrellas. As one might've expected. It was a signature trait of the born and bred native to show a level of unconcern with the climate. For most it was simply an overnight guest who'd outstayed the welcome, yet sadly was showing no sign or desire of wanting to vacate anytime soon. Those with northwest blood in their veins just understood; that Seattle and rain just went hand-in-hand together, like the old lovers they were. It also made it easier to differentiate between the locals and the tourists. You merely looked for the umbrellas or an unnecessary abundance of outer winter wear.

Still, Christian couldn't help but wonder if after meeting this killer it wouldn't be his body turning up in some rain-soaked back alley downtown. As he headed away from the café, he smiled through his darkly twisted thoughts, a reminder that he had yet to begin his novel. Who knew, police might find his remains before the book could gain a voice and its direction, long before an editor's red-pen notes could be scrawled amid the margins.

Chapter Two

CHRISTIAN WAS BORN into a family with proper history and substantial wealth. This made him stand apart from most of his peers in public high school. None of that truly bothered him though. Not even when he was teased and ridiculed because of every quality which made him different instead of all those similarities actually shared. He would occasionally hear the tittering remarks as he passed: that odd boy who everyone suspected would end up being someone firing a rifle into the commons. Glinting gunmetal sparks from the safety of the university clock tower, or hidden amongst the kudzu of a secluded grassy knoll.

College would be easier, he told himself. He simply had to learn more patience. It crafted his personality early in his academic career and made him seem cool and reserved, like a studious professor, instead of another everyday kid struggling to obtain his first PhD. That alone was enough to ostracize him, and he was often reminded how it could've been far worse. Because he knew he at least still had his looks. How much more difficult high school could've been if he'd been a pudgy, pock-marked loner with a bully target on his back like a kick-me sign.

Most students would recall the image of Christian Maxwell carrying an armload of books through the common areas, occasionally dropping one and having to stop and reposition his stack before hurrying off to wherever students like him traveled to. People would tell the stories later, and as each one did, they became infinitely closer to Christian socially than the actual truth allowed. Everyone wanted to be famous, if only by affiliation. No one understood the full distance of miles between Christian and the usual crowds. If they did, they wouldn't say, or they hoped anyone hearing their tale wouldn't make the connection.

He was bookish at times, although he considered it scholarly. He appeared morose by his silence and still demeanor, but to him, it was just observation. His grandfather, who'd been more like him than any other member of his family, always offered the best advice, ultimately becoming the strongest influence over how the boy would turn out. Christian remembered him saying once that it was more important to watch others for a long while before you approached them. When you did that, you learned their personal strengths and flaws and were better informed of their character before you were formally introduced. Although he'd only been a boy when he heard that, he took it to heart, foolishly believing it gave him a social advantage, when in reality it just made him seem a little creepy to those who didn't know him.

One might assume high school was a tougher road for such a socially awkward boy, but it was actually his time spent at the university. Cruelty comes in many forms, and as Christian was already considered odd by some, it drove a wedge hard into his soul as he ventured into his own maturity. Sitting in his dorm room, staring out to the quad, he used to watch couples cross mowed emerald lawns, hand in hand, and he would hate them for being in love and for having someone so close to walk with.

Nothing much had changed since then, although right now, even though he was alone, excitement coursed through him at the thought of seeing Church again. By the time Christian had left the Cherry Street Grinder, he'd already arranged for his next sit-down visit with Church. It was decided. The next meeting would be in two days' time at a downtown hotel that Christian would rent for just that sole purpose. The writer was never to ask his subject what he did between their sessions, a key fact that Church seemed adamant about, and for the writer at times a little unnerving in itself. It was Church who had set the conditions for their meeting, and he had suggested it with a sly twinkle in his eyes. To Christian it sounded dangerous and sinful, like arranging some adulterous, clandestine affair. The prospect of having unrestricted access to the killer was rousing. Without interruptions and outside distractions, there was no telling what secrets the man would divulge.

Brushing past the quirky tourists and the closed farmers' market booths, Christian maneuvered his way along busy streets. He could barely contain his excitement as he headed home. He wanted to race home and jot down some questions. He would have to be subtle as he interjected them into Church's stories; he couldn't risk unsettling the narrator and possibly losing the interview.

Church's question of God flashed into his mind. So random, so alien that someone like him would ask such a question. How could a murdering sociopath have an interest in religious conviction? Christian had realigned his earlier principles of an all-knowing father some years before. It was another reason he never crossed the threshold of any church. The question of his morality coming from a sadistic killer simply irritated him. In

Christian's view, we were a species that could not help but destroy our own gods. We were a race of pagans once and believed in many deities. We were heathen and eventually learned to discard those beliefs for the one true son of God. Now even that faith was falling by the wayside. Every religion became a castoff eventually; we found our spiritual side uncivilized, unholy, and savage. So we just shook it off like a dog drying his fur from the rain. Then we moved on; we calibrated our convictions and then changed our idols. We were nothing if not predictable.

But hearing the killer's input that a belief in God was intrinsic to their time together was surprising. From the beginning, he wasn't sure what he could expect from his time with a murderer, but his question on God wasn't something that he could've guessed. As if to awaken him from a dream, someone rocked his shoulder as they passed, bumping him, and startled, he caught the wafting aroma of marijuana smoke from the walker who'd passed him. It was Seattle, and not uncommon to see the health-conscious urbanites who always appeared more part-time hippies or seventies rebels just beyond the edges.

Christian was only a couple of blocks from his condominium by then, and just in time. The mist was getting heavier and his hair was beginning to plaster to his head even beneath the protection of the awnings of the stores he passed. He didn't seem to mind it though; it simply made him appear like any long-term native of this glorious wet city.

He'd always had a fascination with human psychology. It had nearly become his profession, but the thought of sitting behind a desk, listening to others spew out and whine about their lives, had been less of a draw. Creative writing had been his true calling, so after graduation, he'd started working for a high-end publishing house. His double majors in arts and humanities and psychology had given him an edge over much of his competition, although his vice president status was more honorary than from years of service.

It was his affinity to the dark and mysterious reasoning of the brain that drew him to Church and, of course, by sheer twisted chance of life. He couldn't think of anyone more qualified than him to write the story of a killer, and do so in the murderer's own words. It had been done before; it was old hat in psychological terms when interviewing a subject for a thesis or field study. There were many students who sat across from a killer to gain insights for a paper they intended to publish. But no one had done it with a killer who had yet to be captured or convicted. This was his signature and his alone. He had the good fortune to speak to a serial killer about his crimes before the police even located him. It put him in a precarious position with the legal system, but it was a risk he was willing to accept.

His attraction to the actual crimes, and maybe even his fascination with the killer, had overcome his rational mind. He'd wanted to be the first to talk to someone so unique...and his interest seemed more than academic. As he turned a key in his lock and entered his modest loft, an explosion of overhead light illuminated his living room. He hadn't entertained in a long while, and the area was used more as an office these days. At the far end of the living room was a whiteboard sitting on a precarious metal tripod. Black notes scribbled with a marker lined the length of the board and sat in tidy columns covering a majority of the blank void. Next to the whiteboard was newspaper clippings pinned to the wall, some haphazardly across older more crinkled clippings covering an area nearly an eight-foot perimeter. There were hundreds of articles that were either pinned, taped or tacked for viewing. It spoke to his obsessive nature that Christian had located so many newspaper clippings from so many newsprints about homicides throughout the US.

College had taught him the value of research, and Christian loved research. He had used every medium at his disposal. There were online articles that he had printed out and hung next to print clippings. There were photocopied excerpts from books he'd gotten on loan from the library, and they too were scattered along the wall. He dropped his notepad on a table by the whiteboard and slung his coat over the back of a nearby chair. That familiar table was where he ate his supper and paid his bills, but mostly it was where he read, researched, and clipped articles about any news accounts that interested him and seemed somehow connected from the same original root.

He had done the impossible—he had located a serial killer before the authorities. His responsibility was clear. He should notify the police and wait for the story to break in the numerous news mediums he loved. But that wasn't going to happen. He was going to get the story at the source before attorneys and prosecutors rebuffed him and doors slammed shut in his face. He had found Gabriel Church. He was not going to stand shoulder to shoulder in a throng of reporters and biographers and beg for his exclusive story. He was going to get it first, and to hell with the others. This was his accomplishment, and no one would take it away from him.

Christian reasoned that if he had contacted the FBI with his research, they would have considered him a loony. They, no doubt, had their share of psychics and crackpots along the way of their investigations. Plus, he didn't know how many murders they had linked to a single killer. He had made that connection because he was clever and could see the single strokes in the broad canvas...probably better than most. He could see how the crimes held a union, a tiny correlation to other murders, but mostly because of the type of victim and the seemingly random nature of the killings themselves.

It hadn't been an easy task assembling the facts. He had scoured multiple newspapers across the continent, and all in his free time. He'd collected a database of horrors. And it was only possible after the advent of the World Wide Web and the ability to track any minute detail of whatever one decided to hone one's gaze upon. For his part of the research, it was in the murders. A string of bodies regularly occurring across the nation which hadn't been inspected closely enough to define any individual connection to a single killer. He had become so skilled in the gruesome hobby that he could train his focus to a spot on a map of where he suspected the next body would surface. Based upon the last homicide, he might be able to put a thumbtack into the Rand McNally that he also had pinned close to the whiteboard. On that map, and in that vicinity of that thumbtack, would be the next death; a murdered victim would be unearthed. He was more right than he was wrong.

It was easy to see the locations and patterns, but his aim was even straighter; he could actually distinguish the profile of the next victim. Something no agent of any FBI task force had done in this case. Christian remembered the exact moment that realization exploded in his mind. He remembered uttering "Fuck!" as he stood back with a recent newspaper clipping of an unsolved homicide from the city of Sedona, just outside Flagstaff. The article recorded the death of a beloved high school principal whose body was discovered in the weeds of a remote industrial park. Christian read the story, which bordered too closely to an obituary due to the small city newspaper and even smaller-minded reporter. He'd been about to tack the clipping to the wall alongside its brothers and sisters, and he recalled how just days before he had envisioned the next victim, and this James Peterson, now deceased, fit that image in his mind.

He'd pulled up a chair and sat before his knees gave way under their failing support. He'd remained silent, staring abstractly at his "murder wall" just to absorb it. The repercussions had not been lost on him. He had picked the victim type because of what he suspected he knew about the killer, and this meant the two were thinking similarly. It seemed it had been a random guess but one that had inevitably become a reality. He had successfully crawled into the mind of a killer and could tell, with some certainty, who would be murdered next. That insight was chilling.

On that particular evening several weeks before, his obsessions became something very real and tangible. He was a man sitting in a chair in Seattle, Washington, while in another barren red state hundreds of miles away, an unknown serial killer was hunting humans. It was as if a secret had been revealed, and an immediate trail of light spanned half the country and shot from man to killer and linked them by a tether. Unknown to him, at that exact moment, a killer's head turned as if a draft of wind had blown in from some unknown source to distract him and sent a tiny shiver down his back.

Even from behind the safety of his locked condo doors, he'd felt those tiny spiders crawling up and down his spine. He wasn't a fool, and he'd purposely taken a wayward path home, stopping several times to make sure he hadn't been followed. He understood that he didn't need a serial killer to be acquainted with his zip code. But Church's eerie presence seemed to invade his privacy and unnerved him in the quiet of his room. He felt like he'd been fighting the perception he was sitting on the edge of a knife, but he pushed back his fears and decided to open his laptop and pull up information on nearby hotels in the downtown area. There were quite a few since Seattle had a popular tourist trade for good reason. Choosing the Mayflower Park Hotel because of its old-world charm, he retrieved his cell and opened his wallet for a credit card. He wanted a room on one of the higher floors. The picture of he and Church sitting beside a high-rise window and watching the beautiful skyline of the city appealed to him, but he didn't know why.

After reserving a room, he grabbed his notepad and began jotting down some questions for his subject. He became mired in his thoughts and fixated on his future date with Gabriel Church but was brought back home when he felt a rumble in his stomach and realized he hadn't eaten in many hours. A typical occurrence, he thought, since he knew just how obsessive he could become with his projects. It wasn't uncommon to miss meals over deadlines, or forget social engagements when a topic or a theme pulled his concentration. The entire course of his last few months were testament to that with the wall of newspaper clippings and a growing favorites list in his computer's files.

Obsession wasn't Christian's only flaw; he was fastidious as well. His residence remained immaculate with every coffee-table book stacked and fanned at his exact preference. Dust was never allowed to rest for long on his tables or knick-knacks and every pillow was fluffed, just so. He kept a clean home however cluttered his mind was at times. If dinner was necessary, then a shower was as well. Regardless that he'd just arrived home, he decided on a quick rinse, and then he would grab a plate at one of his favored spots. Chinese sounded good to him and then maybe a quick drink at a pub on his way back home.

One of the things that he'd noticed during their conversation was how well rested Church appeared, while he carried a beleaguered, somewhat harried look about him. Christian wondered if murder could be considered a form of relaxation. There was a serenity oozing off the killer, a peaceful confidence that made sense. It gave the impression that all was right in Church's world. As Christian skimmed the menu at the Kuai Crimson Palace, he found his usual fare uninteresting, while reminiscent images of Church fingering the lip of his wineglass seemed unable to be pushed from his brain. Eventually he decided on a Masala chicken bowl for his dinner and a side of pork dumplings and a glass of iced green tea. It might seem odd to have iced tea from a Chinese restaurant, but the whitewashed American cultural palate of oriental cuisine was too predictable.

He had spent time in the south, where tea only came sweet and filled with ice cubes. He didn't consider himself adventurous with food necessarily, but he'd enjoyed many meals from every corner of the globe via the sprawl of diverse cultures spanning the streets of downtown Seattle. He lived alone and didn't enjoy cooking, so spending time in every café and restaurant along the boulevard near his loft had occupied many of his evenings.

He ate with friends on occasion, but his social life had become stagnant and ordinary. He had never found that innate desire to be coupled, or even be a part of any social clique. It was a curse he bore but one he had acclimated to years earlier. Christian's life circled around work and his personal interests and studies. Even after graduation, his nose was frequently buried in one too many books or he was strolling independent bookstores and literary cafes for that next great addition to his library. He was well suited to his profession and was able to speak with a modicum of knowledge on Seattle's literary world from every angle. He knew up-and-coming authors, he knew the best bookshops, he knew the trends of publication, and deftly maneuvered the waters like a skilled merchant seaman.

But the positive aspects of his life were painted with dark oils. The same studious traits that should have made him popular crafted a socially awkward loner. His ability to converse with comprehension was also the trait that made him laborious to others in his field. Although physically attractive, well-educated, and trained with fine skills, he was too frequently left off the guest lists for cocktail parties or five-course dinners. Christian Maxwell had a lot to be thankful for, and held a clear understanding of most things that surrounded him, but he couldn't see his loneliness...that old adage of the forest for the trees.

Clever people can often be extremely ignorant of their own weakness, and although Christian was cognizant of his love of books, and his sometimes-antisocial behaviors, he couldn't join enough pieces of the puzzle together to show the picture—the image of a sad and lonely man. It was impossible to make that connection because he had never understood how others truly saw him. His biggest flaw might've been his oblivious nature, or his inability to see just how insulated his life had become.

We all weave the patterns of our lives by our actions, and possibly by the desires we maintain to be with others similar to ourselves. Christian had made himself inaccessible to others; he'd forged the walls he intended as protection, which sadly only held him captive and distant from those who could've loved him. The real tragedy wasn't the compilation of brick by brick construction, but the fact that Christian never even saw the wall.

Sitting in a Chinese restaurant drinking tea and eating dumplings alone, he couldn't imagine any another existence. He had found some comfort in reading the backs of menus while he shoveled in forks of shredded pork, content in strumming a newspaper while he filled his belly... It was woefully normal to be so alone.

BY CONTRAST, GABRIEL Church didn't like to be alone. It would seem more logical that a nomadic killer with deep scars of psychosis would be accustomed to his own isolation. Who else could relate when your mind was blatantly fragmented and scattered to the floor...when you were surrounded by those who suffered the same humanities as the rest of us...while you were bereft of those same compassions. Emptiness locked in an endless cavity that nothing could seem to fill.

However, he was a social creature. He liked the looks he received from others and being a benefactor of someone's salacious desires. Gabe was a confident killer; he understood the sexuality he exuded. He would break a tiny grin as he walked down the streets and observed pretty secretaries or dental hygienists turn their heads to watch him walk away. Graced with a full head of dark-brown hair flecked with an occasional sexy strand of gray, even he knew he had won his good fortune in the looks department. He had a physique earned from years of hard toil and maintained by his infrequent visits to the gym at any local YMCA. His chest was broad and defined, and he enjoyed thrilling the female staffers and patrons of any establishment he visited. He liked the image of pulling his shirt off and wiping the sweat from his glistening chest with the bundled garment. He was more metrosexual than he cared to admit.

But bodies were merely bodies to him; his real strength came in his personality. It was a honed craft of knowing when to smile and look away with a mischievous glint dancing through his eyes. It was something he'd mastered, one he found great success with. He knew when wetting his lips looked sensual and inviting, and when it looked ridiculous. His ability to acquire bedmates would have been legendary had he stayed in one place long enough. Instead, he had chosen a life on the road and the repeated sexual conquests of a man with nothing to lose and much to offer.

He'd even noticed men staring at him at the workout facilities and gyms; ones whose eyes lingered for too long on him as he ran through his routines. It seemed the males had lost their ability to smile or speak as they gazed longingly in his direction. He had seen that expression many times, and although he was heterosexual, he didn't mind another appreciating his form or the adoration plastered to hungry, lust-filled faces. When you were as strong and confident as he was, those limp-wristed faggots who trailed him across the gym floors and dawdled at the shower doors were merely a distraction and proof his efforts were valued.

He currently questioned whether his biographer was queer. The look of this "Christian" was suspect. But he didn't care. It was nice to have someone positively dripping with excitement at his every word, someone whose expression seemed to indicate the sun rose and fell at his feet alone. If he'd been uncomfortable with his writer, he'd never have agreed to the interviews. But his stories would get told, his vision clearly revealed, and his words and ideas tossed out into the universe. Maybe his life had been preordained to this one single act of defiance? Maybe by confessing his sins before God and the universe, and doing so before he was forced to, he was celebrating his final "Fuck You, World!" moment.

He had watched others of his ilk, those who'd been unlucky or stupid and found themselves spilling their guts for detectives on the opposite side of an interrogation room table, eulogizing about their crimes and blaming an unjust society or a vengeful God. Gabe wasn't that laughable or foolish. His sins would be openly decorated by his lack of remorse, and his misdeeds would find their own very personal voice, long before some nameless reporter could upend his plans and become some fucked-up ventriloquist for his personal ideology. It was a wise decision to allow Christian Maxwell to write his story. Besides, this day to day existence was becoming rather mundane. Even killing was beginning to lose some excitement.

It had been over a month since he committed a murder. And that last time had even failed to arouse his cock, as it had in those earlier days. He had run aground with the idea of murder—the tensions were no longer as crisp, and the sensation of every stimulus wasn't as powerful. He remembered those first few adventures; how the air had become electrified around him, how the scents that reached his nostrils were intense and familiar. He remembered pulling his blade or holstering his gun and smelling the pine from a nearby preserve, or the stench of a landfill rising from many miles away. Even the air itself carried recognizable aromas from vast distances. He remembered the tingle and itch of his flesh, remembered how every gust of wind brought every arm hair to stand at attention. It was a drug he allowed himself to drown in, and it was the greatest ecstasy he knew.

Lately, Gabe had been drawn back to his childhood, wanting to chronicle it as some explanation for his crimes. But he wasn't a writer, he knew that. That's when the idea was first formed to bring in his autobiographer. He had spent countless hours pulling back painful memories to have that corporeal gift of story in which to offer Christian. Because his occupied thoughts waylaid his mind, other thoughts of murder were back-burnered...and whether he would ever know it or not, Christian had done his own part in the prevention of murder. Without any concise understanding of his own influence, Christian had saved a life.

Chapter Three

THE FBI HAD clear definitions for the types of serial killers: Medical Killers, Organized Killers, and Disorganized Killers. It was easy to break them down into subcategories such as Thrill Killers, Spree Killers, Mass Murderers, and Lust Killers. For Gabriel Church, the pigeonhole slots didn't fit his particular mold. He killed with organization, but he spent marginal effort on planning. He killed for lust but never sexually assaulted or tortured any victim, and actually, sex played only the smallest role in his impulses. He killed across the board; different sexes, different races, and all ages. There was never a favored distinction of victim, nor did he ever seem tied to a *Modus Operandi*, as detectives or profilers might say. He was opportunistic. He used whatever was handy; a rope, a gun, a knife, or whatever tool or implement happened to be close at hand. His victims were only chosen by a single intangibility, by an iridescent white light that seemed to draw his interest.

It came without warning, without the twitchy need of a meth head in need of a fix. He didn't fight the urge to kill, as did so many other plagued killers. He didn't hear voices, he didn't have a deep-seated hatred, and he wasn't out to make any political stand. He killed because he could. And his enjoyment was linked to the ease in which he killed and the good fortune of not getting caught.

There had been one man, a single person with the bad luck to come across Gabe in a convenience store, of all places. As Gabe had walked toward the double doors of that 7-Eleven, the white light emanating from the man at the counter nearly dropped him to his knees. The figure was obscured in the radiance of white heat, and Gabe had to catch himself before he stumbled and gave the appearance of being struck by an inspired vision. He gulped in air and forced a congenial smile on his face as he looked straight ahead while passing. He hoped the man hadn't noted his surprised expression though he couldn't be sure.

He had just paid the clerk for gas, so he sprinted to his car at the pumps to refuel quickly, hoping he could get enough gas in the tank before the man exited the store and became lost to him. He got close, but as the man walked out of the store, Gabe was forced to stop pumping and leave the fuel paid for, but untapped. Cramming the nozzle back into its slot, he jumped in his car and followed the man and his vehicle, as if it were just the smallest of coincidence that they were heading in the same direction.

Gabe trailed the man for a time, ending up at what he surmised was the white-lighter's home, a modest box of nondescript banality. He had to follow the man, to see if that radiant light ever dissipated. When it didn't, he knew this was the one he needed to kill. But nothing Gabriel Church did was easy. He had to survey the man's movements and activities just to ascertain who lived there in that crappy paint-peeling shit hole with him. When he was confident that he knew his target would be alone and had chosen his entry point into the house, he left to get supplies and then waited for the dead of night.

He broke into the home via a window in the rear of the house. It wasn't difficult; the single-paned window and rotting sash and frame construction proved no deterrent for thieves or killers. The man had a dog, as did most folks. In preparation of this he had picked up two items; a week's old online order of prescription strength Seconal which he always maintained a ready stash, and at the store, he purchased a beautiful raw T-bone steak. *God this is a fucked up country*, he'd thought as he ordered the drugs with a credit card in his own name. Having tossed the steak out onto the fenced lawn just an hour before, he then made his controlled, leisurely stroll into the man's backyard. He jimmied the window open with nothing more than a screwdriver. It took all of five minutes. When he entered the house, he became his own shadow, moving through unfamiliar surroundings with confident poise. He did enjoy this part of the undertaking.

To his advantage, the floors were covered in carpeting—he needn't worry about the boards creaking as he slipped down the hall. He passed one wall covered entirely with cheaply framed photographs: a family's life captured in black-and-white and Kodachrome. Each picture seemed sappier than the last, he thought. And with a disdained curl of his lip, he surveyed all the smiling faces and unfettered bonds displayed therein. It only served to remind him how few Church-family vacations at the beach had been, how scarce the camping trips or long drives through the national forests.

He passed tiny empty bedrooms and a room used for either an office space or storage, because it was stacked with cardboard boxes and debris from many years in the same ratty dwelling.

When he found the man's bedroom, he could hear the sounds of heavy, restful breathing emanating from inside the stranger's room. Gabe wasn't armed, save for the screwdriver he'd pocketed in his jeans. He rarely carried weapons. The sport came in the chance of misadventure and the risk of getting caught. He stood in the doorway of the man's bedroom, hidden by shadows, but not so much that a waking man wouldn't see him standing there if he just focused his gaze.

Gabe stood calmly, leaning against the doorframe, watching the man sleep. His target was in his early fifties, he guessed. His breathing, congested and raspy, was that of a man not in the best of health. But he didn't question the veracity of the radiant light's choice of victims then and he never had afterward. It was what it was.

Each murder was different. Some were exciting, while others were ordinary. Some, as this one appeared, would be quiet, low-key, and almost routine. This man's death would be like his white paint-chipped home, old and outdated, dull and unoriginal. Moving swiftly but surely, Gabe walked over without disturbing the white-lighter and then picked up a pillow from the opposite side of the mattress. He shoved the downy pillow hard onto his face. The man awoke with a startle. Naturally, he struggled; they all did, but he was no match for Church's strength as well as being caught completely by surprise. He fought to escape the pillow and pull in the burst of oxygen necessary to continue his fight, but he couldn't have known how ill-fated that struggle would be. He was never meant to win. Gabe held the pillow tightly to cover the muffled screams, and in just three minutes, the scuffle was over completely. It was then it dawned on Gabe that throughout it all he had been smiling.

When, and if, he recalled the incident for Maxwell, he knew there would be the question of "Why?" The man had died because Gabe wanted it, and the only explanation was the white light that surrounded the victim. Even to Gabe, it sounded ludicrous, and he wasn't the writer Maxwell must be. There wouldn't be adequate words that could justify his actions, or get the writer to understand why he murdered someone who appeared so innocent. Gabriel enjoyed killing, it was just a significant part of his own dark mythology. It was something he was good at. But he didn't have a substantial reason to offer as the real motivation. It was just there. The same cold intensity that made it obvious in the mind of a killer was hopefully satisfactory explanation to others. In reality, no others needed to understand, but somehow he wanted Christian Maxwell to. He needed him to. He just couldn't pull that reason into anything tangible to hold.

CHRISTIAN LAY AWAKE in his bed, arms crossed behind his head, staring up at the ceiling. He couldn't get the cool, composed serial killer out of his mind. There was a huge contrast in personalities here. While he was an educated man and understood servile obedience in a civil society, he knew Church was not, but he did have the confidence and self-assuredness of a man in control. Qualities, by his observation, a killer shouldn't have. Being an individual who always appeared anxious, even when he wasn't, Christian possessed character traits of a socially awkward, bookish soul. But Church appeared like a man who couldn't be ruffled so easily, maybe a necessity for someone planning a homicide, but a quality that was very alien to the biographer.

He needed to outline his thoughts on how the book could be shaped, what areas he wanted to delve into, and any particulars the audience might find distasteful. But it was too difficult to look at the work from those terms yet...not while the images of the killer invaded his head and seemed unable to be pushed aside. He was excited at the prospect of his next interview with Gabriel. The anticipation was unlike anything he'd ever experienced before. It was unfamiliar and clumsy in his mind. He was a writer yet didn't possess the words to describe his insights.

BY THE NEXT morning, Christian was perched high above the city skyline, staring out at the sea of cars and waiting rather impatiently for Church to arrive. The Mayflower Park was as expensive a hotel suite as he could afford, and it would be worth it. He wanted to see the killer inside this luxury, to see just how he managed within these walls. His air of confidence could be shattered by the exclusive life of the privileged that would surround him. It was more of a social experiment than anything. There was smug stillness in the air until he heard a slight rapping at the door, and he knew his investigation was underway. By the frail tap at the door, he suspected the killer was already out of his comfort zone. He smiled as he slid across the plush, carpeted floor, satisfied by being correct about his subject.

But as the door was opened, he was taken aback as Gabriel Church strolled in with a smirk of gratification on his lips, apparently still breathing in the oxygen of the righteous and commanding his own masculine influence.

"Great choice of digs," he said as he brushed past Christian and left him standing at the door with a faded, tentative smile.

"Thanks. I thought it would be better than that coffee house on Fifth Street."

Christian closed the door and headed to the salon table where he'd arranged his notepad and next to it, a small recorder. There was an aroma that had followed Church into the room, but Christian couldn't define it. A musky, perfumed scent, not unpleasant to the nostrils. It held a smoky tincture of the great outdoors, something that placed the image of campfires and wet pine in Christian's head. Gabriel had already assumed his spot at the leather-wrapped dry bar in the corner of the suite. The Mayflower provided cut crystal glasses and an ice bucket, as well as a coffee pot and an envelope of ground beans. Christian had filled the pot after he first entered his room. He wanted to be prepared for anything the killer may need. Church was seated at the bar filling his cup with the steaming black brew, his infectious smile still leading Christian to wonder about many things.

"Where would you like to begin today?"

Church was dressed in a clean white T-shirt and tight blue jeans. He stomped around in worn out brown combat boots; the same variety he had referenced in their earlier conversation. The type of lace-up boots that had aided in ending the life of that unfortunate poker player in East Texas, somewhere just outside of Dallas. He dressed in a specific style. He sported a confidence that reeked of him walking away from a burning building, still carrying the Zippo in his pocket. He didn't seem to care if there were sirens in the distance; he just enjoyed the blaze and rising smoke.

"I thought I'd leave that to you," Christian said.

Following Church's lead, the writer grabbed a coffee mug from the bar and leaned close to the killer to fill his cup. He inhaled deeply and stepped back to the table to retake his chair.

"I hope you get some good stuff today. If not, this is going to be an expensive coffee." The killer offered with a smile as he blew seductively over his mug to cool it down.

Christian nodded and then pulled the legal pad closer as he grabbed a pen out of his breast pocket.

"I was gonna ask you the other day—how come you don't use a laptop for your notes? You afraid of technology?"

"Some things are not made better with new developments. I prefer timeworn ways. They're simpler...more basic and straightforward."

"Does that pertain to everything?" the killer asked. But Christian only glared back and flipped to a clean sheet of yellow paper.

"Let's begin, shall we?"

"I'm capable of killing in a fair fight and always ready on the draw if someone risks starting something unfair, but even I can't seem to gauge what it is you're looking for in my story."

"I'm interested in what makes a killer I suppose... And to clarify...mostly you kill when it isn't a fair fight?"

Church smiled again at that and fingered the rim of his cooling coffee mug. "Just a turn of a phrase... I imagine you're right, though. I do kill seemingly indiscriminately."

"Then let's explore that." Christian watched the killer crisscross the floor like a seasoned public speaker, pacing back and forth while still holding warm coffee in both hands and that dreamy expression of fond memories revisiting his face.

GABE BEGAN SPEAKING as Maxwell scribbled and assumed his role of a killer's biographer. The words he spoke were chaotic in his head, like a dyslexic's manner of reforming the jumbled words before speaking. He knew if he ranted on about the white-light designation of each victim it would sound ridiculous. But if he was looking for a sign of understanding from the writer, he didn't receive any.

Gabe found himself engrossed in his own story; the memories of each sweet incidence of murder flooding back. He couldn't fashion the explanation of the radiant white explosion that surrounded each man and woman he had been tasked to kill, so he resigned himself to just recall the details, and allow his writer to form his own opinions.

"I've already told you about my first homicide, so I'll tell you about the second." Gabe had to refill his coffee mug again and noted sadly how small the coffee pots were in these fancier hotels.

"Maybe we can have a larger pot of coffee brought up later. Room service sounds nice...a chrome carafe sitting on a tray of lacy white doilies, bowls of sugar and fresh cream. But to begin, my second murder happened just a few weeks after my initial foray into the world of death."

As Gabe began his tale, he saw Christian look up from his notes. The man seemed trapped in an instant of disbelief. He told the story of him being in California. He'd arrived in Fresno after all. But he didn't stick with the job, the one he'd been so hell-bent on reaching. For all that it cost him by the journey, he just didn't enjoy it, so he quit without any notice or by your leave. He didn't like the fucked-up job and after a week or so decided it was time to move on. He had nearly forgotten about Texas by then—the murder was quickly becoming just a bitter taste on his tongue.

He'd been in a town he couldn't remember well enough to know its name, but it was in Southern California, that much he was sure. It seemed the murders had more pull to his memory than the settings where each had occurred. Gabe told Maxwell about the white light again, nodding his head to show he understood how that poor shit in Texas hadn't fit his usual mold, being more an act of vengeance, and not the calling future killings would be. That was why he'd never been awash in that incredible glow like the other victims that would follow. It had happened that first time along the sunny coasts of California. And he'd never be the same again. But since it had never happened before, he needed to better articulate how strange the sensation had been during that particular killing. He had to explain that blast of immediate awareness, and even if the writer didn't understand the white-light concept, Gabe needed to express its importance, and how it had been a life-altering moment in his life.

AS GABRIEL EVOKED some faraway spirit to offer up his account, Christian felt damage come inside the room's stillness. That familiar shudder once again crawled up his back like a quick-footed insect racing up his spine. He had gathered the killer's reckoning that he wouldn't understand the "white-lighter bullshit." That part of his story seemed unfathomable. But even without understanding the motives for murder, he at least comprehended how evil the story must've sounded. Whatever drove Gabriel Church to kill, it had become deliberate and flagrant. He spoke of it as if it were just another pile of papers in an overflowing in-basket on his desk.

"SO THE FIRST time this...err, white light was obvious to you was in your second killing in California. Can you tell me about that, if you remember the details anyway?"

Gabe pulled the story out with patience that surprised even him.

"I remember everything about it, namely because it was a woman. She was pretty and petite, and like all the others, she didn't see it coming until it was too late."

Gabe assumed his spot back at the bar and sat for a moment trying to dredge up bitter memories. He began first by describing the beautiful coasts of the golden state. It had been the first time he'd ever seen the ocean up close. He had been bumming around Southern California, making his way up north. He was pulling petty robberies to survive, mostly picking up purses and wallets off the beaches or out of open vehicles of unsuspecting tourists, off counters at fast-food joints, anything to grab a few dollars here or there—they were just tiny scams with even smaller payouts. But it had been enough to get him moving along with little effort. Gabe never needed the same creature comforts as most. His childhood had given him an edge over most transients. As a young boy, he would run off and spend the day alone as opposed to being in his father's company. He was independent and self-preserving because of necessity. It had taught him how to survive without needing much—a lasting gift from his fucked-up father figure.

The would-be killer's origin story had given him the knowledge he needed to be self-reliant. When you didn't want to ask your dad for money for a movie, you learned to get it by your own means, which to a child meant stealing for what you wanted, or for what you needed. Gabe had been a vagabond from the very beginning. He had no remorse for the victim he'd left behind in Texas, and it somehow came as a surprise when he stumbled onto a fetching young woman who was bathed in light like a Madonna.

Gabe had hung around Fresno for a bit after he left the freight company. He was considering heading to Yosemite National Park, based on some weird notion that he could live alone up in the mountains. He had always fancied himself a wild man, and the image of him sporting a full beard and stealing food from campsites seemed naturally appealing to him. He had already sold his beaten old Chevelle and was bumming with a backpack by that time. He was hitchhiking along I-99, but he wasn't successful in getting many rides on that fateful afternoon. He found himself in some bedroom community; again, he couldn't remember the name, since all the southern and central cities in California looked much the same to him. At the time he was hiking across California, a show had become popular on television called *The Incredible Hulk,* and so his appearance of walking from town to town carrying a ratty backpack didn't seem so unusual to the people who passed him on the interstate. Plus, a memory of the flower-child seventies was still tangible in most people's minds. If you were going to be homeless, that was the best state, the best weather, and in the best time, since aged hippies could still be found living off the land and spending their time smoking grass and hanging in communes.

He was passing little shops adjacent to the sidewalk and peering in at each business with a look of the tourist trade on his face. He had been smiling, he remembered, because he had nothing but time and few worries. He had enough cash for a quick breakfast and considered popping into one of those rural diners with cute names like Lou's or Fat Freddy's, but he never got the chance. Because it was at that moment he spotted a lovely woman headed into a boutique a few feet ahead of him. She'd been exuding a clean white aura that blocked out any of her features with its substantial glow.

It amazed him at first, and he was curious enough to trail behind her and enter the boutique. Fortunately for him, the shop sold more than frilly dresses. He pretended to be shopping, but it was just an abstract motion. He became intoxicated with following the pretty woman who radiated such a beautiful light. He could hear her speaking to a counter girl about something and realized how exquisite her voice was, but if you had asked him to describe the woman, he wouldn't have had the words. She was, after all, basking in brilliance.

After a few minutes, she departed the store without making any purchases. He followed her out and lagged behind as she went through the motions of shopping along the boulevard. Gabe wanted to know her but didn't wish to frighten her by stepping up and introducing himself. The light pulled him like a moth to a bug zapper, and he couldn't understand why. He mistakenly thought it was sexual desire at first but then realized he didn't just want to fuck her, he wanted something more permanent. He quickly tried to come up with some false opportunity of meeting her. He considered racing ahead and dropping something in front of her to enlist a conversation from a well-meaning stranger but couldn't get ahead of her. He considered bumping into her at her next stop but knew that his appearance and that damned backpack didn't make him seem trustworthy to any local resident. Before he could create some false opening, a better option hit him square in the face.

The woman had pulled out a set of keys, and Gabe saw her click a button on her key fob. He heard a beep and then noticed the flash of lights on a

Volvo parked parallel just ahead. He was about to lose her entirely, he thought, but as she opened the passenger side door, he practically tripped over her, dropping his backpack in the process. Gabe wasn't sure what she was doing on the passenger side of her vehicle, but as he stumbled upright, he blathered out hasty apologies and feigned concern over clumsily tripping over such a lovely woman. He was lost in his own head, he told her. He asked if she was all right, and the young woman smiled broadly, a fact he could tell only by the way her smile affected her words, the glow still obscuring her delicate features.

It couldn't have been more perfect an introduction. She asked Gabe if he was all right and the two shared a congenial laugh there in the middle of that sidewalk in some no-name town. Gabe had been even more attractive in his younger days; women were drawn to him despite his unshaven face and unkempt appearance...or maybe because of it. He had a certain quality, and his rough, manly exterior was only heightened by his unwavering charm. He asked her for directions to the highway and smiled innocently as she tried to tell him how close he actually was. He fabricated a quick lie about where he was headed and why he had his backpack with him, and she took the bait—hook, line, and sinker. She even offered to drive him the half-mile up to the interstate, and he languished in the pretense and said that she needn't bother herself. He smiled sweetly as he waited for her to insist.

Thinking back on that chance meeting later, Gabe wondered why it was so easy to charm women into dangerous situations. He presumed it was because he appeared so very normal in their eyes, or maybe because he was so good-looking. Women seem to have a blind spot when it comes to attractive men. They forget that hot guys can be just as dangerous as the degenerate, sketchy-looking ones. The woman opened the side door of her green Volvo, and Gabe reluctantly agreed to be driven the short distance to the interstate. Once inside the car, it was all over but the screaming and crying.

Gabe had transformed quickly from innocent stranger to deadly assassin. He quickly managed to get his hands around her neck—she was unsuspecting, and he was driven by the light that seemed to speak to him, telling him that she needed to die. After a brief struggle, she was blue and lifeless in his grip. He stepped out of the car and casually moved to the driver's side before moving her body to the passenger seat. He was going to drive down one of the nearby rural streets and leave her and her car to be found later. He knew that someone might have seen their unintentional meeting on the boulevard, but they would only be able to offer a general description of a man carrying a backpack, and clearly the police would assume he was just another "drifter," as they did in most homicide cases. He'd found that in this part of the country everyone seemed much more transient than anywhere else he'd visited. People seemed unnaturally untethered, which seemed obvious by the blank empty stares off every runaway and hustler he saw littered throughout the downtown streets.

There would be a generalized sketch of him but not much else. He would wipe the door handle and the steering wheel of any prints, and there would be no DNA to find. After she was clearly dead, her head lolled to one side and her gaze became glassy and distant; he noticed the light that had enveloped her was starting to dissipate. He equated the disappearing aura with the sensation he was feeling at that particular instant: a combination of excitement and delightful adventure. Ever since that second murder, Gabe would see that aura as the draw to every victim, and the precipitance of that pleasure in killing.

AS CHURCH SPOKE about the murder so abstractly, Christian found himself staring in his direction, almost forgetting his intention of listing detail to paper. It didn't matter because he wouldn't forget what Church had told him about the California murder. He didn't think the words or the image of him telling the story would ever leave his thoughts. It was carved into his reality. The awful, unjustified death of someone young and kind and the speculative way he described the events so carelessly. It seemed each time Church recounted another story, it made Christian shiver more. It would have a lasting effect on his personality, but he was shut off from that knowledge for the moment. He once again failed to see the forest for the trees, and every callous or unkind stony thing Church would say to him would just lie flat and fester in his soul.

Chapter Four

"WERE YOU EVER worried about getting caught?" the writer asked.

The question had been the grizzly in the room from the very beginning. It slept restless off in the corner, always holding that tension that it could rouse to become something deadly. Christian wondered why the killer had ever agreed to have his story told, wondered if it had been Church's innocent ploy in finding yet another victim. That it had been his face the killer spotted that had been crowned in white radiance. He was willing to risk the danger so that he could learn all he could of Church. He told himself it was going to be a good book, and that it had been his calling to become a conduit for a famous killer's rants. But he had to concede there was more to it. He couldn't deny his own keen interest in every aspect of Gabriel Church's life. He told himself it was intellectual curiosity or that true crime stories had always interested him or his major in psychology had been the root to his fascination. They were all lies he told himself so he wouldn't question the face staring back at him from his bathroom mirror. He didn't want to recognize that his obsessive nature was bordering on unhealthy when it came to writing a murderer's account of each and every horrific murder.

"Getting caught wasn't ever a concern. If it happened, it happened. And to be honest, I knew I wouldn't. I'm smart enough and careful when I need to be."

The answer didn't really satisfy since most serial murderers had a heightened sense of grandiosity about their own nature. They simply believed they were too clever to get caught and Church wasn't any different. Christian had studied abnormal psychology; it was a defining aspect to his classes that intrigued him and a necessity when planning a career in the field. One of his papers he presented had detailed analysis of research into the subject. He'd utilized everything in his arsenal to get that favored grade. He had discussed therapies in-depth and remembered the four types: psychoanalysis by Freud, behavioral therapy by Wolpe, Roger's humanistic therapies, and cognitive behavioral therapy by Beck. He had smiled as he received his paper back with the kind words scrawled on the side by his professor. He considered it as a sign that he should continue in the field but decided against such a dry academic future, choosing instead to focus on a career in writing.

But his background came in handy when he had first thought of writing about a serial killer through their eyes. Since he was successful in finding Church before the authorities, he felt his participation in the story had been owed to him alone. And apparently Church felt the same. He was standing in a luxurious suite at the Mayflower Park after all. Christian's degree in psychology was a comfortable addition to his writing degree. It ordained him into a select membership as far as Church could fathom. For his part, he knew he was a skilled mercenary, acquainted with more sin than most would ever know. But he couldn't help admiring the writer who possessed those talents that escaped him. He wanted to say as much and then thought better of it because heaping praise on another man wasn't anything he felt comfortable bestowing. Christian was just as driven as he was he reflected, just as fearless. Who else could sit across from a confessed killer without even beading perspiration beading below the hairline he thought.

Christian placed the notepad in front of him and turned his attentions to Church.

"I have to ask," he paused. "You're confessing to crimes that have not been tied to you individually. At some point this story will be published, you understand, so getting caught is either inevitable in your mind, or are we both wasting valuable time here to finish it?"

Gabe smiled a sexy grin of forthright certainty. "Yes, my friend, the story will be told. And you will be the teller. It may happen sooner than you think...and we're both going to accept the chips falling where they may."

"So you are comfortable with this story breaking, accepting of whatever fate the authorities have for you?"

"My fate is my own." The enigmatic riddle fell from Church's smiling lips, creating more questions than offering answers. But the writer understood how little to push there. It was as if he had pulled up the rope from an abandoned well, only to retrieve an empty, dusty bucket as his only reward. There wasn't anything he could wrench from the well. He was forced to accept it, hoping to find better answers later, when Church least expected it.

"Then would you like to move forward, or would you like to tell me your greatest childhood influences?" Christian retook the legal pad and appeared fixed in beginning again with the tale, but Church had other ideas.

"I was rather thinking I'd like to enjoy this comfy hotel suite more, and all it has to offer. I know you're not privy to where I'm currently holed up… but let's just say it's not as nice as this. I guarantee. I won't go into details, but it offers only a dirty shower with incredibly nonexistent water pressure. I'd love to take a tiny break and appreciate the facilities…with your permission, naturally. A blistering hot shower sounds like a little piece of heaven 'bout now."

Picturing Church naked, surrounded by muggy steam, was an image that was unexpected to the writer, but once it had invaded his head, he couldn't seem to shake it successfully.

"I suppose that'd be fine. It's getting closer to lunch, anyway, and I could get something brought up to nibble on—sandwiches maybe?"

"Sounds great. I'll be out long before they deliver it."

With that, Church slinked off to the back like a curious cat in search of a litter box. Christian watched as he explored the rooms, saw him nodding approval as he found the spacious bathroom with its glass-encased shower and slick Jacuzzi tub. Before Christian could make his way to the phone, he noticed that Church had kicked off his shoes and then stripped off his shirt, tossing it mindlessly onto the queen-sized mattress in the bedroom, a room that for all intents and purposes would never have found a use in their meeting at the Mayflower. Christian's nerves prickled like the hairs on the back of his neck. He didn't recognize why; it just unbalanced him to have a killer getting naked in his hotel room and taking such liberties in his company. It was like they were friends, and that somehow intimidated him. The professional relationship was changing from biographer to something else, and it held some alien promise just out of reach of his understanding.

He could hear the water running in the shower, and a creepy picture of Church slipping out of his jeans seemed to titillate him, but he couldn't measure it as a sexual thought. Christian had never been certain of his sexuality or his orientation. In college, he had dated the occasional sorority girl but had no perceptible emotions about it either way. When the relationship invariably ended, he found no guilt or remorse in the loss of it. He was approached only once by someone of the same sex. It turned out to be an inebriated fraternity kid; lanky in frame and sexy as hell, despite his slurred speech and bloodshot eyes. Like most young men exploring their sexuality in college, alcohol became the great conscience equalizer. Everything worked in tandem and it allowed them to sneak off the traditional path. Particularly when that path enabled them to get their knobs wet with spit and another orgasmic release of all that pent-up cum and tension. Casual hookups were something Christian rarely engaged in, even considering how nerdishly attractive he was to some. It just didn't matter to him how often he got off. Unlike his roommate, even masturbation was a rarity. Christian was an oddity from the very beginning.

But the persistent image of that muscular, naked killer, surrounded by rising steam and lathered in soap, wouldn't find escape. The thought of his close proximity to danger was arousing in ways Christian couldn't define. His cock began to grow and unleashed some strange sensations, quickening his heartbeat and the rush of blood coursing through his chest. He was so nervous he almost forgot to call downstairs and have room service bring up a plate of sandwiches and a pitcher of iced sweet tea.

He anxiously paced the floor while listening to the shower running on full pulse. He wandered into the bedroom and noticed Church's discarded shirt and the tossed combat boots scattered on the floor. He stared blankly at the murderer's white socks and followed his trail of cast-off clothing until he was standing at the bathroom door, which was wide-open and inviting. He focused on the steam at first and then noticed the blue jeans on the floor near the shower door. They beckoned to him, and he quivered at the thought of his desire while holding the denim in his fingers and bringing the man's clothing up to his nostrils...if for no other reason than to just smell that wet pine and smoke once again.

He was shaking, and his brain wasn't functioning properly. There was nothing but memory flashes crossing his mind. There was nothing focused or decisive about his thinking. If he had perception, he might have known it was that exact minute in which his sexuality had been fashioned, and that he had always been gay, but never until now had that ever held a tangible and fixed notion.

Church was a captivating subject. He could draw someone in with his infectious grin and sensual blue eyes. Eyes that could glint warm invitation and then contrast to a darker, pitiless color in a mere flash. He was charming but still soulless by his lack of remorse or guilt. It was a combination that had intrigued Christian from the start. It went beyond a bad-boy image. It was mature and cold-blooded like a snake that struck out with glistening fangs because it was its only nature. And whatever void hung like a weight inside his core was just as beguiling with his intelligent reflection to his horrific deeds. There had been times when the two had been chatting at the coffee house and Christian had forgotten the man was a killer at all. It was just a friendly conversation with another clever, educated soul. Similarly, there were times when Church could frighten Christian and challenge his interpretation of deep-seated psychosis.

If pressured to describe the killer, Christian would have only had the words *original sin* to describe him, the murder of one brother by another—his personal Cain and Able definition in the sons of Adam mythology. If Church represented the "first murder" then what did that make Christian? He had become a dramatist to the twisted origin of death, complicit only because he had not called the FBI and warned them of a would-be, famous killer in their midst.

He stood there watching the bathroom fill with muggy heat, rubbing his crotch to remind himself of the fabric straining against his own fully engorged member. Was he that fucked up that he'd consider throwing himself at a man who had so easily killed so many folks across this country? Apparently so, he reasoned, because he had yet to move on.

His face was flushed as he stared at his reflection in the steam-bathed mirror, quizzing himself on what he suspected was supposed to be happening here. But he could hear the man moving around under the water's spray and the image was impossible to lose. Fortunately, before he could decide what actions, if any, he would take, the water stopped, and he could almost sense the water dripping from every sinewy bit of flesh. The door opened and Church stepped out, but didn't hear the tiny gasp from his writer as he reached for a towel.

He turned and smiled at the sight of Christian standing there dumbfounded. His expression seemed a form of recognition; a clear statement which implied he knew the game the killer was playing—and solely for his benefit. The two were reading each other well, better than expected, given the brevity of time they'd spent together.

He couldn't help noting those flashes of desire in Christian's gaze, all brought unwittingly to the surface by Gabe's unabashed nudity. But still Gabe made no attempt to cover his swinging dick; choosing, instead, to offer his best come-hither look or flaunt his evocative stoicism while toweling his frame and then running a hand through the loose locks of his whisper-touched gray damp hair.

"So is the grub here yet? I'm feeling a bit hungry, are you?" He asked quietly, compelling Christian to move closer just to hear every syllable.

The question was laced with hidden meaning, and the sudden awareness of it all hit him hard. He was forced to fumble embarrassingly with the answer. "No. Not yet, but soon."

"If you wanted to shower, you could've just asked." Church's terminal smile was still present as he finally covered his manhood by wrapping the towel around his waist and brushing past Christian, leaving a soapy scent wafting in his wake.

Christian barely stepped aside in time, but the closeness was an erotic explosion to a man who'd never been intimate with another male. "Excuse me" was all he could mutter from tightly wound vocal cords, and he walked into the room as if he had been headed to the john all along. It was a ridiculous attempt at recovery, but given his choices, it was all he could muster.

He stood with his dick in hand and his back on Gabriel. Hoping his cock was flaccid enough to allow him to piss without having an awkward moment to surface between the two. It was clear he was embarrassed by the twitchy nature of his movements. He guessed he wasn't hiding that fact all that well, and simply tried to maintain a professional distance from the man. He didn't need to admit out-loud how the killer held some type of unexplained power over him. And it wouldn't be good in the end or even an effective resolution for the novel at hand.

"Just to be clear, it doesn't matter to me if you're queer you know?" Gabe's words were like ice swords slicing through his muscle and vital organs. Losing his grip on his cock, his stream of urine went wild and splashed across the bowl, hitting the floor.

Well, somebody else would be cleaning that up.

He had turned to stone right there, unable to move. It wasn't that someone else had made realizations about him...*it was that he hadn't*. The idea hadn't been completely baked yet, and he was already hearing the word *queer*—what the fuck did that mean? He could have turned around and feigned being aghast at the notion, but he'd already heard some horrific tales from the serial killer's tongue. He'd remained steadfast and passive at worse atrocities. The stories he had already jotted down could have brought a strong man to his knees. How could he hold any pretense that he wasn't gay or that the murderer's intuition hadn't been spot on?

All he could do was drain his bladder, zip up, and turn around.

"Why don't you tell me where in your story you want to go next?" He asked as he swept past Gabriel, who wasn't even trying to get dressed. Church's jeans were still on the floor, but his underwear were nowhere in sight. Church was an alpha and most assuredly could never be found in plain white jockeys or French-cut banana hammocks. Generally, he went commando. And as his father said one night after consuming far too many Pabst Blue Ribbons, *"Just don't box-in your naughty bits, son—because speaking from experience, it's never a good Saturday night when you have to wriggle free of your tighty-whities from the backseat of the ole Pontiac."* As spittle flew from his mouth, he continued, *"I'd say just go ask your mom, but she wasn't the one in the back with me,"* he bellowed derisively. It was like he never even cared how such a comment might sound to a boy about his own mother.

At the time he heard that trailing bit of wisdom, Gabe remembered cringing in anger. Even now, years later, with a world of distance that separated him from Bennett, he still felt the hot scars trying to scab over.

Sitting at the same table where he spent his time writing he pulled out a notepad. It was his shield, his justification for existence and the sole reason he was spending his time with such an expansive character as Church. His hands were visibly shaking; the only way to disguise that was with constant movement.

"If you want people to reason you're not insane, we have to explain your motivations for murder." Christian offered with a noticeable waver in his voice.

"Let's face it. No one's gonna root for the killer in this tale..." Church had already slipped into his jeans but remained barefoot and sockless, and although he'd grabbed his shirt from the bed, he hadn't put it on. The room was ripe with the stifling presence of testosterone, and it didn't look as if it was going to get any easier. Before the two could settle the mood, there was a knock at the door, which startled them both, and they turned to each other in surprise before remembering it was room service with their lunch. Christian swept to the door to find an attractive younger man dressed in a hotel service worker jacket and jeans. He stood before a cart with a covered tray. There were a pitcher and glasses as well as a bucket of ice and bowls of sugar and cream. *The Mayflower did it right all the way to the end,* thought Christian.

Church had made no attempt to slip into his jeans and his broad chest was still damp from the shower and covered in a fine mist of hair. It was unsettling to Christian to have the bellhop there while he was in a hotel suite with a half-dressed man in the middle of the afternoon. It appeared *in flagrante delicto* to some sexual tryst he may have arranged midday, with a stranger he'd met online. It was embarrassing, and he caught himself glaring at Church across the room and hating him for his unabashed lack of concern for his own reputation. Church, on the other hand, looked nearly giddy with the prospect of having someone think he was getting lucky in the afternoon, even if it was with a man. He played it up like a child trying to shock their parents. He walked over and grabbed a sandwich off the tray and bit into it with a grin that nearly screamed how famished he was from an exhausting round of fucking and sucking.

Christian signed the bill and, obviously uneasy, attempted to hurry the young bellhop out the door with a neatly folded twenty pressed into his hand. He was coquettish and that grin of suspicion never left his face as he backed the empty cart into the hall and disappeared behind the closed door of room 1512. This didn't help the image or lessen the rumor and speculation against the actual events.

"That was awkward…"

"You actually care, bud?" Church had picked up on the writer's embarrassment. He seemed to enjoy ribbing the younger man at every turn. "Who gives a shit what that little twat thinks. So he suspects we're up here fuckin'… Who cares? Do you? I mean, really?"

Christian occupied himself with pouring two glasses of iced tea and shaking several sugar packets with one hand. "But we weren't doing it," he said as his voice trailed off like a little kid's.

"And whose fault is that?" The words slapped Christian hard as he turned to the killer. He found him as he usually did, smiling that devilish grin with that secretive twinkle flashing in those damned pale blue-gray eyes.

"Here," he said, handing a cut crystal glass of tea to Church. "Let's get started. We've had enough distractions."

Church assumed a spot in a side chair with a sandwich in one hand and his glass in the other, while Christian sat at the table again, turned on the recorder, and pulled his notepad closer.

"Let's revisit those early days," he said, "back to where you had decided early on to kill. I'd like to explore your motivations for murder…with a more in-depth explanation."

"We can," Church said while munching on his club sandwich, "but no matter how we cover it, it will still be something elusive to the readers of your book."

Church had settled into his story. You could see the mechanics of his memory turning the gears in his mind. His expression became remote as he placed himself back inside those early days. His typical smile had melted into a slight sneer. With every memory, there was something akin to shame carried with it, and he began his tale before California, and that second, pivotal murder.

GABE'S SPEECH HAD become a towrope that dragged the tale of his life. He was pulled along like something caught in the wake. It was a story he could explain but not control. Before California and before the murder in East Texas, he had found his escape from his father and sister and mother. He had left home at his earliest possible chance and taken to the road to find something that comforted him. It had been hard days back then, a struggle to survive, and yet it was wrought with challenges. It was the greatest point in his life because he was doing it alone with his own skill and acumen.

This was back when he had the Chevelle, and he'd filled it with gas and thrown enough clothes into the trunk to head out in search of adventure. He had kissed his sister once on the cheek, knowing he might never see her again, then waved goodbye to his mother and the man she still lived with, Bennett Church.

The first thing he noticed about freedom was his fight for food and shelter. He slept many nights in his car; he stole whenever the opportunity arose, and when it didn't, he settled somewhere long enough to find passable employment for a time, just to earn the money to carry him to the next town and future endeavor. He worked a week or so to make the next few tanks of fuel and oil. There were many lazy afternoons spent killing time at national parks and on lakefront campsites or down deserted rural roads, barely drivable. All to keep under the radar and away from those who might mistake him as homeless. In his mind, his home was wherever he wanted it at that particular moment in time.

It was at one of those lakefront campsites on a Sunday afternoon in the first few months of his journey where he first considered murder. He'd parked just off the roadside, on a slight rise of land that overlooked the lake. It was a beautiful afternoon, warm enough to consider swimming, but cool enough to know that you shouldn't. There was a crisp, freshness that afternoon, and Gabe had been sitting in his car with the driver's door open and the radio playing while he ate a convenience store burrito he'd purchased for his lunch.

Another car came around the bend. It was an ancient black pickup truck; years of abuse dinged at its sides and along the wheel wells. Paint was chipped and fading, and it appeared one light was so foggy with age that it might not even shine with sufficient light anymore. Gabe took no heed of the truck, assuming it was someone who was coming out to fish for flathead catfish or smallmouth bass, or possibly a driver from the interstate who'd pulled off just to take a piss. But his concerns were raised when the pickup chose to park next to the Chevelle instead of passing him on the bend or choosing any other campsite close by. It was always unsettling when someone chose to be close to him or invade his very personal space.

Gabe could see the driver. He was a man in his late thirties by the look. He had a decidedly local feel, farmer or trucker type, and by the smile he offered as he turned off his engine and parked, he looked dense and uneducated. Gabe nodded once in his direction, wondering why out of all the possible places to park, he'd chosen a location so close to another vehicle. Turning his attention back to the serenity of the water, Gabe bit into his tiny burrito and then finished the rest in a single bite. Glancing back, he could see the pickup truck's driver was still staring at him, and he still had that ridiculous grin on his hayseed face.

Gabriel Church wasn't a stupid man; whatever he had not been granted with, he had learned quickly in his travels. He surmised this must be a secluded location where closeted queers met up for sex. By the hungry look on that older man's face, he had unwanted designs on him and his junk. It was aggravating knowing that he was perceived as looking for sex just because he had unwittingly chosen a nice spot to park and kill time with his lunch. He didn't even know what the sick fucker would expect of him—he wondered what the protocol was for such weirdness. Was he expected to pull out his wanger and flash it like some waving checkered flag: *Pull over here to get on top of this cock?*

Was he expected to trail off into the underbrush, expecting the driver to follow? What did fags do once they were alone; did they paw at each other like hungry lovers? Did they drop their pants and just wait for someone to climb aboard and slobber on their knobs? He had to wonder if he himself had a stench of queer on him. Why else would someone mistake him for someone who'd want cock? But the black pickup's driver still sat smiling a few yards away, and both seemed to be waiting for some signal to announce their intentions, some opportunity to occur that might create their race at each other with open arms, like paramours who hadn't seen each other in months.

The agitation inside his chest grew steadily. He was angry at any queer who perceived him as his equal. The mere thought pissed him off, and it wasn't better that his mood had changed once his privacy and solitude were invaded. He wanted to cause the stranger harm. He wanted to throttle him by the neck and be the agent of that aforementioned force. *That image alone made him smile.* Regrettably the other driver mistook this as some kind of proposition and opened his door to approach. Gabe wasn't unfamiliar with the concept of truck-stop sex, or "*cottaging,*" as some queers called it. You didn't drive from one coast and back again, or be forced to sleep in your car one too many nights, without being able to claim knowledge of how some animals preferred to hunt. He understood the pleasure that each encounter was more driven than the last, that every act became an anonymous exploration in unbridled lust. Gabe had seen the sweaty faces of strangers and the nervous glances over shoulders as they'd sought a safe spot to blow a man whom they'd never met.

Almost in reprisal, and with a little knowing nod, he exited his vehicle and advanced to the tree line and bramble of overgrown field grass. The other driver tentatively followed, trailing him into a scraggly grove of oak and cedar. Gingerly, they made their way through the brush, lifting overhanging limbs from their path until both men were hidden from that vantage of an open glade. Seeing a patch of minimal foliage, Gabe waited for the man to catch up before turning to face him. Nesting quail had taken flight at the disturbing sounds of breaking twigs and crumpled leaves until the two men were standing toe-to-toe in absolute silence. The other driver appeared reasonably attractive and looked married. He possessed that settled-in carriage of someone who'd given up on impressing anyone other than his own wife. Wordlessly, Gabe began unbuckling his belt, just as the sensation of electricity coursed through his shaky thighs.

This whole event felt alien to Gabe. But, like most new experiences, he enjoyed watching them from a distance, curious at how it all might turn out. He was fascinated by the protocol of it. It was nothing like picking up women in a bar, he reasoned. This was a dance without subtlety or decorum. It was solely for twisted fuckers who were held captive inside their own influences, albeit addictions, sex, alcohol, or gambling. Maybe even the constraints of some sick fetish they couldn't completely wrestle free of or escape. With their boots nearly touching, Gabe could feel the other man's hot breaths of arousal, feel the excited electrical charges passing through the air between him. With pants unbuckled, Gabe saw how stimulated the man had become, and for a brief second, there was that defining tacit that fairly screamed "Okay, you go first."

He presumed the thrill came from that fear of arrest. But in such a desolate place and hidden among the undergrowth near a lake that drew few visitors, it didn't seem like much of a danger to him. Then again, maybe it was the anxiety of risk. The fear one feels knowing they could get all their teeth knocked down their throat at any minute, and from the hands of some redneck asshole who thought their manliness was somehow tied to bashing a fag. It just as easily could've been a honey trap with nine fleshy inches of solid shaft as bait.

Gabe was intrigued by what was happening, almost to the point of allowing the stranger to suckle on his dick. But he had no real desire to reciprocate and didn't relish what other twists could follow. Moving with surprising speed, he advanced on the man, grabbing him by the shirt and throwing a fierce hard right with his fist. It struck his jaw hard, stunning the lusty stranger like an exploding bomb. Gabe was stronger and younger and accustomed to fighting. His blow nearly brought the man down with a single punch. As he staggered back, dazed, the man-made guttural noises as the blood and spit flew like wayward bullets from his lip and nose. It dawned on Gabriel that he'd never had an occasion to fight while sporting an erection and wondered what it must be like to be in the man's shoes— dick and man both surprised by the attack. He wondered which might go down first.

Once the pickup's driver collapsed to the ground, Gabe lit into him with all his might, striking him again and again. But the man simply cowered under each blow, with his arms flung wide for protection and a display of willing surrender. Gabe kicked him in his sides, making contact with kidneys and vital organs on every punt of his boot. The entire assault took only seconds, but it left the grass and earth covered in blood and piss. A noticeable gash on the man's forehead was the cause for most of the bleeding, and Gabe had to *will* himself to stop...understanding just how close to murdering him he'd gotten. Both were breathing heavy and the gurgle of blood from the stranger's mouth was bubbling in and out with every expelled exhaust. Gabe hadn't said a word during the attack. He hadn't shouted "faggot," or offered threats of even harder abuse. He remained quiet and appeared reasonably content, given the circumstances. The man would live; he told himself, but only if he walked away then before the damage was irreparable.

Leaving him to recoil in that tiny clearing spewing god-awful sounds of pain and agony, Gabe made his way back to the Chevelle and drove away. He wasn't exactly sure why any of it occurred like it had, but it still felt strangely satisfying to him. He'd gained an abnormal reward from the beating, though it wasn't vengeance or sadism that cured his mood. And even without ample words to describe it all, he knew it was something he could someday do again if he chose. The proof for that was in the rise inside his denims and the exuberance he was feeling. It teased and taunted him. It suggested there was more of the same to follow. And as he pulled onto the interstate and headed out of town, he never felt a single ounce of remorse for anything that happened in that secluded woody nook by the lake.

Recalling that story for Christian in the Mayflower Park, he himself absently rubbed at his own crotch. By the time the realization hit him that he was even doing it, he was captured with the notion that maybe there was something inside him that intermingled violence with sexuality. He noticed how Christian was fingering the denim of his own jeans as he listened; grinning at him from the safety and comfort of that overstuffed chair he'd been lounging in. It was almost like they were standing toe-to-toe in silence, and he wondered if this outcome would be any different than the story he'd told.

In his lifetime, Gabe would only ever have two opportunities to discuss his deepest, darkest secrets—one with a fat kid in Beauford and much later with a closeted writer in Seattle. There might've been other opportunities he could have taken, but he didn't. He had to choose his timing, it had only ever been exactly right with Dermott McCoy, when he was just eighteen, and then later with the mysterious Christian Maxwell.

Chapter Five

EVEN THOUGH HIS birth name was Dermott McCoy, he'd always gone by the simple moniker of "Fatbacks." The name was born in the teasing he received in elementary gym class. He'd been a big kid even then and grew into a good-sized teenager, much to his mortification. Even he saw the weighty hang of his tits falling lazily over a fast-developing paunch. He'd been surprised and saddened by how genetics had come to fuck him, particularly given what he saw at home were much thinner parents and atypically sized siblings. His whole life had been one long caravan of hurtful taunts, made worse when the coach demanded they play dodgeball and then divided the boys into shirts and skins. No matter how he secretly prayed...he invariably got the latter. And as bad as that was, he knew it'd only get worse with time—tiny, rural schools weren't meant to prepare those kinds of outcasts for the world that awaited them.

"Hey, we don't want Fatbacks on our team." They'd howl at one another with laughter. The mocking and derision were never as silent as the boy himself. It became his shield and his survival, hanging one's head and keeping a tongue as his best line of defense. Ostracized because of his weight, he developed into a loner. And no one, including teachers, counselors, or his priest, would ever see the sharp way his brain worked or the fantastical way he worked out problems without having to put pen to paper. He might've become a writer one day; his potential to become anything had zero limitation. *Tabula rasa*, as they say; if only it hadn't been for all the childish hurts.

Torturous insults carried him all the way to high school graduation. He was decidedly more grateful than most to never have to walk those high school corridors, or hear sneers and catcalls whenever he passed. However, overweight kids from the sticks were not always awarded better futures, and no matter how hard they tried, some simply failed at life's challenges. His parents support was modest, so any prospect of college was remote. Escape seemed like a wall he couldn't breach, being far too heavy and weak to ever scramble over.

Everything changed considerably after he ran across another lost soul by the name of Gabriel Church. He met him on a Saturday evening at Ray's, a local burger joint west of the railroad tracks. They were comrades-in-arms, awkward, alone and excluded—Gabe because he was a new kid in the area and didn't know anyone, and Dermott because he wasn't. And while others were partying with friends or burning rubber around the old Indian graveyard on the southern skirts of the city, they were able to scratch out some well-deserved months of hanging out and having a buddy to call their own. None in the student body ever invited Fatbacks to the graveyard to party with them or their friends. Or anywhere else it seemed. They invariably lacked the courage to buck a system as ingrained and rigid as their own conformity. However, Gabe didn't mind the young man's company; there was something pitiable about him, but he was easily manipulated. And since they weren't always in the same proximity, neither of them felt they had tangible reasons for maintaining a substantial effort to remain close. With that little skin in the game, the losses were more readily forgettable. So Fatbacks and he occasionally ran around together, whenever Bennett released him from his curfew and long list of chores. They'd grab a pizza, or hit a matinee, or merely sit on the hood of the Chevelle and stare up at the stars to kill time. They drank beer and talked about all the places they wanted to see, or girls they thought were hot or doable. No they weren't real friends per se—just like-minded travelers who'd found themselves passing through the same void, and at the same time.

The custom of hard partying happened nearly weekend. Cars positioned like circled wagons around a campfire, with windows down and music blasting. Scaring the local fauna and causing the tree limbs to shake. Smoke from the community fire mingled with cigarettes and joints. Beer cans littering the ground like the fallen soldiers—no doubt where that old adage originated from in the first place. And even though the cemetery had roots extending back nearly two hundred years, the lack of reverence for the stones or the men, women, and children buried showed an astonishing lack of maturity. Every marker saw desecration. Some headstones defaced with painted graffiti to the point of obliterating an entire family's legacy, making it impossible to read the carved names or dates anymore, while others were kicked off their foundations and lay smashed into shards at the exact spot where they fell.

Dermott felt a pang of regret for what his peers destroyed. As a class assignment, he once had to recite a poem and he chose Robert Frost's "In a Disused Graveyard." And as he recalled, it was a sad little piece, but it spoke to him on a very personal level.

As the Beauford youth can attest, it became a sacrament for them to admit they'd partied at the boneyard. Many young people lost their virginity there, and over the years numerous traffic accidents originated from that same spot. It was life and death personified. Far too many people had been killed as they raced from the unpaved rural roads to the interstate that headed back into the city. It'd even become a known procedure for the local police not to come blasting down the country roads with lights and sirens blazing, no matter how much they wanted to quell the teenage drinking or force the kids to drive home sooner than they would've liked. They'd learned early how inebriated youth can possess a grand-scale lack of proper judgment. And on more than one occasion spirited youth tried to outrun the law to save them from a minor traffic infraction, only to spin headlong into other cars or crash against the trees. The loss of life had been an education, making them realize it was often better to leave them undisturbed, but alive.

"Is this what you and your buds do for fun around here?" he asked. "Get drunk, party, and try to get the prom queen pussy to crawl in the backseat with you?"

Fatbacks laughed, too over-animated to seem comfortable. *As if*, he thought, not wanting to admit he was a virgin, or that he didn't have many friends. They both gobbled up burgers and drank their drinks from a picnic table outside. This was where Gabe first learned the local legend of the ole Indian graveyard and its importance as a rite of passage. And once he heard the story, he knew he had to see the place in person.

Fatbacks rode in the passenger seat of the stranger's Chevelle and directed Church on which roads to take. With windows down and the wind hitting Dermott in the face, he recognized just how truly happy he was in those moments and maybe simply because he'd made a new friend. He didn't know why the new boy wanted to see the graveyard in person; it wasn't dark enough to find anyone partying there yet. Regardless though, secretly the idea of hoping someone would see them there together did present a certain unspoken appeal to Dermott. It might've revealed he wasn't a total loser after-all, and even he could advertise that he was popular enough and had balls enough to skip class with the best of them.

THERE WAS MORE to it than both might have realized on that sunny afternoon because it had its lasting impressions for Fatbacks, and equally, it had unseen meaning for Gabe. If someone had asked him years later, possibly while in a downtown, luxury Seattle hotel, if he'd ever had someone whom he'd considered a close friend...then Dermott may have been the first name that came to mind.

The Indian graveyard was all that Gabe had imaged. Desolate for miles, and tucked far off the highway. As they drove the farm-to-market dirt roads, they passed clapboard homes surrounded by whitewashed picket fences falling into disrepair, acres of untilled soil and scarce enough cattle for the residents there to ever justifiably call themselves ranchers. They were single income homes, the kind of houses meant to fade away like a black-and-white Kodachrome from a long forgotten past. Most worked in granaries or factories over an hour's commute from Beauford, and if they were lucky enough, the wives occasionally found work at a local school, library or bank. But receptionist jobs were hard to find those days, so that part of the city was fast-developing a reputation as the poorer side of town.

It'd been an enjoyable drive for Dermott and Gabe, and far too long since were in the company of one they hadn't needed to actively impress. It was nice. A pleasing distraction for Church and his exuberance spilled out and intermixed with the delight that Dermott felt. They laughed about the things young people found hilarious and relished in their freedom. Gabriel had nearly a full tank of gas, and with food in their bellies and no particular place they needed to be, they were racing their futures to their limits. It was learning experience where the young needed to understand the journey, far more than any whatever ultimate destination they'd find in store. There was always time for those things later.

Following Dermott's guidance, Gabe found a spot to park off a well-worn path, where a thousand cars traversed over many late nights of crazy revelry and drinking. Jumping out, they decided to explore the scenery, ribbing one another openly in the bliss of it all. The chubby kid's company had been an unexpected treat for a young man who seemed driven by an unfathomable need to find something—even if he didn't exactly know what that something was. Fatbacks had only been there a couple of times, always alone and never with a six pack of beer in the car. Those times he never got out of his vehicle. Never had a buddy at his side to explore the spots where popular kids hung out. Since it was midday, he figured they weren't going to see anyone from school. The cemetery was a nighttime passage for more attractive people always surrounded by wasted friends and prettier girls. Dermott wanted to walk around and follow in the footprints of those he envied yet never be able to emulate. He knew the difficulty of being the overweight, shy outsider and discard off the top of the deck which separated him from all the rest. It was early in the day and the smell of fish from the lake reached his nostrils. It had a pleasing and earthy scent, he thought. An abundance of birds called from the treetops, proving they weren't the only living creatures hanging out that afternoon. A cool August had greeted them, and he suddenly felt the happiest he'd been in months, rambling the grounds and taking in all the quiet and isolation of natural surroundings. Stepping over numerous bent aluminum cans and used condom wrappers, he noticed the black charred wood from one of the bonfires others had built before their arrival. Vandals had been there as well, broken headstones and smashed markers lay like half-buried bodies in the deadfall and leaves. There was a sad finality in it all—one lived and died, and even the earth where one gets buried becomes another forgettable place on no one's map. *It's been transformed somehow, a place for unruly teenagers to drink, screw, and to forget about the futures that lay ahead. At least I can say I was here*, Dermott thought. As if anyone ever cared to ask.

Gabe stepped past him and began leading the way, pushing aside branches and creeping through the overgrowth. He allowed Dermott to dutifully follow in his wake, as if he alone knew where all the trails would end, being the more experienced Boy Scout camper or woodsman. When Gabe learned there was a party mecca in Beauford and listened to the stories of sexual conquests performed there, his first inclination was to ask Fatbacks if he'd ever brought a girl up there. A courtesy perhaps, since he figured he already knew the answer even before the question left his lips. He wasn't surprised when an obvious virgin stammered out his explanation and nervously stared off in the direction of the shoreline.

For a time, they sat talking on a large flat rock that overlooked the water, skimming stones and quietly sharing stories. Gabe asked about Dermott's parents and then waited patiently for the kid to spill the missing pieces of his childhood in Beauford. Maybe it was Church's way of determining just how unique his own upbringing was, or maybe it was merely to find another connective point that made two very different souls so intricately bound as companions.

THE ODDITY BEGAN a couple of hours after they'd arrived, as dusk was just beginning to break across a glass-like lake, still of any waves. Church began to offer his askew perceptions and views on life, and as he spoke, Dermott noticed a faint edge to his words. He hadn't caught it before then, but Gabe sounded angrier than he should. Even his pale eyes had changed; it seemed like a shadow had fallen over him and the air grew cooler in his presence. Despite his rising dander he still nodded approvingly when Fatbacks talked about his life and dreams of a future. They were old war buddies with too many scars on the inside, and sometimes sharing stories of their upbringing was all the commonality they had. Eventually it turned into a contest where Gabe would interject, beginning a tirade like *"You think you had it fucked! Let me tell you something…"*

Dermott understood it was wise to change the subject and tried in vain to lighten Church's mood. He tossed a stone far into the lake and dared his new friend to throw one a greater distance. But Church was already ghosted, his mind trailing off without a guide or explanation for its departure.

He began to confess that there were times when he wanted to completely "kill the world." And how society was so screwed it probably deserved to be obliterated. He even reflected that if he'd been able to detonate a bomb someplace, where many in town gathered, he doubted anyone would ever care about the loss of life it caused. That good-looking young stranger was quickly beginning to transform right before Dermott's eyes, and his expression faded from that infectious grin he once displayed. But what Dermott noticed first, were those pale irises of Gabe's turning from an iridescent blue-gray to abysmal black.

Church professed to think about murder a lot those days, more than any other time in his life. At least until much later, long after Fatbacks McCoy was in his rearview, before Seattle turned out to be a real point in his transition. Listening to his ramblings, Dermott felt a chill creep across his skin. As bad as he thought his life was, Gabriel seemed to have it worse. He'd never actually considered taking anyone's life before, even with all the taunting, bullying, and shunning; it just never seemed an option that'd pop up in his brain. Suddenly he wanted to escape; as much as he liked Gabe, he'd felt his mood sour and his only thought was that he really needed a shower and break from their time together. But Church was his ride back into town. Unnerved or not, he needed to bear it for a while longer. And if there was one thing Dermott had learned over the years, it was how to suffer in silence.

He thought of a disruption so he looked around and located the largest stone he could hoist and walking to the water's edge he tossed it in. The splash was loud, shattering the silent gap that'd been wedging its way between them. With all his stomping and animated gestures of strength and wiping the imaginary sweat from his brow, he appeared more like a comic version of a giant lumbering around frightened and scurrying tiny villagers. He burst into laughter, causing Gabriel to join in, and before long the mood had gone back to where it'd begun. Eventually they decided it was time to head home, as the first inkling of stars were revealed in the sky.

And for what it was worth, a chance meeting between Dermott and a would-be killer would prove its own set of consequences—a minor point where both would eventually find themselves drawn back to over the many years ahead.

Chapter Six

"I'VE BEEN CAREFUL not to ask before now, but how many would you say you've killed?" It had already whispered in his brain. There were ramifications to the answer that he didn't really want to explore. But how could Christian complete his manuscript without knowing the answer?

"An actual accounting? I suppose I can understand why that number might be important to you, but people who become victims are not necessarily just numbers in my eyes. Think of it as a journey, and they're not people...but mile markers."

With that cold, analytical retort, Church had once again slipped into another persona. His grin faded with every flash of memory he was forced to relive. His posture seemed guarded and closed at first, then as he reclined back into the salon chair, his naked chest exposed and the writer's eyes darting uncomfortably back and forth. And another unseen personality found its way to the surface. This one wanted nothing more than to unbalance Christian and gain some sadistic enjoyment in watching him squirm under all that unspoken pressure.

Church rested his head inside the crux of his massive intertwined palms and set out to witness Christian dance under his manipulations. Church was reminded an old tomcat he once knew. Old *Butchie* loved to catch mice, and after pouncing on one he'd spend nearly a full hour batting the poor creature from paw to paw, the tiny rodent panting hard with its final labored breathes from numerous and failed attempts to escape its own death. Eventually that old barn cat would tire of his own game and pull the mouse's head off with a single bite before dragging it off to the shadows, presumably to eat. It was just like the game Church enjoyed playing with him. And as it went...was proving effective. Christian didn't like being in Church's company when both were relaxed, when both could shed the professionalism of their relationship and become friendly. He also did not like the distraction of such a tantalizing figure sitting so close to him. He expected by now he would've been more composed and calm, and given it all, it was rather amazing just how collected he appeared, given that Church was still just a few feet away.

It had only been a couple of hours. The tea pitcher was draining and the sandwiches were growing stale. He'd hoped by then he would have gotten used to being in the killer's company, and that he'd be accustomed to the sensual way Church would bite his bottom lip when he remembered something painful, or that he didn't get a tad panic-stricken when the man would brush past him or reach over him to grab another quarter-cut club sandwich from the tray. But time refused to alter his nervous state.

"I think the readers would like to know if there had ever been time for romance during all the killings." Christian carried the pretense of writing and never raised his head.

"Yes. I'm sure the *readers* want to know that…but I would have to tell them I never had much interest in what you call romance. I got laid. I found occasion to blow my jizz wherever I wanted, yes. But 'romance' is for fourteen-year-old schoolgirls, don't you think?"

"So, during the height of the murders, or before, there was never any person who you were involved with? No one who might have altered your…err…homicidal course at any time?"

Church stared over the rim of his glass of tea at Christian. There was an unfamiliar look in his eyes. He seemed to be both exploring the man's question and considering for the first time the possibility that someone he might have loved could have changed his destiny, for the better. But the black cloud reassembled somewhere on his face.

"I was never in love, so the point is moot I suppose. Since I have never loved another *person*, then I guess my destiny was, as they say, preordained. I didn't become a better man because no one ever mattered enough to me. Then again, that works on the assumption that I'm not a good man, even currently…doesn't it?"

"Do you consider yourself a good man?" Christian decided, rather resolutely, that he wouldn't get answers to all of his questions, but he traveled the path forward and trained his eyes on the killer to await a reply.

"*Good* is a relative term. I'm good at what I do, I don't hurt the ones I kill *unnecessarily*…so I suppose it's up for debate."

"I beg to consider that the families of your victims may not agree with you."

"Unbiased are we? You speak of morality now, but your question wasn't whether I consider myself moral or not; you asked if I was good."

"Semantics…" Christian folded his hands on the notepad he placed in his lap and leaned back to allow the discussion to reach its apex.

"Morality is reserved for stupid men of the cloth. It doesn't suit the rest of us, those who crawled out of the mud and then learned to climb trees, all until we could stand upright to fashion tools or weapons."

"You said in the beginning you believed in God."

"Incorrect. I asked you if you believed in God. I said it may prove somewhat providential as our talks continued.

"Then we are back to square one. Do you, Gabriel Church, believe in an almighty God?"

"If there was a God, you wouldn't need to be having this conversation with me now. *I would simply not exist.*" Church curled his lip into a barely noticeable sneer. It was his rebuke against the whole point of it. He believed he had indeed become the singularity that disproved a greater God...but to the writer he sounded more like a lunatic than someone with a measured ideology. Being a man with a rapidly failing faith, Christian could only stare blankly at the killer across the room. He was dumbstruck how maniacal the man was becoming while right in front of him.

"So there is no God, and Gabriel Church exists...then what is his purpose? Why does he exist?"

"I answer to a calling. In truth, I don't know if it is God's or the devil's or some alien influence...but I am here, and my purpose is to answer the white-light commands. Beyond that, I don't know my purpose."

"So you, like the rest of us, still wrestle with the big picture issues... interesting."

"I'm a murderer in your definition. I am not inhuman."

There was little reason to travel that road further; it might nullify their unspoken contract and most assuredly get the killer riled up. Christian placed the pad on the table and grabbed his pen.

"I'd like to go back a ways and look at your influences. Do you mind?"

"Your dime," was all Church said as he repositioned his body for a longer discussion. But even though he acquiesced, it didn't appear that he enjoyed where that might lead.

"You began with your father, Bennett. Was he the first influence? Were there others you'd like to share?"

GABE CONTEMPLATED SLOWLY before speaking, pulling back images from a past he didn't enjoy discussing. His feelings for Bennett Church had been laden with revulsion, and there were many stories that he had yet to bring to light where Bennett might appear even less a savory character.

He began telling Maxwell of a time when he was only eight years old. It was a period of confusion he described. That boy he'd been who was just beginning to recognize how dangerous a man his father truly was. Gabe had been a lonely child, he didn't have many friends, so therefore didn't go to their homes for sleepovers or camp in their backyards in pup tents while telling ghost stories. Because he didn't have those companionships, he equally didn't see how other boys reacted to their own fathers, or how their fathers were supposed to act with them. But there had been one time he remembered.

It was during the annual street carnival, aptly named the Spring Fiesta. The community he lived in operated the carnival each year as a fundraising event for the local charities. There were church booths and tiny rides, cotton candy and sodas. There was a dunking booth, where a popular minister might be placed on a pad and positioned above a tank of four or five feet of water. Youthful sinners might rejoice in tossing softballs at the bullseye ring just to submerge their favorite pastor in the smallest bit of water. There was laughter and bliss for the religious; one would never find a person of ill repute running a booth or a ride. There were never any drugs or drinking allowed. It was good wholesome fun. At least until the year Gabe was eight and ran excitedly to the carnival, hoping to ride the tilt-a-whirl. He assured himself he would go on it over and over, even if he puked.

The boy had raced ahead of his sister, leaving his mother trailing both of them. When he hit the midway, he saw the tossing games. He spotted the brightly colored booths with the overstuffed, plush neon animals tied up with string at the top of booths set with basketballs and straw buckets, rings over bottle tops, and bean bags and bullseye paddles to throw against. He was delighted. But in less than a quarter hour, while he was running around like any eight-year-old released inside a carnival, he then ran smack dab into his father, who had shown up unexpectedly.

He first noticed the stench of bourbon and then his father's hand as he grabbed the boy by the hair just to steady him from falling when he bounded into him.

"Whoa there, little camper," he said as his big hand palmed the boy's scalp. From a distance, it might have appeared sweet, in a traditional sense, but then again one needed to be standing close enough to smell the booze, as Gabe had been, and to have known how mean his father could be when drunk.

Bennett had never attended the carnival before, even though it was close enough to their house that one could walk there. He did allow Sissy to take the children each year, and each year she would return with two exhausted kids, only to find Bennett drinking bourbon or beer on his comfy chair in the den. Whenever she found him there and realized he'd been drinking for hours, she'd backstep into the kitchen and then quietly herd her children off to their rooms to sleep. She would do exactly the same by seeking refuge under the covers of their marital bed, lying there in anticipation of his changing mood.

To see his father at the carnival was shocking; to run into him headlong was unfortunate. Bennett crouched down and gripped his son tightly in his arms. To the casual appearance of any passersby, it seemed he was happy to run into his boy, excited to see him happy and so full of life. But Bennett Church was a master of deception.

He smiled as he leaned forward and whispered to his son, inaudible to anyone close, "You're one little fucker who should be in bed by now. You know, son, this is a big carnival...a little boy could end up hurt, or even dead here, and nobody would be the wiser."

Gabe's face drained of any color, and he stopped his squeal of delight instantly.

"What do you think people would say if they found a dead little boy crammed into the mechanics of one of these fun little rides? Ya think anyone would be shocked at the dead little boy?" Bennett chuckled sadistically under his breath but never once lost his smile or the tight way his arms encircled his boy.

"I'm going home now. I expect to see you and your sister in bed by the time I get home. If you're not there...the preacher's gonna be giving me some pretty condolences for my recently dead baby boy. You understand?"

His voice was cold and matter of fact; he meant business, and even though Gabe had never gotten a chance to win a toy, or ride the tilt-a-whirl, he raced home past his mother and even past his sister and then crawled under the covers in his room and cried himself to sleep. The next morning Bennett was sober, albeit grumpy. He never acknowledged threatening his son, never once apologized, and although the boy never told his mother, he knew...somehow she knew. He never went back to the carnival again and vowed then that one day he'd kill his father.

THERE WERE OTHER stories Church shared with Christian, some worse than others, but each one was sad and pitiful. Christian wrote silently as he told each story. He knew Church wasn't asking for understanding, and he wasn't requiring his sympathy. He was fulfilling his part of the contract by telling his account exactly as it was, unvarnished, open like an oozing sore. Christian wasn't going to pity him. It was what it was; a factor in the development of a sociopath, and it was as expected as any segment making up the whole. It was simply a fragment of that shattered psyche that was Gabriel Lee Church.

It was getting later in the day; both men felt a little weary from either writing steadily or sitting for too long in one position. Church suggested they take a break, and Christian agreed. When Gabriel stood up, he stretched his back muscles and raised his arms high, pulling at each elbow to ease the tension in his shoulders. Christian was struck silent by what he saw—the figure of a true sense of masculine authority standing before him. He looked up to see Church had caught his gaze. The man was smiling, as if the two shared a common secret...and it was delicious. As Church finally pulled the shirt over his head, he mumbled something about getting a drink at a bar down the street. He said he could use a stiff one, and his smile reappeared from over the neck of his pullover. The game was becoming old, yet somehow, every time, it still grasped Christian's heart and held it tight in an icy grip.

Chapter Seven

THE CITY WAS bustling. The streets of Seattle were filled with cars, and even in the midafternoon, there was a rush of vehicles heading everywhere. Both men had decided to walk the short distance on the downtown streets to locate a pub or a bar where they could get a drink and take a breather from their efforts. The mist of rain had already come and gone by then, and the crisp, clean air was exactly what they both needed. Walking beside Church down the city sidewalks seemed odd to Christian. The man was a killer, yet somehow they were becoming friends. Gabriel was bigger and walked with the smooth confidence of a man who knew his own skin. Christian always moved cautiously, without the same certainty of the man beside him. He was educated, professional, and not hard on the eyes, but he still had timidity in his carriage; he hadn't fully shed those years in school where he was tagged a loner and a socially awkward misfit.

Church also spoke louder than most. Surely louder and more boisterous than most people the writer had ever come in contact with. He seemed to beg others to notice him and possibly to just enjoy the view. Christian wasn't mousy, per se; he just felt that tinge of discomfort in being singled out in a crowd—exactly the opposite of Gabriel. His fraternal experiences were limited; he'd never hung out with the cool kids, never been one of the rowdy bunch of miscreants who drank too much or enjoyed sports to an unhealthy degree. He was crafted in a serious, scholarly mode. But as he walked down the sidewalk with Church leading him forward, he had to consider he'd much rather be more like Church than the person he'd become. It must've been nice to be so comfortable with who you were, to never have to live with doubt or uncertainty. But the blessed were ignorant, he guessed. It seemed those who didn't know better were just oblivious to life's little challenges.

Yet he couldn't deny Church was intelligent, thoughtful in a way. His mind may have fractured yet nonetheless it retained a sense of divine control. He was clever about those around him. He had spotted something in Christian he hadn't seen in himself and done so with a lesser degree of effort than one might imagine. He understood how influence and manipulation worked, apparently; the games of seduction he employed were just that, games, and only for his amusement.

Listening to him joke about everything around him as he bounded ahead of the writer excitedly, or watch him grin like that enthusiastic little boy racing to the Spring Fiesta, he was something indecipherable, something mysterious. Christian had to consider that being in awe of the man in his company was an affront to life. It slapped at the cheeks of each and every family member of Church's victims. By enjoying aspects of Church as a person, he was invalidating his criminal activities, nullifying the lives of the men and women he had murdered. But still, it was impossible to reconcile against the sexy fucker whose wake he seemed to be pulled in. There was a gravitational force to him that couldn't be defined. It made him realize the job ahead would be difficult. He would try to put a face on his murderous exploits, and to do so, he'd need to grant respect to all those victims, their families, and partially to Church himself. It wasn't going to be easy.

Just ahead, Church stopped in front of a sports bar and smiled broadly at Christian, which suggested without words they try there for a drink. He appeared that childish boy, pulling at his mother's skirt hem, begging her to enter the aquarium doors, or dancing impatiently in front of the human oddities show at the state fair. He was beckoning in so many more ways than one.

The bar was what one might expect: crowded, loud, and crawling with bar staff racing around wearing green lapel jackets, each covered with bright pins and dangling ribbons—personality they called it. Numerous monitors showed every game one might desire: both college ball and professional soccer, and even one screen in the back showing horseracing. Nothing, it seemed, could slow the friendly wagers over scotches, not in a state made famous by gambling.

It was filled with college-aged kids and just a few businessmen who had outlasted their late lunch, deciding to linger after one too many pitchers of beer. Everyone seemed engrossed in one thing or another. These were the types of bars that wanted people to feel like they had walked into a party already underway. Christian could tell by the way the servers spotted arriving patrons but tried to initially ignore them that it was a ridiculous farce of a concept. Church never waited for one of the pretty young girls to show him to a table; instead, he chose to head directly to the bar. Christian followed his lead like a dutiful son.

It was hard not to notice how pretty waitresses and young girls, sitting with friends, would turn their attentions in Church's direction. He was a wanted man in many ways. His cool confidence was a drug that had the potential to lure. Christian knew that their gazes didn't linger on him as he walked past tables heading to the bar. He considered what it must be like, having eyes focused and trained on you. For someone like Church, who knew the value of remaining unobtrusive, it must have been a challenge. It was certain that he liked the response he received. But how does one deal with the salacious, hungry looks all the time?

His sexuality was a coat he could wear around town. He could feel pride in the looks he attained from strangers. And it was a coat he could just as easily remove if needed. Christian imagined if Church had the flu or walked into a bar hungover and appeared out of sorts or dressed inappropriately or shabbily, he would still see admiration on ladies' faces...and maybe even a few of the men's. Anyone could see that Church would be a fun fuck, even from a distance. His very movements suggested athletic energy that wouldn't be wasted in the bedroom; he had full lips that screamed out how he wanted to wash you in long, wet kisses. He was built strong, suggesting the trail down his muscled frame would be an extensive and satisfying trip for someone's hands. His overpowering size suggested he would hover over them while tiny beads of sweat fell on their neck and face and he pounded harder, just like a rutting animal, forcing himself inside deeper with every thrust of taut ass muscles.

But with all the physical attributes he possessed, it came down to that smile, a twinkle of mischief appearing in those damnable pale eyes that always closed the deal. If they'd been words, they would've screamed a boisterous truth upward to the heavens, reminding everyone around him that Church wasn't like others around them. He knew things some never wished to know: like how he was the finest example of a stone-cold killer and hidden behind the bland. That half-bent smile and fiery sparkle of his eyes were mere implements he used to get closer to his victims. Gabe's true disguise came in an ability to shed his outside persona like an old coat, allowing it to fall off his shoulders quickly and with ease. It came as an effective glance, a twisted smile and even a distant gaze of pastel blue tinted with flecks of green; charm personified, and he needed only to flash it once before the killing began. It was his murderous gift. And none knew that better than Gabe and the devil himself.

Church reached the bar first and took the initiative in ordering them two tall drafts. It was his familiarity that Christian couldn't reason through. Alphas typically take the lead or overstep their authority, and forget to ask for the same considerations: *Would you like a beer or a drink my friend?* Church made those decisions for others. Where it might've been offensive coming from anyone else, it was sexy when it came from him. People approached Church first as a rule, long before acknowledging others in his company, a detail that would've been irksome for some but quite appealing to others.

During their time at the sports bar, Christian measured how others treated him and acted in Church's presence. A waitress might approach Church to tell him a table was now ready in her area...if he'd like one? She would nod and smile as she acknowledged Christian, but even he could see the wheels turning in her head. *Is this guy a coworker? Are the two of them close friends or just casual acquaintances? Do I have the chance of getting my phone number in the big guy's pocket unnoticed?* It was painfully clear how special Church was in other's eyes, and not so coincidentally, how bland he was by comparison.

His laughter was animated and his gestures broad; he was once again begging to be seen. It didn't bother Christian how others changed in the killer's aura. He knew something they didn't, and he shared a bond they never could. The two men talked about everything except the book. He offered nothing more on his life before the murders began. It was informal and easygoing like two friends simply out on the town for a drink. Church occasionally reached out to grab Christian at the elbow while he spoke. He was engaging, and he pulled his audience in, ensuring his companion heard every syllable that fell from his mouth. He tugged him along with his stories, but Christian found that odd because he never considered Church a man who was in the company of strangers very much.

Christian reached over and pulled up an empty barstool and slid it close. Although he had taken a seat, Church seemed satisfied with standing, as if nervous, excited energy prevented him from staying too long in one place. Christian could see that Church enjoyed his time with him, and this made him happy. He had stopped making his sexual innuendoes to unravel Christian, but it represented a slight bittersweet resolution; however uncomfortable the insinuations and overtones had been, they would be sorely missed.

"You ever considered us going out together on the town? I mean, we could hit some bars and get our drink on, ya know?" His smile reappeared, and he leaned so close Christian could smell the hops and barley on his warm breath.

"Don't you think we should get back to the book? I only rented the room for a short time, you know?"

The killer seemed adamant in tempting him out for a round of drinks. "It can wait, we have time, *and you have me as long as it takes.*"

The words cut a serious hole into the writer's chest. *I have him as long as it takes.* There was so much inference embedded into that phrase that it reminded Christian of his own manhood, which was stirred to life in his Levi's as Gabe offered prospects of greater glory in his company.

"It doesn't even matter what type of bar it is. I'm game for whatever thrills you, buddy."

It seemed every word the man uttered dripped with suggestive ambiguities, but then again his reference to "type" of bar made him a little nervous. Church was making obvious implications that he needed a gay bar to have fun. Christian had only been inside a gay bar once, and that had been on a lark with friends who dragged him there after already hitting one too many drinking establishments one night. Although he hadn't known it at the time, what seemed just a harmless bit of fun had actually been a test by his so-called, well-intentioned friends who had deep suspicions about Christian's sexuality. They hadn't stayed long, and to their dismay, pounding house music and spinning disco lighting failed to pull any hidden personality out of their companion. He didn't break into song while singing verses from "Finally" by CeCe Peniston or the Weather Girls, but how would he deal with such as untidy a subject as preference with someone like Church?" If you have someplace in mind, then lead the way. I'm new to clubbing, so I'm not familiar with the trendy spots of Seattle."

"I say we let our passions pull us. We'll stop into any bar that strikes our fancy. To hell with trendy or chic. We're just two fuckers looking for fun!"

Christian threw a twenty on the bar and then opened his arms to suggest Church lead the way. There might have been a couple of waitresses sad to see them leave, but Church was in his company now, and he was going to let his caution fly, allow the man to pull him wherever he wanted to go...even if that meant pulling him under exotic waves. As they hit the sidewalk outside, both men took a lasting glance in all directions; the world lay at their feet and now the only decision was which way to go. Church chuckled at the options from lights and sounds rolling out of every nearby bar and pub. There were many downtown nightclubs in the vicinity; the only option not available was if Church wanted to hit a titty bar. They were hidden on less favorable streets, far from the safety of downtown.

Choosing to go left, they walked close enough to hear each other talk, and Christian had to hurry his pace just to keep up with Church, who was racing ahead with an excited thrall. They eyed each bar they passed and would look at each other with indecision, before Church would shake his head in over-exaggerated fashion, a slight sneer curling his lip, suggesting a better, livelier spot may be just ahead in their journey. A couple of places drew their interest, but only for a single cocktail. And even before the ice in their glasses melted away they'd again find themselves outside walking the streets and joking pleasantly with one another. And this was how their evening progressed for a time. It seemed their own company and the derision they found at each establishment was the bond that tied them together. They were enjoying walking alone together with an intermittent beer or drink, before choosing to travel on.

At one point, Church grabbed Christian by his arm and forced him through the doors of a loud oyster bar with an inviting patio. They ordered a tray of the white mollusks and a pitcher of draft. They leaned against a railing upstairs on a patio that overlooked the street. They talked while gobbling down their snacks with Tabasco sauce and balsamic vinegar. It was either the consumption of mixing spirits and beer or the company, but Church began offering tidbits of information about his childhood. It was as if he'd forgotten he was speaking to his biographer, which was perfection to Christian. He spoke about regrets he had leaving his sister behind and confessed it had been many, many years since he'd made the effort to call her just to see how she was doing. Christian asked him how long it had been since he phoned his mother, and he professed it had been even longer.

Christian had lifted the veil. He'd seen into parts of the man's core that had been previously concealed. He saw aspects of the man's soul, which, had you asked him earlier, he might have sworn didn't even exist. Amid the glassy-eyed effects of drink and the pain of distant regret, Church was quickly becoming less of an imposing figure and more of someone who needed something other than a quick lay. Had he been anything other than a killer, Christian likely would've pulled him closer and hugged him, comforting him as any friend might do in the same circumstance.

But one thing he could always hold with Church was whatever mood he was in wouldn't last long. His face changed suddenly, as Christian had seen happen on numerous occasions, and he looked up and smiled, the wash of remorse dissipating like fading storm clouds. He was Gabriel Church once again.

He drained the last guzzle of his beer and looked encouragingly up at Christian from his bent posture over the railing and said, "Is it onward and upward, my boy?" It was simultaneously a question and a command. The words "my boy" dawdled in Christian's head. It would be nice to be considered a possession of Gabe Church; the thought made him smile outright.

Without words, the writer trailed Church down the stairs, brushing past patrons squeezing up to visit the patio, smiling at each inebriated college student as he descended and they headed up. The ever-constant mist of rain had come back, but it was too faint to worry about—it was Seattle after all. The drizzle was enough to dampen Church's hair and plaster his locks to his forehead. Christian noticed himself becoming aroused at the seductive image. It reminded him of Church standing there in all his glory just out of that steamy shower. He considered what he must look like, but forgot himself as Church tugged at his sleeve and pulled him under the awning of the nearest outdoor café.

"This looks like the spot where we first met up," he said as if fondly reminiscent of his first meeting with Christian.

"I doubt they serve coffee here, but where next?"

"Back to the Mayflower," he said, rather coolly.

Instantly, the writer suspected another burgeoning personality arising in his companion and then settled on the idea of them being alone in a room together that he'd rented for the evening—a room currently housing a large, inviting and empty bed.

"You sure? We can always try that place across the street with all those pretty lights and the crowd of hot younger people who just seem confused standing there by the front door?"

"Hotel," was all Church said. The lack of his former enthusiasm seemed to suggest he had indeed changed into somebody new, someone who Christian hadn't yet met. They turned back in the direction of the Mayflower Park and walked with their heads down to avoid the rain. The laughter was gone now, and Christian felt a foreboding to Church's mood.

"You feeling all right, buddy?' he asked with genuine concern and the trepidation of what response might follow.

"No, it's all good. Maybe the beer got to my head faster than I thought. I just wanna slow down a bit, and that sounded like the best plan."

He lifted his face and smiled slightly when he said that, relaxing Christian to know whatever transition had occurred hadn't been the onslaught of some violent mood swing to shadow his earlier jovial disposition. They walked quietly back the three or so blocks as the drizzle increased and drowned out any chance for their conversation. Christian was tense with the picture of them alone together. He was unprepared for what might happen, and he didn't trust himself not to make some unwanted advance on the man who was quickly becoming his friend.

Back inside the luxury of the Mayflower Park room 1512, Church had peeled off his wet shirt without a word. He kicked at his boot heel with his other leg and discarded his shoes haphazardly on the floor beside the door. Christian was amazed at how comfortable he'd become in his writer's expensive digs. His torso was damp from the rain, and his matted chest hairs licked at his broad muscles. He immediately sank into one of the chairs and asked if the hotel room came with an honor bar.

"I'm sure it does. I hadn't looked yet...Do you want something strong to drink?" Church nodded briskly like a child being promised if he was good he could visit the circus. Christian pulled two miniature bottles of terribly expensive alcohol from the fridge and grabbed up the glasses they'd used for tea.

"The ice is melted I'm afraid, but I'm sure there's a machine on one of these floors."

"No need to stand on formalities, my friend...just pour me something straight up."

He was a picture there, resting back in a dainty fabric salon chair, all wet and half naked. He had pulled off his socks, and Christian couldn't help but see how little denim there was to protect him from being completely nude. He was nervous while he handed Gabe his drink of bourbon, which he had mixed with a can of cola from the same fridge. His reach was tenuous as Church whisked his glass away; it seemed Gabe could tell just how unsettled he was in his presence.

"Let's get something clear. I can see you're a little anxious, and I might hazard a guess as to why...but I don't want you uneasy." Church contemplated his next words carefully, almost as if he were counting an exact number or assessing a thing to determine its value.

"You guessed correctly because I am straight. It's an easy assumption to get to—just as certain as I am that you are not that straight." Christian turned quickly and moved toward the nearest chair, lest he risk his knees buckling under the weight or have Church witness the expression of panic on his face.

"I've never actually been with a dude, but granted I have let one drop to his knees to try to suck me off," Gabriel said. "I'm sure you remember me telling you that before. But if you need it, I mean really need it or think that's important just to continue our work...well then I'd be agreeable I suppose. I like you, Chris, more than I figured I would've. And I'm not really sure why."

Christian fell backward into his chair and appeared spent or exhausted. Slowly he brought his shaky hands to his lips as he sipped quietly from Bourbon that suddenly didn't seem nearly strong enough.

Chapter Eight

STARING IN CONFUSION at his companion, Christian was dumbfounded with the ease in which someone might offer their body like some sacrificial gift of cock. He'd never actually been with a man himself. But throughout every minute he spent trying to gain the killer's trust, he'd already noticed his cognitive brain slipping farther and farther down a rabbit hole. He'd found himself preoccupied. Thinking about how it should've felt more unfamiliar or peculiar than it actually had. He was dealing with some pretty overpowering sexual fantasies at the time, and they invaded every thought while dancing nonstop and willy-nilly through his thoughts. He hadn't planted them there. He never intended for them to grow, let alone to flourish. But there they were, undeniably alive and running on a loop through the hollows and between every random thought he claimed to own. He knew they shouldn't exist, nor did he want them to. But even he was aware just how much control he was losing by being in Gabriel Church's atmosphere.

"I don't think I ever asked you for a fuck, mister." His words came out colder than he wished, and he could see the glint disappear from Church's eyes. Was it regret or was it resignation and sadness on his face?

"I think I've offended you. Not my intention, you understand." Church got up and emptied the glass with one full gulp, then walked over to the honor bar fridge for another miniature bottle.

"I think, for the moment, all I want is your story. I'm willing to continue if you are? But it's up to you...naturally."

As Church twisted the cap off the little bourbon bottle, he plopped back down in his chair and refilled his glass.

"Straight bourbon. You're a better man than I." Christian said with a smile.

"Then let's begin with that," Church whispered. "Let's talk about being a better man."

Christian rushed over to pick up his notepad and pen from the table while Church began speaking and that distant, remote look reassembled on his face. He brought up Bennett Church again...not unsurprisingly. He claimed that he'd always wanted to be a better man than his father was. His head dropped sadly as he confessed he hadn't been too successful. He admitted the first person he ever wanted to kill was his dad, but that had been years before the telling white light first came into being. He wondered now if he'd successfully located his father, and he was still living, would Bennett Church have been bathed in that same white radiance. He just knew, without a doubt, he wouldn't be. So killing him would be something personal, but other than that, would have little reason or purpose.

This was the enigma of Church. He'd begun his killing with a strong emotional need, but none of the killings since then had been the same. The way he spoke about wanting to kill his own father, one might assume by now that his father would already have been dead by his hands. When you have left a river of victims in your wake, one vile, dead fuck wasn't going to unbalance the scale by any degree.

"Have you ever tried to look your father up, if for no other reason, than to test your hypothesis?"

Church had turned to look out the window overlooking the city as if he were tugging back something so far from reach that he had to concentrate just to get it in focus.

"*No*...and I don't want to. I don't want to know that he wasn't chosen. In the same light, as much as I want him dead, I don't want to be the one who takes his life."

"Interesting... Do you want to elaborate for your readers?"

It was obvious he didn't. He got up to stretch and absently peered out the window at the skyline of Seattle and the hundreds of cars below. Christian stared at his naked back and the way he raised his arm to rest on the window's edge. He wondered if he'd made a mistake not taking him up on his offer of sex.

"My father was a cruel and sadistic man," Church said, "and he left his scars on me and my family, but tracking him down and killing him would completely end that pain for me. And I must be a masochist myself, because I think I rather enjoy the bittersweet horror of him being present in my life...even as a bad memory."

Looking at Church then, it was easy to forget his murderous trek across the country and the numerous victims he'd left behind. You could almost feel a certain sadness for him. He was a killer, and his reasons were screwed up and perverted, and mostly came from his own distorted reasoning, but he felt things very deeply. It was hard to imagine someone so thoughtful being a murderous, sick, twisted man. Christian had previously considered sex with the man, and now his mind raced to the idea: What if that was just a prelude to Church killing him?

"You said sex wasn't a factor in your murders, but have you ever killed anyone you've had sex with?" Christian asked quietly.

At that realization, Church turned quickly around, and the grin was back and his eyes danced with fiery curiosity.

"There we go. You were afraid it wasn't just a suggestion of sex. You thought it was something sinister, didn't you? You assumed I was gonna murder you, instead of just getting you naked."

"It crossed my mind, of course not until now, which tells you how stupid I am."

Church chuckled under his breath and threw his body back into the salon chair with animated force, spilling a couple of beads of whisky, which flew like raindrops in midair.

"Baby...that was never the plan. And besides, sex was never a property of murder in my eyes. Of course, sometimes the thrill can give me a slight rise in my nethers, but no..." His voice trailed off under his smile and became something imperceptible.

Christian's crotch was thankfully protected by the legal pad, and his own smile protected him from Church thinking he'd been frightened. He had no real fears of being murdered by him. He did have to admit that if he were going to become one of Church's next victims, at least he'd get to see him naked one more time. There was that anyway...and the word "baby" the killer had whispered, seemingly unintentionally. It was sweetly unexpected and strange, but somehow right in his ear.

The fabric between the men was at risk of tearing, and at that moment, Christian could feel it unravel and fray in his grip. He could see the strong man across the room was sinking under waves of his own making, but he was wise enough to understand why. He had hurt him when he suggested Church could so easily murder him. It had only been a hint of a joke, but one he could see Church took as real. He began to wonder why he hadn't seen it more clearly before—the man truly wanted them to be friends; maybe the first in a tragically long time.

Church blinked, as if trying to snap himself out of his bad mood, and then stood up and headed in the direction of the bedroom. As he brushed past Christian, he was unsnapping the top of his jeans, but he never looked down. Surprised, Christian felt the rush of air as the killer passed him, smelled the scent of the man, and glimpsed the smallest extract of sadness in his eyes. Turning to watch the killer from behind, he could see the denim beginning to fall from the killer's hips and noticed the rise of taut ass cheeks as the jeans fell to the floor.

"Are you coming?" Church said stoically without turning around.

Christian could hear his own oxygen being pulled in and felt his heart freeze from an icy-cold grip. He watched dumbly as the killer walked naked into the hotel bedroom and then disappeared. He looked down at the legal pad in his lap and noticed his hands tremble with apprehension. This wasn't expected, and he didn't know what steps he'd take next. The seconds seemed to turn to hours in his mind, and he was afraid. Church wasn't in the same frame of mind as before, which meant he could be anyone other than the last man Christian had seen. Maybe this man was the killer Christian had yet to meet?

He could hear the sound of Church rustling across the comforter as he crawled on top of the mattress in the other room and wondered what exactly was expected there. Desire took the wheel, pushing aside reason and logic for something that smelled more like danger and sweat. Christian stood up and placed the notepad down and then pulled his shirt over his head and kicked off his shoes. His body was trembling slightly as he stepped over Gabriel's discarded jeans, and he did what he'd seen done; he unsnapped his jeans and let them fall to the floor. Unlike Church, he wore underwear, though he yanked them down past his knees with great haste. The image of his engorged shaft bouncing anxiously, like an excited puppy, only made him smile. He didn't care though; he knew there was little that might diminish his mood or lessen the growing excitement in the air.

He stepped into the room and spied Church lying propped up in the bed. Unlike Christian his cock was soft, but even flaccid, it was impressive. *If he wasn't aroused, then what were they doing there?*

"I only know one way to kill tension. I also wanted to show you that it was important for me to be friends with you."

Strange words for a stranger picture, thought Christian. It sounded as if Church was offering himself to him out of some weird gratitude, wanting to be liked, as if the only way he could get Christian to stay was to allow his self to be fucked. For a second he considered saying nothing just to get the sexual promise he'd been dreaming of.

"Not to break ambiance or lose any of my chances for a good time but I'm curious, why do you want this? I mean really what do you expect of this?"

"I only know one way to kill tension. I also wanted to show you that it was important for me to be friends with you."

Strange words for a stranger picture, thought Christian. It sounded as if Church was offering himself to him out of some weird gratitude, wanting to be liked, as if the only way he could get Christian to stay was to allow his self to be fucked. For a second he considered saying nothing just to get the sexual promise he'd been dreaming of.

There was a pause that stayed too long in the air, but eventually Church said, "Yes, I do, but only because it's you, and only because I think you understand me."

"Neither one of us have ever done this, apparently. So what now?" The distillation of Christian's nerves and the sight of the masculine fucker lying naked on the bed closed the gap in his mind of who he was inside. There was no doubt which way he was swinging now—the blood in his erection told the truth. Without waiting for Church to change his mind, Christian moved to the bed and stood beside it, unsure of how to follow that up.

Church, as if sensing his uncertainty reached out and lightly rubbed his palm against the writer's thigh, sending shivers upward that Christian remembered feeling only after Gabe had spoken about the murders he committed. Looking down at the prone figure on the bed, his eyes traveled from the killer's face to his broad, muscular chest, and then trailed, like the glory patch of hair, to the man's generous shaft nestled in a dark bush. He could see the pulse of excitement stirring the killer's manhood, and it seemed suddenly clear what would happen next.

For a first experience, Church seemed surprisingly adept at knowing what to do. His hands understood where they needed to touch to obtain the greatest sense of satisfaction. He took no shame in bathing Christian in long, wet sensual kisses along his chest and neck. He hovered over before grabbing Christian in his oversized hands and then running a tongue along his partially open lips. For his part, he was worshiping at an unseen altar. A writer drinking in the experiences that would eventually become the raw material for several works he was absently planning in his mind. Every secret fantasy broke apart the reserved, cool detachment he'd fashioned from his childhood. He was lost in the need to rake his hands along Church's sides, to grip his cock in his hand, and know him in every detail. Unapologetically, he returned each kiss with considered passion, and when the time came, it was Church who entered him.

Christian was on his back with Church riding over him and supporting each leg in his massive arms. As he thrust and withdrew, he did so hard and quick, but during the parry of their lovemaking, Church never took his eyes from Christian's. They were locked by their gaze. Christian found himself staring into pale eyes that didn't seem to want to blink; there was a void he could fall into and risk never finding his way home. The only sounds they made were the grunts of effort and the slap of skin on skin. Although Church's sex was physical and forceful, his face remained cold stone. His expression was fastened on Christian's, and both seemed unable to pull away from peering into the vastness, as if searching for answers they both desperately needed.

Neither man could have said how long they fucked. Time had sat motionless on the bed beside them...just to watch them play. Christian's attempt at his first fellatio had been remarkably effective, mostly because every unknown yearning had risen to assist his labors. He wanted Church more than he could've imagined. He wanted to burrow into him like a lovesick tick and find solace in his crotch. He could live there, that he knew for certain, whether that be an hour, a day or even a week. It didn't matter and there was no there to dissuade them. Before long their muscles were spent from all the climaxes, they were lying side by side staring at the ceiling and regaining their breath.

Christian wanted to roll over and rest his head on Church's skin, wanted to open his body with a blade so that he could crawl inside and never be forced to leave. His body was soaked in perspiration, as was Church's, but he didn't want to shower until he had pulled every possible sensation out of this single greatest experience.

"Well, if you hadn't done it before, you can't ever say that now."

Christian could feel the hidden smile edged on Church's words. He smiled himself and somehow knew Church could sense it. However glorious this time was in Church's company, he had to study what this would mean for the book he'd set out to write. How much would their sexual act change the outcome of the manuscript? He wanted to mention that but reconsidered breaking the silence in the warm, sticky afterglow of their lovemaking.

HISTORIES WERE LIKE settling dust to Gabe. He could run a palm across it, rearrange the sediment, and even produce tiny swirling clouds with every motion of his hand. But sooner, rather than later, he knew the past would always come back to haunt him...because it always had before. It encased everything inside a thin layer of filth and grime—everywhere it landed. He could run his finger in the dirt, draw a line, and leave a mark. But even that would eventually disappear, buried beneath a multitude of microscopic cells consisting of discarded skin and residue, and hiding everything.

His own history was something he fought hard to escape. And now he was forced to relive those memories even though he'd assumed they were long since dead and buried. He had his stories to tell, though each one angered him more than the last and caused him stress brought on by old regrets. *Surely that was a ridiculous notion; after all, that was a lifetime ago and well into his past.* Whenever Church's anger exploded as it sometimes did, Christian had to face a real fear for his own safety. Being in Church's company implied a measure of risk; though it was never a consequence Christian thought he'd ever experience or therefore confront. It would come unexpectedly, he reasoned, but it was still something he didn't desire seeing. He hoped he'd had an impact on Gabriel because he was locked inside a belief that he'd somehow changed Church for the better. That he'd become a substantial friend and someone the killer might be able to trust. Yet he couldn't escape the impression that he was misreading the unfolding events; that sex could still be misconstrued as an act of violence. If true, he would simply have to deal with it, or at least until he could repair the damage and again regain some footing with the man.

Gabe's mouth was parched dry, but he didn't relish moving, choosing to bask in every second before the guilt had a chance to rise and stare at him inquiringly, demanding he explain his actions.

Chapter Nine

"WHAT ARE YOU gonna title my book?" Church asked, as he opened his arms and let his fingers play on Christian's shoulder, running his thumb and forefinger along skin and watching the nerves make ripples under the flesh. He'd nestled Christian in the crutch of his arm, and the image was one of contentment, if not normalcy.

"Too early to say…"

"I think you oughta name it after me," Church said.

Comically Christian didn't think that such an unusual response, particularly when the suggestion came from a killer with highly defined confidence and a fucked sense of morality. Christian smiled at that, feeling for a minute he thought he knew the man well. He could've guessed that's what Church would've said; he was predictable about some things, while so many other aspects seemed exceptional and erratic.

"Let's just do the work. We can decide that later, together." Church had answered his fears of what sex had meant for the book's outcome. It was obvious he still wanted his story told, but that he hoped Christian could still be professional and unbiased, given what he'd just done with the subject with tongue and mouth.

This is some illusion, thought Christian, *something unreal in the grander scheme.* He wasn't lying next to a sexy stud after a strenuous round of fucking. This wasn't really happening. It had been a dream he slipped into after he and Church had gone drinking. Maybe he'd passed out and this was the lasting effects from an overabundance of alcohol. If it wasn't real, then looking down and seeing the naked Gabe lying so close was something he preferred not to wake from.

He listened as Church's heavy breathing starting to subside into a relaxed pace. He could still feel his heart slowing its race from inside its muscled cage. And he could smell the intoxicating scent from their lovemaking, remember the odor of wet pine and smoke. He could die here…and if it happened at that moment, he would still be happy. But he could feel that Church had other plans; he was becoming restless and slowly attempting to extricate himself from the bed and away from Christian.

"You okay?" He could sense a dark cloud on the horizon.

"It's cool. I just need a drink. Your skin has a way of pulling out all my spit and passion." Although there was a smile, the storm cloud couldn't be ignored. His cock bounced as he jostled out of bed, and it fascinated Christian to watch it. He hadn't been around many naked men, and even those rare times he'd pushed himself to a gym, he'd averted his eyes and refused to partake in those sideward, but expected, glances. Being naked with another man was freeing.

Church moved from the bedroom and disappeared, arriving back seconds later with a cola from the honor bar fridge, making some comment about how expensive this room was turning out to be. He lifted his can and took a man-sized swallow of cola, standing naked by the bed. His manhood had become flaccid, but even soft, he represented a man many should envy. His body hair started at his chest and covered his stomach until it dusted along his strong legs. He was uncut, and Christian hadn't had much familiarity with uncircumcised men. His foreskin dangled beyond his prick head, and his balls nestled in a matt of dark, inviting fur—he was a picture of a Greek Adonis, only with hair.

The brusque maleness of it all became an intoxicating sensation, partially by being naked and exposed, and partially by being in the company of someone so sexually stimulating. A memory flashed in his mind of a time when he was a boy of ten or so; he'd made a friend from school that his mother didn't much care for; she had told him to stop hanging around that Wilson boy; he was trouble, and she made some half-ass comment that the only reason Christian liked him was because he represented trouble. She had chastised Christian for making poor choices in friendships. She'd said, *"Stop hanging around with hooligans. You only like them because it's childish hero worship."* Since the abstract vision had entered his head, it must have had a purpose. His mother's voice seemed pulled from the past, telling him he probably liked Church for all the wrong reasons: he was trouble, and it must be hero worship.

He couldn't argue with that. He seemed to admire Church because he represented all the qualities he lacked in abundance. Even his unashamed way of strolling around naked was liberating. Even alone back at his loft, Christian always found himself wearing clothes instead of just walking around with his dick swinging. There was no particular reason for it; it just seemed an engrained indignity that had been the lasting contribution from provincial parents. To him, Church's nudity wasn't a product of shame; he just recognized it for what it was.

It's probably easier to be so unabashed and brazen when you're sporting such a sizable dangle of man meat, but his confidence went beyond his God-given equipment, it went to the very makeup of his personality. *What makes a man?* Christian wondered. *What gives some males the ability to raise their heads above the shoulders of those lesser mortals in their presence?* Whatever it was, Gabriel Church seemed to have it, and his mother's warning of overindulgent hero worship may have had a bigger impact because of their encounter.

Christian didn't know what it was like when women loved other women, but he started to wonder how many gay men weren't really as gay as they wanted to believe. Maybe it was male adulation, more than an actual desire for sexual congress. Ancient Greeks carved statues out of marble and fashioned figures in bronze, more males than females. They appreciated the manly form, its strength as well as its beauty. Staring at Church, in that instant, made him appreciate the virile, machismo of the man in his hotel suite. He couldn't help but feel the tantalizing flow of blood engorging his member and stirring the heat in his chest to a slow, steady boil.

"I'm going to hop in the shower," Church said, shattering any chance of Christian's hopes in running his tongue along that animal chest and tasting the salt from his straining muscles.

"Sure, why not?"

He watched Church's ass bounce and quiver as he headed to the bathroom stall. He wanted to crawl once again between those hairy, masculine legs and find his shelter. Instead, he decided he too was thirsty and jumped out of bed as the water began to pulsate from the adjoining room. He hadn't got much work done tonight. However, it had been one of the greatest evenings of his life. It had set the standard and opened doors that once had been closed, but he still had a desire to pen Church's story, hoping he was a proper writer and could present something more than a sadistic killer to his readers.

Christian reached for his jeans from the living room floor and then quickly discarded the idea and chose to remain naked—the gift from Church still giving. He grabbed a cola from the fridge like Church had done and walked to the table and spotted the notepad staring back at him as a reminder of the mammoth tasks yet to come. His notes were sparse because his years at the university had taught him how to use the smallest scribbles to refresh memories and complete his papers for finals when necessary. Ever since Church secreted his notes at the café, he had begun writing in a code that only he could decipher. He did this for privacy. He didn't relish the idea of having to explain his thought process to the unlearned. He stared at his rough scrawls that only he could define, suddenly worrying what Church would say if he had successfully broken the code. The look in his eyes would have been unbearable.

If Church had seen what Christian was penning about his perverse nature or his personality traits and abnormal attachments to misshapen ideology, then he might've been upset. But then again, Christian would never have allowed him to read even a single word, citing the work as unfinished, unformed, and not yet ready for an audience. But secretly there were other factors for keeping Gabriel from reading what he wrote. He feared the truths that would be spilled, knowing they could tarnish their burgeoning friendship more than he was prepared to handle. And no risk was worth that, he thought. No matter how much he cared for the man, he couldn't form the right words to describe how he felt accurately enough. They blocked him at every paragraph and sent his mind spiraling to find the correct narrative that might explain it better. There were no disguises in the madness he could use, even during the relative normalcy and lucid moments, like when they fucked in Chris's hotel room until the room completely filled with ripeness like a well-used brothel.

He could look at Church in several ways. He was the point of his research, the subject of his novel, an enigma, and a danger...but he could be more than that as well. As he gently thumbed the papers of the pad, he considered how much his affinity to Church might alter his viewpoint and his explanation of a killer he'd set out to explore. He wanted his book to show the sterile, analytical representation of Gabriel Lee Church, but his eye would be jaundiced and askew because he'd recently had the man's cock in his mouth. As much as he loved their lovemaking, he hated himself for allowing it to change the perception of the novel in the making.

Christian was too lost in thought to hear Gabriel slip up behind him. Apparently the shower had washed some of the dark from his eyes and improved his spirits because he wrapped his massive arms around Christian, startling him. His lips grazed Christian's nape, and his breath was warm and inviting. The smell of Irish Spring soap flitted to his nostrils, and he decided without question that he could melt there and puddle to the floor, happily.

"How long do you have the room?" he asked without moving his mouth from the crux of Christian's neck.

"It was supposed to be a one-day deal. Looks like I'm extending my stay, though. I have no desire to race to checkout now, at least not while your dick is brushing my ass cheeks."

Christian could feel the satisfaction from his companion; it was obviously what the man wanted to hear. The image of a young Church playing with Hot Wheel cars on the linoleum of a kitchen floor hit his mind, in contrast to the same brutal, sexual creature standing engulfing him with his strength. He would have liked to have known the man from the beginning, to have been that fly on the wall of his childhood. He would have to settle with Church's recollections and stories for now. He would include all of that in the manuscript—people needed to understand the killer before he became one. It was quickly becoming very important that he show Church as he was then, and not just the thing he had eventually become.

"We still need to work tonight, but only if you haven't got better plans," the writer whispered over his shoulder. It was painful to think that the story could take precedence over just lying naked with the man in that inviting bed. But time was ticking, and his desire to know the man wholly was as strong as his desire to be with him intimately.

"I suppose we could. We have time for other things later too. But you have to give me some time. Sex with you can be exhausting...but nicely exhausting."

With that, Church disengaged his hug and strolled over to the chair where he'd begun his stories. He plopped unceremoniously into his spot, still naked and slightly damp from his shower. It was going to be difficult working undistracted if he remained unclothed, thought Christian. He had forgotten his own nudity but become anxious with the realization that Gabriel might see his own shaft, witness it rouse and awaken, as an uncontrollable gesture of his excitement in seeing a naked Gabriel within his grasp.

God, he thought, *who is this man in my head?*

Everything was changing too quickly. If you'd asked him a few days ago what he wanted, he wouldn't have known what to say. Now he was like a kid in a candy store, drooling over the colored delicacies within reach. His time with the killer would have lasting ramifications on the man left behind.

"Tell me a story about Gabe as a little boy," Christian said without looking directly at his subject. He wanted to jot a few memoirs down before those invasive images of him and Church lying naked in each other's arms found a dwelling.

"It was a different world when I was young. You remember what it was like. No bottled water, a world without cell phones or iPads, no social media or YouTube. I was born in Kentucky, the back-ass-end of this country for sure. But Bennett had to uproot the family when work dried up in the region. For us that meant moving to Tennessee, where fortunately, Bennett found electrical work and a steady paycheck. I hated leaving the Bluegrass State and learned to hate Tennessee even more. But there wasn't much work for a mechanic after the plants closed. By the way, Bennett was a mechanic. I'm not sure if I mentioned that earlier…"

"Let me stop you for a second. You call your father by his Christian name. Did you always do that?"

"Only if I wanted a beating," Church offered. "I started calling him Bennett when I was sixteen, and since then, I couldn't think of him as a father anymore. He was always just Bennett Church after that." The reminiscent gaze had returned to Church's eyes, and he yanked memories out with a look like he'd swallowed kerosene. His distaste for the man had been clear from the beginning. It was a source of shame and pain, but one he knew he had to talk about as if it was cathartic therapy with a headshrinker. He told a story about Bennett, which Christian found both hard to believe and chilled him in ways he couldn't bear to hear.

A TREACHEROUS LOOK had taken over Bennett's face one night as the family was sitting watching their sixteen-inch Zenith television. Sissy Church was in the kitchen, cleaning up their dinner mess, a place she seemed to find comfort in. The young boy had often wondered how many dishes really needing cleaning, since his mother always seemed to be washing and drying plates, gripping sudsy glasses, and staring out the kitchen window with a faraway, distant look overshadowing her face. Gabriel had been sprawled on the floor engrossed in an episode of *Hawaii Five-O*, one of his favorite shows at the time. As Gabe recalled the story for Maxwell, the distinct image of the god-awful shag carpeting and the dim lighting of a living room from the late seventies came into his mind.

Bennett had been guzzling beer, sitting on his worn and frayed throne of a Lazy Boy lounge chair. He had been unusually quiet for the whole of the day, and now, watching TV with Chrissy Church sitting on the couch and Gabe lying on the floor, his mood seemed a dark, quiet presence in the recesses of Gabe's memory. Gabe was a year older than Chrissy. She still had that pigtail innocence that Bennett had yet to blemish with his angry outbursts. Lying there on his elbows in the glow of the Zenith, he should have been captured by Jack Lord's version of the stalwart Steve McGarrett. Instead, he felt the tug of frightening pressure building, and his chest became encased in something too tight to measure. It should have been an alien sensation; he was a just a boy of eleven and in the comfort of his family home. But it was there, nonetheless, and the boy turned his head slightly to see if his father's beer had awoken a grizzly without warning.

It was clear, that subtle yet disturbing look, as his father seemed focused on his daughter sitting so sweetly across the room. An unfamiliar glimmer sparked Gabe's concern. It was a look he didn't recognize. But he'd learned quickly to be more wary of those flashes from his father that he didn't understand. Trying to describe the look now to Maxwell wasn't easy; he fumbled with the words even though both men understood the sense all too well. Gabe wanted desperately to convey the childish innocence gained by his eleven years of life; it was pivotal to his account. Bennett's hand went absently to his jeans as he repositioned himself unaware. Young Gabriel had seen the gesture, understood instantly what it meant, and panic seized every fiber in his soul.

What the preadolescent Gabe couldn't have known were the secrets from his parents' bedroom. The lackluster sexual activity Sissy suffered as a curse or the manipulations of hungry, yet uninvited, hands. He couldn't have known how Sissy had suspected the overwhelming sexual drive of her then boyfriend, how she had forced that image from her mind when she heard him propose marriage. Or that a picture of wedded bliss could sometimes make a woman forget what she should have remembered most before accepting her vows.

There was a heartrending wisdom within young Gabe that day. He recognized it would only take time before his father found his daughter to be a desire he couldn't control. He wondered where he would be when it occurred, taken it was a given that it would come to pass unless Sissy found the strength to change that fortune by leaving Bennett. Lying on the living room floor watching *Hawaii Five-O* was the first time he assured himself that one day he would kill Bennett Church. Of this, there was a certainty.

Gabe never allowed Chrissy to be alone with their father after that. Whenever she needed a ride and Bennett was her only transportation, Gabe could be found close by, begging to go with them. Even when Chrissy would be dropped off at her girlfriends' homes for a visit, Gabe would create some pretense of riding along, agreeing to walk the remaining distance to the mall or the movies. He wasn't sure if Bennett ever suspected his true motives, but he figured he did. It became the unwavering resilience and bravery of a little boy against greater odds and created both a sadistic killer and the man who wrapped loving arms around a writer in a downtown hotel room. It was pieces of the puzzle Chris was assembling for future readers, as much as he was for himself.

Gabe had finished his story. There were no more painful reminders he wanted to unearth that evening. He turned his gaze toward Chris, who was filling his pad with furious writing.

"I want to go to bed," Gabe said, a smile glimmering just below the surface. He was back in the Mayflower now, and his baggage remained at the train depot sitting like a lonely traveler waiting for the next five o'clock and headed to parts unknown. He watched as Chris laid the legal pad on the table and took in the full image of him like it was his last bit of refreshing breath. Desire tugged at his heart and substantial lower organs. He sat with one leg tossed over the armchair, naked and welcoming. His grin flashed suggestive cravings that mingled with Christian's temptations. There was a strong moment between the two—it couldn't be shattered or disturbed—that lay there ominously as each second turned into hours.

The only chance where that moment could've been violated was with speech, and it was left to Maxwell to do the betrayal.

"Sounds like a plan, mister." He stood up at the same time Gabe did; however, neither turned to go. Both faced each other, as if some unspoken dare had found its naissance; birthed there between them was a mixture of excitement and sweet hesitation. Eventually, it was Gabe who broke the atmosphere by reaching over and grabbing Maxwell by his hand before pulling him behind him into the bedroom.

There was another round of sweaty sex to finish their long evening, but it was the comfort of having another body to encircle that rested there the strongest. It was something that had been years in the making, far too long for the priest-like, inexperienced writer. Their steady breathing and faint heartbeats acted like a metronome, lulling them into satisfied slumber. It was a critical time for both men in imperceptible ways. A closeted writer had found his footing, and a killer had found a reason not to kill. This wouldn't be apparent to him for a significant time, but it was there, embers in the ash waiting for a burst of oxygen to stir life anew.

Chapter Ten

HER NAME HAD been Jane McCullough, a married mother and a nurse at Kindred Spirits Medical Center, specializing in the cardiology unit, a job she'd held for over fourteen years. Her daily schedule kept her running at a harried pace, but she had grown accustomed to the demands of her profession, labored against those of a doting mother with teenage children and a husband with equal burdens. She couldn't have imagined she would have encountered a man like Gabriel Church. It was out of the realm of possibilities she might run across a serial killer who became noxiously drawn to her. It would've been surprising news for her to learn she had been swaddled in white radiance. She lived an ordinary, tediously mundane existence in her own eyes. Gabe would find her determined and strong. He would feel great admiration for her as his knife sliced a bloody grin-like gash in the softest line around her neck. And he would feel great sadness at the loss of her.

It had been like all things tragic: ironic and accidental. It was an encounter with horrific outcomes, but to Gabe, it seemed more preordained. Six months had come and gone since the two strangers had chanced to meet. Jane had made the deadly mistake of passing Gabe in a supermarket isle as she stopped to pick up necessities for a quick dinner, intending on a family celebration for some ordinary event in her daughter's life. Maybe it was when her girl had joined the drama club, or maybe it had been cheerleading. The details would all fall unnoticed whenever her husband or children revisited the circumstances. They were life's particulars that no longer mattered once the bigger picture came into a hazy focus.

Jane and Gabe came from different places, and they were separated by unique conditions. Both held individual passions and their points of view were unique, depending upon which side you stood. They couldn't have been more dissimilar, and yet they became indelicately tied together for reasons that should never have been. To watch, as an outsider, such a small and insignificant event blossom into such vast tragedy was without comprehension. Jane absentmindedly pulling cans from shelves and reading the ingredients from the back of boxed dry goods, and Gabe walking past as he headed to the pharmacy in the back of the store to pick up aspirin. The two strangers would be only feet apart, and for mere seconds, but it was a close enough proximity to alter Jane's life for the worse. It was such a diminutive moment, such a minor twist that would place Jane McCullough in the same supermarket at the same hour as Gabe, as inconsequential as the occasion, yet so horrific for Jane's family and friends.

As Gabe looked up and saw her standing there, casually immersed in that familiar glow, he was struck silent and immobile. It was that same building anxiety he'd felt whenever he came across a white-lighter. It was a strange sensation of heat and tension creeping from his stomach and eventually gripping his heart in a tight, vice-like grip. Forcing himself to pass her as inconspicuously as he could, he rounded the isle and turned to follow. Gabe followed Jane into the parking lot. She was still wearing scrubs from her earlier shift at the hospital. She was easy to follow and surprisingly easy to abduct as she loaded packages into the passenger side of her Audi. If Jane had committed any offense, it had been shopping in the vicinity of a serial killer, and for that, she would pay an ultimate price. She struggled naturally, but was no match for the stronger Gabe. Coming up from behind her with lightning speed, he placed his hand over her mouth to stifle any scream then forced her into her Audi. Gabe had learned early just how much a victim's astonishment could become his greatest implement in his cause of murder.

It would be many months before Gabe would meet his biographer, Christian Maxwell, but even as he struggled to control the middle-aged nurse in her own vehicle with his breath warm on her neck, the only difference from that kill and this moment was the terror one of them felt, and of course, the inevitable outcome. Had he met Christian before Jane, the fait accompli may have led to a very different resolution.

Jane fought admirably. Gabe noticed the car keys dangling from one of her clenched fists. The way the moonlight glistened across a tiny attachment of the ring caught his attention. He thought he saw a tiny picture fastened to her keys—the type of nondescript little item that one might purchase at the counter at any five and dime to house a picture sheathed in cheap plastic. Though a small detail, after seeing the light bouncing off the fob, it became the only focal point Gabe could concentrate on. Had he seen the smiling face of a child reflected back at him, he wondered? While his eyes strained to make out the image, both killer and victim grappled for control in muffled yet disturbing silence.

Those keys were the only weapon in Jane's arsenal. Unfortunately, though her father had bought her a tiny can of pepper-spray for such emergencies, Jane had never attached the can to her key ring, partially because she assumed she'd have to lose the picture of Celeste if she did. For her, the bulk of the can added to picture and all her keys made it unmanageable to pull from her purse while heading to her car.

But Jane was clever and knew the value of what she possessed in her hand. Once she found an opportunity to free an arm, she seized her moment and drove the sharp edges directly into Gabe's neck with all the force she could muster. Being a nurse she knew to aim for a major artery and hoped that alone would give her an advantage. Even though Gabe felt the stabbing pain, it hadn't been uncomfortable enough to cause him to loosen his grip. He was too far into the gravity of that deadly moment. During those split seconds, Gabe was suddenly struck by how much he admired her. She fought harder than many victims he'd met in his past and he was overcome with a strange wave of pity and pride for Jane, even though it was insufficient to alter the outcome, or lessen the tightness of his massive fingers from around her tiny throat. She wasn't weak. She didn't lack determination. But she was still no match for someone of Gabe's size and strength, and because of that, she wasn't able to put the brakes on his long train of murder or able to make it home that evening to her loving husband or sleeping children.

When Chris had asked Gabe about the victims he remembered, his mind sparked on the image of the nurse and her parking lot death. He remembered all of them. There would never be a single face he wouldn't see in his dreams.

The next morning both men woke, still naked and wrapped like a cocoon in each other's arms. It had been glorious. For Gabe that occasional fuck with women he met along the way was satisfying, but he had never awoken the following morning still in their company. He preferred getting it up then getting it down before ultimately making it out. It was a personal mission statement he lived by, and one which suggested it was wiser to never get any closer than what the single act required of him.

He was surprised at how comfortable stirring from his sleep could be while in bed with a man. It was natural and comforting to him. It had been Chris's irregular breathing and increasing movements as he roused from sleep that brought Gabe back to life. The moist heat of their combined bodies created a shift in his blood stream, sending much of it southward to a twitching penis that had awoken simultaneously.

THERE WAS COFFEE and breakfast and even a shower where the two men stood side by side under a warm spray of water. Christian phoned the front desk that morning to extend his stay, requesting the same suite if possible. With his accommodations made, he dressed in the same outfit as yesterday, knowing that he would eventually have to make a run back to his loft for more clothes and any overnight paraphernalia. Throughout it all, he wasn't yet comfortable with Church knowing where he lived, and he understood without asking that Church felt the same. If they stayed longer in that hotel room, it would prove an indelicate maneuver, separating so that each could retain their own secrets of where each called home.

The oddity of such trivialities, when both men had done lascivious sexual acts on each other, wasn't lost on them. But there were bigger considerations: Church was a killer on the run from getting caught, and Christian wasn't confident enough to allow Church greater access to his life. Church wasn't exactly the boy one brings home to meet the folks, and Christian had already seen the transformations occur from one side of Church's personality to the other.

Their earlier lovemaking had made them both famished, so they decided to grab a late breakfast at a nearby diner. Church ordered a large plate and ate like a hungry dog, forgoing any semblance of manners and etiquette. He shoveled forkful after forkful into his mouth and drank at least four cups of coffee. Christian's mind gnawed at the notion of what it would be like if Church wasn't Church or he was the type of person he could introduce to family and associates. If only things could've been different.

"Slow down, Gabe; there's plenty of food in the back if you're hungry."

"They don't serve breakfast in hell you know. There are no biscuits or eggs when you're surrounded by the rubble of your own sins..." he said. "You should get every plateful when you can...while you still can." His grin was slathered with wetness and a small trail of gravy still hung at the corner of his smile.

Christian had to fight the urge to wipe it away with his finger or the bigger desire to lick the gravy away with his own tongue. How was it possible this man-child could be such a dark thing, with even darker stories, as he'd described in their time together? His youth may have been torturous in a fashion, and he'd chosen to give back every single pain he had endured in kind. But there were other more horrific stories, more sadness by other victims who hadn't chosen to murder, hadn't taken out their frustrations against an unworthy society with homicidal means. Loner students with guns had become a part of our culture, a calamity we were learning to cope with. Marathons in Boston where sick people destroyed lives and movie houses where crazed men opened fire at the innocent, but these were gratifyingly rare. Christian was sitting at a table eating eggs with a side of ham steak with one of those outsiders—it seemed as pretty as peach pie.

An elderly man was eating near their table. He was sitting across from a lovely woman in her early twenties, and Christian hoped secretly it was his granddaughter. The old man was wearing an ugly green suit, the likes of which he had never seen. It was outdated, atrocious, and gaudy, but the pretty blonde girl seemed unconcerned with his attire. She smiled sweetly in the old man's direction, craning over her plate to hear him, yet keep their conversation from becoming too disturbing to other patrons. It was obvious to the writer, from what he gleaned from their conversation, this was a rare outing in public, and it was entirely possible that his cantankerous mood had developed after his wife had passed some years before.

Their casual conversation hit Christian's ears, and he surmised it was indeed a grandchild taking her favorite relative out for the chance to see an outside world. Apparently she was as honeyed as her hair and worthy of a long grand life. Christian wondered how similar she might be to any other of Church's victims. He wanted to lean in close then ask if someone like her could be cloaked in that same fucked-up illumination he'd spoken about earlier. Instead he changed his mind. He didn't want that *other* Church to reappear, and he was having too nice a time to spoil it with him

The killer had prying eyes of his own; they flashed inquisitively in all directions, and he was taking everyone in who sat beside him. It was an innocent look, mindless in a way, but as Christian watched, he felt it laced with overtones. Was he seeing someone he would call prey? Was it curiosity or quarry? Nothing seemed easy in Church's company.

It was nearly midday in Seattle. For the tourist trade, it could prove to be a fresh adventure, too late to thoroughly enjoy the farmers' market at Pike's Place on the waterfront, but still early enough to see the space needle or to stand in the shadow of the great Mount Rainier. Deciding to walk off their breakfast, Church led the way, bounding ahead as he did—like a dancing Jack Russell terrier excitedly pulling at his leash. It was anything but indistinguishable from the man who'd stepped out of the shower earlier with Christian. Someone who had explored his wet body like a horse trainer sizing up the flanks of a quarter horse about to race, running his hand through every nook and cranny of Christian's ass and thighs, just as if it were the sensual touch of a stallion's mane and withers.

Church was a riddle that was certain. Maybe it could be considered a functional form of schizophrenia, but Christian doubted the illness ran that deep. He could be a man of many faces, but one never overshadowed the other or blocked the other personalities from access. He was a sexual beast, and he was a child; he was clearly methodic and at times rational and lucid. He had love in his heart, a benefit few psychotics could offer.

You could tell his excitement didn't originate from the busy streets of downtown. Gabriel, for one, had seen too much life to be amazed at the newness of it all. It was Christian's company that made him smile, and the writer was beginning to feel the same. The sun was high overhead, and he was thankful he was in the Northwest where the constant rain kept it cool and clean and the winds from the ocean always blew stronger, pushing back the oppressive humidity he hated. Church wanted to visit Pioneer Square. He claimed he'd never visited the underground tunnels and thought it might be an enjoyable distraction for the afternoon.

In its heyday, Seattle was a chaotic place to live. After the Great Fire of 1889, city planners wanted to raise the streets and improve the drainage and sewage problems that were abundant prior to the fire. Travelers to the city could usually locate walking tours and visit the submerged storefronts and dilapidated sidewalks, taking a glimpse into what life was like during the late 1800s. It could be fascinating, but Christian was surprised to see Church so interested in the historical aspects of the city. They didn't have a guide and didn't know when the tours were scheduled, but they headed off in the direction of Pioneer Square nonetheless, hoping they might stumble onto a tour. If not, they would have fun in the journey.

They walked the city's sidewalks, slowly heading towards the twenty or so blocks that comprised Pioneer Square. Christian watched Church bopping ahead, pointing at each and every detail that interested him, and wanting to share every thought that crossed his mind. It was lush and green along all the streets that circled the square. Wrought-iron fences and lampposts carried the emerald patina of age; even the bus stops were floating under huge iron overhangs in that same picturesque, bygone era. *They certainly did it right for the tourist trade here*, thought Christian.

Church was utterly different from what he thought a murderer should be; like when he first took an interest to discover what a killer was like from the safety of his condominium with news articles scattered across the dining room table. Although he made it a point to follow the murders as they occurred, it still felt rather abstract. It wasn't real until that second he sat across from Gabriel and saw it reflected in his eyes. Because he killed in nontraditional ways, the police were unable to tie each murder to one another. Some victims were stabbed, some strangled or shot, while a select few were beaten to death. The police didn't make the connection, but Christian did. It was all displayed on that whiteboard in his loft, and it had given him the city where he suspected the next victim would be unearthed. The hard part wasn't in finding where Church would strike next: it was finding Church himself.

The last victim on his whiteboard was Fenton McCoy, middle-aged and a middle-management wannabe. Fenton was as nondescript a victim as one could imagine: a father of three grown children, a deacon at his church, and widowed within the last two years. He had no enemies, was not robbed of his wallet or possessions, and yet was found by police after making a routine stop to investigate an abandoned vehicle parked on the side of the road with the driver's door still propped open and inviting.

The murder of a middle-aged man without even the thinnest of motives should have alerted them enough, he thought, but it didn't. It wasn't a robbery and it lacked the usual suspects, such as known affiliations to dangerous vices like drugs, sex, or money. In fact, the murder missed every mark of the ordinary. The death generated little press and left little lasting in the way of tragedy. After Christian read the details, or lack therein, he immediately became intrigued. He began his research into unsolved murders in the region that carried the same characteristics. He found more than he would've liked.

Fenton McCoy was found by a passing black-and-white patrol car. He'd been propped face up in the front seat of his car. The only indication of murder was the thin blood trail circling his neck. He had been garroted and had drawn his last breaths less than a day before his discovery. His tongue was protruding from his mouth, his eyes staring at some unknown distant spot, and the smallest dribble of red squeezed from that dirty gash along his throat.

The police were confounded without a motive and such a nondescript victim profile. They only could pass it off as a murder by an unknown assailant, or assailants. It created little press, but to Christian, it signified a specific killer. *Who garrotes their victims?* Its random nature may have caused consternation for authorities, but it spoke volumes to Christian, enough so that he would make a request for the police records. Like the tragic code of fate, Christian would stumble onto the killer quite by chance. His investigation into the murders piqued curiosity by the police and, as it turned out, the killer.

Christian never asked Church what first drew him to choose him has his biographer. But whatever the reason, it began the descent into the maelstrom of a dark mythology. It was as if they both knew that fact from the onset and tasted it early upon their lips. The authorities hadn't found Gabriel yet, and Chris hadn't tried to identify him to the police. The act of complicity alone felt like a cold hand reaching out from the grave. Christian had been reading recent articles on the murders while he sat at a café staring into the screen of his laptop. Someone brushed past him; he hardly noticed, but the gentleman stopped long enough to invade his personal space and lean over his table, his pale-blue eyes almost beseeching him.

"You're not going to find your killer by looking at the murders that way," he'd said with a devilish twinkle and a faint smile partially submerged under a cold exterior.

His words caught Christian by surprise and the stranger's close proximity was as unnerving as one might've imagined. "Excuse me?" he said, with his concentration broken and his amazement drawn to unwary eyes.

"I know the killer you seek. I thought I might offer some assistance to you, and a bargain to benefit both," the man had said, leaning closer and creating an alarming tension in Christian Maxwell, whose head turned quickly to ensure he wasn't alone.

His visitor was a large man, imposing in size, with the ruggedly handsome features of a collegiate quarterback who could've gone pro but clearly hadn't. Maybe it was his scruffy-bearded face, or the telltale markings of old welts, but it all alluded to a life worn down to its foundation. His hair was cropped close to the scalp and Christian perceived that between the battle scars and intensity of his gaze, he might have been former military. Christian was shocked by the exchange and words refused to follow his bewilderment, but the stranger's eyes and his stern but cordial expression pulled him further into the fray.

"I see that you're interested in the murders. I've done some research into you, and I know you have published books before. I presume your interest is due to some literary work you have planned on the gruesome subject. I want to propose writing from the killer's own words; that is, if you are interested?"

"You know who the killer is?" Christian asked with shaky voice and a hollow timbre of apprehension and fear.

"*I do,*" the stranger said as he quickly took the chair opposite Christian and sat down without invitation.

"You know me. I don't know you," Maxwell offered as he took another glance in all directions, hoping he was close enough to other patrons that the man wouldn't attack him in public.

"Am I correct that you are researching the murders for a book?" the man asked straightforwardly.

"Let's just say it was a consideration. You know the killer's name, and you want to connect us together for a book?" he said, piecing the puzzle together in his mind.

"You are sharp. I figured you were—you looked smart."

"Um...thanks, I suppose. I guess the next question is what's in it for you? I mean let's say I meet with the killer; we write a book...from his or her perspective. What do you get?"

"Not as bright as I figured. You know your killer, you're enjoying his company at this exact moment, but you knew that really...right?"

Frozen with fear, Christian's hands began to tremble. His only saving grace was that he was in public. If he was sitting across from a killer, at least there were witnesses to whatever would happen next. He thought about raising his voice, bringing other's attention to his circumstances with loud, boisterous conversation, one that might force others to remember the incident if later questioned by the police. He thought about standing up and quickly and briskly walking to the door, hoping no one would follow, and that he might make it out to the protection of a busy Seattle sidewalk, but he couldn't move. He had turned to stone in that moment and lost any ability to decide his own fate.

Chapter Eleven

IT WAS LIKE the last remnant of a waking dream, the images in his head of how he first encountered Church and how he appeared to him in that little café. He understood that he'd have to explain how they met somewhere in the manuscript, but he guessed few readers would believe the story. There were ramifications to their meeting, both legal and more alarming ones. He could assert that he doubted the stranger who introduced himself as a killer and even written him off as a nutcase with little experience in death and murder. But the question still lingered in the air: Why had he not called the police when he began to suspect Church was the real McCoy?

Christian had a good attorney, but this was not something he could fly by his old friend James and ask, "What are my jeopardies here? What are my responsibilities with this type of scenario?" Of course, he would first need to complete the book. Before ever submitting the final draft to his publisher, he would forward a copy to James for his legal advice, even though he suspected he wouldn't listen to the obvious answer he already knew as truth.

After their initial meeting, Church and Christian had tethered themselves to a common goal He already knew James would tell him not to pursue publication and to avoid the risk of retaliation just walk away. But he knew after meeting Church that had become impossible. He would follow this path wherever it took him; he would try to be aware of every danger or implication and consequence, but he was on that path already, and there were few things capable of pulling him astray.

Gabe had stopped to admire a totem pole that sat in the square. There were numerous totems in the area; tourists had become enamored with them, and they had quickly become an iconic image for the Northwest. In truth, the carved poles were not exactly indigenous to the local tribes, and although some of the prominently named poles so characteristically sitting in the square had been there for over a century, the first one had been pilfered from another state and transported to the square under false pretenses.

In 1899, the first totem pole was erected in Pioneer Square. It had been stolen from Alaska by a group of businessmen who claimed to have stumbled onto it in an abandoned village and sawed the totem from the tribal chief's hut on Tongass Island. Although a legal case was established against the thieves of Kinninook's pole, it was later dismissed, and five hundred dollars was raised and sent to Alaska in reparation. It never reached the tribe, but the totem remained as the first erected in Pioneer Square, setting the false representation of life in the Northwest region, and now there were many.

Gabriel rested his palm on the smoky-black cedar carving, smiling back at Christian as if in invitation to join him. He was beautiful there as he stood in that dewy, crisp afternoon, looking like some lumberjack under the shade of tall trees. The tree line had been converted to the shadowy overhang of concrete and steel and the natural splendor broken by fat tourists with cameras and screaming children holding caramel apples and spilling sodas on clean concrete. But with all the distractions, Christian couldn't help but see the godlike apparition in front of him and admire him, if only for his beauty.

The air was strong with the moist harbinger of rain. It was getting warmer as the mercury rose. Christian knew there would be a shower soon, something to wet the ground and saturate the fecund growth of lush greenery. Rain came suddenly here, but never unexpectedly; everyone understood the price of that inconvenience was the verdant green overgrowth covering the town. All seemed to accept it, happily.

There was nothing material in watching Church palm the totem with the sun beating down on his face under the shade of yellow copper beech leaves. He was wrapped in something intangible that Christian didn't understand. There was a vague uncertainty to Church.

All circuits are busy. Your call has been placed on hold and will be answered shortly.

Christian's mind seemed to be playing games with him, because while staring at the killer with only a cup of coffee to separate them, he noticed Church eyeing a patron's young son at a table a mere four feet away. And Church was smiling. There appeared genuine kindness reflected in his eyes. Was that an expression of someone who could just as easily kill an innocent child as he was to embrace him? But that was too deep a thought to decipher in the moment.

Observing Church, while a throng of excitable tourists circled around he thought how nice it would be to see the man in very dissimilar surroundings: possibly spending quality time alone with him at a cabin in the woods, away from a more civilized society and void of any prying, judgmental eyes. That image sounded intoxicating, he thought dreamily. To be so close to absolute perfection and so near a window that one could almost yank the leaves from the earth outside if it weren't for the obstruction of glass. Strange, he thought, how heady he'd grown in the man's presence, and so quickly, considering he was very much a stranger. Add to that, he was a man who had already confessed to murder... extraordinary how that hadn't figured into his equation.

Church could be the punctuation to every sentence, finality with the monumental change that alters the very meaning of every paragraph. He must have proved an awful finality for a lot of people who had been unwillingly forced under his command. He could be a fucking nightmare for some, and the same boyish thing bounding excitedly ahead, just as much as he could be the sensual beast with wet desires in a downtown hotel.

Why did Church choose him to write his story? Why didn't he have any fear of the outcome should the book ever see the light of day? He started to hear the ground rumble with marching feet somewhere over the horizon. Something was coming his way that he wanted to push far from his mind. Something Church may be planning but not yet speaking about.

Did his killer have some exit strategy in mind? wondered Christian. Would he turn himself in and leave Christian behind to pick up the pieces? He could visualize himself sitting in a room with FBI interrogators, someplace small and confining, stale and repellant—men in suits with sour faces who would ask him intimate questions about Church and make accusatory conclusions about the depth of their relationship.

Maybe Church was intending to take himself out, but to Christian, he didn't seem the type. If Church allowed that outcome, he would choose "suicide by cop"; there would be a hail of bullets and some shocking picture worthy of the five o'clock news. Church was too full of his false bravado to ever think he could be taken out easily or quietly.

"I don't know where you disappeared, but wherever it is, I would've liked to have been invited along." Christian was pulled from his thoughts by Church's simple words and his sexy, crooked smile.

"Sorry...kinda got lost for a minute. And besides, I'm sure you wouldn't have liked to tag along. My daydreams can get...somewhat dark."

"Consider who you're with, my buddy." His smirking chortle couldn't be contained; it happened even when he amused himself. There was an energy filling his eyes and bursting out that seemed to beckon to his fellow traveler.

"The next tour isn't scheduled for another hour and a half. We could walk around the plaza with all these lovely overweight folks from the square states and wait in line behind their screaming kids, or we could step off and find the nearest bar with a nasty and disreputable clientele... Your call."

"I must say, writer boy, I like the way your mind works."

The two men broke from the herd they'd been pulled along with and then headed across the street to find an acceptable sports bar or pub, a place where they could sequester themselves from the milling crowds and loud noises. Church claimed he didn't do well amid the unwashed masses, but he'd seemed to be enjoying his time with Idaho strangers and their homespun vernacular. Christian had observed the killer's grin as he helped a tiny boy up the steps and leaned in for casual conversation with the boy's father—no doubt an insurance salesman who lived in a state where you could drive twenty minutes along long stretches of road between white farmhouses with large yellow sunflowers planted in the lawn.

Church had seemed cordial and earthy, starting up conversations with strangers in line. Highly contrasting the picture of a killer Christian had already created in his head. He was astonished with how many faces the man kept hidden under his belt. He might never get used to the personalities Church could pull from his cape and flash as his own. But for the moment, only he knew what the man was capable of, knew how deadly a charming smile could be.

Finding a pub called the Owl 'N' Crow, the two men grabbed a patio table and waited for a waitress. Church was in his element here as well, a handsome face in a rustic Irish pub. There weren't many places he wouldn't fit in, Christian suspected. Being a killer and a man on the fringe of society, he must have learned how to blend, how to manipulate his surroundings. Christian could never do that. He couldn't shed his own skin to fuse into the moment; had he had that ability, he might have used it in school. He could've been a popular man about campus.

Church's hands stretched across the dark oak table. Fingers splayed millimeters away from Christian's own, as if they begged to touch Christian but couldn't escape the guarded apprehension of public displays of affection. Church wasn't gay, so he wasn't comfortable with his sexual desires like Christian seemed to be, even though he himself was a burgeoning queer. Both men were a wealth of personal issues.

To Gabe, it was easy to understand the appeal he presented to Christian. He knew he was representational of a bad boy personified. He exuded danger and was cognizant of every trait he possessed...and why some people became weak in the knees at first glance. Usually, they were traits he used like weapons; reserving them typically to those women he was interested in bedding or assets he knew he had a use for, like money or a good alibi. He didn't care whether it was male or female. As long as their stomachs turned to jelly, he knew he had them. It reminded him of a cat pawing over a half-dead mouse—just for kicks, or just to pass the time.

He was strong and had a firm physique. He was gifted with a cock many men would be envious to call their own. He had street smarts and was proud to call himself a survivor. All of this made him special—that much he knew. If he doubted it, he need only to see his reflection through the condensation of a bathroom mirror at any motel where he'd ever stayed; or even when his face was covered in shaving cream, one couldn't help but notice that slate-blue eyes piercing through the steam. Yes, he was beautiful in a manly sort of way. And he knew it. Confidence was king in a world of the insecure, he reasoned.

But as much as he enjoyed his own good looks, he also admired Christian for the traits he possessed. All those qualities Church had been deprived from birth. He was smarter than Gabe—that much was clear. He displayed a pained sadness through luxuriously green eyes—which to him seemed just as iridescent as what others have said of his own. From what he learned of Christian's childhood, he already knew he came from money. He knew he'd had loving parents, and even his grandparents were still among the living. He was bestowed all the presents denied the younger Gabe. But he wasn't jealous because the sadness in Chris's eyes overshadowed any desire to hate him for what he had.

Church was fascinated with Christian and that wounded-child persona he carried like a shroud. Like him, there were unknown hurts hidden just below the surface. And yet, the two men couldn't have been any more different if they'd each been carved by very distinct sculptors.

That white-light radiance surrounded him, much like it did with many of Church's victims. But Christian was nothing like them. Should he pass beyond the mortal coil, Gabe knew he wouldn't be gone completely—not for him anyway. Not like the others whom he'd known so cruelly throughout his lifetime. And Chris looked like he'd already danced too close to the edges of his own environment. He showed his expressive nature and it appeared to lay somewhere above the grave. It was sadness, but with resilience. He was his kind of survivor, living through a seriously long battle and many protracted wars. He had something Gabe desperately wanted, and getting close to him might enable him to see inside his own nature...maybe to even to find some forgiveness hidden somewhere in the darkness.

When a pretty redheaded waitress showed up, she smiled too overtly and appeared too genuinely interested in Gabe. They both ordered a tall draft of imported beer and a plate of wings. As they drank their ales, Gabe took the opportunity to find out more about the writer he'd chosen to pen his story.

"What makes the subtle plot points of the young Christian Maxwell's life? We've done the nasty, but you mentioned earlier you'd never been with a man. Ever come close to it?"

TURNING BACK TO Church, Christian considered his question. "Never really wanted to. You should be proud I chose to do it with you."

"You have no idea. Pleased as punch I was to be the one to draw first blood. But surely you've been asked before... I mean, you're a foxy, studly dude and all."

Christian turned his head away upon hearing Gabe speak so frankly of him. Partly to hide the hot blush he felt rising in his cheeks and partly to catch his breath without showing his embarrassment.

"I've never really placed myself in that situation; of course, in college there were times when the offer must have been laid out for the taking, but I guess I didn't want it bad enough."

"Would your parents disown you or somethin'?"

"No, my folks are pretty cool, they might have suspected a few things by now, and I never married and was never engaged. In my world, that pretty much solidifies my orientation. Of course, they've never even asked the question." Christian edged closer to take the chance to learn more about his prize. "What about Bennett? How would he feel if he could've seen you in action? He already failed you as a father, but what would that have done to your fucked-up relationship?'

Church took a long distant look across the plaza; his eyes veiled a twinge of sadness at his recollection. "I don't think it would've mattered to him either way... Remember, he had his own bent ways; even *he* couldn't have judged me too harshly."

"And your mother...your sister?"

"They are lost to me now. I don't think the image of me fucking a man would've shocked them in the least. I doubt that if they knew my other crimes that'd surprise them much either."

"Regrets? You ever want to look them up, or are you afraid of them knowing what you've done? I mean, if you get caught, what do you think they'd say about it?"

"They'd say good riddance to bad rubbish." His face drained of the preoccupied, dreamlike quality and again turned cold and impassive. His mood had changed quickly, as it usually did, and Christian suspected some form of bipolar affect had taken hold of the man somewhere in his lost childhood.

"What's the plan here?" Christian asked as he braved reaching across the table and began lightly running his fingers along the back of the killer's hand. "Are you going to turn yourself in before the book comes out...or do you have something other than that in mind?"

The words were weighted gold. He wanted his answer because it was important, but they were heavy and rested like anchors in the moment, dragging them both under dark waters. Church had again turned his head, ignoring the question, and he pulled his hand away, reaching for his glass of beer. Men had secrets; they carried their thoughts like they carried their possessions. They learned to hide them in their shadowy caves and hoard them mysteriously. Church was male in every sense; nothing metrosexual existed in his personality. He guarded his past, and he stockpiled his plans. It was clear Christian wouldn't get his answers today.

They finished their beers and ordered two more. They nibbled at their buffalo wings but only as a distracted afterthought. They were relatively silent after that. The writer had overstepped, and the killer had closed up shop to the curious. It would take time before the mood could be reestablished. Christian asked Church if he wanted to head back to take the next walking tour, but the man scrunched his nose in derision. He wasn't the same little kid who left the hotel room with excitement; the cloud had taken him, and he maintained a cautious dullness on his features.

"There's always the Mayflower?" Christian asked with a sheepish grin.

It was only that suggestion that enabled him to yank Church back to the land of the living. Christian's proposition offered a promise of sex and sweat, and that obviously appealed to Church more than any time spent under Seattle sidewalks. He reached his hand over and placed it over Christian's. It was the most pronounced display of affection he could offer, but it had been sufficient in cresting both men's interests. They walked back to the hotel slowly, side by side, cavalierly chatting about nothing of any significance—they both had other things on their minds.

Chapter Twelve

IT HAD BEEN an unusual day all around. Justin Mackavie left home headed for work, and he hit every green light along the way. After arriving at work, he found an open space for his Acura right beside the front door. He was pleased to find every request for documentation from his borrowers had been replied to, and his email was overflowing with the necessary documentation to close almost all the loans in his queue. It would prove to be a profitable month if he could finish all his loans and reap the benefits of his commission bonus on each one.

Justin was in a good mood that morning; he even smiled at the underwriters in the other departments as he strolled in with his steaming coffee in hand and his Walkman plugged into his ear. Things had been looking up lately, or maybe they just appeared that way when his outlook had changed. He had recently met a young woman and begun spending time with her. She had a child from a previous relationship, but at least the little girl was barely out of diapers. She seemed to enjoy playing with Justin on the living room floor whenever his new girlfriend found the time for a date.

Overall, things appeared more promising; he had a job he felt comfortable with, one that enabled him to support himself and the eventual family he'd always planned. He was dating a lovely woman and the sex was good, and he'd doubled up on his car payments and applied every tax refund he could, and now he was nearing a glorious payoff date. Although he had only been renting his condominium, he was considering purchasing; he was only waiting for that voice in his head to push him forward and a woman at his side who was screaming at him to do it. However, his good spirits would not save him, and on any mundane day, as today, when things were looking like they were peaking, he would find his hopes dashed and fortunes altered. Justin Mackavie was acquiring every aspect of his own American Dream, but regrettably, he would not survive past lunch.

Two days earlier, Justin had encountered a man he was not prepared to meet. In actuality, they hadn't met per se, they had merely passed each other, as many of Church's victims found their fate. There was a ghostly aura ebbing from Justin, one he had never noticed and others seemed equally unaffected by. But for Gabriel Church it was a sign, a call to action, and Justin's outcome became considerably shakier at the happenstance of brushing past Church in a restaurant.

Neither men ever faced the other, nor ever shook hands or acknowledged knowing the other. They couldn't have been any more different. Justin carried a paunch of settle at his waist, even though he was only in his early thirties. He was an innocuous man, considered attractive only by his mother and his new girlfriend. He worked and he planned, and his only enjoyment seemed to be that rare party he attended, or his weekend warrior activities with his band of nerdy cohorts from school. The only thing he had working on his behalf was a glow that would pinpoint him as being someone special in another's eyes.

It would be another eight months before Church would meet his writer and settle in a luxurious suite at the Mayflower for his first sexual encounter with another man. Whatever happened in that Seattle hotel would eventually transform Gabriel Church in ways he wouldn't understand until later. But as Justin wouldn't cross his path for nearly a full year, his fate was irrevocably sealed before it even had a chance to evolve. He would be followed to his office, and he would be watched for hours by a man who had slipped easily past security and shadowed him to the fifth floor. After drinking two cups of coffee, Justin would need to relieve himself. It was a predictable sequence of events as seen by a man who studied the patterns and behaviors of others. He would be followed into the men's room, be standing at the sink washing his hands when a stranger would come quickly from behind holding a garrote of wire to end his life.

Justin's body would be found behind the doors of a closed stall, propped on a white porcelain throne with blood staining the front of his button-down shirt. His murder would be investigated, but eventually grow cold. He was a man without enemies, leaving detectives at a loss for motive and reason. No one was captured on video, and no one could say whether they had seen an unfamiliar face roaming the halls on that fateful morning. And since he was unmarried, the only notification his new girlfriend would get about his death would come from a news account on the television while she folded clothes at the kitchen table later than evening.

BACK AT THE Mayflower, the two men roused more leisurely than one might expect. Like the perfumed scent of a slow-burning incense, they decided wordlessly to remain locked in each other's arms and fully enjoy their morning. The suite had become their fortress of solitude, that blissful place where anxieties were kept at bay and firmly secured behind the bolted door. Neither man seemed to be in much of a rush to extricate themselves or untangle their bodies from their satisfyingly giftwrapped slumber. Parts of the prior evening had been an exercise in physical acrobatics, with more than a single climax attained per man, and as a result, they were wallowing in their exhaustion as the first rays of sunlight peeked through the heavy cotton drapes. It was a safe bet that neither of them had ever once slept a whole night wrapped in another man's embrace, but it somehow felt splendidly natural to awaken in such a fashion.

Christian stirred only slightly when Gabriel's chest hair tickled his nostrils and forced him from his dreams. Looking up, he saw those pale eyes were already open.

"Morning, you sleep well?"

Church merely nodded his approval and then asked, "You like resting under my arm, don't you, babe?"

"Yep, it feels like meaty goodness," Chris said jokingly.

Both woke hungry and desperate for caffeine, sticky and raw from their previous frolicking. Gabriel's shaft had started to stir to life at Christian's backside, alerting him that if he didn't jump from the covers, he'd be stuck there for another hour. He showered alone this time, stretching under the pulsing water and lathered with suds. He called out from the spray to have Gabriel phone down for a fresh pot of coffee to be delivered. "Dial 99 for room service," he screamed out while poking his head out from the shower and over the din of the shower jets.

Christian watched Gabriel pick up a complementary white bathrobe from the hook and head to the phone. "Do you want food brought up too?" he called out and visibly started when he turned to find Christian standing behind him with only a towel wrapping his neck. Gabriel's eyes traveled down his wet, naked torso. "Err, sorry...didn't know you were done. Do you want food too?"

"No, let's find something in town. This is going to be frightfully expensive as is."

"Is this going to be our last day in paradise?" Gabriel asked.

"That depends on what you consider paradise as being," Christian offered with a smile before kissing Gabriel's mouth and indulging in their first morning embrace.

"You know you're getting pretty comfortable in my presence these last few hours. Maybe too comfortable..." Gabriel broke away and turned his back on Christian who had grown to accept his usual transmutation of mood and only smiled broadly.

"You are correct, sir, but I'm enjoying the moment because there might not be many great moments to follow. It's nice here... Allow me to keep it." He reached his arm out and permitted his hand to graze the back of the robe as if entreating his lover for acceptance.

"Let's make it a late lunch and work a bit over coffee. There's more about me that you need to know."

Christian nodded quietly, even with Gabriel turned from view; words would only be a distraction now, since both felt their answers, even unspoken. By the time the porter rapped gently at their door, Christian had pulled on his jeans and was wrestling into a shirt as Gabriel opened for a young lady in a starched white top. She smiled sweetly as she pushed a cart with a large carafe of coffee, four fresh cups, and a silver bowl of sugar with a small matching pitcher of cream next to it. She bowed her head in servitude as she positioned the cart in the center of the room, whisked out a pad for a signature, and then backed out professionally, closing the door with a grin of acknowledgment as she departed.

As Christian filled the cups, Gabriel wrapped his arms around him and nuzzled sensually at his neck. "Maybe you should lose the clothing and make yourself more comfy."

"If I did that we'd never get anything done," Christian said, beaming with appreciation.

"That being said, where would you like to begin today?" Gabriel asked as he blew a cooling breeze across his unsweetened coffee.

"We've tiptoed around the subject of your victims for a time now. I'd like to go into that if you're comfortable with it. Namely, how many...and in what states."

"Right to the bone you cut today, even with my scent still dancing around your nethers. Okay, let's go for it." Suddenly Gabriel's eyes became glassy as he tugged for exacting memories, and Christian could see him making a grisly count inside his head. After a long pause and two sips of his coffee, he turned to the writer and said, "Forty, but that's only my initial guess without putting pen to paper and working out the details for accuracy."

"You're saying you have committed approximately forty murders in your lifetime?" Christian couldn't help but pull a round of oxygen in then reach for a nearby chair-back for support. His knees were wobbly with Church's cold pronouncement, and he considered once again the legalities of him standing in a room with such a prolific killer.

"Forty..." The word came out again, and Christian found himself dropping into a chair inattentively.

"I said that was my best guess without doing the math. But I figure it's very close to the right number. It's kinda amazing how I haven't been caught yet, huh?" Gabriel had twisted a grin to his face without the humanity of understanding his own confession. He was recalling numbers, not faces. Simple data was forced from memory, yet there were no remaining family members, grieving friends, or shattered lives wrapped in his words. He had come up with the analytical figure of forty, and that was all it was to him in that moment.

Christian sat dumbstruck with Gabriel casually standing behind him, void of the benevolent remorse one should feel. He couldn't speak words and stared off into space, trying to measure what he'd just heard. He had never really trawled to find that exact figure of homicides before then; maybe it was because he suspected the truth would be overwhelming. Or maybe because he just didn't want to know.

In his eyes, everything seemed to blur and lose tangible substance in his company. He was enamored with a man who'd openly admitted to being more than mere serial killer, and that was disturbing enough to warrant introspection. Gabe had confessed to an inordinate amount of sin, He had confessed to inordinate sin, which Christian understood even he lacked ample words for description. Forty was a number that might've been linked to the sum of deaths in a factory explosion in Jakarta, not the single acts of a lone killer. One had to reserve that number for catastrophes, not those of an executioner acting alone. If he'd taken an assault rifle and multiple rounds of ammo to a high-perched clock tower, there would still be significantly fewer victims than Church just admitted to.

IT TOOK A minute before Gabe sensed a need for empathy. He fought back confusion and placed his hands on Chris's shoulders. The man had resolutely asked for a number, and he'd been given one. Why then he wondered, did his friend be unable to comprehend his answer? After all, it seemed clear to him.

"Sorry...I hadn't figured you wouldn't have known that."

Gabe's voice may've sounded conciliatory, but they couldn't break Chris's state of awe.

Time didn't just dawdle then; it nearly stopped completely. As Chris absorbed everything he heard, Gabe was left to stand silently behind him while resting his palms on the same shoulders he'd run his tongue along hours earlier. It was odd that Christian seemed so weighted by the number, he thought. But he dared not risk making it worse by giving more, or delving into the graphic details of each individual kill.

"The accounting is inconceivable to me," he said. "After lunch, why don't you take some time and come up with an accurate figure? I'll leave you alone with a pen and some paper and let's see what number you come up with then."

"Fair enough," Gabe said. This wasn't what he expected of Christian today, but if he was anything, he was adaptable. Maybe he should have fudged the number, he considered. Maybe then he wouldn't be staring at a pained expression with no words to diffuse the situation.

Chris stood up and gently pushed the chair under the table. "Let's get dressed, 'cause I could use some sustenance. We can pick this up later." As he said that, Gabe could hear a hole in his voice, absent was the tenderness he was accustomed to hearing while in his company. He'd heard concern in Chris's voice before, but now he sensed a cavity there, a cavernous void where Gabe was left to stare into it alone. He wondered if he could repair the damage because he wanted more than anything to keep the man close. Or even something more if it worked in that direction. It never even dawned on him that Chris was quickly becoming the only true companion he'd ever really known.

They hadn't accomplished anything of importance that morning, but even without any note scrawled on paper, the effects would be lasting. Gabe would've liked to have turned the clock back, to have kept his mouth shut, or to have simply lied, but what would that have done for the story, he thought—he was burrowed somewhere under a rock and between a hard place. His fucking of Chris had altered things, but not in the ways he'd expected—it was the truth about his murders that risked unraveling the bindings. Would he lie the next time such a question lingered at the door, one that might shake his friend and threaten losing him forever? Or would he accept how he truly wanted his story told and choose not to shy from the cold realities of the killings? Would he permit his new friend to grow to hate him and fear him more than he did today? He hung his head as he headed back to the bedroom to recover his clothing, sadness oozing from him like an open wound.

They had accomplished nothing that morning, but even without any note scrawled on paper, the effects would be lasting. Gabe would've liked to have turned the clock back, to have kept his mouth shut, or to have simply lied, but what would that have done for the story, he thought—he was burrowed somewhere under a rock and between a hard place. His fucking of Chris had altered things, but not in the ways he'd expected—it was the truth about his murders that risked unraveling the bindings. Would he lie the next time such a question lingered at the door, one that might shake his friend and threaten losing him forever? Or would he accept how he truly wanted his story told and choose not to shy from the cold realities of the killings? Would he permit his new friend to grow to hate him and fear him more than he did today? He hung his head as he headed back to the bedroom to recover his clothing, sadness oozing from him like an open wound.

Chapter Thirteen

YOU COULD NEVER tell what someone was running from, what demons hid in dark corners of their minds—such was Gabriel. He was the baddest of the bad. However, Christian had agreed to walk his hallowed halls, contracted to peer inside...even though Gabriel was someone who should have been studied in a clinical setting, possibly from behind the protection of iron bars and bulletproof glass. He would be a heartbreak that was clear-cut, but for Christian, the question was, to what degree?

Gabriel seemed to possess an abundance of traits that should have made his life run smoothly. By contrast, he was void of many attributes he should have had: shame, remorse, humanity, greed, and even pity. Whenever Christian looked into those grayish eyes or stared at that wrinkled, sexy grin, he found himself confused by the realism of it all. Over lunch, he was lost inside his own head, but Gabriel seemed to respect his solitude and worked hard not to engage him. Double digits had killed the good spirits he'd woken up with.

It's not like he ever lied to me, Christian thought. *Not like I didn't expect there to be horrific truths in his telling.*

God this is fucked up!

It brought to mind the image of him sitting on the floor of his living room as a child, where he first learned there had never been a Santa Claus—nobody but his parents had ever brought gifts to rest under the tree. It was sad when you lost innocence, that much was certain, however necessary it was to growing up. However, it was difficult looking at his friend with adoration, or something akin to love, whenever he pushed the images of the victim's faces from his mind, just so he could look longingly across a room or feel comfort in his embrace.

Forty...the number couldn't be ignored or shelved aside in dusty recesses. It was there already, and it demanded to be heard and acknowledged. Christian glowered over his lunch plate, wondering if he could ever continue with the book after hearing Gabriel carelessly mention the number that was now screaming in his head over and over.

Forty murders. Forty murders!

Whether it was bravery or some version of compassion, Gabriel tenderly reached his hand over to graze his forefinger along Christian's resting hand. The gesture shattered his concentration, and he pulled away more quickly than he would have preferred, as if brushing too close to a hot branding iron.

"You look freaked out. I am sure I preferred the other look. You know...the one where your face was buried in the pillow. You looked happier then, at least from behind."

Christian seemed pulled from murky waters with Church's comment; he even allowed a half smile to break the darkness. He needed to shake it off. He raised his head and forced a deep examination of Gabriel's eyes. They were the one feature the man possessed that could drag one down like a siren's song. It could be the melody that licked at your center yet drained you of drive and stamina. It could be a fatal feature to some, and one Christian would have to be wary of. Driving his mood back, he decided not to think lest he allow Church to see him open like night-blooming jasmine for just being in his company. His face lightened, his chest expanded, and he opened his posture invitingly. He had been enrapt with the killer's gaze, but he shoved those thoughts aside; he would have to disregard the siren's lament just to continue on.

"Sorry about all this. I guess I wasn't prepared for it, but I'm coping...at least, as well as I can."

"No worries, my buddy, I guess I raced when I should've idled." Gabriel attempted reparations by allowing his fingers to crawl along the table toward Christian in silly spider-like fashion, creeping closer and begging a smile from the writer. It appeared to work, and Christian finally let loose a tiny chortle from under his breath and smiled, opening petals even more.

YEARS BEFORE THIS moment, somewhere between Gabe's first killing in Texas and his last one to date, he had met a man he thought was a stranger. By chance, the man was actually Gabe's own neighbor, even though he didn't know that at the time. Gabe had been holed up in Flagstaff in a ramshackle boarding house. He had been living the gypsy existence for so long that he had forgotten the creature comforts of a steady address. If you asked him today the name of the shithole he once lived at in Arizona, he would've said he didn't remember. He had forgotten it for good reason. The floor was dirty and stained; one could almost see the vomit and blood the super had failed to eradicate. There were roaches and termites under every counter, and the sink had deteriorated to a rust-colored chasm where dirty dishes always seemed to dwell.

His name was Stuart Hennessey, and he'd arrived in Flagstaff only a month before Gabe. He'd found the same boarding house by the sign sitting on its tiny patchy grassed front lawn: ROOMS FOR RENT – REASONABLE RATES. They were more micro-apartments than traditional boarding house rooms, but they were, as promised, reasonably rated. Of course, the sign neglected to mention the infestation of creepy-crawlies and rotted terrazzo, equally failing to note leaky faucets and sickly tenants who would be sharing the same floor. Each room did possess a bathroom, with a shower so confining Church had to crouch extremely low just to fit under the nozzle and allow poorly pressured water to fall on his shoulders. But at least it was the type of place that didn't ask questions, require legal documentation, or hold one to a lengthy lease term. A rental contract would be a waste of paper for the transient types who chose to live there—it quickly became a pay-as-you-live residence.

Gabe never bumped into Hennessy at any point during his two-month stay. It was merely a twist of irony that sanctioned both men to live so close in proximity yet never have an occasion to meet. Had Gabe ever spotted him in the halls, possibly carrying an armload of groceries in small paper bags, at any juncture during his residence, things might have gone drastically different.

Stuart Hennessy had his own story and his own demons. He had recently been released from the Arizona State Prison Complex in Yuma, and that rathole of a boarding house was all he could afford with the wages he earned from a local grocery store while working as a stocker. He had his own dreams and aspirations, stemming from his two-year stint in a correctional facility. He had not been a bad man when he was arrested and then later convicted of petty larceny, but he'd had to work hard to shake the corrupt side of his nature; the same trait he'd learned to acclimate to while suffering prison. He was rebuilding his relationships, working on his character, still oblivious to the white light that surrounded him like a ghostly brilliance. The one only Gabe could see.

Gabe might not have encountered Hennessy at the rooming house, but he did at a bar, never recognizing him as a neighbor or as being in the same timeworn and frayed circumstance as he. Gabe had stopped at a dive called the Cheyenne and ordered a draft to quash the Arizona heat from his throat. It was only a glance over Gabe's right shoulder that would change both men's destinies. Hennessy exited the men's room slathered in a white, hot shine that needed to be addressed by the killer's bent perception.

The tidal wave of crashing light that overtook Gabriel was not unexpected; he had been witness to this experience many times before. Stuart Hennessey wasn't the first of Gabe's victims, nor would he be the last. This pudgy little man may have been overlooked by most of the strangers he passed, but to Gabe, he was the epitome of something life altering, a pristine opportunity to answer some unknown call.

Each time Gabe took a life, he watched the radiance dissipate; it washed over him as it slipped away, leaving him feeling sated and clean. It was as if he could almost reach out and grasp the tangible glow as it left the host, before seeping through him as the universe took it, pulling every dark nugget of his soul and taking for a long ride. Gabe wouldn't even hazard a guess as to the lasting effects, the origin, or the meaning behind it all, and it would be years before he would even try. Sitting in a Seattle hotel room with a man he barely knew, he voluntarily attempted an explanation for his deeds. But Gabe didn't have true words to express himself or get his damaged point across to Christian. He knew how it sounded—it sounded that way to him as well. But he couldn't discount the feeling, or negate those emotions. So with, or without justification and clarity from others, he would be compelled to relive the moment, over and over again.

Gabe sat stunned for a moment as he watched Hennessy returning to his table. By his reckoning, the man was enjoying a happy-hour cocktail with a coworker or some other unimportant associate that never factored into his plan. It didn't matter to Gabe; his white-lighter was incidental in the grander scheme. He too would be forgotten soon enough. Or at least by the time the next murder was calling him and begging for a release of all those pent-up sins he'd amassed. It was his gift, he figured, that ultimate contribution that only he could bestow—and he intended on doing that presently, but only after completely absorbing what energy the white-lighter possessed before hastily imparting back into an unforgiving cosmos—a universe he was rapidly learning to despise.

Stuart Hennessey ambled out to his car after only a couple of drinks. *What a lightweight pussy* Gabe thought, as he watched him wave goodbye to his drinking buddy before fumbling awkwardly with the car keys he'd pulled from his pocket. He hadn't noticed the stranger coming up behind like a shadow. Like so many others before him, he'd failed a valuable lesson of those very basic rules for his own security. A large hand ensnared Stuart quickly, covering his mouth as Gabe shoved his massive frame like a boulder pinning him against his car. With his movements restricted, Hennessey became yet another victim easily dispatched by a swift and experienced predator. Forcing him off his feet, he dragged Stuart to a spot behind the Cheyenne's dumpster. It was safe there Gabe thought, hidden in an alley where only bartenders ever came to toss empty liquor boxes. Say for that occasional drunk frat kid who slipped outside just to drain the old lizard rather than having to face a long line at the urinals.

The expression on Stuart's face must've been a mixture of surprise and fear, and it was surely made worse by the sight of glinting moonlight sparking off a raised blade. He didn't know his attacker and remained gratefully unaware for any motivation of such a violent assault. Robbery never even crossed his mind when the knife was plunged deep into his chest.

The feeling of powerlessness wasn't lost on Stuart. In the seconds before his breathing stopped it scattered across his brain like buckshot. But by then, it was too late to reflect on much, because the blade was being pulled from his lungs before being forced back in hard, and with amazing force. He felt every penetration, witnessed the blood flying from his torso in bright red spurts like a ghastly sprinkler on high, but the pain was more removed than he could've ever had expected. You can consider your untimely death as it happens, or you can spiral into the belief that as humans we are all vulnerable. And in the end, we are all weak. Stuart chose the latter.

Within too few lapsed moments, he was undergoing a sense that his own body was rising. He saw himself suspended in the air watching the melee from above in eerie astonishment that told him he had mere seconds left to live. He didn't have any enemies and never carried much cash with him. He had a great deal still left to accomplish before his ticket was to be punched. No, there wasn't a single reason for him to be there, experiencing his own mortality one final time. In the tragic end, it never mattered. And while being soaked with his own blood, even he couldn't pull a foundation for the things that were occurring...*and then he was simply gone.*

The powerless feeling of such an event wasn't lost on Stuart. In the minutes before he stopped breathing, he observed the knife being pulled out and then brought down again and again with amazing force. He felt every penetration, witnessed the blood fly out in bright-red spurts from his body. But the pain was something more removed, because his mind was already locked on the abstract notion of how alone he was in those seconds, how weak and vulnerable the human body truly was. Before he knew it, he found himself rising above the melee and staring down in astonishment at the eeriness of it all. He didn't know the man. He didn't have enemies, didn't carry any cash, and had too many things to do before his clock was punched. There was no reason here, no sanity, and before he could pull some foundation for what was occurring in that moment...he was gone.

Gabe felt the man slump lifelessly in his arms, and he released his grip sufficiently to raise both arms to the heavens and throw back his head. It was a look of crucifixion, but it was more. Gabe became a sponge, soaking in every drop before it vaporized back into stardust, drinking in whatever balanced the scales of our souls. He would appropriate whatever essence existed before it was gone forever...because he was a thief in that way. The fading brilliance had always been his meter. Once the light was gone, it was too late to lap up what was left. Hennessy's glow didn't last long, but Gabe had taken every portion he could before it left that dirty alley adjacent to the Cheyenne Bar.

BACK AT THE Mayflower, Gabriel had assumed his spot on that salon chair, just as before. Christian occupied his hands by fixing them a drink from a bottle they'd purchased when headed back from their misspent time looking for a walking tour. Christian's efforts to remove the dark mood had been only slightly successful. It still weighed him down like a magnet hold, dragging him to the earth. He couldn't help but picture the expression on Gabriel's face as he killed—he hadn't seen it, thankfully, but he imagined it twisted and grimacing as if he were a skilled predator who enjoyed sadistic games. He couldn't balance the scales from killer to the man he'd made love with hours earlier. It seemed incalculable he could be both men.

Gabriel rose from the chair and grabbed the bourbon and cola that Christian handed him. With his free hand, he unsnapped the top button of his jeans and then placed his drink on the table so that he could pull off his shirt.

"Put it out of your mind, Church. Your moment's been infected."

"Don't embarrass yourself, junior, I'm just getting comfortable. I'm not an animal. Even I see sex is not always the best cure-all remedy." He yanked his pullover over his head and discarded it casually on the floor. "I'm just a little warm is all." Gabe plopped down and Christian could see his damp chest hair indicating he'd been telling the truth. He absently strolled over and turned the air conditioning down, starting an immediate breeze through the suite. He turned and faced Gabriel, sipping his drink with a methodic deliberation.

"You know, when I was born, I had a hole in my heart." Gabriel sat staring at Christian with cool detachment as he began his story. "It's called ASD, or Atrial Septal Defect." He let the words hang for a minute before continuing, "Poor ole Sissy Church was the first to notice her little baby boy had blue, swollen legs and occasionally suffered with shortness of breath. She wrapped her baby up and headed into town, but doctors are a stupid lot, and they calmed her fears and sent her home with a consolatory pat on her back and a promise that all was well. Later she decided her doctor was fucked in the head and took me to another specialist who diagnosed me with this ASD crap." Church took a long sip of his drink, and Christian took a chair at the table, concentrating too much on Gabe's wet, full lips as he told his tale.

"It's nothing major, you understand; it just means eventually I might need surgery, but the likelihood is that it will someday just give me a stroke. Alcohol exacerbates the problem, but I do enjoy a stiff one now and again...as apparently you do as well." His smirking grin was back and that twinkle of seduction flashed again in those pale blue-gray eyes. A recent memory came back; it hit Christian's consciousness where it had previously gone unnoticed. He remembered lying with his head on Church's chest after they'd completed a rousing sexual bout, both had been breathing hard and languishing in a recent satisfying climax. He remembered listening to Church's heartbeat and feeling an odd sensation that something sounded strange. He wrote it off, discarded it, and allowed it to blank from his head. But the awareness came back as Gabriel told him about his condition.

It had been the heartbeat...it had sounded different, louder than it should have, straining arteries aching to pound closed.

"You didn't mention this before. Why?" he asked.

"Wasn't an issue actually. I'm only telling you now because I want you to understand me." Gabriel leaned back, and Christian had to take note of how sexy he was, sipping bourbon, his shirt off, jeans seductively open at the waist showing that hint of hair beckoning to be touched.

"Understand you...meaning what?"

"Meaning, I have always lived with an hourglass over my head. The sand was tipped from the moment of my birth, and although I'm super fine at the moment, I think that ever-present ticking clock has affected how I look at life."

"I don't mean to sound harsh, but that sounds like something bordering on an excuse. Maybe even a fish for pity." The words came out more severe than he'd intended, and he immediately wished he could jerk them back. To be accurate, he did pity Gabriel. He also felt a wave of depression hit him. The man of his obsession was even more greatly flawed, and he'd become human once again. Looking across the room at the man he was exploring, he realized he didn't want him to die, didn't relish seeing him after a stroke, or finding him blue and cold on the bathroom floor. *Am I losing my friggin' mind?* he asked himself.

"I wanted you to know about this. Not sure why I needed to tell you, 'cause if you think it's a pity I want from your sweet ass then you haven't learned anything about the real me during our time together."

Christian bowed his head, a shamed child who'd been admonished for doing something he knew had been wrong. "Sorry."

Gabriel nodded his head, his eyes staring at the floor. Was it derision or forgiveness?

"I was hoping you'd know me better by now. Didn't our fucking so well mean anything?"

He didn't even wait for Christian to respond, choosing to stand and head back to the bar to refill his drink. He seemed disgusted in the moment, but as Christian watched him from behind, he couldn't help but feel something close to adoration. His mother may have just made a shitty remark, but had she been right? For someone who'd never felt these types of emotions, they were wholly unfamiliar to him. He realized it did make a difference knowing about Gabriel's condition. It seemed appropriate that a killer would have a hole in his heart...that it would be congenital. Like some predestined gift that would make him unique to those around him...lacking something everyone else seemed to take for granted. Maybe the void where heart tissue should have been was the exact cavity where the human soul sat? Maybe this was another reason Gabriel had become a killer, a loner, and fated to some gruesome end.

He was glad to know he'd at least been as attuned as the young Sissy Church. He'd noticed something unique about Gabe's heartbeat early on. He just hadn't enough experience resting on the man's chest. But he did want to rectify that. Being in Gabriel's presence made his insides unsteady. He found himself flooded with strange emotions and kept noticing how blood coursed more southerly than it usually did. His desire demanded his attention. He positively needed to lie intimately beside Gabriel one more time, or risk feeling incomplete. The killer had broken his friend's mood by his quiet confession to a normal deficiency, making him appear mortal and imperfect. Forgetting his more deadly defects for the moment, this news was something he could grab onto, something he could understand. He walked over to Gabriel, who stood pouting like a little boy, his back turned. Wrapping his arms around him, Christian rested his head on the big man's shoulder.

"I only know one way to break tension," he said, and then Gabriel turned and accepted his friend's embrace. They walked silently to the bedroom, and even though they were alone in the suite, Gabriel closed the bedroom door behind them.

Chapter Fourteen

CHRISTIAN WAS PRAYING for time to crawl, to retain those minutes one typically wastes without much thought or concern. He needed a chance to lie undisturbed in a silent room while still being present for the things that happened around him. *Gabe hadn't lied...there was a missing beat. It seemed to echo louder because of its absolute absence,* Chris thought. It somehow lacked the usual follow-through one might expect to hear in a normal heartbeat. He labored intently atop his lover's chest and listened for that strong steady thumping of a healthy organ. But he was alarmed by every faulty sound he wasn't hearing. It dragged like a sticky valve that needed oiling, something that had to work harder than the others just to properly close. He found himself anticipating the rhythm, waiting for the next report like measured sounds from an old metronome. He held his breath, hoping the next sounds were the typical crashes of tiny atrial flaps banging shut. But he recalled thinking later that it was the things one doesn't hear that become louder whenever one needs them most. It was like Gabe's heart was whimpering in pain, a noise strangely deafening. Particularly from someone one loved and never wanted to watch die. It was loud enough that he figured he might've recognized it from way across the room...*thump...whiny...thump* and then all over again. His defect was real indeed, and lying there, breathless, Christian tried to match his heartbeat against Gabriel's. But the strain was too clearly evident to compete for long. Especially after sex, when it sounded the roughest and most anomalous.

Perspiration glazed Gabriel's broad ribcage, with odd sensations of combined testosterone and sweat wafting toward Christian's nose. They were both panting from a fresh climax, spilled semen left crusting dry across their abs. He never wanted those minutes to end, choosing to bask in the languid moments between every life and death struggle that'd become Church's life.

"Gonna sleep real good now, baby, thanks. I'm still not sure I'd willingly choose a man over a woman yet, but you certainly opened me up to new vistas."

"You better not choose anyone else," Chris offered mockingly. "But you're welcome for getting a new way of thinking. You're one sexy motherfucker you know that? And I love what you do to me, particularly from someone who claims he's never done those things before."

"Likewise," Gabe replied, squeezing his lover's arm tighter. He was right after all, Chris deduced. Sex between them was a rare thing of beauty. He lay his open palm across Gabe's furry chest as if he was patiently waiting for the steady knocking as a response and allowed his mind to wander. It trailed from moment to moment, between their lovemaking to that hereditary flaw buried under his skin. As satisfying as those moments felt, he still couldn't let go of the sadness it represented, like watching a winning lottery ticket you'd just purchased getting blown out of an open window by an unapologetically strong breeze.

"Is there anything you can do besides surgery for your heart?" he asked cautiously.

"Not a damn thing! But it doesn't matter anyway. I was always racing toward a quick death...and no one deserves it more."

They both decided words would only shatter the moment. Without knowing the true breadth of their connection, both men seemed to become in sync with the other's emotional state. They rested in silence, as men occasionally did in other men's company, and Christian's palm tightened over Gabe's massive chest. Desperation ebbed freely like a weeping sore, sufficient for both to see it plainly displayed. The mood transformed from relaxation to bittersweet melancholia before they both slipped into a restless sleep.

FITFUL DREAMS INVADED Gabe's slumber. He was remembering an incident or possibly misremembering it. It was a dream after all, and even in the dream, he recognized it as a sleep-filled play performed for his amusement. He had met a man, years before, and now he pulled that picture back from memory. It had an air of familiarity, but much was different than how it truly happened. It had been somewhere in the Midwest. Traveling as he did, he couldn't rightly remember all the names of the cities he passed through. This was one of those no-name towns in some visage from long ago.

It had been just outside a bar, which was a familiar custom for Gabe who liked to spend much of his time drinking alone late at night. He had stumbled out, still reeling from the effects of too many glasses of beer, followed by a few shot chasers. He'd wanted to be drunk that night; he'd set out as that being his purpose. "Self-medication" he called it—a chance to push aside those irritating thoughts that continually plagued his mind.

He practically tripped over a group of men just outside the bar who seemed as drunk as he was. They had circled another fellow and were taunting him with verbal assaults, shoving him from man to man, like stoners passing a joint for each smoker to partake. He had become some plaything for inebriated assholes that had cravings for violence. Gabe didn't know what the ruckus was about, had not heard their argument with the slight man they were batting around like a cat with its half-live mouse. Whatever the commotion, the slightly smaller man was gravely outnumbered. But out of all the men, he seemed the least inebriated one.

Gabe never liked to get involved with the petty residue of the unwashed public. He didn't much care what others did around him, but as he faltered out the door of that seedy bar and was hit with the stench of urine and rising fear, he knew he couldn't escape the commotion without at least knowing the cause. Lurching up to the crowd of drunken hayseeds and the man contained in their circle, he heard one of the men call the slighter man a "cock sucking faggot!"

Nobody took much notice of Gabe lumbering up behind them, their concentration was trained on their smaller target, and in their beer-induced volatility, they were finely focused on the beating to come. It wasn't a fair fight by any means...not that anyone cared. Someone had made an assumption about the cocksucker in the center of the fray—it was certainly an incorrect assumption, because even wasted, Gabe knew that no queer would be stupid enough to make a proposition at any of these loud fuckers...not in that type of bar, not outnumbered.

Gabe wasn't completely blotto. He was sober enough to judge the circumstance for what it was: wasted country bumpkins picking on a smaller man. Too much beer, hot-blooded tempers, and stupid, uneducated fools, but they had made a bigger mistake than just picking on some tiny fellow, even if he'd truly been a cocksucker and dropped to his knees in the bar's dirty piss-stained men's room or placed his hand on the leg of some flannel-wearing redneck. They had made the mistake of allowing Gabe to walk up to the scene.

Without a word, Gabe grabbed one of the rowdy assholes, who had yet to notice his presence, and swung him around wildly. He slammed his fist into the man's jaw, and rendering him shaken before he could be surrounded by the remaining goons, he swung again, this time missing his mark slightly, no doubt an effect of the alcohol. But he missed by mere inches. He'd intended his blow to be square to the chin, but it made contact with the side of one confused hayseed's head. With the two men dazed and attempting recovery, his mind flashed to the remaining three. All were larger and fatter than he was, but each appeared the type of hillbillies who'd let their waistlines stretch and their minds shrink. None of them individually were any match for Church.

Gabe had been raised in the sticks. He had fought kids from the first time he could walk. He enjoyed a good fight and had learned how to manipulate his swings and his footwork to ensure his success. The man in the center of the attack had fallen to his knees; he seemed as surprised as the men Gabe had set upon. Gabe swung again, but he'd actually anticipated his swing going wild. His true motive had been to unbalance his target as he dove low to hit the hole he'd made under one man's arm just as that man raised an arm to strike back and defend himself against Gabe's wild swing. With the fat fucker unbalanced, Gabe elbowed him hard in the center of his back, hearing the man lose all his oxygen with one quick jab. Then Gabe swung back around and laid his fist hard under an already stunned chin.

The brawl had been so surprising, and Gabe's actions had been so swift and unexpected, that one of the bullies looked flabbergasted; this was not the fun he'd originally planned for his evening. He stepped back and threw his palms up and out, indicating he'd rather not be the brunt of this stranger's next attack. But his companion wasn't so wise.

He advanced on Gabe with spit spewing off his lips and with a mixture of agitation and red-hot revenge burning in his eyes. He was a bull on the charge and with sufficient mass to upend Gabriel if he reached him. But even drunk he was smarter than that runaway train barreling down the track and so he deftly stepped right just as the man dove for his midsection. His intention was to allow the bull to miss him by inches yet close enough that he could bring him down before he flew by. That was the plan anyway, and it went just as smoothly as he'd judged it would. Gabe brought his elbow down hard onto the bull's neck, and with as much force as he could muster. He nearly severed the man's spine in the process and all by nothing more than a rapid response to an unexpected attack.

The free-for-all was over as quickly as it began—with one man unconscious at Gabe's feet as the others were receding backward in an attempt to salvage their own skin and retain some small semblance of their failing pride. Gabe had become a caged animal, dancing in the center of confusion practically begging for someone to advance on him. His lip had been split in the fray, though he hadn't yet tasted his blood in his mouth, he was all but certain he wanted too. He desperately needed for one of those fat shits to make a run at him. He was practically demanding it. To his amazement none of his tormenters stepped forward, fearing the sheer amount of rage represented in the big man's sadistic grin. His pale eyes couldn't be clearly seen due to the alley's dim lighting, but the expression on his face was sufficient to cause them trepidation. Slowly they began backing away, cowering in the shadows to diminish themselves as possible threats. Two even spun on their heels and raced back inside the bar without a word. Some men foolishly misjudge their own their prowess, while still others know just when to turn-tail and run for safety. The focus of the battle had been one undersized victim who'd finally found his footing and had begun rising to his feet. Moving closer to Gabriel he smiled through his embarrassment and did the only thing he could, he extended a hand and stammered out his appreciation as plainly as possible, *Thank you, mister...thanks for all your help I mean!"*

Turning to acknowledge him Gabe instantly recognized why the others appeared to hate him so deeply, "*Fuck off, faggot!*" he said as he spun and sauntered towards the parking lot and his waiting car.

Gabe had all-but forgotten the incident, pushing it back as just another unimportant memory of his life. But now, in the hours before he fell unconscious with sleep, he could see the faces of each of the attackers just as clearly as he saw the younger man he'd chosen to protect. He remembered his delicate, dark features and wide expansive eyes. First they'd flashed with fear and revulsion and then they shined with outright, unabashed gratitude. The face reappeared from time to time, though it'd been ages since he recalled that part of his ancient history. He never truly understood why the image seemed to remain with him, or piece together why he'd rushed to the rescue of another vulnerable, weak homosexual. It flew against the grain of his nature; particularly after he'd practically beaten one faggot to death on a lakefront cruise area not so many years earlier. Both were portions of his character he assumed, just separate sides of the same coin. They may also be an unspoken explanation for something yet to come he thought. One never really knows.

He contemplated it only briefly before discarding the notion altogether. Sometimes it didn't pay to thoroughly examine things in the cold light of day. Not when they should remain concealed, buried and dormant somewhere. Never to be spoke of and especially never in the mixed company of strangers. This was a lesson he'd learned early on in his life. Though for the life of him he couldn't recall exactly when or where he discovered that little piece of wisdom.

THE MORNING SUN broke through the cracks in the hotel's blinds, hitting Christian squarely on his face and forcing him awake. He opened his eyes but didn't move, waiting to see if Gabriel would stir. He listened to his partner's breathing and watched the rise the fall of his lover's naked chest. It was glorious waking up next to such a sinfully beautiful creature, he thought. He just knew he could lie there all day long and be as happy as a pig in shit. But his movements shook Gabe from sleep who then made a sudden grunting noise as he stretched his arms and strained his sleepy muscles into life. Rolling over he offered a quick dry kiss on Christian's neck.

"Morning, boy, you sleep well?"

Gabriel's use of boy seemed oddly titillating in Christian's ear, since he was effectively only a few years younger than Gabe. But as incongruous as it sounded, it was still nice hearing the word. Chris decided then and there that he'd acquired a new and favorite moniker. He wanted to crawl beneath the man's massive arm and be sheltered there under his protection. *Is this what being a subordinate is supposed to be*, he wondered? Everything he'd been feeling lately seemed off-putting and a tad eccentric to his old life. It was like he'd been trying on different disguises and hadn't settled on the person he was destined to become. Everything felt new and every desire was an unaccustomed visitor you never wished to turn away. He liked being swaddled in Gabriel's adoration and somehow knew if it were taken from him he'd lose an important part of who he's supposed to be.

"Yeah, pretty well...and you?" he asked lovingly.

"Had a few fucked-up dreams but waking up with your body heat warming my cock was nice." He smiled broadly, mainly to himself and then jumped up and out of the covers with a start.

"Daddy needs coffee..."

Christian's gaze was drawn to his nakedness; that flaccid shaft with its overhang of foreskin, his brown furry chest, and his wild, manly bush of pubic hair. He could see a twinkle in Gabriel's eyes and a grin being subtly established. It was clear this man enjoyed having his body worshiped from afar, seeing a lover's eyes fill up with the same adulation and lust that he must be showing in this moment.

Facing his lover still tied in knots of the comforter Gabe flipped his extended thumbs outward.

"*Hey – eyes up here buddy*!" He said with a grin.

Christian looked back sheepishly then barely above a whisper he replied, "Mia Culpa my love," as he averted his doleful gaze away like a puppy who'd just piddled on the carpet.

"You look horny, baby. You want a ride on this love rocket"? Gabe asked flaying his open hands around his junk like it was an invitation.

"What I want is a shower and a big dose of caffeine. Then, as much as I'd prefer lying naked with you all day, I know we have a lot of work to do."

"My baby boy has turned down my gifts, it seems. Will wonders never cease?" He flaunted an expansive grin and then turned, with a little bopping dance, and headed to the shower. Watching him walk presented the best gift he could've given Christian that morning.

Chapter Fifteen

"YOU REMEMBER EVERYONE you killed. Do you remember everyone you ever fucked?" His question came from nowhere, and his eyes fell to the cup of coffee he was stirring. Gabriel looked up, surprised, and then leaned in closer to Christian.

"I remember everything I've done that was worth remembering. I could tell you stories, but remember, they were all with women."

It began as a peaceful morning for the two men. They'd showered and then taken the elevator to the café downstairs. The Mayflower boasted a simple elegance to their dining hall, but in truth, it was just a café that had seen better days with a finer reputation. Called the French Hen, it served a country breakfast in European style, but it was a café that tried too hard to be special.

Christian had thrown out the question as if it was an afterthought, but he could see the look on Church's face showing how interested he was. The idea of Gabriel being with others was strangely titillating, and Christian wanted something to gauge his own lovemaking with him against. Was Gabriel the same sensual animal with women that he'd been with Christian?

"I'm just a little curious," he said, trying to appear disinterested as he sipped gingerly at the hot cup.

"I BET YOU just wanna know if I like fucking them as much as I do you. But if you'd asked me this upstairs, we would've been an hour later for breakfast." Gabe smiled and leaned back against the chair and scanned the few guests still lingering over breakfast or an early brunch. He decided, as he was showering, that he would be more careful with what he offered Chris today—he didn't want another reaction like yesterday. This conversation held that possibility, so he decided "less was more."

Gabriel Church liked women. He may not have always understood them, but he knew the cool parts they brought to the party, and that had been enough. He had never had to try too hard like other men, pouting about how they couldn't get enough pussy; he could drown in it if he wanted…which wouldn't be a bad way to die, he thought. But since meeting Chris, he'd had stirrings that should have felt stranger to him than they did. Gabe never looked at Chris as some dick-hungry dude who wanted to simply guzzle on his hose, he saw him as something better. He enjoyed everything they did in bed. He loved the hard wrestle of being with another man and not having to be as gentle. Chris was a sexy form he could maneuver however he wanted, throw him this way or that way to reach purchase. Dominant sexual control over another man pleased him in ways he couldn't comprehend. It made him feel powerful and godlike, and that was something Gabe could gravitate to.

He doubted that he would ever be with another male sexually after Chris; it just wouldn't be the same. That concern flashed something forward—*life after Chris*. He'd never allowed himself to be fully aware of that concept, yet there it was. Would he ever be without Chris? He knew he'd awoken things in the writer that he'd never experienced, but it was an inevitable conclusion in his eyes. Chris was queer when they met; he just hadn't made the connection until being in Gabe's company. The thought of his new partner being with another man had never come to mind, but it rested there, hidden in the dark holes underneath. The picture in his head was unpleasant; he didn't want to share Chris, and didn't want the man to have a life outside of his adoration of Gabe. He knew he could be selfish that way.

"I just wanted to compare the Gabriel I know now to the one before I met him." Chris was still on that train and just wouldn't release his grip.

"What does it matter now? You got me, baby. Why do you care who I mighta fucked before?" He pushed back his plate—the eggs benedict had been too runny and seemed bland after yesterday's long bout of drinking.

"You're probably right. I don't know why I wanted to know, but you seem like someone who has changed a lot in the last couple of days, like someone finding his footing for the first time."

Gabe decided he didn't have words for that, and his head tilted slightly with a look that implied some playful disregard to Chris's line of questioning.

"Shouldn't you ask these questions back at the hotel with your trusty legal pad?"

"I decided I can remember everything you tell me. By the time it hits the noggin"—he said while tapping at his skull—"I promise I won't let it go."

"Besides, you no longer need that distance...and that pad of paper as your protective barrier, between a killer and a writer...am I right?"

CHRISTIAN SMILED SHEEPISHLY back at Gabriel, realizing how much he so often took Church's wit and intelligence for granted. It was another reason to admire him. He couldn't feel the same about Gabriel if he was just a beautiful imbecile. Smart was sexy, and that flash of intellect shined brightest in those pale eyes.

"Call it what you will, but it was wise to keep a professional remoteness to our conversations."

"You kinda fucked that up now, didn't you?" Gabriel said, cutting him off in midthought.

"You helped. You shouldn't have taken off your shirt, remember? It was all over but the sweating and panting once you did that." They both grinned like devils at the recollections.

They had eaten their fill and pushed the plates aside as Christian grabbed the bill and stood up to pay. His eggs hadn't been as tasty as he'd hoped either. Both suspected the French Hen would only be a place for coffee in the future, if there was a future. Christian had already decided to check out that morning, but the prospect left him numb. If they didn't have the Mayflower Plaza, what did they have? No sumptuous sex or waking up in cool, clean sheets with nothing but time to fill their days. It had been something of a vacation for him, and he still wondered if Gabriel would ever confess to where he was staying. Originally, he knew Gabe wanted that to remain secret, but that was before...before they'd done the glorious nasty with every finger and with each wet tongue. Would he slip away after their conversations to some out-of-the-way hole and fade from Christian's life forever? It was time to address that question.

"So you remember I was going to check out today? Actually I need to do that pretty soon. I was wondering what we were doing after that." His hand grazed Gabriel's back as he stood in line to pay for their dismal breakfast. "I have a loft here, not far... You could crash with me until my research for the book is...well...underway, if you want?"

"Get real, baby, you're never gonna have everything you need on me. It would just be days of fucking, and you know it," he whispered the words over his shoulder as an addendum, but the prospect incited Christian's shaft to stir in his jeans, and a smile formed as he pulled out his wallet.

"No. I think I will head back to my place tonight. We can arrange some schedule of meeting somewhere to talk," Gabriel said with sure confidence.

"Hooking up just to talk? Is that all you want now?" Words that were meant for Gabriel's ears alone, but the breathy question hung like an albatross around his neck.

"Worry naught, my baby boy...you *will* ride again."

Even without turning, Christian could sense the killer's power over him. He was a child being denied his prize, and he curled his bottom lip in a pucker, thankful Gabriel hadn't seen it.

THE FUTURE WAS a ridiculous consideration for either man. Both were trapped in the final hours of their daylight, only they didn't yet know this. While Christian reflected about the possibility of a life spent with Gabriel, the killer was measuring out his irrevocable, unalterable days. Gabe had lived his life by a single motto: *Everything crumbles and dust eventually takes it all*. He could appear playful in Christian's eyes, he could smile and joke about sex, but only because he saw the finality of it all...recognized the fate that would befall everyone, knew his future was locked into place, preordained. And it wouldn't be a good ending.

Gabe understood you couldn't take a life without first understanding just how feeble life was, how tentative and weak it stood alone. If you desired murder, you held a life in your hand. Whether you released it to grant life or gripped tighter to end it, it was at your command and discretion.

HER NAME HAD been Sandra Hodges. She was round and fair-skinned. Her blonde hair hung at her shoulders with a smile that made one forget her plump size. Lovely was a word her friends and family used to describe her, but it was her personality that made her special, in a not-so-special shell. Four years before Washington, Gabe had been traveling through California. It was there the two strangers had met.

"Don't be too afraid to be weak," he whispered over her shoulder calmly, just as she drew her final breaths. The look on her face was something Gabe would remember for all future days. It had not been sadness or surprise...maybe it had been acceptance.

Gabe had come closer to getting caught with Sandra's murder than he ever had before. It was in the timing, or the lack of it. As the fat woman trembled in those last breaths of life, Gabe barely had time to sop up her essence before his escape became compulsory. He hadn't chosen well, the spot where he took her. He was a vampire who needed sufficient time to drink, and he had rushed with her. He'd had no plan for the blonde's ending, and it nearly caused his undoing. He had only left the carwash stall seconds before another car pulled in. The water jet lay dripping suds from its nozzle like a bleeding artery.

He'd first caught sight of Sandra as she was standing next to her tiny red Prius shooting soapy streams on her new baby. She was alone. The light enveloping her held its usual brilliance, causing Gabe to weave his vehicle slightly, unexpectedly. He raced to the next corner and took a hasty U-turn to make it back around so that he could park in the adjacent stall. Excitement surged in his chest as he grabbed a familiar blade from under his driver's seat. His tension bubbled up and his nerves jangled as he shoved the blade in his jeans and opened the door under the pretense of washing his road-dirty car.

It was early dusk. There had been no traffic on the streets next to the Suds-Stream Car Wash. He wondered why a single woman would ever choose to wash her car in such a remote and unsavory area. It was as if she didn't respect her own safety. He wanted to mention that to her before he killed her but chose to hold his tongue. Taking a long look around for cameras and pedestrians, he calmly walked into the next stall, spotting her smiling as she held the wand over her windshield. He offered a pretense of asking her if she had change for a single or knew where a change machine was. She was cordial, naturally. Gabe could barely make out her round features because of the light that blinded her face.

It was over in seconds as he encircled her quickly, placing his massive arm around her ample breasts, the other covering her mouth to quiet her scream. She was wearing a pink, frilly sweater, forcing Gabe to wonder why fat girls always dressed as if they were still in high school. He could smell her perfume slathered over her buxom tits, and he felt remorse for what he speculated was her type: never invited to the dance, playing the good girl, all smiles, but only because no one had ever asked her to play anything else. Claiming to her friends she had to babysit on Saturday nights, when the sad truth was no one ever asked her to do much. She should have lost her virginity in the same ratty back seats as her girlfriends, but she had become a caricature of daddy's little girl, grasping her virtue with tight, fat fingers. It was a tragic disguise to everyone but her that her chastity had never been a prize of value for any of the boys in her grade.

Gabe held her tightly as he drove the blade into her chest, breathing heavily in her ear, almost sensually. Her pretty pink sweater started to ooze a bright-red stain between her breasts as the air in her lungs escaped with a grisly sound. The cable-knit flowers on her sweater ran from pink to a dreary blackened red, and Gabe felt her full size as the oxygen finally escaped and she became nothing more than dead weight, like a marionette once her tiny strings were severed.

"Don't be too afraid to be weak," he whispered again.

It seemed the best advice he could offer her, and she appeared to open with his words in her ears, at least until she was nothing but fat girth in his arms. Gabe laid her gently on the wet ground as suds intermixed with blood, and he noticed one of her equally frilly slippers had fallen off one foot and now rested on the drain. The swirling soap bubbles intermixed with a wash of bodily fluids and red. Staring at the slipper. he was seized inside the image, noting it too had been a lovely pink as well.

Sandra Hodge's remains were discovered less than a quarter hour after she'd been disposed of at the car wash. It happened when someone pulled in to run a wand over their filthy hubcaps. She was hard not to notice, a plump figure lying face-down in the water right beside a pretty red Prius, which from the outside seemed amazingly clean already. Gabriel would pass several police cruisers shortly after depositing the woman for a stranger to find. He noted the first wails of sirens as he maneuvered his truck at a leisurely pace. All in all, it was a very uneventful drive, but he took it with his window down and the car stereo playing on low. He couldn't help enjoying how his life was turning out, just as he enjoyed the way the warm night breeze danced through his hair.

Chapter Sixteen

CHOOSING SIDE STREETS and mixing into crowds with other pedestrians and tourists, Gabe couldn't shake his cautious side. Several times he glanced over his shoulder to ensure he wasn't being followed. He half-expected to see Christian's head bobbing into view, mixed in with the faces of laughing sightseers and normal Seattle residents. He pictured Chris ducking in and out of the throngs of people as he worked to provide his best impersonation of a gumshoe detective tailing a suspect. When he left the hotel, he'd left strict instructions that Christian wasn't to follow him, but the man possessed the curiosity of a cat in a house of closed doors. He enjoyed spending time with Chris and he had to admit all the sex he'd been getting wasn't anything he'd be complaining on anytime soon. But even at this early stage, this type of relationship required a fair degree of work.

It took thirty minutes to finally really reach the safety of his tiny, dismal temporary residence. Time he needed to spend by taking back alleys, or meandering aimlessly along the length-long blocks while slowly checking out the businesses along the way. From the outside, he was just another native who had interested in the merchandise of the businesses placed there to pull-in foot traffic. But actually he was surveying his own reflection in the windows, seeing if there were faces which popped out of the ordinary or with too much frequency. He was also checking to see if Christian was behind him. Weaving through the mob like a bad actor from an old black and white gangster movie, trying hard to appear incognito for an audience who couldn't believe it.

After basking in the luxurious Mayflower for two days, his place looked even more wretched than he'd remembered. He would've been embarrassed for Chris see his shithole he thought. But then again, there there was still a great deal the writer wasn't aware of; like the times he had to sleep in his truck or woke up burrowed in the underbrush of the nearest park because he'd been dead-ass broke. Or even the times he'd taken some fugly women home just to gain access to a hot shower and clean sheets. It was what it was, he reasoned. He needed a break today because he could feel himself losing perspective. The introduction of Christian, the chance to enjoy room service at a five star hotel, it was all too much. It was quickly become that temptress encouraging him of his chosen path. He didn't want to forget his old life exactly, just the respite he received in the warm embrace of something new. But he had to get back to his roots...because relaxed hunters can often make terrible mistakes.

They decided to stay apart for the day or rather Gabe decided it for them. He suspected he'd miss Chris's company nonetheless; like hearing that honeyed voice as he called from another room, or the sight of his eager desire to please or even those sweet tactile touches as they lay in silence on the bed.

He also liked how Chris could occasionally be the angel on his shoulder, that voice of reason and morality from all of his grisly deeds. He thought it odd that Chris was so hell-bent on finding some kind of answer to the events described to him. Odd particularly since Gabe thought it was a clear and sensible conclusion for him to have done the awful things he had. Sometimes it's just an appropriate response to insanity to go completely insane yourself. *He knew that, so why didn't Christian?*

Gabe pulled the crumpled telephone number from his jeans and tossed it on the nightstand beside his bed. The air seemed stale and rank from a lack of circulation, so he pushed open the French doors overlooking the courtyard. The doors were New Orleans in style, just as the courtyard was. It was the single feature about this hovel that made it passable. He pulled his shirt over his head and dragged it under his armpits before tossing it on the mattress and standing by the window for whatever breeze he could find.

He was forming a plan. Although abstract, it was developing a tangible edge, and Gabe had been playing with it ever since he and Chris had last fucked at the hotel. There were things he'd never told Chris, and those secrets were materializing now in his quiet, rented room as he stared out at fireflies beginning to dance in the air of the plaza. Gabe had always held a belief he would never get caught. He would never be tried and convicted for his part in the murder spree. That was never his destiny. If he was going to get arrested that white-light radiance would have been somehow different than it was. How was it possible that his victims were so distinctly shrouded in the familiar glow? They were distinguished for identification. This was some master plan that was working in the background. He was sure of that. He assumed when it ended, it would end poorly, with him eating a bullet and Chris writing a novel about who he was—why he'd done the things he had.

From the beginning, Gabe had wanted his stories told. He'd always harbored a secret desire that his legacy might be published in a book somewhere. Something you could pull off a shelf and physically hold in your hands. Even he had to admit that his life had been one train wreck after another, but to see all those accounts from psychiatrists or articles from reporters all gathered in one spot...well it just felt right to him somehow. He knew any assessments would be made long after his incarceration or even his death. Simple eggheads trying to explain the unexplainable when they'd never even faced him in a solitary room and then asked the important questions...like *why?*

He may not have had any control over his growing emotional attachment to Chris; that was true, but he could control how his story ended. And this became the switch he found himself continually turning on then off again in his head. And if he eventually ran those notions to their bitter finality, then the proposition of asking his new friend to participate in the next taking of a white-lighter seemed like a perfectly logical assumption to him.

BACK AT HIS loft, Christian gathered his notes on the dining room table. He surrounded himself with all the papers, articles, and his recent notes from his stay at the Mayflower. It was a daunting task, but he knew the book had to begin with an outline. He would use his usual process of drafting his framework and push those ideas through the grinder of his brain. It was his custom to work in this fashion; he liked to see the gristle and fat left in the bowl. It was how he'd written before, although he'd never written about a serial killer, nor had he ever written anything close to true crime. This would be a challenge.

He suspected the book needed to completely catalog each homicide, and he wanted Church to confess to his crimes, every one. He wanted to research the victims, their backstories and their families. It was important they have a voice throughout his manuscript. What he hadn't considered from the onset was his desire to make Church more engaging, more human. Originally that had never been the plan.

Christian Maxwell may have been one of the first to connect the unlikely homicides to a single killer. The more he'd read about the murders, the more intrigued he'd become. Even he could see the shrieking pathology of the crimes, mainly because there didn't seem to be one...at least an obvious one. The more articles he read about the string of unsolved murders, the more it seemed a construction was hidden somewhere inside their lack of relationship. It was as if the killer was speaking directly to him because he saw the random nature of the murders more than any other investigator. He would stand staring at the news reports he'd cut from papers and pinned to his whiteboard, but the more he added to his collage, the more they whispered to him to look closer.

The writer would feel like he was weaving dangerously through traffic every time he faced the whiteboard, and his heart would race at the thought of how close he was to seeing the full picture, which seemed forever just out of his line of sight. It was never enough to alert police; he had nothing more than they did, just a nagging itch in the back of his throat, suggesting he was closer to finding their killer than they were. He'd tried to visualize the faceless killer; it was easier than standing in his shoes because the motives were still too far from his grasp for understanding. That shocking realization only hit him when he placed a pin in a map and knew without hesitation the next victim would be discovered there. His hands trembled when he was later proven right, cutting the article from the paper about the latest unsolved homicide to pin on his wall map, right next to his whiteboard.

But that had been before he met Gabriel; now everything was different. Now as he sat surrounded by old print newspapers, his laptop sitting open, his trusty legal pad there, fixated on the mountain of work ahead of him, he would list every homicide on paper to go over with Gabriel later in a conversation he knew would not be pleasant. It would be difficult trying to perform the task so analytically; he would need to force the faces of all of Church's victims from imagination. But he didn't relish the idea of picturing their bloody smiles staring back from his writing like a constant reminder he was crossing over an unimaginable line.

Christian's hands refused to work the keys. He mistyped many words and found his thoughts straying just out of reach. He kept hearing Gabriel whispering over his shoulder, refusing to allow him any solitude to work. He was making ridiculous statements and running his tongue along the writer's ear in an effort to distract him. He was an impetuous child demanding to be noticed: *Look at me, Daddy...hey, watch me!* Christian had to turn around a couple of times. He knew he was alone in his loft, but he still felt that breathy awareness at his nape and ghostly perceptions standing behind him, telling him Gabriel was directly behind him, staring over his shoulder, reading every word he typed, and pouting disapprovingly.

Even without the killer in his presence, he was haunted. How could he construct a book about something as horrific as murder without picturing Church dancing around a bonfire covered in blood and visceral like a mad man? It was an image that seemed to occupy his every waking thought now.

YOUNG OR OLD, female, male, it never mattered to Gabriel Church when choosing his white-lighters, as long as they offered the usual signs. "Everyone was a potential victim," he'd said as he described one event to Chris one afternoon. It had been a hitchhiking marine, but this had been years earlier, when hitchhiking was more of a safe way to get around than it was considered today. He had introduced himself as Lance Corporal James Macabe. He was an attractive, solidly built young soldier who had been headed back to Camp Pendleton after a long weekend pass. Gabe hadn't noticed the customary radiance, as he usually did when spotting a victim. He had pulled over and offered a ride, merely out of kindness.

It wasn't until the young man gratefully opened the passenger-side door and Gabe saw his effervescent grin, as he tossed the duffel in the back seat, that Gabe first noticed a beautiful smolder of growing embers beginning to surround his new passenger. Gabe knew how to assimilate, smiling as the younger man regaled him with stories of his weekend pass, drunken parties, and the women he'd met. Alpha males had that familiarity to other males; it was ingrained into the marine from basic training, and for Gabe, it came from years of practice. For a young man taking the dangerous trip back to camp with only his thumb, he was required to talk pussy right off the bat, signifying his orientation quickly and effectively removing him from having male drivers making advances on him. There were a lot of sick assholes out there, he understood.

Gabe had no such designs on the soldier in his car. He smiled in return, joked, and laughed in accordance with every tale the man offered. His distracted air was there, covering bigger concerns in his head, which were currently racing on the prospect of how to kill him. The man was strong; he would represent more than a just a challenge. He was younger than Gabe, and he'd applied those muscles to more recent activity than Gabe had.

Playing out every element, the killer began performing the stage play in his mind, checking for possible outcomes. He couldn't kill him while driving, so he had to get him out of the car, and that wasn't going to be easy. He suspected the soldier smoked pot, and he seized an idea that may be his best option yet, but he discarded it when he noticed a truck stop ahead. It was perched just off the interstate, beseeching him with its own inviting smile to pull over.

Glancing down to his fuel gage, he could see that he wasn't running on empty yet, but it may be sufficient reason to carry his pretense along—he was, after all, resting on a quarter of a tank.

"Hey, Lance Corporal, I really need to refuel. Mind if we make a quick pit stop just ahead?" he asked.

"Not only do I not mind, but I really gotta take a strong whiz myself. I've needed to piss for miles now," he said with a grin. Even as he nodded in agreement, all Gabe could recognize was the glimmer of highlights surrounding his next victim. *Shame*, he thought. He was such a pleasant soul and someone who appeared could've one day been a genuine hero in the making. Not that it would've interfered with what Gabriel was already planning.

After pulling up at the station, Gabe left the driver's side door open as he propped the gas nozzle into the tank. He then walked behind his soldier who was bounding off to the men's room in that desperate gait of a man in need. They chatted casually as they pissed in the dirty urinal of the dimly lit bathroom with the cracked mirror and broken air dryer. This was a different era. In future days, bathrooms would have locks; they would be well illuminated and have cameras just outside the doors to monitor the rooms for sick fuckers looking to hook up or a safe place to shoot up their heroine, but this wasn't that time. We still possessed a few ounces of innocence splashing around near the bottom.

Macabe shook the dribble from his meat and then stuffed himself back into his jeans. It was like wrangling an angry snake into a far too small box, Gabe thought. Before he could turn to wash his hands, Gabe was on him with the ferocity of an uncaged beast. He'd already played out every scenario and chosen his implements of choice when he slipped the blade from under the driver's side seat as he jumped out of the truck. Decided that would be unnecessarily messy, he passed over the knife before running his fingers over the homemade garrote he used only occasionally. It was constructed of large-gauge wire tethered to two metal rods, each about six inches in length, and it was a substantial killing tool.

The young man was strong, wiry with muscle, and his height became the inducement more than the challenge. Killing such a man with a knife seemed a feminine effort; the thrill would be in overcoming the soldier with brutal force and his own strength and physique. He seemed a man worthy of a masculine death.

FOR A FEW seconds, it could have gone either way. Macabe's surprise at being attacked from behind was quickly liberated when his training and instinct took the wheel. Wisely, he attempted to twist his body, compelling his attacker to lose his footing. If he could spiral free from the hold, it would be a much different outcome. Face-to-face with his assailant, he stood a stronger chance. For Macabe, there had been more fistfights before he'd enlisted than all the time he'd gone through basic. And since he'd been released for weekend passes, he'd had several more in town. But his attacker was strong himself. He had pushed him back against the porcelain sink with all his might; his toes scraped the concrete and begged for purchase, but the killer prevented him from gaining an upright stance. The garrote was cutting a bloody ribbon into his neck, and his loss of air was as big an impediment as the forceful thrusts of the driver he'd just met.

Macabe's face was inches from the killer's, and he could feel the man's hot breath being blasted into his own gaping mouth—it was the only air hitting his tongue. It was the expression that startled him, or lack of one. The man's eyes were blue, yet edged with black rings around the wide pupils. He was straining with some effort to yank the wire taunt, but he wasn't grinning nor was there any malice on his face. He had become someone who was performing a task with great exertion, a mechanic turning a tight bolt with an unwieldy wrench. He didn't hate the tool...he didn't hate the bolt...he just accepted it as a chore needing to be done, one he must complete before he could move on.

Sweat began beading on the killer's forehead, and the sounds of ghastly death filled the tiny bathroom. Macabe tried to push his attacker off, but he was already starting to lose consciousness without oxygen to revive him. One arm went up in defense while the other was pressed back with one palm still gripping cold porcelain at his rear. Blood was merging with the perspiration at his chest, and the gurgling sounds became infrequent as the soldier pulled in his last opportunities for survival. Before he blacked out completely, he stared soulfully into the killer's eyes. He could see wonderment there, the sheer enjoyment of this stranger witnessing his breath in his final seconds of life.

THE SOLDIER SLUMPED like a ragdoll in Gabe's arms, but he refused to release his tight hold on the garrote until he was certain the man was completely gone. He then heaved the marine to his feet and dragged him into the empty stall. Propping the young man into a sitting position on the toilet, Gabriel turned the man's face skyward with a gentle brush of his finger. There was a faint smile in his eyes as he dusted the man's shirt and straightened his appearance before locking the stall door and then closing it behind him. The dead soldier wouldn't be found for a while, so he felt safe to enter the station and pay for his gas with the smiling girl behind the counter whose smile seemed to be a signal of interest. He drove away and then headed in the same direction as previously, before he met a military soldier hitching a ride along the roadside.

Chapter Seventeen

THE WRITER WAS someone Gabe liked. There were few who could easily fit into that category, and it was because they were friends that he didn't want to make him into a monster. Christian represented life before the murders began—he equally represented what it could have been like if Gabe had never taken his darker road. But he had, and that was an inescapable truth. Half of him wanted Christian held pure of the same ideologies he possessed because it wasn't a healthy way of living, but the other side of him knew he needed to bring his new companion into the fold or risk losing him completely.

Standing on his balcony wearing only his shorts, he breathed in the aroma of the courtyard; the scent of honeysuckle and lavender wafting to his nose. As decaying and decrepit as his lodgings were, they belied a history from a much grander time. Gabe wouldn't have known it, but untold starving artists had once rented apartments in his residence. One writer spent years living there before eventually becoming a national treasure in his own right, but never reached fame before his own death. But no one boasted about those parts of the legend and he wasn't even aware of the hodgepodge collection of painters and poets who once called it home. Now it was disheveled and falling into disrepair, but once there had been talent housed there, living another impoverished life under duress as most talent did. Gabe wouldn't have known the history and was never blinded by the morality plays and parables he'd been lied about at St. Ignatius, choosing to see the ramshackle rooms for what they were—a rest stop in a longer journey.

His palms rested on the wrought-iron railing of his Juliet balcony. When he'd chosen the apartment, he'd asked the heavy-set, middle-aged leasing agent what they were called when you had French doors but no balcony to stand on. He was surprised the fat fucker knew the answer. He supposed it came from Shakespeare's work, but he thought he'd rather prefer having a balcony he could sit on. Still...it was available, it was reasonably cheap, and they didn't require a lot of paperwork. Gabe only worked sporadically, so his income derived from robberies and intermittent jobs and day labors. He also made it a point to lift whatever cash he could from his victims.

FOR THE FIRST time in days, Christian slipped under the covers alone. It seemed oddly foreign not having Gabriel there to draw close and feel the heat rising off his body. It was difficult letting go of those tantalizing images, but he needed sleep more than dreams. He couldn't help wondering what Gabriel must be doing then; questioning whether he too was just crawling into bed and thinking of him in much the same way he was Church.

But whatever peace he may have desired was shattered by a series of awful dreams. His mind was locked on Gabe, but regardless of how he tried to manipulate the pictures in his head, inevitably they turned sour in his brain. Instead of hallucinating about a loving tangle of flesh and sex, he watched as the Church personification turned dark and grotesque with still frames flashing across his mind. When he saw a smiling picturesque shot of Gabriel, it suddenly transformed into a hideous adaption of a grinning, savage Church as nothing more than a deadly assassin. Although he'd never actually witnessed the monstrous realities of Church's murders, his mind played them out in shadowy black-and-whites whenever he was unconscious. It had happened from the very beginning of their friendship, and it continued irritably even today.

An ugly performance was playing through his head; a multitude of faces representing the whole of Church's victims, each one pleading for salvation as Chris stood by speechless, unable to help them or prevent the atrocities they must be suffering through. This was the first time he'd imagined the expression on Gabriel's face in those twisted minutes during the murders, and it wasn't a picture he enjoyed. Though even he had to know that it wasn't real, that he would never have known how Gabriel looked or what had to be going through his head in those terrible split seconds when he was fulfilling his sick need to waste another human soul. He witnessed seemingly random brutality and watched Church kill with impunity. Chris attempted to regain control of his self-induced nightmares by furiously rolling around in his sheets and trying to jar himself back into awareness. But his body was no longer his own. It was suddenly imprisoned with every muscle chained in a hellish perdition which his brain was creating with lightning speed. All he managed as a fruit of his efforts was to stain the pillowcase with sweat, built from a sensation of being confined inside a nightmare and when nothing you could do would free you from its horrible outcome. At one point during his shadowboxing Chris knocked the clock radio off his nightstand with his flaying arms, but even that didn't free him from his prison. He called out to Gabe, both in his delusions and aloud, but there was no one there to hear or even comfort him.

Fortunately, the next morning he couldn't remember all the facets of his nightmare, but he did see the tangle of damp sheets and tasted a tinge of bile on his tongue. Bounding up, he raced for a shower, hoping it could clean as much from his mind as it did from his body. He would have had too much difficulty connecting the person in his dreams to the man he'd made love to or followed through the Seattle streets like a loyal puppy. But few of us could ever say that we'd slept with a serial killer, or known the duality of a kind soul who turns into a deadly predator. Maybe there *was* a book there: the story of the lovers, friends, and families of murderers; those who could lie next to a killer during the height of their spree and never suspect a thing.

After showering, he stood facing the bathroom mirror. He ran a palm down the mirror, streaking a visible path to allow him to shave. Looking at his naked form, he wondered what Gabriel saw in him that he didn't see. He was attractive, but so were a lot of people. He had an average build but possessed no spectacular features to draw in another's attentions. Yet Gabriel seemed fascinated with him. While he had run his rough hands down every part of the writer's body, Christian had seen Gabriel's eyes glaze over. He had felt the transfer of bemused awareness on each fingertip that raked his body by their light touch. He could question it, but he chose to just accept it willingly, gratifyingly. He smiled as the razor made sharp lines in the cream on his jaw.

Before he could finish shaving, he heard a substantial knock at his door, and his heart jumped excitedly at the prospect. It could've been his neighbor Ruth; she often stopped by in the mornings to share a coffee and gossipy conversation, but he hoped, not so secretly, that it would be Gabriel. He grabbed a towel from the hook, threw his razor haphazardly in the sink, and raced to open the door, smiling from ear to ear.

"Sleep well...?" was all Gabriel asked as he stood there engulfing the doorframe with his steel-gray eyes and unshaven face. He was a god dropped to earth for the masses to enjoy, and Christian could barely contain his thrilling pleasure at seeing him standing there.

"Not so, but I'm glad you found my place."

"Naturally you are," Gabriel said, absently brushing past the writer but stopping short as he entered the room to take it all in.

"Nice digs; not the Mayflower, but it's nice...simple."

Peaking adrenaline mixed with the uneasy tingle in his stomach to make Christian seem frozen. He had forgotten the shaving cream that still marked his face or that he was standing there in a towel and wet hair. His surprise finally subsided enough to allow him to play host. "Make yourself comfortable. I was just finishing getting ready." Heading back into the bathroom, he pulled the towel from his waist and wiped his face dry. With his back to the room, he shouldn't have sensed the look, but the cold blade was burrowed deep, and he became awash with the knowledge Gabriel was staring at him as he stood at the bathroom sink rinsing his hands.

He was learning enough from Gabriel to become as content with his nudity as the killer was. He suspected he was an entirely new human; years earlier, there would've been shame or embarrassment, even if he didn't understand why. Shame was a gift Gabriel had not been bestowed. He was comfortable in his own skin, and this was a quality far removed from the writer's custom. Glancing over his shoulder, he could see his companion staring at him intently from the shadows there in the center of his living room. Although his face was obscured by a lack of morning light from his shaded windows, he could sense a heat coming across the room in waves of hungry desperation.

"You want to go grab coffee and breakfast?" Christian asked as he dried his hands.

"That was the plan...but that may need some alteration now," he said, cool as ice, yet belying a hint of innuendo. Gabriel wasn't moving; he'd become a living statue rapt with attention. Christian stepped from the restroom and breezed up to Gabriel to see his head tilting slightly to the right and his twisted grin of seduction. They pulled each other into their arms and then kissed. It was both sensual and male, and Gabriel's hands moved to Christian's neck, holding him tightly in his massive arms. He darted his tongue around the younger man's mouth.

Christian's head was held taut in those two strong hands, forcing him to look up at the taller man, leaving him to stare into those dreamy eyes, which held a vastness that seemed impassable. This was Gabriel—one couldn't ever fully comprehend what bounced around in that head of his. Like looking at a beautiful painting of a stunning model, the faraway gaze was displayed, but there was no inkling to the subject's inner thoughts...blank and yet still gorgeous.

Church ran his tongue over Christian's face like the lap of a happy dog, but as he did that, Christian knew it wasn't out of joy; it was a signpost that directed the trail. There was animal lust here. There were no gentle explorations like fifteen-year-old girls testing their bodies—this was firm, concrete, with a clear unabridged resolution. Gabriel required his adoration before pounding all his strength in rabbit thrusts of his hips. He vigorously shook the semen from his body before they both lay exhausted but sated in Christian's bed.

They forgot about their morning coffee, and by the time they rose from the mattress, it was closer to lunch than to breakfast. But it was good, and it was necessary. It became a fire that needed the stoking from a poker or the billows of oxygen to ignite into something violently dynamic before fading into the tiny embers of a lover's embrace. It helped them clear their heads so they could continue the afternoon without the hanging presence invading their conversations.

Chapter Eighteen

CHRISTIAN PALMED THE mouse to light the screen. It awoke with a beautiful landscape scene. Immediately he opened the file on his desktop that held the Word document containing all his notes on Gabriel Church. He preferred writing from his legal pad because the keystrokes had a way of breaking a mood and destroying the silence between interviewer and subject. He only used the laptop to refresh his memory on various points. He allowed the pointer to drag over dates of recent murders and then copied those dates on his ledger.

"I'd very much like to build your story around the dates of each of your murders. I have a few in front of me. I was hoping you could fill in the details, cities, what you remember of the victims...things like that."

Christian had assumed his professional role. The cold and clinical monotone edged his words as if he was something removed from the murders. In fact, he felt like he was standing behind Church during each one of his kills.

"WHATEVER..." THE WORD hung there as a temptation, begging to be explored. Gabe was perched on Chris's sofa, wearing only the skimpy boxers he'd pulled on after their sexual pastime, while the writer had pulled on a burgundy bathrobe. Gabe told himself *this part is necessary. The legend needs a concise origin story*, but he hated having to relive individual murders. He didn't like how the Chris's countenance changed whenever he heard how Gabe murdered.

By discussing each kill, it added another dark aspect. One kill was sufficient, but having Chris hear all the details somehow made him directly complicit in every crime, and anything more meant there were two sociopathic killers engaged in a single conversation. The dialogue continued, it was just no longer held in the swanky surroundings of the Mayflower Plaza, having been replaced by Chris's modest digs. As the writer offered dates from his notes, Gabe would nod in acceptance.

"Yeah that was me," he said with certainty of his involvement.

Occasionally he supplied additional details for each victim named as Christian watched him intently. Gabe knew his expression was hard, chiseled, as he tugged back old memories he preferred to remain undisturbed.

Is this Catholic school penitence? Is Christian my priest confessor sitting behind a curtained wall of adjudication? Am I supposed to feel shame or remorse?

He didn't like this new arrangement of their relationship. He much preferred Christian acting as his lesser, and not the judge and jury he was quickly becoming under the premise of the book's research. Christian's disgust was showing at every edge, and he twisted and turned, as if he had sat for too long on the sofa.

CHRISTIAN COULD FEEL the tension building; he knew he was losing Gabriel to the minutiae of dates and names.

Leaning back in his chair, Christian decided to take a different tact. He needed to build the story of what city Gabriel had been in and then tie those directly to murders committed there. If he dragged the man through the mud of memories, he would lose him for sure.

"How did you feel about yourself when you were not committing murders?" he asked coldly. He watched as Gabriel turned his way, seemingly spellbound by his question. Even with a surprised expression, Chris was still utterly fascinated by those gray eyes staring back at him.

"What the fuck? What are you asking?"

"I was curious, as I'm sure the readers will be, what you felt like when you were not killing...or targeting a victim or spending your time enthralled by the single act of it? Did you feel good about yourself? Did you feel whole?"

Church sat upright, and Christian could feel the venom building.

"You make it sound like I'm some sick psycho...that I needed to kill to feel good about myself." His expression was ice, his gestures abrupt. "If you think that, then just go to hell!" Standing, he paced nervously around the room, scanning the room as if he'd misplaced something. "I could use a smoke... You wouldn't have a pack lying around would you?"

"I didn't know you smoked, or I would've bought a pack."

"Only when I'm pissed...and you're doing a great job of getting my back fur up."

"Then I apologize. I actually do have a pack I think. My neighbor likes to come over for coffee and chitchat—she smokes like a train. I think she left a pack here for emergencies. Try looking in that big Crock-Pot on the counter."

Gabriel moved to the kitchen and rummaged through a brown pottery jar holding cooking utensils. He located a crumpled half-pack of Marlboro Reds hidden in the jar and then pulled a cigarette from it. Turning the gas stove on, he popped the smoke in his lips and bent to light it off the blue flame. It occurred to Christian he'd never had a man in his place who generally walked around in just underwear. The sight of him moving around his living room so cavalier and acclimated to his environment made him feel like he'd missed a great deal of life before Gabriel. It brought a tinge of sadness to his consciousness knowing that being in a man's presence, one with whom he'd fucked, was something he could have easily adjusted to. It seemed comforting in a way he had never known.

Waiting for the mood to lighten, Christian decided to make them coffee. He worked best with his nerves jangled from the caffeine. Gabriel watched as he filled the pot from the tap and spooned grounds into a filter. Both men could sense the air change from agitation to the static nothingness of anger being pushed aside.

"I hope you understand that the readers are not going to see you as a sympathetic antihero. There are horrific crimes to consider. If I ask difficult questions, it's not me being an asshole. I just want to unearth reasons why you killed and the person behind the mask."

"There has never been a mask to hide behind. Every rotten thing I've done has been with clarity and without subterfuge." Gabriel was back on the sofa, but his temper wasn't far below the surface. "I would hope by now that you'd have understood me better!"

There was a distance between them that Christian attempted to bridge. "I'm trying...truly I am."

"So how would you feel watching it?" Gabriel asked. The question seemed random, but it was clear to Christian that Gabriel knew the hefty weight of his question.

"What do you mean, watching it?" Christian was incredulous—he couldn't fathom what Gabriel was asking. "I'm already at great risk by just knowing you have murdered and I haven't called the police... What do you mean *watch*?"

Gabriel had crossed the threshold, but Christian couldn't pull the question back, and it dangled in the air taunting him.

"You could watch me next time. Be there to witness yourself what happens when a marked person dies."

With the words out there, he was trapped—there was no going back now.

"I don't understand..." Christian began fumbling with cups from the cabinet, conspicuously moving quickly so that the question would just go away. His stomach began to spit acid back into his throat, and no matter how fixed he was on his activities, he couldn't escape the frost building between them.

"I'm suggesting you accompany me next time I get the call...to be there and see it for yourself so that you'll know I'm not completely crazy."

"What's crazy is you asking that question!" Christian had already arranged cups on the counter; he'd pulled out sugar and cream, but his hands were empty and begged for something to do.

Why won't the coffee finish brewing, for fuck's sake?

"I know what I'm asking you, babe. I know how it sounds." Gabriel moved closer to Christian, but he pulled away, distracted and nervous. The aroma of smoke billowed around Gabriel, making Christian miss the scent of wet pine.

Why can't he smell that way again, he wondered?

"I wouldn't ask you if I didn't think it would help both of us." The bigger man reached out to grab Christian by the arm, regardless of his resistance. Possibilities raced through Christian's mind. He was initially confronted with the idea Church was still actively killing. It had been an awareness he worried about. But somehow he'd managed to dodge the theory, sweeping it over the edge like it had been nothing at all. But he was losing the battle because it entered his head more and more with time. Certainly he hadn't killed anyone since they met; that would have been impossible, wouldn't it?

His new lover was asking him to watch him as he murdered someone! That simple phrase carried all kinds of damnation. But surely Church understood that? He already assumed he was becoming a coconspirator just because of his current knowledge of the crimes. It was insane that Gabriel would even ask this of him. The acid in his throat was turning to bile, and he almost considered throwing up right there in the sink. He was gagging back whatever demanded a release, trying hard to suppress the onslaught of sickness.

"No one but you and I ever have to know you were even there—it will be our secret, something between us," Church offered. How was he still speaking? Didn't he understand the lunacy in the words?

"IT WILL BOND us together forever. You will understand. It will all finally make sense in the end." Gabe was pushing too hard, he knew, but in for a penny or a pound; it didn't matter now. He tried to wrestle Chris into his arms, confident if he held him tight the writer would relinquish his obvious fear. But the man wouldn't be held. He pushed Gabe back with his open palm, and the look on his face seemed overwhelmed in confusion. He was trapped inside the confines of the finite space of his loft; there seemed no place he could run to or hide.

"I have no intention of discussing this. I'm already going to hell in a hand basket for just knowing you, not to mention allowing you to fuck me."

He paced the floor, hands fussing at the front of his cotton robe. He'd become a nervous child awaiting the inevitability of punishment. It was clear he had been pushed to the brink, so Gabe backed away and leaned against an empty chair, hoping to release some of the tension he'd created.

"Relax, baby...we don't have to talk about it anymore. Just settle for a second and take a chill pill."

"*Relax.* You might be even more insane than I thought. How can I relax? Not only are you still talking about murder...but you want to drag me along, like it was some fun activity we could share as a couple. You asshole!"

Chris was unyielding in his outrage. He marched back and forth with his arms gripping his elbows tightly. He was far too distracted to calm down, so Gabe crossed his arms. It was best just to surrender, he thought. He was careful not to move too abruptly or show any interest in changing Chris's mind. But he had thrown it out there; it was his heavy stone tossed in the lake. It would make its own ripples and waves, but eventually, they too would diminish into nothing. But the rock rested at the bottom now, and would always be there. He'd accomplished that at least.

Gabe moved to fill their coffee cups, straying to look anywhere but in Chris's direction. The only Band-Aid available was time and distance, so he occupied his hands with their drinks in silence. A faint smile crawled across his face as he stirred in extra cream and sugar to the writer's cup, remembering how Chris preferred it. He couldn't remember the exact date of his sister's birthday, didn't know if he'd ever had all of his childhood vaccinations, but he remembered how Chris liked his coffee. There was something in that. For someone like Gabe, it represented an aching itch of remorse. How much had he missed out on in his lifetime because he hadn't seen it clearly? How different would his life have been if he'd met the writer years before, or someone like him?

"I come bearing gifts," he said as he presented his offer of coffee under a consolatory smile.

"But you're still an asshole."

"So I've been told," Gabe said, turning his back on the man and taking his spot in a nearby chair. He had overstepped, pushed too hard, but one thing he was quickly learning was how to influence the writer in subtle ways.

"When's your birthday?" Gabe asked apathetically. "I know a lot about you, but I don't know that?"

His random, off-the-cuff question had broken the austere moment, and Chris turned, surprised. Gabe observed the merest hint of a smile breaking somewhere on the rocks; he was truly a puppet master when it came to this one.

"February...the twenty-seventh actually. Why? Planning a party?"

"Just good to know... If we're still around in February, I think I'd like to take you someplace fun."

"Plan on *not* being around? That's only a few months away—the book won't even be in final draft by then."

"I wouldn't mind taking you to the mountains. You deal pretty well with the cold?" he asked blatantly, ignoring Chris's earlier question. "I know a place near Takhlakh Lake. It has a killer view of Mount Adams. We could rent a canoe and camp out under the stars. How about that, could be a pretty cool birthday?"

Gabe sat sprawled in his chair, scratching nonchalantly at his balls and watching a faraway gaze building on Christian's face. He could see he hadn't needed to ply the writer with many stories; he could see Chris was already there. He could almost see the blaze from the campfire reflected in his eyes and almost see his breath billowing out in tiny frosty clouds.

"Sounds fun I suppose...a bit on the nose maybe. I keep getting flashes of *Brokeback Mountain* with two men in one tent, but it could be all right."

Gabe had effortlessly corrected his misstep. He had turned it around with a smile and a casual, deft maneuver. He was good like that. You couldn't commit grisly murders for eighteen years without getting caught and not possess confidence like tempered steel. He'd set out to lay the question at Chris's feet—he'd never expected an answer right away. For him it was something that needed to build...or in Chris's mind, to fester there.

"Then it's settled. We hit the mountains for your birthday!" Gabe's deep, resonant voice boomed with excitement at the prospect. His words broke the silence that had filled the room with his inappropriate line of questions, and everything began to fall away to a better vibe.

God, I am good!

"It'll be fun, having you alone and all to myself," Gabe continued breaking the frozen water that had been icing up between them. He backed away to refill his cup, but it was merely the distraction that would create the safety of distance between them. If Christian wanted to ask him questions later, he'd have to lie about his answers. He couldn't risk having the water refreeze, not at this crucial point.

BLOWING A HOLE in the steam, Christian sipped his coffee gingerly. He immediately noticed a sugary sweetness hitting his tongue. Gabriel had made his coffee exactly as he liked, which meant his companion paid attention to small details, particularly about him. That sensation was as saccharine as his drink, and he smiled secretly over the heat rising off his cup.

"So, babe, what's up for the game plan today?" Gabriel moved around unceremoniously and began to nibble at Christian's neck while holding a steaming cup in one hand and wrapping his other arm around the writer's waist. Standing so close, Christian could feel Gabriel's soft, yet impaired heart beating even through the heavy cotton of his robe. He began to doubt if the void would ever be something he'd get used to after now knowing Gabriel's condition. He worried that someday soon the hollowness inside that irregular drumming sound would just stop altogether, and he feared Gabriel would simply turn blue and then fall to the floor. If Gabe stopped breathing while in his presence, he would be shattered. He didn't want to be there if it happened.

His anger was subsiding, but he still didn't relish Rodd idea of sitting down with Gabe and discussing the murders in greater detail. He was no longer in the mood to hear his accounting of the bodies he'd left in his wake, nor was he considering having sex at that moment. So for them, what was there left to do, he wondered? Church must've felt his unnerved detachment, though, from his lack of response and decided to chisel deeper into the ice nonetheless.

"I think both of us could use a distraction. What would you say we forget about the book today and do something just for us?"

"What did you have in mind?" Christian asked.

"We could take a stroll through the city and talk; we could use the time to learn more about each other...not for the book, but just because. I would love to hear more about Christian Maxwell's childhood. There's a great deal I'd love to hear."

Breaking his embrace, Christian turned around and faced Gabriel, staring into those slate-colored irises and considering his proposal. Yes, he thought. The idea of spending time with him while removed from the book and the stories and that continual stench of death was something he wanted very much indeed. He recalled what a good time they had during the underground tour because it wasn't all about the book or the murders. He thought the distraction was a pleasant one, so he readily agreed.

"Why not," he said matter-of-factly. "Let's get dressed and face the city."

They kissed lightly and then both broke their hold to track down their discarded clothing. They would head downtown to see what wonders they could find together and hope the atmosphere shoved back all the drama of Church's sick proposal. Christian wouldn't allow his mind to wander over what he'd been asked by the killer. Just the thought of it made a rank taste on his tongue and brought waves of shame and regret. It had been too easy to picture Gabriel as anything other than a killer most times; he was falling into that trap and watching as the door was closing overhead. It was a desperate attempt to hide from reality so he could admire the man for something good and proper, but it was a lie he was telling himself, and he knew it.

Chapter Nineteen

ALTHOUGH NEITHER MAN was a native of Seattle, they had seen the hot spots already and chose to skip the touristy crap like visiting the Space Needle or observing the city skyline from Kerry Park. Christian drove them downtown, only a few blocks from the Mayflower Plaza Hotel, and found an empty parking space to pull into—both preferred strolling on familiar ground. The conversation was purposely light and breezy, and they walked side by side, close enough that they could whisper to each other and still be heard over the sounds of city traffic. Gabriel was peppering Christian with questions about his childhood: what schools he'd attended, the relationship he maintained with his family, and his current job, from which he had taken a hiatus.

Christian answered each question as best he was able, having difficulty only with what had prompted him to take a sabbatical from his job to write that next great masterpiece of a novel. He stammered out his expectations of the book, trying to steer away from discussing the project in detail, which was quickly becoming a sore subject for him. He smiled as he recalled stories of his childhood for an eager listener. Gabriel seemed fascinated with learning all he could about Christian, which was pleasurable. At one point, it seemed a meaningless fable in Christian's mind, acting like the two were fresh lovers with endless possibilities. But Gabriel was not the type of man you took home to meet the folks.

He hadn't thought about his family at all recently; he would have to come clean with them about his own sexuality now, but he wasn't concerned with their feelings about it either way. His relationship with his mother had always been a tad chilly, too severe for a normal mother/son relationship, and his relationship with his father wasn't much better. Christian had learned resilience and independence, but not from his parents' teachings—more of a cold distance that created a personality separate from his upbringing. Love and support came in the form of the scrawled *I love you*s at the bottom of Christmas cards and occasional phone calls to keep everyone informed of routine changes in their everyday lives.

Christian's mother would be too embarrassed about not being in the loop with her children's lives, more than by her actual interest. She was constrained by propriety and decency, but it was also her shield, and it was a shield she intended to carry until her own bitter end.

He wasn't sure that his parents had not already suspected something unusual about his orientation, since he'd never been engaged and had rarely introduced them to women in his life. But he knew they would never broach the subject directly with him; that would be a taboo subject and a minefield his mother would never willingly cross...even with a few glasses of Chardonnay under her belted cocktail dress.

Trying to describe the essence of his childhood to Gabriel, he suspected it was something strange for him to hear. They were polar opposites by their upbringing, and he hesitated to even recite stories about his rigid parents since Gabriel's stories held such darker edges. How could he explain the frosty way his father had been with him after hearing Gabriel offer dismal stories of his father's abuse and the mental anguish he'd constructed?

But Gabriel didn't take offense at the stories; instead, he lapped them up with a smile and an eager excitement with follow-up questions like: "Do you think your dad would understand your newfound lust for the male form?"

He chuckled as he asked, begging the bigger question of whether Bennett Church would understand his own son becoming a fag?

They walked the city streets with unplanned expectation, peering into shops and bakeries along the way. It was a casual afternoon of killing time, and with every block they strolled, they pushed the earlier emotions further back. Gabriel had a way of physical contact when he spoke; he would poke a joke into Christian's ribs with a hearty laugh, or he would place his hand on a shoulder or in the center of his back if he spotted something he wanted to share. Every time he made the gesture of kinship with Christian, the writer's heart would race, ever so slightly. Having such a stunning man be so enwrapped with him could be intoxicating. He'd never been on the receiving end of such admiration himself, nor had he ever given as much as he'd been granted before now. It made for a pleasant walk, and both men laughed more than they had in years.

They passed a patio bar, and Gabriel turned to his friend with a glimmer in his eyes. "Hey, do you know any gay bars in the vicinity? I've only been in one so far, but I think I'd like to have a drink, that is, if you can find one."

The prospect seemed intriguing. Although Christian had been in gay bars with friends from college, he'd never visited one with someone who looked like Gabe. He wondered what effect walking into a club with a studly creature would have on his ego, deciding the experiment might be worth examination. But he wasn't familiar with the area, particularly with gay bars.

"Not sure we will find one, but we can try. Let's keep our eyes peeled for a place. Just look for a window with too many hanging ferns. Remember you can't tell by just looking on a man's ring finger now, 'cause now you don't know which state he mighta been married in—it could be Washington or it could be Idaho." They both chuckled at the absurdity. It was a new world, and they weren't the only ones feeling their growing pains.

It was true. To the naked, undiscerning eye they were two Joes simply walking down the streets side by side; neither appeared outwardly or flamboyantly gay, but their differences in size and carriage made them uniquely interesting to watch. It was their informal camaraderie and the way they leaned in to talk that made them appear like casual lovers on an innocent evening out on the town. But for the writer it was a watershed moment, one where he didn't feel that gay panic of walking among the crowded streets without a fear of shock and reprisal. Besides if anything untoward happened, he knew he was with a man who could hold his own with the very best of them. He couldn't imagine anyone dumb enough to fuck with them, or call out derogatory implications of "cocksucking queers on their knees;" after all, he was walking with a cold-blooded killer, and anyone stupid enough to hazard an altercation would find themselves in greater danger than they could've ever foreseen.

He observed women turning their heads with satisfied smiles as Church passed. He had to wonder what it was like to be so beautiful and so desirable. He saw men's heads turn as well; the hungry anticipation and sexual longing displayed in their eyes. Christian understood he was a handsome man; his Roman features and the delicate symmetry of his face wasn't undetectable when he shaved every morning, but it was different in Gabriel's company. It was more than just being handsome or pretty— Gabriel was an awe-inspiring study of perfection.

They didn't have to walk very far before they stumbled on a club both easily recognized as gay. The Pony was a throwback from the seventies. A renovated gas station sitting on East Madison, it was clearly a gay club even seen from a distance of a quarter block away. It might as well have had ferns in every window or possessed a festive awning that fairly screamed precious. Church turned to his companion and beamed an enticing grin. *He's fearless*, thought Christian. Nothing seemed to intimidate him. They both broke out in an excited snigger, and they quickened their pace to reach the main entrance.

It was a tiny bar but filled to capacity, even during that early hour. Everyone was bouncing around to music or engaged in loud conversations at the bar. Masculine men wore faded jeans and torn T-shirts, but the majority of the bar was an amalgamation of twinks in skinny jeans and flashy tank tops. There were women there as well, though Chris couldn't tell if they were lesbian or just random fag hags. The place was filled with the acrid scent of a fog machine that had gone off recently, and as if it were standard issue queer, he saw the spinning disco bar suspended above the dance floor. It was all just a bit too trite.

Gabriel took the lead and grabbed Christian's hand in his before weaving carelessly through the throngs of people. He headed in the direction of the bar, nodding and smiling at each individual he passed. A child discovering Christmas, he seemed transformed. Christian watched as he was pulled along excitedly; he smiled as he observed men from every niche in the bar begin to take notice of the strangers who'd just arrived.

The bartender was a studly man in his midtwenties. He was wearing only tight, white underwear and combat boots. Black calligraphy tattooed his ribcage with some sentimental devotion to someone who'd passed away, and he smiled a toothy grin as Gabriel reached the bar first.

"What'll it be, hot stuff?"

It would have been impossible for Gabriel to appear nonchalant or indifferent to his surroundings; his infectious grin and shimmering eyes belied any attempt he could've made to appear blasé about where he was standing.

"What you drinking, lover?" he asked as he turned to Christian.

It was effervescent to hear someone call him lover, particularly one such as Gabriel. Although Christian had never been the type to wait by the phone, or to need that validation and connection by another soul, he realized now what he'd been missing. He leaned in to Gabriel, allowing their bodies to make physical contact.

"Beer for me, baby."

"Two Buds for thirsty travelers my man," Gabriel bellowed out over a smile.

"Weird, huh?" Christian asked, leaning into Gabriel's ear over the blaring music.

"Weird being here, you mean?" Church asked. "I think it's cool. I also think it's what we needed all along."

Scoping out the bar, the killer's gaze scanned one area of the bar to the next. He always appeared to be assessing the clientele whenever he entered an establishment and Chris couldn't tell if it was his inquisitive nature or something more macabre. And that alone unnerved him.

Pulling a twenty from his jeans he tossed it on the bar. Although he didn't know what beers ran in such a place, it didn't matter. The whole experience of seeing it through Gabe's eyes was worth every penny he figured. The bartender whisked away the money after dropping off two cold beers on the counter as he turned and headed down to the other end to check on other patrons. Christian could see he wasn't pleased to see the stranger had already gotten paired off with a date, dashing any hope of a quick fuck later.

Strolling through the tiny establishment, they walked hand in hand, turning to look at everything like out-of-town tourists. Christian, for one, had never been comfortable with public displays of affection before then, but in this instance, it seemed promising. He liked knowing others saw them as a couple, regardless of the disheartened expressions on a few faces in the crowds. Knowing they didn't stand a chance picking up his companion.

They stood by the dance floor watching younger patrons spinning recklessly to the music; all appeared high but outwardly triumphant. They were young and filled with abandon, and Christian wasn't so ancient that he couldn't understand that. It hadn't been so very long ago that he'd felt the same youthful jubilation with something as genuine and inherent as being young and alive and unrestrained.

"You dance?" he asked Gabriel, even though he suspected the answer.

"I have." Gabriel smiled up at him as he leaned over the railing that divided the dance floor from a path of heavy foot traffic. That was surprising to Christian; Gabriel didn't appear the type to move ungraciously around a dance floor. The image it created forced a chortle to bubble up from deep inside.

"Don't laugh, you little shit, I can dance... I just haven't done it in a long while, but don't ask me when I'm sober—you wouldn't wanna see that."

Gabriel was one of the hottest dudes in the bar at that moment; all other eyes seemed to loiter for a split second in his vicinity. But there was a tall fucker dancing that everyone seemed equally fixated upon. He wasn't as attractive as Gabriel, but his obvious erection drew focus from the multitude of guys standing in awe by the floor. He had an enormous cock snaked down his pant leg for all to view; even his dickhead was easily distinguishable through his tight denim jeans. He had stripped off his shirt and waved it around like some gay flag. His eyes were glassy from too much booze, and his manner told people how fucked up he truly was. But his endowment drew much attention, and Christian wondered how anyone so drunk could get such an impressive erection. He surmised he had to be on something vaguely pharmaceutical.

There were two young males and one girl dancing around him—obviously they were friends. They raised their hands in joyous uproar at the music, lost in their own chemical-induced euphoria. Others seemed fascinated by his dancing, or more likely the denim covered python reaching to his mid-thigh. Christian observed how others where whispering and smiling at the image of the horny man in his middle thirties losing his mind on the dance floor. Everyone seemed drawn to the picture of him, except Gabriel.

"See anything you like?" Gabriel whispered over the music as he stroked Christian's hand on the railing.

"I got what I want."

"You know you do, baby. Most of these assholes are butt ugly...even duct tape couldn't mask these unattractive drunks."

"But it could muffle the sound when they try to talk," Christian offered with a slight smile before instantly regretting what he'd said, wishing he could've pulled back his meaningless joke before his words hung in the air. He was conversing with a murderer, and he'd simply forgotten that. The reality hit him squarely in the face; he was in a place where even trivial quips could offer something darkly evocative and dangerous to someone like Gabriel. He relaxed only when his friend chuckled back absently "You sick bastard" and then turned his gaze elsewhere.

"This bar is filled with cum-dumpster queers and fag hags, but for some reason...I think I like it," Gabriel mused. His reflection came out unintentionally harsh, but at least he'd broken the stillness surrounding Christian's unfortunate remark about duct tape. His head turned this way and then that; he looked captivated by all unusual sights and sounds.

Christian wondered how different this place had to be for him. He would probably be more at home in a biker bar with outlaw meth heads and transient women who wore excessive makeup on their faces, just to disguise the years of self-inflicted abuse that'd become their existence.

Standing by the DJ booth, Christian noticed all the soft-core, erotic, black-and-white photos plastered to the walls behind him. Each scantily clad model appeared a ghost from an era long since dead. Gabe wouldn't have known it, but that age of the seventies produced a look that died a fast death in the wake of AIDS. Bushy mustaches and unshaven chests standing like fools in nothing more than leather police caps and jock straps. Everyone poised next to heavy equipment and oversized trucks. There was a great deal of history he'd missed, but the images on the wall represented men who wouldn't stand a chance in today's fast-paced, social media entrenched world. The dichotomy of the seventies set against the hipsters of the new millennials carrying cell phones like shields and playing on Grindr for quick anonymous sex with a stranger. It was just the kind of thing that made Christian feel headily outdated and older than his years implied.

Gabriel downed the backwash of his Budweiser, and both men headed back to the front to that attractive and nearly naked bartender. Faces turned to watch, as they were strangers in a strange land. The Pony was a tiny bar with friendly regulars, but whenever a new possibility walked through those double doors, heads would spin and their interest pique. Gabriel received smiles from everyone he passed, but Christian only noticed the hungry anticipation and longing in their features, and he quickly closed the gap between them like a jealous dog marking his territory.

Gabriel paid for their beers, surprising Christian. Maybe this was his way of getting face time with the young server because the glint in his eyes became clear insinuation of flirting. His butch companion's eyes darted from head to toe along the bartender's frame, lingering for too long at the young man's skimpy underwear and significant package. He accepted both bottles with one hand and returned the young man's smile with his own contagious grin. The hairs on the nape of Christian's neck rose to life.

"Don't poke the bear," he whispered as he accepted his cold bottle over his own smirking grin.

"How do your attractive eyes turn so green so quickly?" Gabriel asked with a sneer. "So are you up for a three way? Then again...maybe you can't handle healthy competition?"

Christian scowled back, but he understood he was being toyed with, then nodded slowly appearing to actually consider Gabe's proposal.

"Sure...Bartender Boy, or do you have someone else in mind?"

Gabriel batted at his prey with delicate paws.

"No, not him, fish in a barrel that one. I was thinking about someone else. How would you feel if it was female?" Gabe's head went down, appearing as if he were trying to avoid the barrage of buckshot spray he anticipated. To Christian, he seemed fearless. "I'd even let you choose the pussy."

Even dated disco, playing loudly from every corner speaker couldn't displace the silence creeping between them. Christian knew how Gabriel liked to force a shocking revelation; it was one of his favorite pastimes, but it spoke to real concerns. And even a simple, teasing jest had overtones that Christian would one day have to address.

"Sounds like a plan, but remember I get to choose the woman and the place where we get it on."

Christian was learning to be the same intrepid, plucky force of nature his companion was, adapting to the same fearless approach he'd seen in Gabriel from the very beginning. It was his lover's turn to be shocked. He may've tried covering it with an audacious smile, but there was little lost on the writer. He grinned back savagely. He was edging closer to his own metaphysical line in the sand. And he wasn't pulling back his toes now, he thought.

Game, Set, Match!

Until recently, Gabriel had only known intimacy with women and Chris was no virgin, but it'd been years since he'd been with anyone. The last time had been a work function. He recalled seeing her across the room and found her short auburn hair and pale creamy flesh appealing. She moved effortlessly through the crowd smiling at everyone she passed like their old friends separated by years apart. Christian always sought others who possessed the qualities he lacked. The woman was sophisticated and engaging and it was her ability to charm others in her gravity that most captivated him.

There had been an abundance of alcohol throughout the party, and the wine was free flowing from catered servers who were always underfoot. The young woman edged closer and closer to the spot where Chris had found solace in hiding. He was never any good at those types of gatherings and came off colder than he ever really intended. When they finally spoke and made idle conversation about one thing or another, both parties seemed to feel that electricity building in the air between them. Looking back on it now, Chris assumed it was more inebriation than any actual desire he'd been feeling. It hadn't taken long before they found themselves sharing a cab back to Christian's loft. They were barely inside the door before she wriggled free of her cocktail dress and Christian fumbled with his belt under the influence of one too many glasses of expensive wine. There appeared a promise of wet warm kisses given passionately as they stumbled into his bedroom and each wrestled free of their clothes. But it was bittersweet and achingly far too brief a moment in time for her.

She bucked and whimpered in concert to his every thrust, but the wine was as much a detriment to her as she assumed it had to be on her date. Until eventually Chris felt the tiny radiating quivers of her muscles as she slumped across his lap, a satisfied grin beginning to show in the moonlight. He doubted she ever even climaxed. But he was a novice and too prudish a lover to think of asking or even to have known whether she reached or not. He may've been new to casual sex, but he was learning. One had to question whether it was having very dissimilar instructors where the problem rested.

Naturally, Gabriel's proposal had to be considered. But fucking a woman, or having someone else watch himself getting fucked, well, they were two separate and altogether unaccustomed sensations for a man like Christian. He feigned interest in the crowd as he and Gabriel wove through the throng of drunken partiers. His mind was playing through the scenario where it was he and Gabe and that yet unnamed player on the field, but what he hadn't even considered, when Gabriel asked him about sharing a bed with someone else, was a tenacious statement that had never occurred to him, one where he could have simply said "*No*...not today. I'd rather have you all to myself tonight."

Chapter Twenty

THE WORLD USED to boast of seven great wonders, but even those great feats of architecture, artistry, and beauty were falling away...as Gabe was fond of saying: "Everything crumbles." His relationship with Chris would be challenged and altered, and it would come from the smallest of women. Her name was Shea Baltimore, and she'd lost her mother to cancer when she was just entering the tender age of eight.

Gabe had always had a complicated relationship with God and the divinity. His father, Bennett, claimed Catholicism was their chosen religion, but he rarely dragged his family to church on Sundays, usually because he was still hungover from Saturday night. Even with his wavering commitment, he would extol the virtues of religion like some misguided saint.

"Do as I say, not as I do!"

Still, it had been inside the walls of the St. Ignatius Parish Cathedral, on one of those infrequent visits, where a young Gabe would first see the stained glass windows. The beautiful artistry of saints and angels reproduced with colored, cut, and soldered glass. With every representation of angel or saint, the boy noticed the halos of gilt and gold that surrounded their heads. He remembered it well because his mother, Sissy, had grabbed his tiny finger and pointed it up to a side window where he could see a robed figure with wings and that same halo of gold, and she'd whispered, "That is the Angel Gabriel," confiding with him under her breath that was how he'd gotten his name. It had been at St. Ignatius, so many years before, that the notion of the white-light radiance, which would later surround each of his victims, was first born.

If you asked him today, he would not remember the pews, the song selections, the ceremonial standing before kneeling. All of that had already left his memory, pushed purposely backward, so there was no opportunity for a connection to be made inside his mind to all his later victims and a nearly faded and forgotten memory from his childhood.

During one of their so-called interviews, Chris leaned in to Gabe with a serious scowl on his face before asking him what he thought his victims might have said about being chosen or how they might feel about their *white-light* designation. After a minute of contemplation, Gabe surprised them both by simply saying, "I didn't choose them. God did."

Gabe's victims couldn't be objective, since they didn't know their place in God's design. They couldn't see their own radiance. If you didn't understand that you were chosen, you couldn't understand that no homicide had been committed. By being occluded from seeing the grander picture, they had little to offer in the form of an opinion. He knew they couldn't blame Gabe, because he had not been the one choosing them. "Blame God," he would say.

Gabe was merely a player in those events, one whose role had been preordained by the Almighty. And Chris would never have the courage to ask him if it wasn't really something he had just created in his mind due to some weird enchantment he fashioned after staring at stained-glass windows nearly thirty years earlier. But the angel Gabriel's strongest role, as described in the book of Daniel, was the role of *revealer*, and he carried that role out in later books. Gabe saw himself as very much the revealer of all of those he saw bathed in God's light, who, in his waking mind, he knew he'd murdered. But in his deeper soul, he understood he had committed no crimes, just fulfilled a prophecy and listened to his heart.

To date, there hadn't been anyone who might've changed Gabe's mind regarding his participation in the murders. Even Chris sat on the sidelines, a bystander to every killing Gabe instigated. His newfound lover hadn't tried to alter his course; he sat in judgment, naturally, but he did so from the comfort of the Mayflower, or from under the sheets of his own bed. Then again, Gabe had yet to meet Shea Baltimore...although she had seen him from across the courtyard of their apartments and made a mental note to get to know him better if she could.

A DOLL-LIKE FIGURINE, Shea Baltimore had been a tiny girl. When at eight her mother succumbed to cancer, she was left alone with her father, DeWayne Baltimore, in a less than modest home in southwest Seattle. She'd suffered the loss of her mother, and DeWayne suffered the devastation alongside her. It created a gaping distance between them, one that should never have happened, but it had. DeWayne tried in vain to raise his daughter well as a single parent, though he lacked skill. It was more than fumbling fingers over hair ribbons and bows; it became the awkward handling brought on by his sadness and regret. No matter how hard he tried, he seemed to fall short in every area, and Shea was left to fend for herself far too early.

It was irrefutable evidence that some fathers cannot function without the help of a woman in their life. Without a guidebook, DeWayne wasn't able to give the same support to Shea that he longed to offer her. He loved his daughter greatly, yet the weight of raising a child after the death of his wife felt overwhelming to him. Some men just can't handle the responsibilities that fatherhood requires. His grief was insurmountable and it left a little girl in the wake of his departure as it fast drifted away under the guise of depression and alcoholism. He wanted to be the best father he could, but his personal demons always seemed to intervene, and there were many nights when a young Shea would play alone in her room, while her father sat in the dark living room stacking aluminum beer cans in tall columns beside his chair.

Mercies can often abound in even the darkest of places; held together like the strands of a spider's web in the corners of the inner sanctum of Shea's bedroom. Being so alone didn't kill her; it merely made her stronger. Shea Baltimore wasn't raised by a father in denial; she was raised by her vision of how she saw things. She would stare innocently at the beauties that only an artist could distinguish and would eventually become a soulful inspiration for her next great drawing or painting. Her isolation became her steadfast companion and enabled her to become quite talented, even if there was no one there to tell her such things or ever show a parent's support or love.

As she grew older, Shea found she was preoccupied, maybe even slightly shielded, by her ability to draw. She spent her teenage years sequestered from peers at school and never joined in extracurricular activities like band or the drama club. "I have duties to attend to for my father," she'd say to others on those rare occasions when she'd been invited to come along. Her charcoal pencil and empty sketchpad became her release of sorts, a pathway beyond the drudgery of a tired and meaningless life. Even as a diminutive child, she had been lovely, though; a mere whisper of a girl far too pale and shy to not draw the attention of the adults and teachers she knew better than the students. She represented a particular pity they that would bubble in their insides. They knew her mother had passed, and what they didn't know of her father many were already suspicious. They pictured a child playing with paper cut out dolls and eventually moving toward the easel and inside they would practically weep. Nevertheless, Shea Baltimore was no shrinking violet as many regarded her; she blossomed and grew even in the absence of a parent's love. Proving too many who knew that children could be remarkably resilient—even when left alone to their own devices. Some young people just know when to find their way through the darkness because kids can be terribly elastic and in many ways stronger than the adults they eventually become.

Shea's life had been such a self-imposed prison, it was harder for her to move out of her father's house than she'd ever imagined. He relied on her for so many things she worried, what would become of him when she wasn't there? Without her there to cook his dinners would he even take the time to eat? Or without her running his towels and clothes through the washer, would he even care about his appearance anymore? Who would be there to pick up the empty aluminum cans which typically littered the space around his dilapidated old La-Z-Boy, she wondered.

But Shea did find the courage to move away; knowing her life would only have meaning once she'd fulfilled her dreams of becoming a great artist and possibly even moving to New York - and to whatever acclaim that might mean. And even if her job as a checkout girl at a local grocery didn't pay well and it made all her aspirations of attaining her goals a near intangible reality, she still believed in herself. She maybe young, and she maybe too naïve, but somewhere along the way she'd burrowed out a spot inside her soul to punch in a small degree of faith...even if that was all it was, hope and faith. Part of her understood how all artists she'd ever admired were prone to suffering for their talent. And if she had to live in some dank, dingy hole in the wall, she knew at least it would be hers. It would become the first of many stairs, a mere riser step on an ambitious path to success, she told herself.

She first observed the For Rent sign as she was driving around looking for a place she could afford. But it was the courtyard that enticed her to pull over and check out the grounds and the buildings. Shea thought it was all positively lovely, overgrown with wild honeysuckle and with its unusual architectural design. She even liked the failing plaster from its exteriors. In her artistic eye, it appeared to her to look like snow melting into the earth from an unseasonably warm spring. It reminded her of one of those old Spanish villas she'd read about because she was just young enough to be impressionable, and sheltered enough to see things with much younger perception.

The rosy tint of youth and inexperience allowed her to see many things, not as they were and how she might imagined them to be, and she never even noticed the crumbling walls or broken drains. It was destined for decay and overrun by invasive weeds and ugly foliage. It was a property that practically guaranteed it would be razed one day soon, but to her, it was gloriously charming and retained great possibilities. If she had doubts about moving there, the overweight leasing agent squashed them quickly when he mentioned that back in the day many well-known Seattle artists had stayed there. He said this as he fumbled with an oversized key ring and hobbling over to the empty unit for an unapologetic showing. Once the words left his lips, she was smitten, and there was little he could've said that would have deterred her from signing on the dotted line.

She recalled rushing home that night, excitedly wanting to break the news to her father, while simultaneously being afraid he might not allow her to move out until he'd walked through the apartment himself and given his go-ahead. She knew if he saw it, he'd grumble about how tiny it was or how it was probably infested with roaches or rats. She didn't need to hear that. She didn't want her dreams shattered by a man who couldn't see the good in things that she did. She decided to stop in at the store and pick up some pasta for a nice meal. She hoped that a bellyful of spaghetti would change his mood to something positive. Anything to help grease the conversation she knew they'd have to undertake and one she worried about.

Three weeks later to the day, Shea had settled in her first apartment ever. She worked whenever a shift became available and carried her groceries on the bus or when she had the extra gas money drove her old car or even purchased painting supplies whenever she could. It may have sounded dull to most people, but to her, it was that representation of freedom, the tiny first steps of a child learning to walk before they ran.

And her isolation aided her immensely—her work was represented with female nudes and portraits of each face she encountered during her daily travels. Every face she sketched held a powerful sadness and a longing of its own, and every dark pupil in every eye seemed to be staring off at some unknown horizon as if they were pining for some nameless desire or some lost love. Shea noticed the new tenant shortly after he moved into his tiny, furnished unit. She spotted him as he crossed the courtyard, and she lingered there at her window, watching him unlock his front door and slip inside with a backward glance, which looked suspicious.

She thought the new tenant was a striking figure of a man. His manly appearance suggested to her that he was some kind of carnal beast who surely possessed a dark and tragically concealed heart, one which only she could pull back into the light and by using all her skills of empathy and kindness. Of the few failings, Shea possessed, her greatest was her inability to learn mistrust or picture the worst in strangers. Her fascination with him hadn't lessened as the summer days grew even longer. Her observation of his movements and the way he strolled across the courtyard when he came home or left all became inspiration for her artistic eyes. He was fast becoming one of her favorite models and she spent immeasurably long evenings reproducing his image on paper. He never had overnight guests that she could tell, and she never saw him carrying in groceries or even holding a basket of laundry. All of this made him even more mysterious, and an enigma worthy of closer examination.

In her mind, there would be a chance meeting. She would accidently drop contents from her grocery bag at or near his feet. He would smile in return and bend over to retrieve what she'd foolishly allowed to fall. He would think she was more of a character in an old Hepburn movie, too young to understand how he saw right through her fumbled attempts to get to know him as if she were crafted from nothing more than gauze or lace. He appeared more brutish than cavalier and seemed to be one of the few single occupants of the courtyard not currently riddled with drug addiction or saddled with the sallow continence of someone living beyond the edges of anything she might consider normal.

But getting the stranger to notice her was hard; he kept irregular hours and never had a smile on his face, making him unapproachable. Still, he was a man, and she possessed what they all wanted. It would happen to her if she just made herself available.

One evening, the young woman watched the courtyard for the man's return, and when he did, she was trapped in the image of the stranger standing at his balcony in his shorts and nothing else. It was unseasonably warm that evening, and each room was only equipped with tiny fans instead of window air conditioners. She could easily understand why he'd removed his clothing and stood there begging a breeze in, but the picture he made of masculine symmetry could have been a charcoal drawing worthy of framing.

Even from across the plaza, she could see his expression. She caught what she surmised as a look of anguish painted across his face. She suspected he was a man in transition; the inner turmoil clearly visible in those lovely eyes suggested the man had complicated stories, and knowing that made him even sexier than at first glance. *How heavy the crown*, she thought. He must have burdens and responsibilities that he didn't have the confidence to share. He had a face that implored for a woman's soft caress, and she figured she would make as honorable a choice for queen as any other lady-in-waiting.

SHEA COULDN'T HAVE been more wrong about Church. Although he may have been weighing lofty decisions that night, he only appeared kingly because of his masculine energy. He wouldn't turn out to be the noble beast she'd hoped he would be. He was a killer with a twist, a villain from a dozen lives rolled into something fresh and dangerous. It wouldn't benefit her life to be a player in the play where a man bends to help a lady in distress and their longing eyes meet with that suggestion of intimacy. Meeting Church would, at the very least, break her heart, and at worst, it created the events which would ultimately become her undoing. Whether it was sadistic trickery of the sisters of fate or all-knowing God playing pranks with mortal lives, she would not know the real Church...at least, not until it was too late to turn back.

AFTER LEAVING THE Pony, Gabriel and Christian walked back to his car in the rain. The dampness plastered Christian's hair to his forehead, but he wasn't concerned with the warm northwesterly rain, not when he was in Gabriel's company. They turned on 13th Avenue, just off East Madison, and headed back in the direction of downtown and Christian's car. They were not the only patrons from the bar who'd chosen to leave at that time. There were obviously gay men skirting the rain, either heading from the Pony, or heading there to make the late-night crowds.

Gabriel's shirt was clinging to his form like a rubber skin, and not unlike Christian, he didn't seem to care. It wasn't like they couldn't dry off at his loft. They heard the distant horns from ferries along the Lake Washington Ship Canal, which connected the fresh water to the salty inland seas of the Puget Sound. Gulls screamed overhead, but their calls became lost on the winds and mists from the Pacific. The breeze carried the aroma of fish and red seaweed, but it wasn't unpleasant, smelling much like freedom and the carefree abandon that came from stories of pirates or seafaring traders.

Mount Baker was an illumination of white crests in the backdrop of their walk, bringing to Christian's mind a serenity he had never known while strolling the city streets. It must be the jovial nature of his companion combined with Seattle's splendor, he thought. Throughout their day, Christian had shoved back every dark reflection of Gabriel as a serial killer. It had been a great day. He didn't want to spoil the mood with questions he didn't really want the answers to. In that moment he was seized with a newfound concept of simply scrapping the book. He'd never understood what motivation Gabriel had for allowing his story to be told anyway. There would be fallout if the book ever reached the public. It would end their budding romance forever, and for the first time since they had met, that had become an unacceptable resolution.

His heart expanded uncomfortably in his chest, and even with Gabriel chatting nonsense in the background, his mind raced with the impulse to just leave the horror of the book behind. He would have to get Gabriel to stop his murders of course; he would push him to seek professional help for his sickness. They would learn to date, slowly. He would go back to work. He would do everything he could to try to normalize Gabriel—wipe all of what he'd learned from his mind, like steam from the bathroom mirror after a shower.

He could do that; he knew he could…if it only meant he'd be able to keep Gabriel in his life.

Turning and interrupting his companion in the midpoint of some lame story, he asked, "If it meant that you and I could be together…would you ever consider stopping everything…no more murders, so you and I could remain together…free?"

GABE SEEMED STARTLED by both the look on his lover's face and the urgency in his voice. "Jesus. What are you talking about?"

Rambling back with a harried pace in his words, Chris continued his line of inquiry. "Our lives converged for reasons neither of us could've understood. But we're here now. I can't face losing you, not now. So far, you haven't been caught. Doesn't that mean anything to you?"

They both stopped walking; gratefully noticing they were isolated from bystanders. Turning to face each other, Gabe could see the younger man getting agitated, like he was pushing a hefty load inside a wheelbarrow uphill. But just minutes earlier, he'd seemed fine. *What the hell is going through his head now?* Gabe was stunned by Chris's quick transformation.

"Chris, calm down. I think you were having another conversation in your head. Maybe you should let me into that; maybe just give me a chance to catch up?" Gabe took Christian by the elbow and pulled him closer, but the writer couldn't be pacified easily. His breath was coming in rapid succession, and his eyes darted nervously.

"When we met, we were both a hundred miles from anywhere. We got a chance to meet under...err, terrible circumstances, *but we did meet,*" Chris said. His expression seemed genuinely intense and even a little panicked. As if he'd awoken from one of his nightmares, the ones that Gabriel invaded and changed with nothing more than his presence.

"All I'm saying is that we could put it all behind us...just slip away. But only if you put this aside, this...sick cause of yours...at least to give us an option at a stable life...together."

He was rattled, and it hit like a floodgate swinging open. Gabe recognized this wasn't the same man he shared a beer and conversation with some twenty minutes earlier. Gabe had to step back and take a breather. The same nervous energy coursing through Chris was jumping like electricity and desirous of a willing close conduit. It crossed the vacuum between them; it hit him in his gut and traveled up and outward. It held his heart firmly in a cold grip and prevented it from beating freely. He was instantly anxious and uncomfortable. It wasn't that he hadn't thought about it before, he admitted secretly. The words hadn't been sufficiently formed, and certainly they'd never allowed the word to spill out with that kind of ease. He was shocked to hear Chris spluttering out those things he hadn't allowed himself to consider. It was like bringing voice to a once-hidden hope and that alone felt wrong on so many levels.

"What the hell are you talking about?" he said, making more pretense than acceptance. No matter how much of the shock he fabricated, he couldn't cover the lie with simple expressions.

CHRISTIAN COULD SEE that Gabriel had dreamed of that likelihood before then. Maybe he'd even contemplated it and after realizing it wasn't possible he let the notion slip away without a thought. But Chris could see that Gabe had thought about it, at least at one time. The writer had become familiar with those pale eyes by now. He could see things Gabriel tried to conceal—their time together had given him that.

"This is nonsense," Gabriel said, turning away, trying to disengage. But Christian was already deep in the waters and there was no going back then. He grabbed Gabriel by the arm and twisted him back around by force.

"It's possible...I've thought about it. I just never allowed myself to bring it up because it was just plain wrong. You think you had reasons to murder those innocent people, but you didn't. Each and every victim deserves to see justice for your crimes, but I can't imagine life without you now."

Christian was relieved to finally shed the garment he'd been wearing since the two had met. Exhausted from carrying it around, it now lay at his feet, leaving him breathy, confused, and tangled in ways he couldn't understand.

"You may've been some dark figure that I was never meant to fully understand, but you are more than that to me now. I want to be with you. But I simply can't imagine only seeing you through thick glass and bars."

GABE STEPPED AWAY, trying to gain some perspective. As they'd been walking, twilight had fallen, and the expansive sky of robin's-egg-blue was quickly turning dark. Lights twinkled from the boats on Elliot Bay. The water tours were underway, and the horns from sea traffic beckoned from a distance. Gabe looked down at the pavement, confused. This was not how he wanted to close their evening. All he wanted now was to fade into nothingness, leave Chris standing there less than a mile from his car and a quarter mile from the coastline. It hadn't been that long since he'd asked Chris to join him on his next killing, but now Chris was asking him to stop altogether. He began to get angry at the man who'd thrown some wrench into his plan, which had always been to have someone else see that he wasn't completely mad. Someone who had the wherewithal and knowledge to prove that fact to others—a writer who could tell his story as it truly was, so that it didn't fade into the annals of history without someone knowing he had been right all along. Gabe didn't like confusion; it was a rare occurrence, and he was unaccustomed to how angry it made him.

How could such a good day turn so horribly bad, so quickly?

CHRISTIAN TRIED TO bridge the distance, moving tentatively closer to Gabriel. He wanted to pull the man into his arms, to get him to understand just how much he wanted to stand next to him. Maybe even to show him he had a chance at a very different life—if he'd only make a step in that direction. But even after that misting of humid Seattle rain, Gabriel had turned ice cold. Neither man could remember a time when there wasn't this very question hanging between them. They had forgotten all their time in the sack, holding hands at the Pony, or those sweet moments spent at the Mayflower Plaza. It was just this moment in time, and it seemed to drag on endlessly.

"I thought you heard me before, but now I know you didn't," Gabriel said under his breath, barely audible to Christian's ears. "I'm going home...and I'm going *alone.*"

With that, he turned and headed back in the direction of downtown, on foot. It was clear that Christian wasn't supposed to follow him as he stormed away. Gabriel never turned back around, and even now, yards away, the writer could sense the emotions coming off him in waves. Gabriel was angry and confused, and now it had been Christian's turn to say something that broke the mood.

Christian stood alone and watched as Gabe's image became smaller in his eyes. His heart finally began to beat at a normal speed, and he hung his head, and in a swell of anguish, began to cry. The sounds of gulls and the ferryboat whistles filled the air. He had overstepped and done so early, but even in his sadness, he knew it had been time to say those things. After what Gabriel had asked him earlier, he knew he couldn't keep quiet any longer. He had to try to stop Church from killing or lose him altogether. As sad as that was, it was still very clear that he had to at least try.

Chapter Twenty-One

IT WAS AFTER ten when Gabe passed through the courtyard headed to his door. But as he reached it, he noticed a large piece of paper tacked opposite side down and squarely pinned in the door's center just below the peephole. In his anger, he suspected it had to be an eviction notice before remembering that he was paid up for the remainder of this month and for the next full month as well. Confused, he pulled down the paper and then fumbled with his keys, wanting to escape inside his apartment before reviewing any legal document delivered from that shiftless landlord. Closing the door and flipping on a light switch, he turned the paper over to find that it wasn't what he expected. It was something different altogether. He was surprised to see that it was a hand-drawn sketch and it appeared to be of him standing casually on the balcony, a distant faraway expression plastered on his face. Whoever had done it, he thought, was remarkably talented. They seemed to capture his image perfectly. From the outside, it appeared whoever drew it really liked the inspiration.

At first, he thought it was some kind of signal from Christian. That immediately pissed him off because it meant that despite his gruff demands Chris had disregarded his wishes and followed him home one night. How else would he have known where he lived? It also meant that Chris had broken their prior arrangement and that he ignored the bare canons of the bond they'd been attempting to build during this book fiasco. But then after more careful scrutiny of the image, Chris realized how it couldn't be a gift from his lover because he wasn't that talented; or at least, he never mentioned or indicated that he liked to draw. And surely that would've come up at some point.

There was an immediate issue he needed to consider, then, if Chris hadn't delivered it, who had? It meant that someone he didn't know was surveilling him, tracking him, following him, and knew his temporary residence. And that raised every alarm bell and began the ringing in Gabe's head. His hatred flashed anew. This was Chris's fault, he foolishly rationalized. If it weren't for him, the hunter wouldn't have allowed himself to become the hunted. He would've seen it happening and somehow prevented it. In his hand he held a large piece of art paper, absolute evidence that someone was investigating him, stalking him, running their own reconnaissance...and what seemed even more paramount to him was that he missed all the signs and neglected seeing it for what it was. All of his life Gabriel had been on the lam, remaining one step ahead of the authorities and doing his best to appear nondescript in every crowd. He'd learned to be a ghost wherever he went because his survival depended on that skill. Standing in his shitty apartment holding the picture only proved to him that he'd failed in that very important skill.

But before his anger took control over his actions, he paused to consider the drawing and the artist who'd penned it. Obviously they were a fan. That much seemed clear by every carefully drawn charcoal line and every smudge to specify shadow and background; and how they deftly worked to capture his essence and even took the painstaking efforts to show him in that smoldering, riveted gaze, or display his features in the strongest and most admirable of light. Whoever gifted him the drawing had done so out of love. That much was testament by the craftsmanship and even by the delivery to his door itself. *The proof is in what I'm holding*, he thought astonishingly.

After walking to the window, he peered through an open crack in the blinds only to see the empty balcony and a ghostly vacant plaza below. The sketch that someone left him seemed to be drawn from an angle and perspective that suggested it had to come from someone down there, he thought. It must've been done by one of his neighbors. With a bemused smirk creeping across his face he realized he had an unknown fan out there, hiding somewhere beneath him. Not that it'd all that difficult to track the artist down, since they'd all but left a practical map back to their apartment. He'd never taken much notice of his neighbors before then, they were all unimportant phantoms, left to pass through his life in that same cardboard fashion that most white-lighters were delegated to become...all save Christian. Stepping out onto his balcony he stared at the darkened windows of the units facing his, and then did the only thing that seemed reasonable in his mind; he smiled and offered an enthusiastic wave. It was a comical gesture, meant solely for whoever had been surveilling him without his awareness. He couldn't be sure if they were watching him in that instant or not. But it seemed likely to him since they'd surely want to see his response at the moment he first stumbled onto their gift.

Then the notion hit him that he was actually being observed, and that slightly unnerved him. If they were watching him, they were witnessing him coming and going. Maybe they'd sat in their apartment, voyeuristically obsessed by him, catching a fast glimpse of him as he exited the shower, a towel wrapped around his waist, or walking around naked as he prepared to leave to see Christian again. Maybe they were sitting in the dark at that exact moment, touching themselves romantically like only an absent lover might do. Watching him as he stood on his balcony waving and smiling like a simple country rube.

The vision of that picture sent a shiver down his spine. Gabe wasn't a prude in any fashion. He was proud of the gifts God had given him, but he had to weigh that out on the cautious efforts of a man who was currently on the run. He always thought it wiser that he keep blinds drawn and his head down where possible; lest it generate undue interest and questions from the curious like the police and the FBI. Having someone he didn't know spying on him wasn't a comforting area Gabe liked to find himself in.

He could carry the drawing across the courtyard and knock on a few doors. But it was late and he was tired. It would have to wait another day because it was already late. Going back inside, he lay the drawing down on the table and smiled. He liked being the inspiration for someone else's talent. It was one of the reasons that the whole book project was first broached, after all. And now he had two people who were interested in him. He mulled over that pleasant idea as he headed toward the shower to rinse off, thinking first he needed to make sure the blinds were adequately closed and the front room left dark.

He suspected he would have to keep his curtains drawn more closely now; after all, it wasn't uncommon for him to walk around naked, and although he didn't much care who saw him while he was in his apartment, he didn't relish the idea they were sketching him in all his glory. He wondered how long it had been since he'd jacked it in the shower and possibly walked around with a hard-on, and wondered who'd witnessed that.

His back and feet ached. It was a reminder that he'd walked a long way home in a hurry and the mood Chris had left him hadn't faded entirely. So he tossed the drawing on his table and headed to the shower. The idea of getting his rocks off under hot steam seemed instantly appealing, and a great way to change his disposition.

BACK AT THE loft, Christian wasn't in any better mood than before. His mind raced with every detail of his conversation with Gabriel. He'd thrown his keys on the table carelessly, unable to shake his frustration. He opened cabinets and pushed back dry goods, trying to locate a bottle of bourbon before he remembered a half-full bottle of vodka in his freezer. *Hadn't it been a gift from Ruth, or more likely a stash for her own amusement?* He filled a glass with the chilled vodka and popped in a couple of cubes, but he couldn't find any clear soda. He didn't like drinking straight booze, but he wanted to shove back questions and regrets from earlier...so straight it would be.

The whiteboard stood like a monolith in the corner of the living room, a constant reminder of what had started his fucked-up journey. The news articles and loose Post-it notes on his wall were not making him feel any better either. They were a recap of his obsessive nature and a memento of just how he far he'd fallen. He couldn't help wondering whether Gabriel had headed to whatever "hole" he called home or whether he'd headed to a bar. It was easy to imagine Gabriel going to a club—he was the type to seek out sex with a stranger as some consolation, a chance to change his mood. Christian hated the pictures that played out in his head, but more importantly, he wished he were the type to do the same. He envied anyone who could fuck so freely without remorse or connection.

If he'd kept his mouth shut, they would be lying in bed together right now, maybe stroking each other or humping like bunnies. *Why hadn't he just waited for the morning to talk to Gabriel?* But as he considered that, his gaze was drawn to the wall covered with news accounts of recent unsolved murders, and the sheer volume of papers littering his wall made him realize how stupid he was.

Christian's memory flashed on a crappy TV talk show playing in the background while he'd been getting ready for work one morning a year or so earlier. He remembered the topic of heated debate had been women who chose to remain with lovers who were addicts. He remembered being disgusted at the panel of sad and lonely women who foolishly thought they had a power of change over their loved ones. Some people are just stupid sheep, he thought as he pulled a tie out of his closet. The show hadn't been particularly interesting enough to want to watch any more, but he was drawn to the idiocy that some folks never seem to escape. "But I could change him," he heard one of the unseen ladies on the dais say just as the audience broke into a cacophony of cheerless laughter. Stupid women, stupid ideals he said aloud as he grabbed his suit jacket and headed toward the door. All he knew was he was far too intelligent to ever allow himself to be trapped in that kind of a relationship. It seemed as inconceivable to him as waking up one day with horns growing out of his skull.

That memory came back to him now, changing his perspective slightly, even though he doubted there had ever been a topic like his.

I'm in love with a serial killer. So tell me, Oprah, what am I to do? How do I get him to stop his murderous ways and stay home with me?

He wasn't in the mood to judge; he'd seen too much and learned too many particulars of just how sick the world was around him. He knew that he loved Gabe, despite what he'd done or all that he was capable of doing, and he couldn't imagine a tougher life than loving someone else when it wasn't addiction to drugs but to killing for God. Those women on TV who pretended to know otherwise had nothing on him. He'd fallen far below their sling-back heels, he wasn't even worthy of pretending he was better than they were now. He was even more pathetic than they could've ever sounded. If he was as smart as he thought he was, he'd pick up a phone and dial 911; he'd sing like a canary for anyone who'd listen, confess his crimes, or even betray a lover. In some ways, he felt very close to coming clean, but it was a desire he knew he'd never be able to follow through with; the repercussions were just too big, the chain reactions too devastating. Was that really an option, though? Was it as stupid a concept as agreeing to write a book about a killer from his perspective? Who the fuck did he think he was anyway?

Dropping onto his sofa caused a few droplets of vodka to fly out of his glass. It seemed to him that everyone wanted to escape confinement that night. One splash landed on his wrist, but he didn't care. He didn't even wipe it clean. Instead, he stared at the wall and the whiteboard with a blank empty expression. He felt like he was being buried under a mountain of new information. That, and the strong emotions he was carrying around his neck like an albatross of a tether. He had more in common with the women on the talk show than he cared to admit. He'd found himself in a strange relationship. If relationship was even an adequate description for what he was falling into. The reality of the situation was that it had only been a few days of fucking nonstop and long, slow interviews about his past. But he had learned a lot about the man. Just not as much as he felt he still needed. He suspected Gabriel cared for him, just as he was beginning to care about him. But he was still an unpredictable animal and could be just as easily backed into a corner of his own making, and that could turn out to be a dangerous place to be near should it happen.

Gabriel was an enigma, a wild, untrained pony that Chris was trying to ride without possessing the abilities of a skilled equestrian. He wasn't the kind of man easily broken; even under the sheets, Chris had seen that in the force of his thrusts and the way he Gabe grabbed him by his wrists and then hovered over him all stony-eyed as he pushed his manhood in deeper. Ever the oddity, Gabriel wasn't exactly a person you could pinpoint with accuracy. If there had been a mold, it had been shattered at the forge. And yet it was incalculable how much Chris could admire while fearing in the same breaths as he did. He looked at him with as much analysis as he was capable of offering, how a man like Gabe can kill without remorse and still reach for a sick justification that only he could ever fathom well. Sinner or saint, he was all about the way he looked at things and that was a train no one else wanted to ride. He got a nauseous pit in his stomach if he looked any closer, but from the outside periphery, against the smooth texture of Gabe's flesh and the muscles hidden beneath, he was suddenly his prisoner. And with his lungs expanded and heart racing from the latest orgasm, it was clear how sweet the penitentiary could sometimes feel.

Even in those tiny seconds of rational thoughts about Gabe, Chris was unable to define his place between the flip-flops of anguish to explanation. There were no excuses or vindications he could possibly find there. If Gabe had been born to some undiscovered Indian tribe of the Amazons, then one might've understood exactly how a traditional, civilized society didn't actually work for him. Gabe was something different, a person who needed to be viewed through a totally different microscope, or held to other standards than the rest of us. He was unblemished, save for his soul—and he was special. Chris knew that Gabriel didn't hate the world, just those parts where he didn't fit in. The victims who suffered under his hands were not chosen because they were terrible people, quite the opposite. From what Chris gathered during their unending conversations on that very topic, it seemed they were specifically unique and important to Church's bent ideologies. Gabriel had crossed many state lines along his murderous spree. Surely he was aware that Texas was a state that practically boasted about how quickly they were able to dispatch their criminals. No, he had nothing to look forward to except a speedy trial in one of those southern conservative courts, before Gabe walked into death row. As righteous and sane as that resolution sounded, it wasn't anything Christian wanted to see in his lifetime. There were few things he felt sure about those days, but that much he was certain.

But even knowing what he knew, he didn't want Gabriel to die. Gabriel had changed him too much too drastically, and far too importantly not to be spared his life, he hoped. Christian had only ever allowed himself to see the future where Gabriel was arrested, maybe even tried and convicted. He had never allowed himself to see a point beyond that inevitability. All of a sudden he had begun to equate himself, rather grandly, to the writer Truman Capote during his writing of *In Cold Blood*. It was long conjectured that Capote became "unusually attached" to the killer, Perry Smith, during the trial and eventual hanging. He wondered if he was to become some twisted death row widower, a man only happy when standing dangerously close to the veil of death. He'd questioned Gabe's sanity several times, but in the last couple of days, he was fast learning to question his own. He presumed that once Gabe met the electric chair, or took the lethal injection that would end his life, that Chris would still be close by his side. Maybe watching from the death room as he drew in his final gasps. It was a painful fantasy to imagine, but in some ways, he knew he was just as guilty...if only because of the complicity he shared with the killer.

SHEA SAT IN her apartment with baited anticipation, hoping the stranger across the way would get her message and come over. But she grew dismal when no came knocking. Pulling back the curtains, she watched as he trudged upstairs and then noticed an irritated expression on his face as he pulled the drawing down and disappeared inside. *Did he hate it*? She actually thought she'd done pretty well with the representation. Sadly, she hadn't waited for the stranger to reappear on his balcony. She hadn't seen him waving and smiling back at her. If she had, her mood would've been greatly transformed.

She didn't have any words prepared should he actually come knocking to say thank you. She couldn't image what she'd say if he were to stand at her door imposingly while holding her gift. Would she invite him inside? Would she simply stammer out her responses like a shy school girl fumbling with her words? Maybe he would've thought a drawing of him was inappropriate somehow, she worried. Maybe it was something akin to stalking, she feared. She hadn't even considered that prospect before that very second and the thought alarmed her. She meant well, she told herself. It was nothing more than a gift to show her talent and a willingness to get to know her inspiration better. The thought of him being angry, standing enveloped within the frame of her doorway was unnerving. And she had to admit it was a tad titillating too. It sounded insane to admit that. It was a little sinful to think about a stranger in those terms, but she couldn't help herself. She'd never approached a man before and never had cause to be interested in many people. But this guy was different. He was sexy in the kind of way that drew her fingers below the covers and fashioned sensual wet dreams where he whispered sweet nothings in her ear, and it made her feel slightly invincible.

She figured the truth was she'd act like a fool if he ever showed at her door. She knew she'd turn speechless and be unable to look as sophisticated as she wanted to appear. But then again there was that portrayal she was crafting in her head, him standing there like a shadow at her door, silent and arresting. Would she have the strength to invite him in and allow herself to know the electric pulses of pleasure coursing from her thighs to her breasts? Would he lead her gently to her bedroom and then lie down beside her in that hollow vacuum of unspoken silence? Could she be the type of woman who could sleep with a perfect stranger?

In the privacy of her bedroom, Shea allowed herself to carry the illusion to a satisfactory completion, surrounded by the all the jars of paint and sticks of charcoal along with her trusty easel standing guard in the corner. There in the dark, she gently moved her fingers lower to the lips of her nether region and pried and explored herself with abandon. The stranger wasn't just her inspiration, she thought, he was quickly becoming something more tangible and the physicality of all her masturbatory imageries.

Chapter Twenty-Two

AUTUMN REDS AND browns lined the trees along the waterways that surrounded the city. It was a good time of year for Gabe, who liked the brisk, clean air of the fall season. He had left the French doors open when he'd crawled into bed the night before, and now the smell of dew and honeysuckle beckoned like a crooked finger, enticing him up and out of bed. His first thought was of Chris, whom he knew would be rising with a powerful desire for coffee. He smiled at that strong image before remembering, almost as an afterthought, that he'd been exceedingly angry at Chris only hours earlier.

But the writer seemed to invade his brain more and more these days, never far from being plucked into view and focused with a clarity Gabe had never known. It had not been a glacial change either, it simply wasn't one day...but by the next, it was. There wasn't a line designation where Gabe could witness the man becoming important in the grander scheme of his life, and it certainly had never been his plan from the onset.

If one were to ask Gabe about his sexual orientation, he would easily say he was straight. If you asked him today he still might make that claim, but Christian Maxwell was becoming important, and he didn't comprehend why exactly. The writer was supposed to be a character in his own play. He'd intended to find someone capable of giving him a solid voice...because he desperately wanted his story told. He also never assumed there would be a trial because after his confession had been captured on paper, somewhere before the book would see print, he intended to snuff out his own candle.

But much like his victims, Christian had become a tangled part of his story and, surprisingly, awoken feelings that Gabe had thought buried. Not about being gay; in his mind, he wasn't really homosexual. But if he had been, it wouldn't have bothered him or changed his course in any way. What was new was how he could feel about another person. He'd felt next to nothing for anyone since the day he slipped from Bennett's grasp and took to the highway. His discomfort with leaving his sister and mother quickly faded through time. They were transmuted into spirits, just a flash from some forgotten memory that no longer had value. Gabe didn't know if either of them was even alive, although he had wondered a few times during his time on the road if his little sister had met anyone special or had ever married.

On one side, he felt nothing for others, but he had felt something akin to indebtedness to every victim he had encountered—the ones who'd been bathed in their white glow—and equally he felt obliged to Chris. They were all fragments of who and what he'd become. The writer, in particular, had some major part yet to play. Maybe that was why the image of Chris bounding out of bed and begging for coffee made him smile. He'd figured Chris's role had always been one thing, but maybe, in reality, it was something else.

He crawled from his bed and stretched his naked form. His arms reaching high over his head to break the stiff, inflexible sleep from every ligament. He turned the water on high in the tile-stained, dilapidated shower of his rented room and bent under the steam to wash his body, using a mostly vanished bar of soap he'd stolen from a gas station restroom. He wanted coffee too. He'd never been much of a coffee drinker before he met Chris, but apparently the young man left his vestige wherever he traveled because he craved morning caffeine and imagined what he was doing in that very instant. Gabe contemplated putting his anger aside and calling Chris to invite him for coffee. The only way this thing was going to work was if he learned to acquiesce more than he usually did. He decided he wanted to see his new lover, regardless of how they'd left it.

ACROSS TOWN, CHRISTIAN had arisen about the same time. Without knowing it, both men had modified their schedules to meet a singularity. Both men woke wanting coffee, both wanted to see the other, and individually, both regretted how they'd parted the night before. It was almost no surprise when, only fifteen minutes later, Christian's cell began to vibrate.

He paused for a beat before he answered. He didn't recognize the number but suspected Gabriel was standing outside at one of those rare payphones one almost never sees anymore.

"Good morning," he said calmly. "I was hoping you'd call this morning."

"I don't want to fight," Gabriel whispered. "I just wanna see you, and I suspect you need a morning jolt of java just like me."

"Well, I have coffee here…" But even as he said it, he knew it came too early. "Then again, I can meet you at that same café where we first—"

Cutting him off, Gabriel said, "I'll be there in twenty. If I'm late, you know how I like it."

And he did, he thought, as Gabriel hung up unceremoniously. He knew how he liked a lot of things. Besides his neighbor, Ruth, Gabriel was the only other person for whom Christian knew the way they drank their coffee. He couldn't remember how his parents drank theirs, or even if they had. But Gabriel liked it black with two sugars. He wondered about something about something as infinitesimal as someone liking their coffee prepared could become so paramount a consideration. He never even wondered why it made him smile just knowing that.

Christian knew only the vaguest points of Gabriel Church's travels before they'd met. He had studied the trail of murders in his earlier research, but he had yet to cover most of that with his killer companion. There always seemed like too much to discuss whenever they were alone. He knew Gabriel had spent his childhood in Tennessee. He knew he'd jumped into his Chevelle and put a backwoods state in his rearview. He knew that he had committed his first murder in Texas and from there he'd traveled out West and bounced around California for a time.

In truth, Gabriel Church had crisscrossed this country more than once. He had gone as far as he could without ever passing the borders into Canada or Mexico. One thing he'd wanted to see was the beaches of Southern California, which he had…early on. Another highpoint had been the highway into the ocean heading to the distant Florida Keys, and he'd seen that as well. But committing forty or so murders takes time, and it takes great distance and many miles. If Church had ever stayed too long in one spot, he always knew he'd be tagged to one of his own murders, simply because he fit the part—aimless drifter.

To get from the hill country of Tennessee to that golden state of California, it takes merely jumping on four or five major interstates. You could trace a line of murder with your finger on a map with Church watching, and he would simply nod and smile as if some great achievement had been met and surpassed. There were backwater towns along the coasts of Texas and rural shit holes that were barely evidenced by the road kill you traveled over, as well as hilly canyons throughout Southern California that looked out to an endless expanse of water. At times it had been glorious, and for Church, it always represented an adventure. Thinking back on it now, Church would never have chosen another existence.

But Christian wasn't aware of all the miles Gabriel traveled, or exactly how many murders he'd committed. He only knew of six he guessed that could be credited to Church. He had been told of one he hadn't been aware of; that being Gabriel's first foray into homicide. That man never fit the pattern of future kills; he simply was there when it all began, and even now he and Church were the only ones who knew who exactly he had already dispatched. Gabriel was the spider web that the writer couldn't quite shake off. No matter how he jiggled, he couldn't shed that creepy crawly feeling from the back of his neck. He was a flicker for which he couldn't distinguish a distance, but it was a light that still drew him like a beacon. It had been his candle in the window calling him home, but even he never believed that was how life was supposed to be. He could see a sickness spreading and the virus was none other than Gabriel Church. But knowing a thing and breaking it from your life were two totally separate occurrences—just ask the nearest standing junkie. And he was addicted to Gabe, though Chris had never been the type of person to become easily addicted to anything before then.

The Maxwell clan were predominately college educated, morally ethical folks from a God-fearing background. But forever being the black sheep he was, Chris had turned into someone immoral and tainted. He'd be more than a *proverbial* embarrassment to his family's good name. He was suspect in a dark spiral that would've made his grandmother roll around in her grave—had she actually passed.

If it broke badly, as he knew it would, he'd be ostracized, awarded the moniker of the "Maxwell Family's Forgotten Son," like Lord Voldemort from the Potter books, he would become the *"You-Know-Who,"* or the *"He-Who-Must-Not-Be-Named."* Partially due to his fledging sexuality, but more so because of those he allowed himself associated with people like Church.

Being alienated from the Maxwell family wasn't, in truth, such an awful consequence to consider, he supposed. At least it would put the brakes of finality on those rather indelicate conversations on his orientation that he feared were coming all too quickly. But it also shielded the fine Maxwell name from being dragged through the papers or becoming the brunt of unprecedented muddy chatter from his father's social peers at the country club or mother's literary discussion group. Certainly it wasn't a conversation he relished having with her. Just reflecting on that prospect, put an icy finger tracing along his spine and sending shakes to every spot imaginable. He could already picture how it'd go; probably in their living room of their old house while she stood with her signature cocktail of gin in hand and looked at him with those striking, but stern, green eyes peering just below the line of the eyeglasses bridged across her nose. He could imagine how he'd stumble through the explanation as he washed over the events of his latest affair as if he were already seated in the confessional, while good ole Father Bachnell clutched his bible across his lap like an obsequious servant finding they were standing in the presence of something satanical or spiritually unclean. He was going to become that corruption every soul feared, he believed.

But he did see some things in the revelation. They wouldn't be discussing religion once they found out who and what he'd been doing with Church. Her astonished expression would've said it all without having to speak at all. His mother's true convictions rested singularly with the family's reputation. Her dogmas seemed steeped in appearance and respect, more than the worry of an eternal damnation of anyone in particular. He would be more likely to go to hell, not by his sexuality, but more likely due to his sordid affiliations and his membership with criminal ilk. She would never consider the deeper pools, the essence that he was "special" or different. Gay people were an accepted effect to the wealthy, but then again, she had to consider that scandal was an entirely separate matter altogether.

As Christian raced to dress for his appointment with Gabriel, his mind played out all the possibilities...but none seemed good. Then again, Gabriel was never the sweetheart one takes home to meet the in-laws. Even with the darker consequences of their meeting, he was excited. A nervous energy was brewing, even before the caffeine. He dropped a shoe on the floor as he sat on the edge of his bed, and when he picked it up, he stopped his harried pace long enough to consider what their meeting would be like. Would Gabriel break apart the stony rocks of their prior conversation, or would he just put it behind them as he had done so many times before? With Gabriel, he could never tell.

As Christian wove through the heavy Seattle morning traffic, he hoped the man might offer up some slivers of insight about his future. Whether he might accept the offer to quit his murderous ways and get far from Seattle with Christian at his side. Perhaps, he thought, we could get out of the country, some Panamanian village or Costa Rican getaway. He couldn't be sure, but he suspected no one was on Gabriel's trail—it seemed he might have gotten closer with his insignificant investigation than even the feds. He had plenty of resources to draw from, and in that part of the world, they might prosper for years.

This was an alternative, but only if the man could swear the killings were behind them. Christian knew if he could be convinced the murders were done, both could move forward and never speak of their past lives or those mistakes and misfortunes that lay buried there. Remembering an article, Christian seized on something he'd read in college about the San Blas Islands off the coast of Panama. There were hundreds of tiny islands, but only about fifty were inhabited. It was a gift now, the flashing memory of all he'd read: the coconut trees and sandy beaches where turtles came ashore at night to bury their eggs, the crystal-blue waters of a vast Caribbean Sea. He remembered reading the soil was so famously rich there that one could grow just about anything worthy of planting. It was as if it were eager to sprout up and blossom or bear fruit, all simply for a person's pleasure and to grace a dinner table with a zealous bounty. He pictured a shirtless Gabriel sweating beautifully under a midday sun, working in a planted field beside a miniscule cabin of cut lumber and under a thatch-and-palm-frond roof of green. It would be a small but homey place, he was sure. Just the kind of place one could call home. Someplace he knew where they'd be spending their daytime playing in the waves or relaxing under the sun, and their long nights fucking and talking like separate halves born from an original whole.

Thinking about such a possibility stirred and twisted his insides, but in a good way. It might be just the type of thing a man like Gabriel would go for. He had to consider the best way to propose such a plan. While he was wondering how much a good satellite phone would cost them, a woman in a white Audi cut him dangerously off, nearly sending him into the side rail of one of the many Seattle bridges and forcing him to maneuver rapidly just to remain on the road. Tires squealed and time froze instantly around him just as he was able to regain the wheel and allow his heart to settle back into place. It wasn't exactly life and death, but it could've been, and that made him realize how tenuous life was. That he might be planning a future with Gabriel at the exact moment where his life was terminated. After his heart found its normal speed, he continued heading toward the café, but conscious now that life had its own set of ironic twists and turns. He was grateful to be alive in that moment, but the near collision had set in concrete that he would make his proposal again...and hope this time the man listened.

Amazingly, Gabriel was already at the Cherry Street Grinder. Christian saw him sitting alone near the large-pane window at the entrance. His expression was pensive and slightly frayed; a look that seemed an unfamiliar garment for him to wear. Still, it produced the smallest of grins once he looked up and noticed Christian arriving happily to greet him. He was a nervous suitor, fidgeting apprehensively as he waited for his date to show.

Didn't that make him Gabriel's date, descending down the staircase prepared to make his appearance by that scenario?

"She was quite a lovely picture bounding down the stairs in her lovely rose-colored taffeta gown and her shy, girlish smile," he recalled.

He chuckled openly at that odd image. Next, he thought how strange it was that Gabriel had beaten him to the cafe. Then again he didn't even know how close he was staying to it. Which was another extraordinary aspect of all this—the question of whether he was there to propose they grab their passports and the nearest ship to another country and finally leave for good. Again he reflected back to that picturesque imagery of Panama and living side by side with Gabriel anyplace other than there. Reality hit him as he reached the table when he suddenly considered that Gabe might not even have a passport. They hadn't discussed that part yet.

"I already ordered you a coffee, baby boy," Gabriel said as he pushed a cardboard cup across the table. He stood up quickly, and before Christian could adjust to the scene, Gabriel was hugging him. It was a typical straight guy kinda hug, that of a close friend or brother; the fast grip and quick release that suggested more familial than real intimacy. Chris was not yet comfortable with public affection. He only found himself secure to be so unabashed when the men were in private. But he would get there in time.

"I'm glad you called me. I wanted to apologize for the other night," Christian whispered under his breath as he yanked an empty chair closer. "But I was hoping we might be able to go somewhere else more secluded later. I've something I want to talk about and thought it best done...alone."

Gabriel exhaled deeply, a look of hurt on his face. *He may have mistaken my urging us to another location as some spot where I could dump him,* thought Christian.

"It's probably not what you think. I just want to talk to you alone. I might have a plan for us, something I want to go over with you."

Gabriel rested his elbows on the table on either side of his coffee and leaned close to Christian. There was pain hidden just below the surface; it was rising, bubbling, and threatening to overflow.

"I got here earlier than I thought I would, and I had some time to think about things myself."

Gabriel always maintained a strong persona. One of the things that Christian admired about him was his self-assured nature and the powerful control he sustained between his childlike bursts of joy and wonderment. But at this moment, he was alarming; whatever words he was struggling to unleash were stronger than even his usual disposition.

"I kept hearing your voice in my head last night...kinda hard to sleep, thanks to you. I know you began all this with an intention of research for a book about a killer, but even I could see it became much more than that. You wanted to know about my mama and my daddy; you wanted to know about my first awkward fuck in the back seat of my Chevelle; you wanted to glimpse deep inside to find out what made me turn out so *friggin' special*! That to me says you weren't just researching the man but...I don't know...falling in love."

Gabriel's head was slumped, a dismal shame hidden in the edges. Christian wondered how a man could feel disgrace or indignity at the concept of being loved. *How sad,* he thought, *that a man would get to Gabriel's age without ever feeling like someone cares for him. How miserable his childhood must have been?* Reaching across the table, he took Gabriel's hand in his and craned his neck to see the face Gabriel tried to conceal.

"I did fall in love...and I still find myself falling," he whispered over the din of the crowd and coffee-clutching patrons breezing past their table. "That's why I wanted to talk to you, hopefully more alone," he said, turning his head from either side to indicate the noisy throng. "I was hoping to offer a way out, a way we could be together and free from all this."

By the time Gabriel responded, his voice resonated over the clatter of dishes and idle conversations around him.

"Before we bounce, I wanted to explain that I was sorry about storming off the other night...but I wasn't sorry for what I said. I thought you knew me better. I thought we were on the same plane...wavelength...whatever. I'm not so sure anymore."

Christian could see Gabriel was putting brick to mortar and building his defenses. If he didn't stop the progression, it would be harder to scale later. "Don't jump to conclusions just yet. Give me a chance to explain myself," he said strongly, "but in a more private fucking location than this!"

He leaned back, disgusted with being in a crowded coffee bar and not able to pull Gabriel into his arms; his public embarrassment seemed stronger than he was. If he could get him alone, he might be able to sway him to consider his proposal. He could break his defenses by holding him close and allowing Gabriel to seize control of the moment. As if in tandem understanding, both men rose from their chairs simultaneously and headed to the entrance without uttering a single word.

Since they had met, they'd only spent a couple of nights apart, but as their feet hit the sidewalk, Christian had to fight the urge to ever be separated from Gabriel again. He was an addict; this much seemed clear. Even in Christian's sheltered, ivory-tower upbringing he'd seen addicts. Two male friends from college had fallen into that hole. He'd seen them transform into something darker before his very eyes. He'd noticed how anxious they became whenever they were about to score. He'd even noticed their blatant erections, barely concealed under denim jeans, as he'd watched them shift nervously with baited anticipation of that next shot of crystalline heaven to their veins. At the time, years before, he hadn't understood it, but walking now on the sidewalk, turning down the street with Gabriel in tow, it all became a filmy haze that was suddenly lifted. He was carrying his own drug, and it was standing at his side.

Drug users frequently mistake the pleasure of sex with being high. Once a dick gets hard, they fail to see it's just chemical anticipation and not arousal. Whenever Gabriel was close to him, or whenever he wasn't, he felt the same confusion. He had that "nervy stomach with butterflies bouncing around his insides" feeling whenever he thought about the man. His cock grew stiff with the expectancy, just like a meth head's. Both drugs were dangerous; both had strong effects and risks of annihilation, but he couldn't control the damage because he couldn't shake the man from his life.

They walked a quarter of a block down the busy sidewalk before either of them spoke. The gusts from the seawall were blowing stronger now, and it felt like there was a storm front brewing and it was headed their way.

"So where do you wanna go?" Gabriel asked as his boots made a steady sound on the pavement. His stride was quick, and Christian had to hurry to remain at his side. It was just like him to expect others to follow at his pace.

"I don't care. I just wanted to be with you, somewhere where we could talk. But I'll put a leash on you if I have to...don't want you running off from me again."

"If anyone gets leashed, pup, it'll be you," Gabriel said stoically, yet barely audibly, over the wind. The frailty of the words Christian wanted to say hung on his tongue, but walking here, unnoticed by the self-absorbed passersby, seemed as appropriate a place as any to begin.

What you've done can't be undone, but whatever we started here doesn't necessarily have to end like we thought. Christian's grim look relaxed a bit, though Gabriel couldn't see it by his straightforward gaze. He continued because there wasn't a stop sign blocking his path. "I was thinking about heading out of the country, maybe Costa Rico or Panama...I was hoping to convince you to come along."

After a pause, Gabriel stopping walking and turned to Christian with an expression the writer hadn't seen before blanketing his face.

"You're such a *shit*..." Gabriel hissed the words, his eyes narrowed. "It's what I was trying to tell you earlier, but you just don't fucking listen!" Turning back to the sidewalk Gabriel headed westward, this time at a faster pace than before. Christian had to practically run to catch up.

"Tell me then," he begged.

"You think I'm some twisted fuck! Even after everything I've told you, you still don't understand that those poor unfortunate shits I ran across were not a product of some thrill-killing maniac. There was something bigger going on. I sought you out because I wanted everyone to know that before I was dead and couldn't tell the truth myself!"

Christian thanked God quietly they weren't standing next to anyone in that moment. His conversation would be hard to explain to the innocent. Grabbing Gabriel by the sleeve, he jumped ahead of him on the sidewalk and gridlocked him in confrontation.

"What the hell do you mean 'before I was dead'? Were you planning on killing yourself at some point while we worked on the book?" He was incredulous at Gabriel's confession. He immediately forgot how to speak and was suddenly lost and awestruck. He couldn't have prepared himself for Gabriel's admission, regardless that it had already been secreted away, shelved but hardly forgotten in the recesses of his brain.

"I just needed everyone to know the truth," he said, ignoring Christian's question. "I'm not crazy—there aren't a lot of screws missing from the machinery. I know how it sounded, but I always hoped you might understand, or at least try to!"

There it is...the exact obstacle to our problems, thought Christian. *The moment that will linger between us and eventually be the cause of our destruction.*

"I want to try to understand, Gabe. I need to. It's just a great deal to understand...the white light...the sensations you get when you do whatever it is you do. It's all just murder to me. They're still heartrending, innocent victims in my head. But I'm trying."

"Try harder!" Gabriel said with a firm shove of Christian's chest before turning his back and heading away down the walkway.

It is happening again, he thought. He was losing the war for want of a single battle. He couldn't hold Gabriel in a spot long enough to get him to understand that he loved him and was willing to forgive him all the fucking sins he'd committed...if he would only stop and let him explain. Just like the night before, Gabriel was leaving him standing alone and confused while he disappeared into a crowd of people. He wanted to race after him, but he'd already intermingled with the attractive, happy faces. Besides, if he ran after him, others might hear some of their conversation, which might place both men in jeopardy. He had hoped nothing he said would challenge the man, but it had. His hope that they would spend the night together was dashed, and he felt remorse for even testing the waters so early. His heart sank with worry that he might not see Gabe again, and that he had pushed back too hard and too frequently. He regretted more than ever not finding out where Gabriel was staying. His fear was that if he had known he would have followed him, but all he would have found was some empty, abandoned apartment...because Gabriel couldn't take his questions anymore. There was an unknown catastrophe gaining momentum; he could feel it in his chest. A wave of gigantic size was heading inland, and if he didn't grab Gabriel and look for shelter soon, he knew it was all going to come to some sad, watery end.

Chapter Twenty-Three

TWO NIGHTS IN a row, Shea had observed the hunk across the courtyard arriving home. She couldn't believe her luck. *Where is he coming from?* She wondered because he seemed out of sorts whenever he arrived home. Today had been her day off, and with no shift at the grocery store, she had been able to spend the day painting, while keeping her eyes trained to the window—a building hope in her chest that she might see her sexy stranger. It was merely by chance that Shea caught sight of him arriving at all; remaining camped by her window hadn't proven all that effective. She had stepped away for a considerable length of time only once, and that had been to take a quick shower. As she reentered her bedroom, wrapped in one towel and twisting another around her head like a turban, she caught sight of him crossing the grounds. He was barely visible as he headed up the walkway, obscured under the shadow of the heavy canopy of leaves over their courtyard. For a second her heart skipped a beat.

Standing where she couldn't be seen, she pulled the curtains back and watched the big man stop for an instant as he opened his door. Her head tilted slightly when she observed him doing that thing again. Strangely, he had taken a look backward before entering his apartment. He appeared anxious, as if he half expected someone to come rushing up from behind him. That was the second time she'd noticed him do that. It was an odd gesture for someone like him, she thought. It might've appeared predictable for her to do that; she was a single woman living in a dangerous town, but the stranger was big, muscular...someone who could take care of himself. *Why would he act nervous? What does he have to worry about,* she wondered?

In her mind, Shea began to fashion stories of mysterious figures and illicit secrets the stranger must be forced to live under. Shea's artistic mind imagined how the stranger might be on the run from the law or hiding out from bookies he owed money to, or maybe he was a contract killer who had arrived in town to complete a job. Every fantasy mused up in her wild imagination should have put her on guard, but it seemed to have the opposite effect by making him even more intriguing.

With the premature death of her mother, the young woman was deprived of certain wisdoms that every little girl should be bestowed from early on. Without a guiding hand in that area, little Shea was left defenseless about men and the danger they might represent. Shea Baltimore had developed into a teenager on her own, and even now as an adult, she was less than skilled in the ways of men, since most of what she knew came from books and television. And surely those had to be clear illustrations of life and the possibility of peril?

The waning light and curtains hid her from being spotted. She watched as the stranger's door closed behind him and felt somewhat cheated by the experience. The overcast skies were quickly turning that bloody bronze of evening, and she thought she would screw up the courage to introduce herself one day very soon. Possibly it was the isolation of her life, the minutiae and daily grind that was becoming her existence, but whatever the cause, there was a confidence that she wouldn't always be that mousy girl from school who never had stories of great sexual affairs or was accustomed to being pursued by boys with flattering attention.

Dreams of being a famous artist had circled in her head for years, but she had never considered her life beyond that single crutching support. When girls at school gave her the cold shoulder, it had been because her perspective was skewed. Because young people were only comfortable when there was conformity among their peers. She was different, and that made her a pariah in certain cliques. She spent her lunch periods alone eating from the risers in the school's auditorium. This by itself wasn't anything worthy of excommunication from her peers. Then again, teenagers are the cruelest of God's animals ever created.

Without malice, Shea had watched as the parade of young girls sauntered through the halls in small but tidy tribes. Clear-skinned girls clutching books to their bosoms and exuding every confidence she lacked but for some reason admired. Each pretty face seemed to beckon to an unseen camera, each one believing they were the star of their own Hollywood scene. But it could have been worse, she considered. There were other young girls who'd suffered harsher fates than even her own. She knew of several who had faced a death from a thousand tiny cuts, until one day they simply gave up and uploaded a final posting on Facebook right before slicing through the ulnar artery of their wrists while languishing in the bathtub. She knew to count herself lucky because sometimes just being excluded was castigation enough. Or at least that what she reminded herself daily just to maintain a sense of sanity and worth. She wasn't the last one chosen for field hockey teams, but she certainly wasn't the first. There was a Hispanic girl, who Shea couldn't remember by name, who had buffered much of the cruelty she might have been given. The girl held the status of top target of the abuse, being poorer than most and culturally different from the norm.

It was hard to say what young people suffered through. Some things were character building, while other damage sunk lower and created the foundation for future bitter wives and mothers. Shea was strong and suffered through it, knowing her way above it all would be due to the talent she was struggling to hone. Eventually she would move to New York and sell her name and her work throughout all the boroughs. She would rise above the trauma and become someone worthy of forgetting her painful upbringing. It was that dream that allowed her to make it from her locker to her next class, to shrug off the callous whispers at her back.

For a time, Shea even had a boyfriend in high school, although she was still a virgin when she graduated. The relationship was just the tentative steps of growing up for her, as well as her beau. It was the small town stuff of movies—fast food diners and school dances—but it helped elevate her from pariah to just being merely ignored, and that helped. She would never see her boyfriend, Cole, after they broke up shortly after graduation. She would never know that he would make it to New York before her...or that he currently lived in Manhattan with his new lover, Steve.

Even with the substantial lack of Valentine cards and photos of friends tacked to her bedroom walls, or the brief paragraphs scrawled in her diary about boys and the uncertainty of losing her chastity, she survived. Despite her alcoholic father and the financial troubles he caused, she endured. If her mother had remained, she would have known pride in how her daughter overcame her challenges with grace and patience.

The soft light from her bathroom blazed a path across the floor of her tiny apartment. It was her only illumination, and it was all she needed. Shea found comfort in the darkness, particularly after spending a day painting or sketching, a TV or stereo playing in the background as her only source of companionship. She always felt drained after spending time at the easel or hovering over her sketchpad. Any talent she possessed seemed to explode onto the canvas with a fury. She was held trancelike, resembling a blind monk translating verses with fervent devotion, running fingers across the braille inside a forgotten abbey. Trapped by both her isolation and dedication.

When the talent seemed spent, she was left exhausted, and the darkness brought its own welcome mood. The young woman understood how much it was like sex, the frenzied build before a final, orgasmic release. Much like the lovers she didn't have, she found the dark and silence soothing. With her brushes wiped clean, her charcoal sticks and pens stored away, it passed like a shower after a sexual encounter…some discreet restitution for her lack of lovers. It was the final act before she normally drifted off to sleep. But at that moment, Shea was not crawling into bed; she was sitting far enough from the window to remain hidden, staring intently into the courtyard and a stranger's door across the way.

Her hands opened the twisted turban towel that covered her hair, and she shook her shoulder-length strands free. She may have been a gangly child, but she had blossomed after graduation. Her brown hair that had once given her a timid, mousy air had changed after her breasts came in. Her locks had become a richer, mahogany tone, and with her bright, green eyes she had taken the appearance of a hellcat.

She was quite lovely, even though her petite size had always been a cause of embarrassment for her. Shea had grown into a woman who any man might overlook at first glance, but if he looked closely when she passed him, he would surely turn his head and smile, if only to consider her feminine features and whether she was indeed a hellcat in bed. But men in her circles tended to gravitate toward other types of women; it was the main reason she spent too many nights alone. But still she was hopeful because of her talent and her knowledge that things would be different for her one day in the future. And she suspected that day was fast approaching.

She was resolute. She would introduce herself to the stranger across the way that very evening. Maybe it had been her dull routine of late; maybe it was just because she craved human contact—voices that didn't begin and end over a conveyor belt at the store as she blanked out making mental pictures in her mind's eye and allowed her fingers to deftly work the register by sheer rote. There had been too much solitude, and a damned long stretch of monotony, and the artistic side of her was craving some excitement. It was settled—now all she had to do was gather it together and dress for the occasion. *What does one wear to a chance meeting encounter,* she wondered?

AS SHE WAS getting dressed, across the plaza, Church was shedding his clothing. He was stepping into his miserable shower and trying to rinse that heated anger from his body. The water pressure was weak, and it couldn't maintain a regulated temperature for long. His entire body engulfed the tiny stall of broken and stained tiles. He imagined this was how Communist or early Socialists had to live just to support their revolutions. It was a threadbare existence, one he might have been used to himself, but for other tenants in neighboring units of this shoddy, moldy villa, it must have been a dismal life. He had always been a rambler from his younger days. He was used to sleeping in places where most women would not squat to pee. He had seen his share of SRO hotels and run down boarding houses. He'd even slept under a couple of overpasses in his lifetime. But he had what he considered good reason to live that way. What were his neighbor's excuses? He became tired of bending his head under the showerhead just to have it go from scalding to ice within seconds; he finished rinsing the soap off and turned the knob in disgust.

Stepping out, he wiped the mirror and stared at his image. His beard, which he always kept close-cropped, had grown disheveled, giving him a wild-man appearance. Grabbing a disposable razor, he began dry shaving his face. He wondered why Chris hadn't mentioned that growth; he was such a fastidious dresser himself. *How strange my friendship with Chris.* He was college educated while Gabe had barely graduated high school before he hit the road. But Gabe had a clever mind and a willingness to learn; he had nothing but time on his hands and a lot of that was spent reading. He didn't want to be considered stupid or unread, and so even without the white-collar advantages that his companion had, he had made do and soaked everything up like a dry sponge.

He liked that others saw him as a brutish fighter, but even more, he liked it when he could surprise them with all of what he'd learned. He'd seen that surprise on Chris's face, and it made him feel as if he had more sides to his personality, and that he wasn't just a two-dimensional character who could be easily overlooked. He'd educated himself because he would never have had the opportunities of Chris's fine schooling, or his social advantages. The writer was everything he wasn't, and that should've irked him, *but it didn't*. He was confident enough with what he'd become and bright enough to understand that each one of us could end up with lives very different than we could've ever imagined.

Whenever he was in Chris's presence, he never felt dumb or uneducated. The look on the writer's face had always been one of admiration, and he felt lucky to run across someone who didn't turn up their nose or narrow their eyes whenever Gabe spoke, as if it was some derisive, scornful look by someone calculating the distance between them. That was another good quality that Chris had. The playing field had been leveled for both of them because each had skeletons in their closets. There were secrets they now shared, which had invariably become a great equalizer. No man could stand above another when both had some part in murder.

Scraping the remaining hairs from his face, he held the razor under the tap before shaking it off. He then dried with the same towel he'd used for his body and walked naked into his bedroom. He had stopped by a street vendor on his way home and shoved a hot dog down his gullet because his annoyance couldn't be quelled to spend time looking for a better meal. He'd hoped he would have dinner or drinks with Chris before ending up at his place for a satisfying fuck before sleep. He was just as annoyed at that not occurring as he had been with Chris for completely missing the point about all their time together. It was strange finding out someone you thought you knew was, in reality, someone you didn't recognize. Gabe didn't like it when things went all screwy on him...and this pissed him off even more, making him sad in knowing his good friend thought he was a fucked up monster.

Before he could crawl under the sheets, he heard a faint tapping coming from the other room. It was the front door. Rage seethed quickly up his throat and left a sour taste on his tongue. Chris had followed him home apparently—he obviously wanted to apologize or some shit. But he was instantly angry at the invasion to his privacy. If Chris could find him, that meant others could as well, and he didn't like people getting within arm's reach of his collar. It was dangerous, and he'd have to explain that rather forcefully to Chris, as well as fight off his desire to punch him in the face just to illustrate that fact. Slipping into his jeans, he opened the door but was surprised to find it wasn't his friend standing there wide-eyed and repentant; it was a young woman.

SHEA COULD SEE the confusion building on his face. She'd caught him unaware. He was wearing only jeans and the top button dangled open freely, his hair was damp and suggested to her he'd recently stepped out of the shower. He stood there sinfully dumbfounded, looking much like a

Greek god in her eyes, masculine and posed seductively in the frame of his door, solely to elicit every secret desire from all her hiding places. All she could do was smile and look stunned.

"YES?" GABE ASKED. "What can I do for you?"

"My name is Shea Baltimore. I live across the courtyard in 180. I just wanted to ask if you got my gift?" she asked with the timidity of a shy mouse.

He had forgotten it, but then it suddenly came back.

"The drawing...that came from you?"

"Yes...I'm an artist of sorts..." she stammered out. The lilt in her voice and the way she offered up her own self-proclamation of "artist" seemed too pretty on the plate, making Church realize she didn't get to make that announcement very often. "I thought you made a nice subject. I hope you don't mind. I just noticed you across the yard and wanted to draw you."

This was unexpected, thought Gabe. What did she want...him to model again? Did she expect to get paid for her drawing? In his confusion at the absurdity, he stepped aside.

"I'm sorry, come in...please."

He opened the door farther, and the young woman brushed past him, unafraid. He could smell the perfume wafting off her hair and noticed she was wearing makeup. He then guessed the girl was wearing one of her best outfits, making him question why she had crossed the yard and knocked so directly at his door. For a man like Gabe, it seemed clear that she had designs on him. Why else would she enter a stranger's apartment just because she was invited? After all, he could've been a killer.

"I must admit I've seen you a few times coming and going. There's not a lot of activity around here, and ever since I saw you, I wanted to stop by and welcome you to the complex."

"So you're the welcome committee?" he asked. "I must say, that's nice."

He could see she was a woman overcoming her shyness with an unaccustomed bravery. She tried hard to appear sophisticated, but Gabe could smell her personal rise from a broken past surrounding her like a cloud.

"You're my first guest, so I'm afraid the place isn't much, and I haven't cleaned in a while," he said apologetically. "I'm not even dressed—"

"Not to worry," she said quickly, cutting him off and preventing him from the awkward sense that he needed to leave the room to put on a shirt.

"I didn't mean to bother you. I guessed you'd still be up...but welcome to the neighborhood anyway." She smiled broadly, arms held wide, hinting at her own nervousness and uncertain where to go from there. But it was Gabe who filled the gap.

"Sorry...my name is Rumsfeld, Chris Rumsfeld." Church pulled the name just like the antagonist had in that old Bryan Singer movie, *The Usual Suspects*. He *Keyser Sözed* it by utilizing Chris's name after seeing a bottle of Bacardi Silver that was sitting on the counter in his kitchen. It was a bottle he'd bought a week ago; it was already half empty, but it caught his awareness just as he extended his arm to shake the young woman's outstretched hand. It was the perfection of casual pretense, and Gabe had always been one to be quick on his feet.

"So you're the artist..." he began. He wanted to break her concentration from his earlier lie and lifted his own arm to indicate she could take a seat wherever she desired. "I was impressed with your talent. I just can't figure why you'd wanna draw my picture," he said with a smile, hoping he hadn't crumpled up the drawing, or left it carelessly discarded where this Shea girl might find it and be disappointed. He couldn't even remember where he'd laid it, but it was Shea who first noticed it, drawn to it like a magnet. She walked over and found it resting on a side table and picked it up with a satisfied glint in her eyes.

"It's not my best work, but you were pretty far away and it was getting dark..."

She stopped at that, probably realizing how much it made her sound like some sick stalker who'd been spying on their neighbor, even though that was precisely the case.

"I think you make a good subject," she said quietly. "I draw portraits mostly. You know faces I like, those I run across that seem to have seen life or are weathered and timeworn. I don't draw for others though...it's usually just for me."

Gabe sat on the edge of the shabby sofa that came with his rented room. "Not sure I have that kind of look, but you're a good artist, I can tell...and I'm not a connoisseur of art, not usually."

SHEA DROPPED THE sketchpad and turned to look at him. Sitting there without a shirt on, a trail of black hairs peeking from his jeans and crawling up to mix with those on his chest—it was an image she believed she could simply bask in. He wasn't concerned with he appeared to others, but she couldn't determine whether it was confidence of just him playing with her, teasing her with s suggestive smile behind those cold stoic eyes. Either way, she had to fight the urge to walk over and run her tongue across his face, slathering in with her adoration and hoping he might pick her to kiss. She looked around randomly, to occupy her brain, but she was thinking how great it would be if he just fucked her there on that crappy beige couch of his.

"MAYBE ONE DAY you'll let me sketch you posed, like a life study. You know nude", she asked with a tiny giggling laugh. "I plan on being famous in the future, and one never knows, it might be a valuable investment someday."

She grinned shyly at the prospect of her future fame and he witnessed her budding like a night-blooming flower right before his eyes. *It must be quite the undertaking,* he thought, *to step out of one's own comfort zone and attempt to be something else entirely.* But Gabe had a skill for reading others fairly well. It could see what a struggle it was for her to attempt a transformation such as it was. Simply walking the short distance between their two apartments and doing her best to tempt him must've been a reach for her.

"I think I'd like that. It might be nice to have a great picture to leave behind." Shea was too involved in her own head to hear the implications that fell from his lips by accident. She was helping him forget about Chris by just her simple presence, and her sheer dress and the lithe way her body moved so effortlessly made his cock stir to life.

"Do you draw many nudes?" he said.

Shea heard his words, which sounded like the run of heavy-laden syrup down her spine. His voice had a quality that could control and his tone was suggestive. She smiled sheepishly at his intimations but somehow found the courage to bat the ball back to him.

"I have," she lied, "but I'd like to do more. Are you offering to model now?"

"Well, Shea...we could start there," he said coolly. Purposely using her name because he understood well how women needed that personal connection from the beginning. But for him, he was just committing her name to his own brain; they had, after all, met only minutes earlier.

SHEA HAD NEVER been so brazen before. But even as unfamiliar as it was, there was still something right in how she felt. The man had a way of bringing to light what was once hidden, and his manner didn't just encourage it...he demanded it. His looks aside, he had some alien gift of shattering her into pieces and watching as the shards of her reserve scattered and circled around his feet. His eyes implored for her to see whatever lies he'd decided to spin and they conveyed strength and assurance that whatever he claimed had sure and certain truth. But his talent to disarm was even less significant than his ability to force a freedom from those he spoke to, begging them to unburden themselves of all the weight they carried around their necks like millstones. Clearly she'd chosen her subject well.

Perspiration made her hands feel clammy. She was caught between being a bad girl and deciding not to be one...and she didn't know exactly which way she'd turn. He was the exact opposite. He sat without emotion and peered directly into her soul; he was calm and reserved. But even that couldn't hide that animalistic thing she had created in her head. She could see he was a cheetah poised to lunge, and each and every defining muscle was starched but eager. His smile crept crooked onto his face but veiled what images were going through his mind. He was tentative but readied, and the seconds between them turned into hours flying by.

"I didn't bring my pad with me, but I suppose I could draw from memory..."

She gingerly untied a tiny string that held the collar of her dress taut around her frail neck and suddenly felt relief she'd decided to wear her best panties and matching bra. He stood up and closed the gap between them, assisting her in the removal of her clothes. He did this slowly and methodically, attempting to keep her from running from the room in horror. But she was already in deep waters and rising from the waves offered little salvation from her drowning. She wanted and needed for all the things she hoped would transpire between them. It was like that life-granting oxygen in the last possible moments before death.

GABE WANTED TO calm her obvious anxiety. She was a gazelle, one that would either sprint away in fear or hopefully drop to his feet in sublimation. He gently brushed a finger across her cheek before picking her up into his arms and to prevent her from bolting from the room once she saw where this was headed.

As her dress fell to the floor, Shea seemed to melt into something weaker, held upright only by his strong hold of her waist. She had to battle the knee buckling terror or risk falling. She was a delicate marionette whose strings with her strings abruptly cut. His lips traced hers as he held her face in one oversized hand while the other supported her back. It was a strange phenomenon, one that would enable her to seduce a man she barely knew. But she had desired him for days, and her life was being quickly transformed into something too small and contained for her to exist. And he represented escape, a departure from that awful feeling she'd always known.

As his tongue wrestled wet against her own, she could detect the clean scent of her perfumed soap mixing with his perspiration and felt his excitement growing as leaned into her body. It was an impressive weighty thing she thought, that shaft brushing against her thigh. Because of her size, it was nothing to hoist her in his arms and carry her to the bedroom. He gently lay her down on the comforter noting it was only a bra and panties that now separated their passion.

Tugging at his jeans, they too fell to the floor, and she lost her breath at the sight of his naked arousal. She was young and had never had a man that much older than her—he was furry and toned, and she suspected he knew many things that could please her. Straddling her body, he raked his rough hands along her frame, deftly removing her panties without any awkward or unskilled gesture. He raised her up and ran his mouth at her navel and bare abdomen while simultaneously unhooking her bra from behind her back, and then rubbed his palms underneath the loose garment and squeezed gently at her breasts. She bent and twisted to give herself sufficient room to wriggle from her bra, and he grabbed it and tossed it over the side as his lips again continued laving her body, softly moving downward.

Shea didn't know what to expect from the man she knew as Chris. She was yielding because he was the one holding the switch...it was his hand resting on the throttle and directing which track the train would run on. He was her chief conductor, the one responsible for all that tangible power, and it was his choice whether they derailed or whether he guaranteed her safe return to the station.

She might have presumed his hands would remain gentle, but they did not. Gripping her at the knees, he pulled her closer to the edge of the bed and drew her slick pussy to his wanting mouth. She had never experienced anything as visceral and primal as his lack of hesitation. He licked at her with his twitching tongue and forced it inside; his grunts of pleasure released even more passion from between her legs. She had a vibrator and used it often, but she had the instantaneous desire to throw it across her room at home and watch as it hit the wall breaking into a dozen tiny electrical parts. She would never believe she alone would ever be able to fulfill her own hunger like he could.

Hanging on the verge of climax, she arched her back and whimpered as his tongue did its job. Before he would allow her to come, he raised her body up with each hand holding firm at her waist. His cock was rigid and taut, practically beseeching her to yield and reminding her of back seat sweaty tumbles after graduation, though this was no youthful and inexperienced lover from her past. He drove his dick in like spearing a lion; it was both painful and glorious. She had become his wounded prey, and the look in his eyes had darkened, telling her he was there to finish what he started.

His thrusts became powerful, quick jabs meant to inflict the greatest satisfaction. He had substantial girth, and she felt every inch of him inside her stretched lips. He didn't speak a word—outside the exhalations of short, strenuous bursts of oxygen, he had remained relatively quiet. She on the other hand moaned to the heavens, loud enough that even she suspected the neighbors were listening. It didn't take long after that; she wasn't sure she could have continued longer anyway. She felt his seed slam into her, and she withered and folded while she watched tiny beads of sweat fall from his chest and forehead.

The beast subdued, he was controlling his breathing then, but he hadn't withdrawn the sword. It parted her and drained her like a bleeding snake. Little then changed about him after that...save for his eyes. She had seen them grow dark when they were fucking but wasn't sure if it was the scant lighting escaping from his bathroom or if it had been a trick of her imagination. But whatever the cause, she could tell they'd begun to lighten and once again retained their brilliance.

GABE LIKED THE fact that during every pounding thrust he hadn't thought once about Christian. But of course, as he withdrew his cock from her, even he had to concede he was thinking about him now. Maybe it was the commonality of the actions of lovemaking, or maybe it was the contrast in their bodies, but whatever it was, it triggered a response that transposed Chris's face atop Shea's body. A quiver sped across his flesh like crawling spiders on his skin and it produced an odd disturbance about the world he understood. All he could think of in that moment was how grateful he was to have already shot his load, or it could've fucked that up as well.

Chapter Twenty-Four

AS GABRIEL TURNED in a huff before disappearing into the crowd, there wasn't much Christian could do but watch him leave, realizing once again he'd screwed up. Maybe this was too complicated a thing to work, he wondered. Hanging his head, Christian felt alone and confused. If he didn't get through to Gabriel, there would be only devastation and ruin, and certainly there would be no thatched-roof hut in the San Blas Islands with Gabriel at his side.

He knew the insanity—being in love with a killer—but as the water from the shoreline blew trickles of mist across his face, he thought the *sanity* was in finally finding someone he loved. He felt dejected because he'd muddled through every inconvenient conversation he'd tried to have with Gabriel. His hand reached up to the bristle on his face; he'd forgotten to shave in his rush to meet Gabriel. He was exhausted, and he didn't know why. The book was so far on the back burner now that it was light years away. There would be no book, no written confession that would only serve to take Gabriel from him...and as horrified as he was at what Church had done, he was sure he couldn't be the one to assist him in his race to find some death and redemption.

He had questioned Gabriel's motives many times in allowing his story to be told. He'd originally assumed it was guilt, before the truth was illuminated that the man simply wanted the world to know why he'd done what he'd done. He wondered how many people out there in the real world might be in love with something they knew to be insane. There might be medications he could be prescribed; perhaps there were therapies that might alter his fucked up ideologies and skewed reasoning, but what did that mean for Gabriel and him?

You might love a schizophrenic, you might care for someone with deep mental scars or addictions, but he was in love with a man he knew to have murdered others without remorse. That seed, once planted, would only bear dark fruit and withered blooms. It seemed a challenge existed either way he turned.

Walking back to where he'd parked his car, he felt alone even in the throng of club goers and tourists surrounding him, taking photos of the Seattle skyline dancing on a rippled mirror across the bay. His heart had sunk too far to be retrieved, and he was crushed under the weight of the man versus all the things he knew. His key turned in the ignition, and he pulled into the side streets to get to his place and wondered if he was ever going to see Gabriel again.

SHEA HAD PULLED on her panties and her bra as her sexy neighbor reclined on his bed and watched her. He hadn't tried to pull on his jeans or hide his flaccid phallus. The man didn't have a tincture of shyness or shame in his genetic material; his DNA was different than any man she'd known. To her eyes, seeing him propped on one elbow, he was a hairy, strong, and beautiful creature, but she didn't trust him completely. She knew that once she'd entered his apartment, she couldn't trust herself, but it had not dawned on her how much she could not trust him.

For her, it was an awkward few moments. She'd just stepped over some cavernous hollow and fucked a man she didn't know, and as she was getting dressed, she wondered what the protocol for her escape was? Do you thank him...promise to do it again sometime real soon, or just apologize...she didn't know.

Those pale eyes stared at her as she fumbled with her clothing. She expected a smile of appreciation, or at least satisfaction, but he was blank like some dark, deep water where she couldn't perceive a bottom. Breaking the tension, she felt she had to say something.

"I hope you know I don't do this with every new tenant. I mean...I'm great as a welcoming committee, but not every resident gets the gift basket you did."

There it was...that tiny semblance of a grin reaching the corners of his mouth. However, no words of comfort escaped. It made her even more nervous, and the stillness between them grew heavy as she wriggled into her tiny dress and bent to retrieve her sandals, which had been discarded under the sofa.

HE WAS LOST in thought, but not about her or what they'd done. Gabe had no guilt in his body to offer. He hadn't considered how Chris would feel about his infidelity because that was a concept beyond his reach. Sex was sex. He had suggested he and Chris get into a three-way once because carnal acts had no boundaries and couldn't be pigeon-holed into anything more than they were—it was just fucking.

But he was thinking about Chris, just not about it with any remorse. Gabe was playing out in his head how much sex could be different with a man, since Chris was the only one he'd had any experience with, he had to use his body as an example. He thought about his want of going down on a woman because it had been a while since he'd done that. The last few times he'd simply screwed outright; there wasn't any emotion or even passion to the act. It was the artless act of getting his rocks off. But this Shea girl had made him want to lap her up like a puppy attracted to a scent trail in the air. He'd been eager to taste her for his own and liked the experience he had. He rarely sucked Chris to completion. He thought it too feminine an act and wasn't totally comfortable performing it. He preferred being a machine, something he could grease up and move quickly through the motions.

"WELL, SHEA, WE should do that again soon...and I still need to pose naked for you," he said with a rich, honeyed voice, breaking the painful silence between them.

"I wouldn't mind doing it again, but you've given me plenty to work with for your drawing." Even as she said it, she regretted it. She would surely enjoy fucking him again, and seeing him naked, laid out before her while she sketched him would be as sinfully delicious as the act itself. Shea was unlike many artists she knew. She could arouse herself with her own process of sketching, which may have been why she started drawing the man across the way as she had. She had felt the dampness growing in her when she first took her charcoal stick to paper and envisioned that studly man in her mind as she worked feverously.

Then it came, the casual ineptitude of strangers after sex, where she did the only thing she knew to do that might guarantee her escape from the moment. She made the groping gestures of straightening her clothing and then walked over and bent over the bed; she offered him a rather innocuous kiss on the lips. She noticed he hadn't opened to her gesture, and she rummaged for excuses of why she needed to leave. He didn't try to stop her departure, taking it in like a sponge and holding it. He did smile back, and he even thanked her again, but he thanked her for her drawing, not what they'd just done.

She knew the man was terribly experienced, as much as she knew herself to be a novice. Why then, didn't he try to help her? He didn't rise to walk her to the door; he didn't offer conciliatory words that might ease the tension she felt. He could have done anything to help her, she thought, but he seemed to enjoy her lack of sophistication and green mishandling of an awkward moment. As she bent down to kiss him, she could smell her own scent: the perfumed mixture of her vagina and her excitement. Her hand fell to his chest to support her, landing on the massive expanse of hair and muscle. She noticed twitching already starting to stir in his manhood, and however brief their exchange had been, she wondered, *Is he good to go again?*

Outside his door, she made the walk of shame back to her apartment, her stomach twisting into knots. She was amazed at herself by what she'd done, but she was excited that she had done it at all. She was evolving into someone who wasn't as afraid of life; *either that or I'm just becoming a whore.* But she was happy, more in herself than what she'd done. For Shea this was an accomplishment, a watermark she would not soon forget. She wasn't sure what it meant, but she was pleased and sexually satisfied despite her reservations.

As she turned the latch in the safety and darkness of her apartment, she leaned her back against the door and exhaled deeply. Part of her felt as if she were a giddy schoolgirl, where another part felt the experience had been a necessary function in becoming an adult. Everyone needs to have a few dirty scandals in their lives, and this might be the beginning of hers. Her thoughts became clouded in that second because as a good girl she had to consider what her mother might've said to her in that moment if she'd been alive. Would she scold her for being such a tramp? She didn't think so. She imagined her mother would hold her daughter in her arms, tell her a few of those intricate secrets of being a woman, and feel the same pride she felt in taking a chance...because life was only missed opportunities and gambles for bravery.

She wanted to shower and crawl into bed in the dark. She wanted to languish there in the sated imprint of her satisfaction. She wanted to play out the moments over and over because Shea believed she had met someone special. In her mind she was already preparing a future for her and the man she knew as Chris Rumsfeld—it would be a glorious love affair. But sleep would not come easily, because within minutes of closing her door, she would see Church one more time that night.

Chapter Twenty-Five

AS ANY TOURIST walking through the hiking trails only an hour from downtown Seattle would tell you, the beauty and lush foliage was a sight to behold. The Vashon glacial ice sheet formed the Puget Sound and the lakes of the region some fifty thousand years earlier. The soil there was rich with volcanic ash from the Glacier Peak eruption that occurred 6,700 years before the time where anyone would walk those trails and become awestruck by the sheer magnitude of its glory.

It was on a beautiful crisp afternoon when the Devlin family from Post Falls Idaho found themselves walking those same trails, laughing as they snapped photos to take back as mementos of their vacation in Snohomish County, Washington. The smell of damp pine and lush foliage mixed with the scent of deadfall rotting on the forest floor, and the sun was midpoint in the sky, but under the canopy of immense branches, it was like walking in the twilight of dusk. The Devlin clan was only visiting Seattle for one week, trying to take in as much of the local sights as possible before attending a family wedding and then returning to Idaho with only their memories of their experiences in the Northwest countryside.

Arthur Devlin, his wife Charlene, and their two daughters had chosen to hike without a guide, since they were on a limited schedule to get back to the city for a late supper before heading back to their hotel. They intended to only skirt the outer borders of the forest, remaining as close to the nature trails as they possibly could. Arthur wanted to keep his family safely near the traffic of backpackers and day hikers, but once they were standing in all that grandeur and overwhelming scenery, it was impossible not to stray a little off the path. Charlene wanted to snap as many photos as possible: more reminders on the living room mantle to show that theirs was a happy clan, ones who could easily afford those occasional outdoor vacations so necessary to finish off the images in her mind; those picturesque images of traditional family with only good things ahead.

But every forest begins by a single tree. Just as every painful memory can originate from the smallest of unpredictable tragedies. Such was the case when the youngest of the Devlin daughters took a few steps away from the trail to photograph a pleasing image in still life. She intended to lean against a colossal old cedar to gain a better perspective of the canyon below. But, as she stepped nearer to the ridge, she stumbled on what she thought was a fallen log at her feet. Looking down, she was surprised to see a man's face staring up at her from a mountain of dead, dark leaves and old pine needles. Her screams shattered the serenity like a gunshot, and birds suddenly took to the skies from every nearby branch.

Within hours, the trail became flooded with state police and park rangers. The bustle of bodies in motion was only a prelude to the crime scene technicians to follow, but for Arthur Devlin, it shattered his faith and rocked his ideal world. How would his daughters overcome the sight of a dead body? And what did that mean for any conversation shared on their plane ride home? He comforted his girls as best he could. He shielded them with a blanket provided by the rangers and folded them up like dolls in his fatherly embrace. Being a parent could have its difficulties as he knew, and this one was just another challenge he needed to overcome.

The unfortunate Devlins were escorted to their car by a few consoling park rangers, telling him that with their statements written down it was doubtful they'd ever be called to testify in any court of law. *"Truly, it's usually quite beautiful here,"* their sad faces seemed to say. *"It's rare we find any dead bodies that disturb the tranquility for hikers and campers alike."*

And dead bodies unearthed in wooded parks were indeed an unusual find, even if they weren't the perfect spot for murder or one of the most effective places where anyone could dump a corpse. Scavenging animals, heavy rains, and dense overgrowth were petri dishes of possibilities. And they all ensured that a victim might remain nameless for many months to come, or even for years. Dead things tended not to fair for long, not among the harsh elements and all the majestic things one likes to see inside those treasures of our national parks. It was only happenstance that young Gina Devlin had managed to stumble onto one so easily.

Their victim was male, mid to late thirties by the look, and would have been lying on that forest floor for at least a couple of weeks. But it would be up to the coroner's office to give a cause of death, if it could be determined, as well as a victim's identity so that detectives could begin a fruitless investigation. Their only job was to work with the state police to secure the crime scene, knowing time and predators would have destroyed any evidence. The muffle of voices and the continuous parade of first responders traipsing along the pathway made it seem surreal against the backdrop of such splendor. But there was gravity in the work with everyone understanding this was a beautiful but lonely location to excavate a dead body.

It would be over a week before the man would find a face and an identity. Carl Whiting was thirty-eight when he died. An electrical contractor living on the outskirts of Queen Anne, he was married with his first child only three years old. There was nothing untoward in his lifestyle, and he had a reputation of a man without enemies. His homicide, as it was determined, was due to gunfire at close range. The corpse could not offer much in the way of which type of firearm was used to end his life, and police could find nothing unusual about his murder, which in itself was something worthy of note.

Carl Whiting may have been without enemies, but he had run across a killer named Gabriel Church when, quite by chance, the two had intersected at a local hardware store in West Seattle. Whether it was a simple ironic twist of fate or some greater providence, that would be a question left for others in the weeks that were to follow. For Gabe, it made perfect sense the two would meet, even if the term "meet" was a misnomer in all respects. Friends did not introduce the men. They did not shake hands in casual greeting, nor was there any solid reason that might influence how the men were thrust together in such a dynamic explosion of purpose.

In all the conversations Christian shared with Church, this murder hadn't been discussed. The writer never knew about this particular victim, or Church's involvement. Maybe they would have reached that in time, but their personal discord prevented many detailed discussions of individual murders. Had Christian known that Church had killed as recently as that week before they met, things might have ended very differently for them.

Carl Whiting had stopped in for supplies at his favorite True Value hardware store. He needed additional twist connectors for wires, which were always in short supply, and recently dropped his crimping wrench behind a second story wall of a new construction in Bellevue and needed a new one. He knew all the counter associates by name; he was a familiar face who always smiled his shit-eating grin whenever he passed the threshold and heard the ding of the bell that announced a new customer entering the store. Carl enjoyed poking fun at the blue-collar freelancers who hung out there between jobs and was known to have an expansive and friendly nature.

Gabe had been in that same hardware store at that precise time. He was buying fifteen feet of coiled rope, laughing with the salesman about tying down a recently planted Judas tree to fight the turbulent northerly winds that threatened to upend his new shrub. He was good with lies—he could pick them as easily as wild bluebonnets in an open, airy field. Both were simple acts that came too easily to someone like Gabe. Catching sight of Carl coming around the counter instigated the usual explosion of ashen glow that Gabe was all too familiar with. It sparked his focus and forced him to train all his attentions in the direction of the smiling bystander who didn't seem to have a care in the world. In that moment, the killer knew, without hesitation, he was facing his next victim.

It was a typical afternoon. While most residents were employed at neighboring offices or shops, the store was littered with tradesmen who carried the daily grind of simple labors. Besides random contractors, the store held a sparse clientele of senior citizens and little old ladies buying birdseed and hummingbird feeders. The sounds of talk radio played over the loud speakers, creating a lazy atmosphere of mundane shopping for all those who had little else to occupy their days but shopping for things they didn't really need.

At the time, Gabe was carrying a Smith and Wesson black Governor .38 caliber revolver. It was effectively concealed inside a tan scabbard holster strapped under his left arm and hidden beneath his jacket. Gabe liked firing guns. He would often take practice shots in the woods just for sport. He liked the kick and the distinctive smell, which seemed to have a lasting impression on his tongue, reminding him of the few good memories he had of Bennett and those rare times when his father tried to teach him how to be proficient with guns.

His dad may have given him only a few impressive memories to pull from, but one seemed to be buried there in those times when Bennett would take Gabe to the woods to shoot out cans or take pot shots at standing trees: "Just for shits and giggles" as Bennett was fond of saying. It was a distant vision but turned out to be one good thing in his childhood...one good memory raised above all the bad. His recollections of the smell of gunpowder after firing the pistol had been particularly strong. He knew it wasn't the smell of cordite or sulfur, knowing no one had used gunpowder mixed with sulfur since the last Great War. But it had an odor nonetheless, and he couldn't quite place the origin, or its sweet smelling glycerin and the pungent scent of sawdust and graphite swirling through the air. He learned to love the smell wherever it came from.

There may have been a cutting, sardonic twist hidden in the training Bennett gave his son on gun safety, but the lessons were certainly the strongest bonding experience between father and son. The thread of commonality between them, a would-be serial killer and the man who first placed a weapon in his tiny hands, may have been thin, but it was palpable. Given how Gabe would turn out, the reality seemed a tragedy of immense proportion.

Gabe preferred to kill using his bare hands. Occasionally, he might reach for something lying opportunistically near his feet. But primarily, he preferred to face his target mano-a-mano as it were. There was something sweeter in completing the task in animalistic fashion and in a heated exchange and performed quickly. Murder by gun seemed a bit too cowardly an act, Gabe thought. Then again, his circuitous reasoning was his and his alone. He also understood that guns were easily traceable. But if it became a difference between his survival and someone else's, then yes, he was amenable to shooting anyone that he needed to, just too make it out unscathed. Yet something had told Church he needed to carry the Governor that day. And so he had. It proved fortuitous because Carl Whiting was a big man and not one as effortlessly taken down as some of the others were.

With a blaring tune bouncing in the hollow of his head, he was sure this was just another sacred cow bestowed upon him for sacrifice. He smiled as he paid for his coil of rope and left the hardware store, but not the vicinity. He chose to lag behind and wait for the one granted him—his exalted prize and another step closer to learning whatever truths were currently eluding him. He felt the trifling weight of the Smith and Wesson at that crux, just under one arm, and assured himself it was destiny. Whatever almighty deity that controlled him and sat conveniently just beyond any reach had *willed* him to carry his gun on that particular day, it had pulled him into that hardware store and yanked the chain that brought him another battered soul bathed in light, and it had seemed fated that it should deliver the cow directly at his door.

Carl spent over twenty-five minutes at the True Value. Contract jobs were obtained by word of mouth, and those mouths usually belonged to other skilled tradesmen. Carl could chat up plumbers, subcontractors, anyone willing to listen as he threw his name out there for the entire world to hear. All the men he encountered would see what a good man Carl Whiting was; he was dependable, trained, trustworthy...and a damn fine electrician. Not an unpleasant bud to work around either: one capable of laughing and joking with the best of them. As he left the store, he carried more than his insignificant purchases in his small plastic bag—he carried new contacts. He remembered how his little old mama used to say "If you're selling it, best put it out on the porch for the neighbors to see!"

The man's size would be a problem for Church; it was daylight and it was a busy parking lot. The man likely weighed in as big as Gabe. This meant he'd have to lift his heavy frame into the cab, and that meant he wouldn't be able to sneak up behind him or wrestle him down in the passenger seat. He'd have to approach this from another angle. Seeing the wedding ring on the man's left hand, he decided unreasoningly that another tack was necessary.

Before the man could unlock his truck door, Church jammed the gun's barrel into his back. "Don't move," he whispered over the man's ear with all his screwed-together calmness. He was standing close enough that his gun barrel touched the man's spinal column; the cold contact ensured the man couldn't turn rapidly around. Both men knew the gun was too close, and neither, especially the man holding it, wanted a random gunfire explosion in the middle of a strip-center parking lot, in front of a hardware store, or during the midday rush.

"We have your wife," he said coolly. "You and I are going to take a drive...but I promise to take you to where we have her stashed. If you try anything, we will kill her." Then he added, for effect, "And then we will kill you."

It was a gamble, Gabe knew. The man may have just gotten off the phone with his wife only minutes earlier. He may be a man who was not particularly in love with his missus, or may know his beloved was out of town visiting the folks and couldn't have been abducted. There were a ton of variables, each one more risky than the last, but Gabe knew he couldn't take the man by force, not in broad daylight, and he couldn't maneuver the big fucker into the cab of his Dodge truck without some kind of guile. There was an abundance of mistakes in play, but he couldn't risk losing the man in traffic and watching another white-lighter escaping his grasp.

"*What the hell...?*" Carl screamed out as if all that was happening was lunacy. It would be normal for his mind to first race to robbery, but even he could tell the man had nothing of value besides his truck, and who would risk their life tangling with a man of his size.

"What have you done with my wife ...? If you've hurt Carol—"

Gabe cut him off and forced a smile to his face. "Not to worry," he said quietly and composed. He had to make the encounter look as inconspicuous as possible, hoping his grin was an effective trick to passersby. He couldn't hazard anyone driving the streets ahead of him and noticing anything strange, just two extremely close friends saying hello. The dodge pickup the big man had headed to after exiting the True Value was parked on the side of the lot. Gabe had observed that detail...as he did most things in his environment. He couldn't be walking as free as he was without him paying attention to every part of his surroundings and he feared any CTV cameras catching him and his soon-to-be victim.

It couldn't be much fun knowing your image was displayed in a grainy, black-and-white footage for all the jurors to see. He could almost imagine their gaze darting from the courtroom television and then back to him, sitting next to a sweaty assigned public defender with the ignominious task of defending the indefensible.

"Carol is fine...for the moment. We're gonna walk around to the passenger side and you're then gonna open the car door and slide over to the driver's side. I will sit beside you with this Smith and Wesson pointed directly into your kidneys and direct you where you need to go. You can be with Carol in no time and I can again so along my merry way." Gabe offered the last part as his indication that he didn't want to hurt anyone particularly. This was a lie he found comfort in giving as much as saying, which was odd to him, since he already had an outcome in mind.

It was clear by the man's dress and manner he wasn't a personal banker; Gabe guessed painter or contractor by the worn coveralls. Waving the Governor, he guided the man to the passenger side and watched as he fumbled awkwardly with the keys. Gabe could tell this Bubba was decent enough an individual. He could see callouses on his unsteady palms and could tell how much he loved his wife by the concerned way his voice shook when he feared for her safety. He drove a fairly new model SUV, so it was apparent that he was successful in his choice of careers. And even though he hadn't spoken a great deal, Gabe detected the twang of good ole southern upbringing

He tried not to consider the white-lighters' lives only slightly. It usually tended to interfere with his plans. He didn't like sympathy and the stories of their mundane existences needed to be quashed early. For it to work to continue, he needed to see them as cardboard cutouts and less than people. He couldn't afford the luxury of seeing them as healthy, responsible individuals with lives of their own. But at times it was harder and usually tied to the expressions on their faces as the proverbial hummer was struck. Everyone was a predestined act, he told himself. No matter how they begged, they were merely cannon fodder which he needed to sacrifice for a greater goal. All else had to be occluded from his brain entirely, lest he find he was developing a consciousness and that would only derail him from the path he'd been assigned.

With his Governor trained on the driver, Gabe ordered him to continue out of town. It began a strange reflection in his mind. One where there had been many killings, but none where he'd ever been forced to kidnap a white-lighter and then take them far from where he picked them up initially. He was doing his best to keep the man calm and complacent. He told him that it wasn't robbery he was interested in, just transportation out of the city. He still couldn't begin to understand what kind of confusion must be bouncing around that ole redneck's brain. It seemed just as strange to him, so it must've felt the same for his driver he decided. This made his wonder if he was losing his ability to control a situation. He'd always been so cool and measured about such things before, he thought.

As the driver wove through traffic under his controlled guidance, he seemed to relax, and Gabe asked him his name to ease his apprehension.

"Carl...Carl Whiting," he said nervously. But then the look on his face appeared too much like a veil being lifted. He was placing it together; that if the man with a gun didn't know his name, why was he being kidnapped? Gabe could see the puzzle pieces connecting in Carl's underused imagination.

"Okay, Carl...truth is I don't know you...and your wife is safe, probably still at home doing some cleaning or something. I admit I lied, but remember I still have the gun." Gabe was stoic, trying to keep the driver's mind occupied. He gestured with the Smith and Wesson to indicate it was still fixed at close range and it would take only a single shot to end Carl's life.

"Let's just say I needed a ride, and you're my chauffeur for the day. You're going to drive me someplace, somewhere outside the city limits, and then you're going to be on your way. It will be a great story you can tell your friends...nothing more. Not to worry big man; *this won't be a scene out of Deliverance I assure you*. Trust me, you are not my type." He smiled over at the driver, anything to ease his tension, and Carl chuckled back, clearly nervous but compliant.

Gabe could see Carl's beefy hands straining to hold the wheel, beads of perspiration dotting under the sleeves of his coveralls. They chatted causally, just as if it was an unplanned drive with a friend to the country...but only because Gabe was forced to. He had to at least try to keep Carl calm and driving. The reality was that Carl could easily veer his truck into a guardrail or stop abruptly, forcing both into the windshield, or he could just accept the bullet that would surely be unleashed if he did any of that. It's what Gabe would have done, if the tables were turned. In his mind killing Carl was inevitable, but not while driving the interstate headed to a secure scene for murder. Dying on asphalt with a gunshot in his side was not how the game was supposed to play out.

But the long drive and the required chitchat had their own effect, because the more time they spent navigating traffic and interstate exits, the more time Carl became a real person and not some soulless cutout he could so easily murder. Gabe was beginning to feel the tide of remorse building somewhere in his chest, but it only served to irritate him more. *This didn't usually happen*, he thought. Normally, he was able to complete the act quickly, and he wasn't required to spend time staring into the faces of each cow before slaughter. But watching Carl's eyes dart anxiously from the road and then back to him, hearing that hillbilly speech, or wondering whether he had kids at the exact moment the sun decided to glint off Carl's wedding band made his stomach turn sick—it all seemed too serious.

He could see the tops of buildings flying past Carl's driver's side window, and they were becoming less frequent until each building became scarcer than before. He could see more and more sporadic clumps of trees with fewer billboards. The car exhaust fumes were dissipating as well, telling Gabe they were even farther out of the city than he guessed. Pointing his gun like a finger, he tapped it in the air, suggesting Carl take the next available exit.

DOING AS HE was told, Carl took every road his kidnapper demanded. He didn't understand what was happening, but he knew he had to play it cool. That seemed the most logical step to take that might guarantee he would see Carol and his boy again. Their conversation had dried up as the man with a gun seemed to be scrutinizing the area, squinting his eyes and trying to gauge side roads that would take them into bushier, more rural, and woody spots.

Carl was grateful the guy said he didn't have plans of a sexual nature with him; he'd never guessed the dude was queer...but why then was he searching for some secluded spot? Did he intend to find some stretch of nowhere, a place cars and traffic were rare? Was he gonna steal his Dodge and leave him standing in the middle of a road, maybe miles from the nearest house? Was that what this whole thing had been about? The guy wanted his truck and just wanted to get him somewhere he couldn't easily get help? Was he gonna be forced to watch as the stranger stole his truck and made his getaway? He felt certain that was about to happen. After all, the man had no call to harm him; they didn't know each other, and his truck was relatively new and in good shape. Why then didn't he just say that? What was all that shit about Carol for?

BOTH MEN'S MINDS were racing; one with questions about motives, while the other was simply scanning for a spot where Carl's body could not be so easily discovered. Gabe's cold calculations were the implement he used, the rudimentary tool that served to occupy his hands so he didn't have to consider his actions. It was his brain refusing to grasp any ramifications by weighing out the minutiae of his simple planning. It was a mind trying to prevent him from caring about what was about to happen to the driver, reflecting on what he was about to do. He'd surprised even himself by growing suddenly attached to Carl. It was true that he was more likely insignificant in the big picture, but he surely was important in some aspect of his marginal world. He may've been nothing but a tiny cog, but he was a cog that moved all necessary gears for a wife, and possibly for his children. He was important in ways that Gabe had never once even considered. Not since any of this began over eighteen years earlier.

Forcing Carl to pull to the side of the road, he guided him at gunpoint out of the car, telling him they were going to take a walk into the woods just ahead. He lied when he promised Carl he was just getting him far enough off the main road so that he could escape. He watched the big man lumber over brush and fallen trees, following closely behind rodd chatting with him as if none of this had any meaning, trying to comfort him so he wouldn't react quickly and try to make a futile run for it. They walked farther into the underbrush, until even the daylight seemed to hide away. Under the canopy of lush vegetation and in the quiet of that forest just outside of the city, he had Carl turn around and face him before he fired twice, dead center at his chest, killing him instantly.

Gabe dropped to his knees as the man crashed backward like a mannequin forcibly pushed to the ground. He needed to work quickly to steal the essence of the life-giving radiance that had so defined Carl at the hardware store. He felt that familiar pulse surging through him, zapping his strength like an electric charge jumping from circuit to circuit, fleeting as it passed from one body to another. Gabe was immediately blinded by an explosion of bursting light, a hand grenade of UV sunlight trapping him inside its bubble. The detonation set off a debris field of white...like standing in the center of an oncoming car's headlights with no place to turn before impact. Even the dead thing in the mossy grass ahead was captured in the beam and emblazed with a brilliance before the light eventually evaporated...leaving one man poised on his knees amid the wet leaves while the other lay on his back, his face staring up at the God who'd unsympathetically taken his life. The roar of the explosion in his ears took several minutes to die away. Equally, it took several minutes for the pounding in his chest to subside and stop racing. It was always like this...both painful and amazing. It left him with hard breathing but sated, like a quick fuck with an enthusiastic and energetic lover.

After regaining his composure, he walked over and looked down at Carl's face. His eyes were open; sadly, his death expression had captured his surprise for all eternity. A wet stain circled his crotch, and any dignity the man once had had been washed away with his final breaths. His chest was stained a bright-red with a patch of wet blood pooling at the big man's belly. Church dragged the body a few feet away to offer it a better cover before rummaging through Carl's pockets for his keys. He stowed the gun in the small of his back and hung his head as he took the long walk back to the truck. He'd drive back into town in Carl's Dodge, and then wipe it down thoroughly, before discarding it somewhere close to his neighborhood. He would abandon the truck with keys dangling in the ignition, just a baited hook with the slim hope someone would boost it and take it for an extended joy drive; anything to help cover his tracks and confuse the patrol cars that'd surely be looking for it later tonight, or at best, by early the next morning.

In his mind, it was something that had to be done. But he still felt drained and regretful driving back to the city, without Carl, while listening to the dead man's stereo playing in the background—anything to break the abyss of bothersome silence and keep him from feeling anything. Things were changing it seemed, because it was getting harder and harder to do what he had to, or maybe he'd just stirred up some unaccustomed feelings because he'd had to spend so much time with this one. He didn't usually know the names of most of the meat sacks that had been presented for his taking, but he knew Carl by name, and he even knew his wife's name was Carol. That was the problem, he thought, knowing them. Gabe turned up the radio and smiled a knowing grin; it was satisfying finding out and exposing such a simple truth.

Next time I'll make it a point not to know their fucking names before I kill them, he thought, *it's all just shit anyway...and in the end everything crumbles away!*

Chapter Twenty-Six

SOMEWHERE BETWEEN TWO and three in the morning, Christian's phone rang, nearly causing him to break a toe racing for his cell that he'd left on the coffee table. It was Gabriel he thought, there wasn't any doubt. Who else would call in the middle of the night and expect him to be home? Even if his father had slipped into a coma after a stroke and tragically died suddenly, his mother would've still have waited until the next morning to phone him. *"Well honey, it's not like there was anything you could've done anyway. It's all the same sad news no matter when you heard it"*, she would say quietly. Probably still sipping from a vodka gimlet as she went about the task of making calls to inform the family members of the horrible news. But it wasn't his mother. The heartbeat racing in his chest told him that much. It'd be Gabriel, and he'd be calling to apologize or tell him he was coming over to talk.

The sting of jamming his toe forced him to limp over and grab up the phone before voice mail caught it.

"Yes..." he said, panting and holding one foot and trying to support himself from tipping over. "Church is that you?"

"Why are you outta breath? You okay...you have company or something?" Gabriel asked incredulously.

But before Christian could respond Gabriel began speaking, obvious pangs of guilt dripping off his every word and producing a loving swell in Christian's insides.

"I'm sorry for bouncing earlier, but even you gotta admit you can be a real douche bag sometimes?" There was a hint of something odd in his tone, and then Christian remembered the well-lubricated words of someone who'd had a few.

"You been drinking since you left me standing in the middle of the street?" he asked, forging past the apologies he would have savored.

"I went home first...but couldn't sleep, so I hit the streets...and then a couple of bars. I decided before they made their last call, I'd make mine." Even with a distance marked in miles, Christian could feel a sloppy smile creeping across Gabriel's face.

"What's this...*a booty call?*"

"Maaayyybee..." he said, drawing out every syllable, hinting at his southern drawl.

"You say the cutest things, mister, but you wouldn't like it over here—all the sex is downright consensual." Batting his charm back to Gabriel, it was now his turn to understand how it felt to be so adorable.

"Only if you're willing to forgive me, that is," Gabriel said, sidestepping Christian's discreet inferences. "Not sure if I could perform though...been downing some fast drinks before everyone closed up. It's raping my brain and might make it hard to rape you...or maybe not so hard." He was slurring his words, but Christian knew the man well. He had to fight his desire to jump for joy at the fact that he was coming over. He wanted only to hold him in his arms, drunk or not.

"Door's unlocked. I'll be in bed," he said before clicking the end button. He had just enough time for a quick rinse before crawling into bed and waiting for Gabriel to slip under the covers and make everything all right.

If there were questions rattling around in Christian's skull about his time spent with Gabriel, or about the frustration of finally meeting someone special—one who turned out to be a serial killer—he was pushing those so far down they couldn't be found. He felt ecstatic running the bar of soap over his body, the tingling anticipation of seeing a person he cared for deeply. He felt as if the scales had been lifted from his eyes, or that his earlier beliefs that he'd been a happy person had been, in fact, a lie. He'd just been blinded to what happiness truly was, and now it lay before him like a banquet set before the starving masses, and all he wanted to do was taste every morsel and fill his belly completely.

He didn't care whether they fucked, because all he wanted was to lie next to the man and listen to that irregular heartbeat before the chance was snatched away by unseen hands. He didn't have to think about hiding his fears, because in that instant, he didn't have any. His chest was still thumping loudly as he stepped out of his shower and ran a towel down his body. He ran into the front room and plugged a tiny nightlight into the wall socket before extinguishing all the other lights. He didn't want Church to stumble and hurt himself in his inebriated state, like he'd done while racing for the phone, but he wanted enough guiding light to draw him into the bedroom. Crawling under the covers, he waited with anticipation, feeling the blood plump up his resting cock.

Within ten minutes, Gabriel was at his door. He listened to the sounds of a drunken man fumbling in the other room, a dark figure desperately navigating the hall as he struggled to wriggle out of jeans and boots. He hadn't called out. Christian knew he thought he was moving quietly because in his head he couldn't even sense the clatter he was making. He found himself smiling as he watched the shadow inching forward. Gabriel may have intended to creep under the covers unnoticed, but he collapsed on the bed in an awkward attempt to find his footing. He was naked as he reached over and pulled Christian closer. The smell of alcohol was heavy on his breath, but Christian didn't care. Their lips were magnetic, and they both found each other easily. Without ever speaking a word, their tongues had found other callings, and they kissed wetly as Gabriel gripped the younger man's face tightly in his meaty hand.

They slept without ever even trying to screw. The night was reserved for close contact and soulful touching. Gabriel didn't last long, the booze had tired him, and Christian noticed when his breathing became something labored and long. He curled up under Gabriel's arm and snuggled in, his ears trained to hear the heartbeat that fascinated him so. It was strange that such a potentially deadly thing could be so soothing, but it was a rhythm he couldn't match to his own heart, and that seemed accurate for many reasons swirling in his head.

By morning both men felt well rested, even though neither had gotten much sleep before Gabriel's arrival. Gabriel's eyes popped open about the same time as Christian's, and again, without words, he pulled Christian closer, this time ready for performing as he hadn't done the night before. It was not the usual sensual pleasures that Christian was accustomed to sharing with Gabriel. The man's hands raked and pulled for his own amusements, tossing Christian on his front as Gabriel placed a powerful hand on Christian's head and his thrusts became frenzied and brutal. The bigger man was driving like a hammer on penny nails, and Christian heard him utter the words, "I'm fucking almost there, partner...hang in there."

For him, it appeared his lover was working out some personal frustrations; he was simply the nearest punching bag for Gabriel's need for physical exertion. As Gabriel tensed, his hands tightening their grip on Christian's body, he exploded his seed like a rocket being released to the heavens. His grunts of animal pleasure were like a cleansing of worry and inner turmoil. After orgasm, it was easy to see the corporeal change wash over him as he fell to his side with labored breathing and reached his hand and yanked Christian to his chest. If his lover had climaxed, Gabriel didn't know and seemed not to care. But at least he became the other man Christian knew, the one who was gentle and protective of the one in his bed, and for the unsated lover, that was enough to last.

After a few fixed moments of lying in their heated exchange, Christian jumped from his bed.

"Coffee...*chop chop*," he said with a smile.

CHRIS'S GRIN SEEMED beckoning as he raced naked to the bathroom. He was a thing of beauty with his perfect ass and his sinewy form. Gabe took a second to scrutinize him as he opened the glass shower door and pulled the knob for water; the steam was immediate, and he watched as the younger man pulled a fresh towel from the rack. Gabe repositioned his body so he could see part of the bathroom and a partial Chris as he showered, but he didn't move from the comfort of the covers. He was considering the difference between lovers in that moment. The little girl Shea versus his Chris: both were more than adequate in bed, but he thought Chris was brilliant and worthy of more exploration.

Shea was innocent and had room for growth, but he seemed drawn to Chris's movements and tiny gestures. He'd observed Chris's lip curl slightly whenever he was writing quickly, trying to pull his thoughts together, had watched him blow cooling air over his hot coffee on many occasions. It was those simple acts he saw that made him want to pull the man over to him and cover him with kisses. Shea was great, but she'd never solicited such emotion; then again they'd only had one brief encounter and one quick fuck. Gabe slipped out from the sheets and headed to join Chris. It would be nice having his body lathered and rinsed with loving hands.

COMBING HER SHOULDER-LENGTH brown hair, Shea stared into the mirror and wondered who was looking back. She'd been proud that she had stepped out of her comfort zone and introduced herself to the man across the way, and oh, how she'd introduced herself! But in the security of her own apartment, she felt her satisfaction eventually drain. But moreover, it may have been stolen from her body because within fifteen minutes of getting home, she'd looked out her front window and caught sight of the man she knew as Chris Rumsfeld. He was leaving his place, and he wasn't heading to hers.

She'd expected he would have fallen asleep after their session of lovemaking, but there he was, leaving in a white tank top and his tight blue jeans and boots. The expression of his face as she stood at the window hiding behind the curtain…well it looked anxious, which was the only word he could use for a good description. When she saw him lock his door, she immediately assumed he was coming to her place. Maybe to sleep the remainder of the evening with her with his big arms enveloping her, but instead, he just walked past and headed out of the courtyard without looking back.

She hadn't dated since high school. *Maybe I'm out of practice*, she thought, because this made her feel discarded and directionless. Their sex meant something to her, but she was beginning to think it meant less to Chris Rumsfeld. Maybe he was just headed out for a bite somewhere, she hoped. Maybe it was her imagination playing with her that the look on his face had been one of drive and need. She'd hoped he'd been as spent as she was, but men were strange creatures and didn't react the same way that women did. Maybe he went out for a post coital drink of celebration, she surmised. There were plenty of possibilities. *Hail the conquering hero*, she thought with a satisfied smirk raking across her face.

She was the hero, though. It had been her seducing him, not the other way around. She had picked the persona she needed to illicit sex. She was the one with the guile, and any story of sexual conquest should be hers to tell. But in a flood of reality, she realized she had no one to share her story with. Shea had wrapped her world around her art and her immediate needs for survival. She had few girlfriends. Her life was so encapsulated in her art that if she'd picked up the phone to gossip, she would have found her contact list near empty. It was depressing.

Running through the events in her mind, she decided it was best to put it behind her and finally go to bed. If she didn't, she knew she'd lie awake wondering what her unplanned lover was up to, or where he'd gone. She turned on the television for some much-needed background noise and got into her nightgown. She was filling her head with too many emotions and plans to notice when the reporter from the Channel 5 news flashed on the TV. She wasn't paying attention as that same reporter informed a wary public about a grisly find in a nearby National Park. Shea hadn't captured enough of the story to hear an unsuspecting family who was visiting Seattle had stumbled onto a body while sightseeing, hadn't heard the reporter identify the victim as Carl Whiting, or that investigators were currently reviewing clues. The reporter's words and demeanor were intended to increase ratings, shock before the awe. The last words he spoke were to tell his audience of viewers that a manhunt for a suspect was beginning.

Chapter Twenty-Seven

THE LOVERS ATE a late lunch at the Sage Café, splitting a soup and sandwich special with tall frosty mugs of root beer. The entire day was spent visiting shops and walking through the district and never once had their conversations turned dark and disturbing. It was a day for each of them to shelve their fears and simply enjoy each other's company. Christian sat awestruck at the sight of an animated Gabriel discussing grand notions of exactly how he saw things, and not the rigid impermeable Church he'd come to know whenever they discussed his past and death. It was a pleasing side of the man he'd never really seen.

"I tell you, eventually the whole universe is gonna stop completely. Man, I read about it. They call it something like...'heat death' for the universe. Can you even imagine such a thing?"

Christian leaned in, surprised at how enthusiastic his companion was on a subject so out of the norm for him. "So you're saying we're all gonna burn up?"

"No, that's not it at all. It actually doesn't refer to temperature. If I remember what I read, it was about the inability for everything to function...like in every sense. It's when you lose the energy that makes all life work. They call it 'thermodynamic equilibrium' he said, happy to sound so astute and educated.

"Who calls it that?" Chris asked, with a too cynical tone in his words?

"Astrophysicists I suppose, I don't know. It's some theory of cosmology or some shit like that."

Gabe sounded exasperated. Partially, he was excited to show how well-read he was but slightly aggravated that Chris wasn't noticing it or sitting there in awe.

"It's also called 'maximum entropy.' I remember reading the term and thought it sounded pretty cool, so I made sure to commit it to memory."

Continuing his rant, Gabe blurted out modestly, "I'm not sure I'm smart enough to correctly explain it all, but you gotta read about it, bro. I think you'd be fuckin' amazed."

There he was again, that childlike kid whose passion and curiosity couldn't quite be contained. Along with the excited tenor as his voice rose and fell with every new impression, he felt a driven need to share. This was another reason Chris loved him, he believed. It balanced out his mercurial personality, which always seemed laced with heartrending sadness and a dark finality. The ideas were rushing out with a speed he couldn't control and he was eager to pull Christian into his story. It had been the first time in far too many decades that he'd had a guest to share the ride, and he was enjoying every second of their time together.

"Screw you, dude, you don't even give a crap about what I'm saying!" Gabe said when he noticed the glassy-eyed way Christian was staring back him over the remains of their lunch plate. It was the only thing preventing them from holding hands, he thought. It was the Great Wall of China. But Christian never enjoyed PDAs.

"Oh I'm listening, dude," he said smiling. "I was just observing you and how much I care for you, that, and all that oozing humanity spilling onto the table."

"Humanity...I don't have any humanity asshole," Gabe barked with a disdainful curl to his lip. "And if I ever did once, I'm doing my level best to rid myself of the sickness...hell I'm the sonofabitchin' cure for that ailment, and you know I'm speaking truth here, brother."

With that revelation, they both broke into subdued laughter, and Gabe, not giving a shit about Christian's public display worries, reached over and brushed his fingers along the back of his lover's hand. It was plain that over the years Church had developed some unusual notions and being able to shed a few of them without fear of judgment put a spark back into those intensely iridescent pupils and crafted a smile that was bent with character lines surrounding his mouth.

TO CHRISTIAN, IT seemed it was a hand extended in invitation, like children holding hands for security as they crossed a busy street. It was Gabriel's summons that the two head out for a thrilling adventure together.

"Dude, if you think about it, and you know we're all gonna just cease to exist one day...then what's it all for anyway?" As Gabriel rambled on, his ideologies became a clear path to why he'd ended up in the life he lived. Christian could see the dots being connected right before his eyes, the curtain withdrawn and the wizard was standing there, shamefaced. *If he really believes all this shit, then naturally, he'd end up a killer.*

"Hon, I don't think you're supposed to live out your life knowing what happens at the end of it all...seems kinda unfair if you ask me."

Christian wanted to keep Gabriel talking; he enjoyed it when he rattled on and finally became excited about something, even if it was inane drivel.

"I just think if the scientists are all right, then we shouldn't have to live by some societal pressure of how we're supposed to behave." Gabriel was adamant in his beliefs, regardless of the ramifications he was failing to see.

"You have to have societal pressure," Christian offered. "It'd be anarchy if we didn't have structure. People would be taking what they wanted...killing whenever they felt like it—"

Christian words were cut short as he realized what he'd said. He had become relaxed and simply forgotten who he was talking to— He regretted those words instantly. He was eating a club sandwich with a killer, but it wasn't bread and luncheon meat in his mouth now, it was the bone and tissue of his own foot. With the statement released into the ether, he was shocked and embarrassed, and there was no denying that Gabriel could see it plastered all over his face. It was Gabriel who picked up the slack and prevented the words from hanging there in eternal awkward silence.

"That's what I'm talking about...the whole thing. You have anarchy and people killing people for no good reason, but maybe that's how it was supposed to be. Maybe we all just fucked it up with religion and expectation and trying to be better men."

In his gratitude that his companion had not called him on his fumbled words, he allowed the conversation to continue. "Trying to be a better person is what this life is supposed to be about, I think—the human condition and all that nonsense."

"There's my boy Christian again...the devoted idealist. I think that's why I love you so much." Gabriel had pulled his hand away but never lost his smile. He seemed unfazed by his own admission, making Christian wonder if he'd meant the words to come out so haphazardly. Although they'd never spoken them, the words had always hung somewhere in the significant dark, just to the rear of wherever the two men were standing. Christian smiled at hearing him say he loved him and was equally glad it had been Gabriel who said it first. He grinned from ear to ear, ecstatic at hearing the declaration, and even his stayed expression couldn't hide his feelings.

Gabriel was smiling, too, eyes bright and contagious with joy. Christian suddenly wondered if he'd accidently said those words. Was he now regretting his stumble, or was it a game used to taunt him? Christian couldn't tell. He needed to know the answer or risk bursting inside. His companion's gaze was leveled over the glass of soda he brought to his lips; he was letting his admission linger unattached, adrift in the water and awaiting rescue. It was clear Gabriel was indeed playing with him. *The fucking bastard*, thought Christian. *He is simply gonna let it lie there and see what happens. How cruel can he be?*

After thinking about it for a second, Christian decided the best way for him to win the game was not to play. He would ignore it. It would serve to frustrate his companion, who simply wanted to bat the half-dead mouse from paw to paw and watch as it drew its final breaths. He would quickly change the subject and test Gabriel's resolve.

"So after lunch, I was thinking we could hit up the Space Needle. You know, as long as I've lived here, I have never gone."

Christian munched down his last bite of sandwich, and as he reached for his glass across the table, his eyes came up to observe. Gabriel was glaring through squinting eyes. He didn't like to lose and fully expected to bait Christian some more. His frustration was coming in waves, making the younger man feel gloriously in control.

But the power was lost in longer moments, and Gabriel accepted his defeat and shrugged his shoulders as if to say "Whatever."

"If that's what you wanna do, babe, I'm game if you are." The battle was over without any real victors, and as the two stood up to leave, Gabriel downed the last of his cola and placed his hand in the small of Christian's back and guided him to the door. As they walked the sidewalk, Gabriel leaned over and completely surprised Christian with a question the writer thought he'd never hear.

"On the way to the needle, we have to pass that rat hole where I'm currently hanging my hat...wanna stop in and see how the other half lives?"

He was astonished to hear Gabriel invite him to his very secret lair. It had always stood as a strong, impassable border between them: Gabriel's privacy and protection, as defined by four walls.

"I think I'd like that," he said rather nonchalantly; he didn't want Gabriel to see how pleased he was just to be invited. It would be one of the last secrets between them, he thought. *After all, there can't be any more,* he guessed. So they chatted briefly as they walked with Gabriel leading the way. It was a farther distance than Christian would've liked to walk, but Gabe hadn't mentioned how far it was. Gabriel seemed so unaffected by walking everywhere, even when Chris wasn't. He was more accustomed to being behind the wheel, even for short jaunts like to the grocery or drycleaners. And yet he knew that walking meant spending more time together, and with no particular need to hurry anywhere, it seemed the ideal way to spend the afternoon with someone who had just admitted that he loved him.

It took an hour of walking to reach the rundown, furnished apartment Gabriel called home. Walking the seedier streets of Seattle might not have been a safe endeavor for most, but Christian was in better company. There was some security as long as he walked close enough to the big man at his side; his lovely bodyguard, his protector. He was curious about how the man lived, and the feeling of sheer anticipation seeped from every pore and brought hairs to attention on the nape of his neck.

Wide-eyed, he gazed at all the units facing the courtyard. He saw the broken stucco fountain, once ornate and lovely, now just a decaying reminder of former glory. He saw the scattering of chairs and tables amid all the overgrown plants. He could see the beauty that had existed there once, now lost, like those forgotten days. He rather enjoyed what he saw. He likened it to being in the company of some diva from the golden age of film; she had been a star once, but now even heavy face paint couldn't hide all the wrinkles. She seemed swathed in costume jewelry, which at one time may have been the real McCoy, but now was just a faint reproduction of its original value. She was draped and gorgeous…if only in her own mind. A feather boa might have been wrapped around a faded cocktail dress as her eyes begged to be taken back to a simpler time. A place from her memory where she reigned supreme and everyone took notice. For a writer like Christian, the building had history, many stories to tell, and no matter how dilapidated she'd become, he was envious that Gabriel had found it first and grateful he was even allowed to visit there.

Where the façade might've been intriguing, Gabriel's apartment was a letdown. Inside, it was bare of any real life, and the furniture was worn and terribly out of fashion. Christian smiled as he entered; trying hard to disguise any shame for his lover he might've felt. He first commented about how much sun Gabriel must get in the morning, gingerly taking steps not to overreach and embarrass his friend.

"Fuck off, dude. I told you it was a shit hole," Gabriel said gruffly.

"Actually, babe, you said it was a rathole, not a shit hole. And as far as holes go, *yours* is nice." He grinned with that. It seemed every word between them sometimes came out as some vague sexual innuendo, even when they weren't trying.

"It's cheap, and it serves its purpose. Remember I don't have the kind of job where I can take a sabbatical just so I can write a book, and I never had folks with money."

"No seriously…it is nice…honestly." Christian walked over and hugged Gabriel and nuzzled his nose under his ear. "I never tried to imagine how you lived, but seeing this is cool. I like the complex; kinda jealous. I should've wondered how you paid for your place at all. I guess I'm just stupid." He broke away and sauntered through the apartment. "Considering you don't work, this place is a fuckin' palace. That's probably something we're gonna have to talk about soon, but for now how 'bout we christen the place with sex?"

He turned with a smile, only to find Gabriel looking sheepishly away. It dawned on him that he'd made some big assumptions that day; his first when he entered Gabe's apartment. And he didn't need any new surprises today, he thought.

"Of course, it's supposing you haven't already christened the place with someone else…" his words faded off to a mumble as he turned his back.

GABE HAD DECIDED not to throw a line in; let the drowning man sink, he thought. He had nothing to feel embarrassed or ashamed about because sex and love were not mutually tied together. It might have been a conversation they would have explored further, but as if on cue, there was a light tapping at Gabe's door. Whatever questions Chris may have stumbled over were about to be answered, whether Gabe wanted them revealed or not.

Gabe stood, without moving; he didn't advance to the door, and Chris was left dumbstruck with a long pause as the knocking continued.

"Well…you gonna answer your door?"

There was no escaping the moment. Gabe already knew who it was. There was nothing left to do but hate himself for bringing Chris to his place. He hadn't ever expected Shea and Chris to meet, and he was equally astonished that he hadn't seen this as a possibility. He'd just never assumed the bitch would come knocking at his door so quickly after his arrival. Theirs had been a chance meeting. This wasn't any different he supposed, but he'd totally screwed it all up when he brought Chris home. And now he'd pay for that mistake. He couldn't decide what to do, and his bewilderment fused him to the floor in solid frozen amazement.

CHRISTIAN BROKE THE stalemate by walking past Gabriel to leave and just as he opened the door he was surprised to see a pretty young girl standing there, her arm raised as if she was interrupted before knocking.

"Hello there," she said, smiling. At first Christian thought she was selling something, Girl Scout Cookies, or tickets for a local church raffle perhaps. There was no other convenient reason for a lovely young woman flashing a counterfeit cheerleader smile, to be caught standing at Gabriel's door.

"Hi there, can I help you?"

"Sorry to bother you but..." and just in that instant she noticed Gabe standing back inside the room, barely hidden in the shadow. She brushed past Christian with an apparent cool and casual confidence. Her gaze was precisely trained on the other man while she shoved her way past Christian.

With a flabbergasted expression on his face, the woman's actions seemed to catch him unaware. And with his hand still wrapped around the doorknob, he stood silent as this young, impertinent girl tried to invade their privacy in an overly animated flourish. Even though he didn't know her, he could sense how her gestures didn't really suit the woman she pretended that she was. She looked too mousy to appear so brash, he speculated. Whoever she was, the scornful expression on Christian's face was indication enough that he immediately decided he didn't care for her.

MUCH TO GABE'S chagrin, the woman accidently saved them all from additional mortification. If she'd simply asked for Chris Rumsfeld, there would have been quite a few long minutes of confusion, leading to pain and embarrassment. But for Gabe, even though he wasn't happy to see her standing there, he'd been grateful Shea had kept her mouth closed and left one particular lie a mystery.

"There you are, Chris. I was worried that I'd missed you" Shea whispered as she entered. She was an inconvenient visitor clearly establishing an awkward and unexpected air inside the apartment. She lingered too long, like a hovering specter one either acknowledged or pretended wasn't even real. Only a second of time passed, but for the men, it felt like eight or nine excruciating minutes of uncomfortable silence.

With inscrutable eyes laser-focused on Gabe's guest, she steadfastly held her ground. "I hope I'm not intruding," she said; knowing full well she was. Gabriel quickly reasoned he needed to assume the lead, and rushing closer, he gently grabbed her by her wrist and guided her into the aura of Christian's company.

"Shea, honey, this is Maxwell, an old buddy from way back. Maxwell you ole shit, this is my....*friend*...Shea Baltimore."

It seemed the sanest move at the time, even though it wasn't. Gabe wanted to prevent his female companion from saying the name Chris Rumsfeld, thinking he could maintain some distance and privacy. But he failed to plan it effectively, particularly when no one there was even privy to his intentions...including him.

When Gabe introduced Chris as Maxwell, he was trying to hide a lie that he couldn't explain. He was hoping that the writer would pick up on his meaning, but Chris was only focused on one new bit of data—the woman Gabe was fucking was presently standing mere feet away. It was an awkward moment, made even more painful when Shea stood on the tips of her toes and embraced Gabriel right in front of him. The hug was bad enough, but when she offered him a light air-kiss against his cheek, it sealed Chris's hatred of her like the vacuum around a mason jar of jam.

CHRISTIAN WAS CLEVER, so he caught the veiled inference that the two lived in the same complex, and the air that was breezing over conveyed the two were closer than he could have guessed. They were lovers! But that couldn't be true. He would have known if Gabe had someone else in his bed...*wouldn't he?*

Christian could only close the door with a slight degree of shock. He recognized whatever was about to happen between the three of them needed to occur behind a closed door.

"I'm sorry...didn't mean to break up the party. I just wanted to stop by and say hello."

Shea was still clinging to Gabriel like some lost love, making the writer fume with hidden anger. Somewhere a line had been drawn in the proverbial sand. This tiny, alien creature, with her awful feminine ways, had slipped into the room and was marking her territory without even knowing the circumstances of their introduction. Christian loathed her—this woman who was confiscating his man inside their embrace, implying a secret affair he wasn't supposed to be privy to.

"Hello, Shea. Like the man said, I'm Maxwell Grant," he said as he bridged the gap between them with an extended hand. Shea shook his grip lightly, and they both smiled engagingly. But under the mask Christian was seething inside. He had been placed in an untenable situation, not knowing why he was forced to use an alias with someone he didn't even know. His grin belied his emotional rage, but Gabriel could see it; he knew that he could. All of those nights curled up in his arms had given him some knowledge of how the man operated, and likewise, he could see that it wasn't lost on Gabriel, who recognized the smoke rising in his lover's eyes.

"Your friend was just showing me his place—never been here before. It's nice. You live here, too, I gather?"

"I'm just across the way at number 180... He's my neighbor, that's how I met my fella here."

He could almost see the word "Fuck" projected over Gabe's expression. He was behind Shea, so she hadn't been able to see how he hung his head in shame. Suddenly he was the kid who'd been caught with his fingers in the cookie jar...more like trying to steal a piece of pie...*cherry pie that is*, Christian mused angrily. He nodded as Shea spoke, but Gabe was more familiar with that smug continence of his. Lord only knew how Gabe had seen it more than once.

"Well *Chris* and I go way back," he said flashing his pearly enamels and grimacing with envy. His bitterness was like gold-plating; it covered his tongue and enhanced the gleaning smile turning it into a sneer. "So how long have you known Chris?" he asked casually, tasting more acrid venom and praying the room would explode and burn this tiny bitch into cinder and ash.

"Actually, we met recently," she said. "I'm an artist, and Chris turned out to be my muse and my model. I gave him a drawing not long ago, and I guess as they say 'that was all it took.'"

What a cunt she is, he thought. She'd failed to mention one important detail; that it couldn't have happened earlier than the other evening. She was letting on like they'd been lovers for years. This pissed him off, particularly since "her fella" was sleeping in his bed a mere twenty-four hours before that. She was a hookup, nothing more. Chris nodded in acknowledgment; branding that permanent smile on his lips while simultaneously wanting to slap the shit outta the bitch and toss her ass outdoors.

"So how do you know Chris? You guys work together?" she asked pleasantly. The woman was beyond stupid, thought Christian. She was a vapid girl pretending to be someone that she wasn't. She stank of the effort, and the inelegant way she tried to maneuver herself into his social graces made him want to scream. She was clearly a small-town girl whose father may've even been the local pastor. "Actually, we are doing some work together. As a matter of fact, we were going to head out to do that before you knocked, but I suppose we could do it later if you two would rather call it a day," Christian said politely as he brushed past Gabriel and headed for the door. He knew he'd be stopped before the knob could turn even slightly. He'd laid the train tracks before his lover's feet; it was up to him to jump aboard.

"*No*, Max. I think I need to head out with you and take a look at it...before it gets dark..." Turning toward Shea, Gabriel grabbed her hands in his. "Let's try again later, baby. I gotta do some stuff with Maxwell, and we're burning daylight... Till later."

Another important second passed as Gabriel's eyes implored some reaction from his female concubine, leaving Christian perplexed and somewhat stranded in the moment. He began to wonder, *What the hell am I doing anyway?* He was acting like they were lovers and not the fuck buddies he knew them to be. He was trying to keep sensible about it, but he was falling into some trap of convenience. This was not him. What the hell did he care whether she went batshit crazy if she assumed Gabriel was leaving with his real lover? He told himself it was his life Gabriel was hiding, not his lifestyle. Gabriel had learned long ago to stay under the radar, to hide rather than be noticed. He was a serial killer by vocation and slipping through the latticework of life unseen was how he survived. Christian told himself again, he was simply keeping up an act for appearance so Shea didn't freak out and draw unwanted attention. However, it was still a fucked-up situation.

Without waiting for a reply, Gabriel hustled the two of them from his apartment as he locked the door behind them. Christian, for one, was grateful the bitch hadn't asked what type of work he did. This awkward subterfuge had already been far too exhausting. For the moment, all he wanted to do was escape. He wanted to get Gabriel alone and have him explain. But he was emotional at times, sometimes overtly so, and he feared the outcome. None of it bode well, he presumed.

Walking far ahead of Gabriel, Christian was racing to get anywhere but the spot he'd been standing seconds earlier. He was in shock at the thought of all of it. It was ludicrous, he knew; after all, he'd only known Gabriel Church a short time. Not to mention he was an admitted serial killer. *Oh, did I forget that already?* He was someone he didn't rightly know, and they hadn't been joined at the hip by ceremonial vows. *How the fuck could I be so jealous of someone like that?*

Finding out your boyfriend was fucking a woman on the side might happen to a lot of people, but he never suspected it would happen to him. He stormed down the street, after bowing out of the conversation with Shea and Gabriel, who, rather comically, the bitch knew as someone named Chris. Exasperated, he believed he'd suffered through enough shockers today. Was it Gabriel's way of directing a pointed finger to the air with a salutatory "Fuck you, Christian Maxwell?"

For him, it was like walking in on the two while they were doing it. It was humiliating and made him question everything he knew about Church. They'd just bumped uglies that morning and this "Shea aberration" made it sound like the two of them were also equally intimate. Was he really fucking one willing partner and then driving across town for another roll in the hay?

GABE SPRINTED UP to catch Chris, having taken the time to get Shea headed back across the courtyard. He would have to deal with her later, too, he knew, but right now he was worried about what Chris was thinking.

"Babe, wait...please!" Even as he called out, he knew what had to be going through his lover's mind. Shea had done a bang-up job of possibly ending his relationship, and just because of a twenty-minute fuck of nonsensical proportion. It certainly would've stung less if she had meant something to him, or at least been nominal in bed. But to lose Chris over this would be a tragedy. Running up beside him and spinning him around, he tried to get the man to stare back into his eyes. He understood the base of his power over Christian originated from his eyes. Chris had all but admitted that one night in bed, so he was left with trying that ploy again. He'd hoped the look, his pained expression, something, might get Chris to stop and give him a minute to explain. But he could feel the pony was tensing to bolt, and he worried he might not get the chance to say how sorry he felt.

"Stop, asshole. Give me an opportunity to talk to you about it before you turn your pretty butt and walk away."

"Talk? What the hell do we have to talk about? You didn't fuck up. I did. It seems all my realities were hinged on the wrong main character. Now all I have to do is rewrite my ending."

"Goddamn, you're quite the drama queen, aren't you?"

Gabe understood the situation was tenuous, but in his imagination, he was smiling; he had predicted how Chris would take it, and by heavens, he was right on the money. "I fucked her, *yes*, but only once and just for kicks. I didn't know the bitch was crazy and thinking we were all dating and shit!"

"Why did you fuck her at all?" Christian's credulous nature came erupting out like a volcano full of lava. He couldn't conceive why Gabe had cheated on him, with her of all things, and his expression was a painstaking exhibition of that. The bigger man could only stare back in silence. He could say the words, but even if everything in his head played out, he didn't think Christian could even begin to comprehend. They were, after all, entirely different creatures. But the words had to come out. As each one did, it was laced with shame, dripping like heavy syrup from his tongue.

"I don't know, because she offered…it was there…what the *fuck* you want me to say. I got a cock. I like using it. You should know that better than anyone else."

"Not better than her, I'll bet!" Christian said with a humph and turning to yank himself free of Gabe's grasp.

"Don't be such a little bitch, Chris" Gabe demanded loudly. "Give me a freegan break, why dontcha?""

It was useless. He'd screwed up their near-perfect day with one more tangled fight, and although he hadn't started it, he was complicit by just bringing his boy toy home to see the digs. He stood there in the waning light of day, scratching his head, a true caricature of dumb confusion. It seemed every time the two men got together, one was storming off in a huff and leaving the other holding his dick in the middle of a street. If this was how it was supposed to be with a dude, he'd rather go back to cunts.

This was an overplayed scene, he thought. *Done that -Got the T-shirt!* If they couldn't make it through two full days without fighting in some heart-wrenching, dramatic, fag-boy fashion, then they had no future to speak of.

Chapter Twenty-Eight

CHRISTIAN LOWERED HIS head in concentration as he headed down the sidewalk away from Church's complex and the love nest he'd shared with Shea. He didn't know where he was headed, but it didn't matter, as long as it was away from here.

It would be a long walk back to his condo, but his anger and frustration would carry him like one of the city's many ferries. Christian's pace had purpose. Every footfall gave him proof he was walking away from Gabriel and his disloyal, wandering cock. He'd never had anyone be unfaithful to him, and he was angry he'd allowed it to be Church—a sociopathic killer of the innocent. In that second, when the girl had breezed past him and headed into Gabriel's arms, he'd felt bile rising from his stomach and wetting his tongue. The flash of realization of Gabriel's betrayal was something he wouldn't forget. A stupid "deer in the headlights" look on his face, and the budding shame of knowing he'd been caught. *Why the fuck did he take me to his place if there was a risk this could happen...that he'd be found out?* It didn't make any sense.

The roar of traffic passed him, but he was so lost in his own head everything was dancing like shadows just outside his vision. He was furious, and there were just too many questions racing through his mind. Why her? What did she have that enticed Gabe to spend time with her? He'd met Shea; she was cute, he had to admit that, but beyond that, he personally didn't see anything special in her. Certainly nothing that could pull Gabriel from his bed, he thought.

Where was that fucking light he was so fond of talking about? Why hadn't it surrounded her? She was a cunt, a tiny thing who expected Church would want her because she had a pussy, and we all know how that controls the world. But Gabriel was his now, or at least, he'd thought he was. He'd decided which path of his sexuality he'd take, and Christian had won the prize. But it was truly fucked up knowing that he'd been wrong, that he hadn't triumphed. He didn't have Gabriel, and it was clear he'd never have a firm hold over him. They would never be more than just friends, fuck buddies, acquaintances who messed around for want of anything else.

With all the anger filling his gut and that bile in his mouth still a fresh memory, he thought if he headed back to his place he'd only go stir crazy. He needed to go somewhere to clear his head, somewhere Gabriel wouldn't show up unannounced like some shamed puppy that piddled on the floor. Then he remembered a small detail Shea had said.

"Just across the way, number 180." It was how they'd had the chance to meet in the first place. If he stormed off, he'd leave the man in her convenient tentacles. In his frustration, Gabriel might just wander over to her place and crawl naked into her bed. The image of that possibility shook Christian to his core. She could get her icy grip around him and hold tight, and Gabriel might be lost to him forever, all because of her proximity and feminine guiles.

That will just not work, he thought. It was clear in that second what he needed to do.

Turning back, he glanced in all directions, a secretive act to ensure he wasn't being followed. He knew Gabriel wouldn't run after him, not that far. It wasn't his style. They had done this play before, and it always ended the same way. Someone would calm down, someone would apologize, and then like rats in a maze, they would follow the same routes that had gotten them to that particular dead-end wall. Neither of them seemed to learn much from the experience. They just seemed fated to reenact the same arguments over and over.

But in his heart, he knew Gabriel was his and his alone. Christian Maxwell had dated in college, and he'd fucked on occasion, but never in his thirty-four years had he ever allowed himself to open up as he did with Gabriel. He'd been ensnared at first glance; he just hadn't known it at the time. He had become another's plaything, subjected to their whims, his body laid bare for exploration. *And how could he not?* After staring upward at those penetrating, steely eyes and seeing perfection he'd never known existed before that. Even after learning what drove the man, his sickness of reason and his dangerous past, it had not altered his feelings about him. It went against the grain about everything Christian knew to be true about him...and had taken all he understood and broken it apart...just so it could be reassembled into something new and strange to look upon.

Even as angry as he was, he was already seeing past his pain. He was shaping the man back into fusible parts, fashioning him into the man he might one day yet forgive. *This must be what it's like*, he thought, *to love someone beyond your better reason. To know that no matter how hard the fight, there remained that steady picture of them standing with you, side by side.* For one like Christian, who'd never been the type to reach his hands to hold someone at the same time as being afraid they might one day yet abandon him, this was something new and alien. It was a sensation he'd never experienced before. But even as unaccustomed as it all felt, it still solidified his brain, telling him over and over through his head, on a loop, that there were things he needed to accomplish. His biggest fear was whether it'd leave a stain on his relationship with Gabe. At least it would finally end that silly dalliance with the figure who'd come between them thought...this Shea character, the girl working to replace Christian with herself.

The sounds of distant ferry horns rang in his ears. The only other noise was nesting birds in the courtyard and music playing too loudly from one of the other units near Shea's apartment. Christian wondered what types of people rented here in the dirtier part of town, thinking it must be artists and minimum-wage workers. They all had to be young and fresh, starting their lives. Why else would one claim residence in such a rundown place?

He was trying to slink in unnoticed, but still not appear like some burglar casing the joint. One thing he didn't need was to bump into Gabriel, who might be heading out to locate him. Hell, that would be awkward, he surmised. He'd reach apartment 180 and then lightly knock on her door, not really sure what he'd find or how he was supposed to react if she answered. Inside, he rather hoped that Shea was home...minus Gabe of course. If she answered the door with that fresh-fucked look and her hair all mussed and makeup smeared, well, he wasn't sure how he'd respond. Part of him assumed he'd drop into a fetal position before evaporating into nothing right before her eyes. But the other side, the jealous side of his nature, thought he could still grab her by the weave and the two would fall to the courtyard and wrestle in one helluva bitch-slap festival.

If Shea was there alone, he still figured she'd invite him in; if only to learn additional details about Gabe she might've been unaware of. It occurred to him in that instant that his was a sickness, a drive he couldn't control, and as unreasonable a response as any he'd ever had with another human. He just needed to understand her appeal and how she managed to acquire Gabriel's attentions and get him into bed with her. It was female manipulation he assumed, and it was the only thing his mind allowed him to hold on to. For heaven's sake, she probably didn't even suspect Gabriel was bisexual. All of that reminded him he also had to remember to refer to

Gabe as Chris whenever the two were in the same room. *Why the hell had he introduced himself by the name Chris Rumsfeld in the first place?* It was mystifying, if not a little illuminating.

His stomach was rumbling, and a nervous anxiety gripped his lungs like a vice. Christian knew how insane this moment was, understood how it made him look like some jealous queen confronting an adulterous mistress. And, he supposed, that was as accurate an assessment as one might imagine. But he *had* to do it! The courtyard was empty; the complex's residents were all either at work or holed-up inside. He was grateful no one was there to witness his fall from grace.

Peering around a poorly landscaped hedge, Christian fixed his gaze on Gabriel's door. There wasn't anybody exiting, and the windows were closed, with blinds drawn. What if Gabriel had brought Shea back to his place? What if he was fucking her at that very moment? Gabriel wasn't the only one capable of murder, he thought. If there was a gun in his hands right then, he understood how easy it would be to fire point-blank at his betrayers.

But his anger was rising fitfully and he knew none of this could be true. He knew if the two were facing him he probably wouldn't have the balls to pull the trigger. For one, he didn't want to kill Gabriel, not really, not even in the slightest. And if he were facing Shea with a gun in his shaking hand, he knew he couldn't do it. She may be a bitch trying to appropriate his lover, but she was still innocent. She couldn't have known the real darkness of the man who'd fucked her. So she couldn't be as guilty as he truly needed her to be, he reasoned. He suddenly felt like a pussy next to Church. How the hell was he able to do all those terrible things that he had, he wondered? When he couldn't even hold a gun level at someone he loathed as much as Shea Baltimore.

That was the crux of it. The idea was forming in Christian's brain, the words never really making perfect sense. Shea didn't know who she had trusted. She didn't know the man already had a lover, never even knew him by his real name or that he was a stone-cold killer. He could help her by letting her know all the things she was about to wade into...just as he had, he thought. He could be the bearer of that kind of news, he believed. Because knowledge was power, and he could tell the girl was weak. Shea would walk away as fast as she could. She'd abandon any hopes she had once the truth was revealed. He felt certain of that.

Reaching the door marked 180, he hesitated before knocking. He craned his neck and tried to listen to any sounds coming from her apartment. Half expecting moans and cries of her pleasure through the door, the same ones that once emanated from his bed, he felt the need to pause and consider his actions for a final time. He was close to running away, close to putting the lunacy behind him, but the robin's-egg-blue paint that was peeling from her door made him grab that reality and pull it into focus. It seemed like a tangible moment one could physically hold within one hand. It was some Sartre explanation of existentialistic crap like he'd read in college. And it couldn't have been any more *real*.

He inhaled and held the air as he rapped on Shea's door. He was still fighting whether to run away or hold his ground, but the decision was made for him when the door swung ajar, and Shea stood there with that same fake smile plastered on her bitch face.

"Hey, Shea," Christian said with an equally sham grin. "Sorry to bother you. I missed Chris when I had to step out to make a call...when I came back, he was gone. I was just wondering if he might be over here. I didn't mean to bother you... It will only take a second."

There it was. The lie he'd have to expose later...*but it if it worked, what the hell.*

"No, Max, I came home when you two left. I thought you fellas would be out for a while, but no, I haven't seen Chris. Maybe he went looking for you?"

God, she is dumb, he thought. "Well we decided not to do that thing we were gonna do, and I was thinking about coming over to invite you both out for a coffee. I could use a cup and wanted to get to know my best guy's new girl." The question in his mind was how dumb was she?

"Well, he's not here, but I got coffee. Why don't you come in, and I'll make some, and you can call him from here." Very dumb...he figured.

He smiled as she opened the door, allowing him to enter. It was a dismal place, he thought, but she was an artist, for sure. There were sketches and paintings scattered throughout. Now if she could only paint her door. Gabriel didn't carry a cell; he said he'd never had anyone he wanted to talk to until now. The cunt didn't know that, and it made him happy just knowing he shared an intimacy with Gabriel that she didn't.

"Well, aren't you kind? I can see why Chris likes you so much." With those words, she turned, and her eyes blazed back in a hopeful dreamy gaze.

"He's a sweetheart, that's for sure, even if we hadn't known each other very long." He recognized then that Shea was attempting to sound more sophisticated than she was. Acting like her reticence on a new and budding relationship was a closely guarded secret, which only smart women understood. She was lying, naturally. But he nodded his head in passive acknowledgment rather than to say anything at all. They'd fucked probably no more than once, he figured. At least if he were to believe what Gabe had screamed at him on the street that day. It was all smoke and pretense and the only guarded secrets tying them all together were the ones that he knew...and she did not.

"Chris told me you were a great little artist. I was hoping someday to see your work; having talent is such a gift. I don't possess one myself, but I like knowing others who do."

What the fuck, dude? Aren't you supposed to be the great author in the family? he heard Gabe whisper in his head.

Chris spent those next few minutes guiding Shea through the motions. She was eager to show off some of her illustrations, and he was able to ingratiate himself into her world. Almost like it was nothing more than a new friend who shared a particular commonality, and might one day run in the same social circles. She busied herself by making a fresh pot of coffee, with him on her couch thumbing through her sketchpads and offering the obligatory oohh's and aahh's once he discovered drawings he enjoyed. It was meant to appear casual; normal conversation among surprisingly modern, new acquaintances. But hidden behind the idle chatter Christian was gauging her value, training his eyes into her very soul. Behind every counterfeit compliment and while gushing over all her detailed work, he was steadily scrutinizing her under a solemn gaze.

As she was pulling mugs from her cabinets, Christian was looking around the room with a cast-iron gaze. Had Gabriel fucked her in her living room? Had she offered him the same innocent ploy of coffee, all to get him entangled in her web? He made random remarks about the pad resting on his knees, asking about her preference for portraits over landscapes. It was all nonsense, but he was fixed on learning what he could, just as he was surveying the possible spot where Gabriel betrayed him first.

"Has Chris seen all your work yet?" he asked sheepishly.

"Actually, he hasn't...he hasn't even been over to my place yet," Shea said, coming around the corner and carrying two steaming mugs. She had foolishly alerted him that she didn't know Gabriel as well as she pretended she did. But Christian was thankful that her tiny confession had shown he wasn't sitting in the same apartment where the two had screwed earlier.

"Well, I think he's gonna like it," he lied.

After a few minutes of banal drivel, Christian decided to up the ante—he just didn't know how to go about it. "You know, Shea…" he began after deciding his tact, "I don't know you very well, and I'd like to call us friends, but I thought, being the kind of man I am, that I'd like to share some stuff with you." He leaned in closer, trying to give her the comfort of speaking with a close confidante. "I really want your relationship with Chris to be all that it should be. He deserves the best, and I'm hoping that's you." He smiled over his coffee, eyes bright with compassion and empathy.

"But I don't want to see you hurt, so I thought I'd share something with you *privately*." There was no turning back now, he thought. If he handled it poorly, she would burst into tears and scream at him to leave her apartment, and it would be the ruination for his relationship with Gabriel.

"Chris is not his real name… His name is Gabriel Lee Church. My name is Chris…actually, Christian Maxwell. He leaned back and readied for the explosion. Instead, she only stared back, confused, her pretty features frozen like a china doll. She had questions—first, being his motivation for saying those awful words. He decided not to let the truth lay there flat. He intended on giving some air to the embers; he needed it to become a blazing inferno. He was left with nothing but the road ahead, since there wasn't a place left where he could retreat.

"I met Gabriel Church because I wanted to write a book about his exploits. He is a confessed serial killer…but despite that, we have become friends."

He threw the truth out there like a discarded thing without value. He knew how difficult it was to hear the words because he'd fought that battle himself. He waited with baited anticipation for her reaction, expecting the worse. But Shea sat silent as stone, disbelieving what she was hearing because there was too much to consider.

THE MAN IN her home was lying; she just couldn't understand why. He wanted something from her, but whatever it was she couldn't see it.

She sat too stunned to move, and she grew suddenly afraid. *If he could say these things, he might be dangerous*, she thought. She had opened her door to someone who intended to harm her, but what did that have to do with Chris…or Gabriel, or whoever?

"You no doubt think I'm lying to you...and why wouldn't you? But I can prove all that I'm saying. I'm only telling you to protect you and prevent you from falling too deeply for someone who you can't truly know or trust."

Her hands began to shake, and she tried to set her mug down on the table in front of her, but she only spilled it, sending coffee flying over the table and beginning a steady drip of black liquid onto her hardwood floors. She never moved to grab the mug, never instinctively raced for a towel to clean up. She was still stunned and intensely afraid of making any sudden movements while in this stranger's company.

It was impossible for her to imagine she had slept with a killer, not someone like Chris. She was still knotted to the idea this man was simply lying to her. But his eyes seemed to say otherwise. He seemed kind and imploring, and there was genuineness to him regardless of his assaults on Chris's character.

"I can tell you, Shea, Gabriel has admitted to over forty murders from before we met. He is a dangerous man... There will be nothing good that could come from you staying with him. If you doubt me, you can ask him. I suspect he wouldn't lie to you. But if possible, just leave my name out of it."

CHRISTIAN STOOD UP and breezed into the kitchen. He found a tea towel hanging by the sink and raced back to clean up her mess. *She wasn't all that bad*, he thought. He even felt sorry for her because he understood her confusion. There was a shared cohesion between them. Both had sex with a killer, and both were forced to admit that they were falling head over heels for him. And no matter what strangers or friends might tell you, the truth doesn't always set you free.

His hands were trembling as he wiped up the stained coffee from the table and picked up the cup that had fallen over. Her smile hadn't faded since he allowed his words to slip out. It must have been astonishment she was wrestling with, he insisted. But the mood was building. He could feel it, smoke from a distant volcano on the verge of a violent eruption. It broke fast as he suspected it might, until Shea rose quickly and then headed directly toward the door. Opening it wide was a signal for his departure, her smile replaced with fury and a disreputable expression flashing in its place. What she was feeling in her gut he couldn't even begin to fathom, and though she never actually offered the words outright, it was still clear she'd wanted him gone.

Wondering how much he'd just fucked himself, he stood and walked silently out of her room. Even for someone like him, there weren't ample words he could use to describe what'd just happened. Whatever she was feeling, whatever battles that were raging inside, he knew she'd have to face them alone. And as the door slammed tight behind him he thought he could detect the first inkling of pity for the strange girl he'd only recently met. Odd, he thought, as he walked through the plaza toward his car. He'd hated the woman the first second they met. He saw her as an interloper, someone trying to steal the treasures he cherished most. But now all he could do was wonder about how sad her life was going to turn out, and how eventually she was destined to change with the news. The same as him, he guessed. And suddenly that realization slapped him hard across the face like dark, crashing waves against looming rocks ahead.

IT WOULD COME much later for Shea, as she struggled with everything that Maxwell told her. She finally reached her own conclusions, though, alone in her dank little apartment, just as it should've been. It came only after she flipped on the radio to distract her racing mind. And amazingly, she'd tuned in at just the exact moment, because a reporter was in the middle of airing a story about a recent slaying that had rocked the city to its foundation. It was one of Seattle's more gruesome murders, the reporter promised. She implied it would be a scar across the city's impeccable reputation and taint us for many years to come. She also mentioned the same reputation was in store for one of Washington's most beloved national forests. The news anchor recounted in detail the tragedy of a group of out-of-towners stumbling across the body of local resident, Carl Whiting. She said the remains were discovered just off one of the more popular nature trails twenty miles from downtown. She even offered her opinion on how it might effect the city's tourism, and she did that before acknowledging the names of all the family members the deceased was leaving behind. Listening intently to the broadcast, Shea felt another cold tremble shuddering its way through her core. She thought it was positively morose. Eventually, the program finished, and once the reporter moved on to other topics, Shea found that she was standing once again, though she hadn't remembered ever rising to her feet. Marching to the radio, she clicked it off with a degree of finality in the gesture. She stood there alone, quiet and confused, which was becoming a sensation she was about to learn all too well, she feared.

Chapter Twenty-Nine

GABE WASN'T GOING to apologize for seizing any opportunity of casual sex. *Particularly since it had been so readily thrust upon him*, he thought, amused. That alone could be considered an unnatural act. He couldn't even conceive of having to apologize, since he'd never had a lover, or anyone he had to apologize too. Oh sure there'd been fucks, all casual, and all too brief at that. But there'd never been anyone he considered a fixture in his life. Therefore, by his reasoning, he hadn't ever needed anyone's permission. Nor had he felt a particular need to remain faithful to anyone. In his head it worked both ways too; because he didn't care if Christian got poked by some anonymous fucker in the back of a steamy sex club or not. Live and let live was his motto.

This was a lie naturally. He did care. More than he admitted to himself. But if he rallied behind that argument he'd find himself standing on shaky ground, so he decided that particular conclusion was somewhere just beyond his reach.

Gabriel Church was like most men, driven by ego and a throbbing phallus. He had always lived by the credo of "if it makes your dick hard, it must surely be fair game." With such a broad doctrine, one might have assumed he would have gotten into a vast array of sticky situations. If Chris and he had ever discussed that part of their friendship, then there may not be a problem now. Then how could he imagine his boy-toy as anything less than jealously guarding him for others who wished to slobber on his impressive shaft?

Gabe didn't have answers for all the unasked questions. He'd been approached by men before, as well as a helluva lot of women through his lifetime he thought gratefully. And he thought he was already beyond shame, but acquiescing to another male who then took to their knees in some back alley or abandoned rest stop, well it wasn't exactly ideal. It made him feel weak and inferior. He understood how the body worked - the blue-ball tension aching for a quick orgasm, along with the building pressure taking control when a man was unable to even jack off in his truck for some relief. These were the reasons he didn't judge more harshly than he did, he thought. Yes, there were faces in his past, men he recalled beating and kicking on just so that he'd feel superior. But he'd only done that retaliation he assured himself, and only after their hungered, lascivious ways in which their pupils darted from his crotch then back to face. Each one hoping a man of Church's stature would finally give in and freely accept the blowjob they really wanted to give.

"Okay bubba, you can go for it – just don't get your seed on my boots."

The truth was; he knew Chris was more pissed that he fucked a woman than him being unfaithful with another dude. Women could be territorial and possessive, but in his limited experience, he didn't think men were all that different in the end. Certainly Christian wasn't. As far as sex went, it was the flip side of the coin: each lover had their own special kink they enjoyed. But what made it different now was not the gender but the person. He cared for Christian Maxwell because there was a lot to admire. He was a strong and fearless man he knew, what he lacked as a good person, Chris seemed to have in abundance.

In their time together, he'd found himself wanting to make the younger man happy, and he struggled with trying to show his best sides to him. He had seen that furrowed look overtaking Chris whenever they had long conversations about the murders. It was pity mingled with horror...*How could someone be such a vile human being?* He'd worked harder than one might think to keep that look from creeping across his lover's face.

But Shea had been pivotal; he could see that now. It was too early in their friendship, and Chris felt betrayed by him fucking someone else, specifically a woman. He couldn't pull back time and fix the screwup, so he was left with trying to get someone to forgive him, and that was as alien a notion as those new feelings he was fighting. He felt something he couldn't put his finger on, but he knew he'd never felt it before, not since trading diapers for short pants. He didn't know quite what it was, and sadly, there was no one in his apartment he could trust to explain shame and humility to him.

If there was ever going to be a book about his life, he knew it would have to say how much he'd changed since he stepped into Chris's sphere of influence and how much more sex had been transformed by simply knowing him. He was questioning things about himself in a new light, and he was measuring feelings he'd never known. He didn't know where the hell this road would take him, but he felt sick in his gut that he might have lost

Chris along the way. The fading light was dimming his living room like a dying candle. He was sitting at a rail-back chair that had come with the apartment and was pulling on a bourbon bottle, drinking it straight. He hoped the alcohol would stamp out his festering mood, exchange one bad spirit for another, this one of 80-proof power. But it wasn't helping much.

His head was beginning to feel like it was stuffed with wet sponges. He couldn't focus any train of thought for very long before he could see it being derailed. But still his mind was playing out possible scenarios of how he could win Chris back. He figured it was time to throw his body into bed and worry about it tomorrow.

Before he could stumble into the bedroom, he heard a knock at his door. Instantly, he seized on the hope that it was Chris coming back to repair the damage Gabe had done. He was smiling as he lumbered to the door because he could already see them lying in his bed asleep. It dawned on him that they'd never awoken together while both were on his part of town. He was surprised to find Shea standing there, and his disappointment was painfully illustrated when he craned his neck around both ways to see if Chris had come with her.

"We need to talk," she announced rather matter-of-factly.

Gabe was startled by her arrival, but he tried to regain composure and pretend her appearance was something he expected all along.

"I want to ask your name." She uttered those words with less confidence, allowing them to spew forth like gagging of the vomit in her throat. "You told me it was Chris Rumsfeld but your buddy says its Gabriel...something or another. *So what is it?*"

She was standing at his doorway, immovable arms crossed, and a resentful scowl half-illuminated by a single lamppost in the apartment's courtyard. It took a minute before Gabe could piece together what she was saying; his eyelids were heavy and the bourbon was effectively stretching time out in a foggy cadence. *Had she just called him Gabriel?*

Even tipsy, Gabe was connecting the wires in his mind. When she first started to speak, they may have appeared as delicate cobwebs, but they quickly converted to steel cable when he heard the phrase *your buddy,* mixed so closely with *Gabriel.* His big hand went to his jaw and rubbed at the stubble of his beard. He was momentarily lost, appearing like a man who'd just lurched out of bed and a long sleep. Still, the words she had said had their own powerful impact. He decided to play on his drowsy look of confusion.

"What...?" he said. "Hey, Shea honey...sorry you just got me outta bed. What did you say...you're looking for a buddy named Gabriel?"

He was a big man who could play on a stereotype: that of a muscular mountain of a man who had the brain of warm broccoli. His only hope was to convince her of his dubious skepticism and run with his lie, if only to keep her calm until a better plan could be formed. He stepped aside, rubbing his eyes and wiping his mouth, the consummate actor building his own contrivance. He was hoping Shea's curiosity would pull her inside so he could see what annihilation Chris had done by spilling whatever he had.

"Come on in, baby...tell Daddy what's going on," he mumbled as if rocks had grown in his mouth as he slumbered. His outstretched arm beckoned her, inviting her to come inside and tell him about everything she was ranting about. His look conveyed the simple emotion that there was no harm in sitting together and getting to the bottom of all this. He walked away from the door to show her that he wasn't about to trap her inside, the way one might entreat a stray animal to come in from the cold—*look, no worries, I'm not even close enough to slam the door and ensnare you in my home.*

Shea took the bait, entering his apartment without even a hint of fear. She closed the door behind her before moving to an empty chair to begin her story. Gabriel considered himself expert at reading people. The reticence in her steps, the emotions seeping from her posture, as well as that begging look behind her eyes, were all telling him she needed him to prove it had been a mistake, or a lie...by someone who had a motivation to lie.

She sat rigid in the chair and told him all about her unexpected guest from the afternoon. Her wide-eyed, kittenish look pleaded for him to explain and to satisfy her curiosity. She had finally found someone she could see herself with, and even he could see she'd willingly chose to fall under his spell, rather than risked losing him completely. He dragged a chair from the kitchen and sat across from her, a distance within an arm's length away. He sat emotionless, listening intently as she recalled what Chris disclosed while all the while trying to appear incredulous. *This is news to me* his wide-eyed response seemed to say. His amazement may've been very real because it was disturbing how much Chris had confessed to complete stranger like Shea. *Does he realize what danger he's placed her under?* he thought. *Does he understand all the after-effects from his fucked confession?* He couldn't even begin to speculate how angry Chris must've been with him, because this was a shitload of trust he was willing to break. It was dangerous for all of them, and he doubted he could even comprehend what he'd done by approaching Shea with his story.

Her words spilled out, and Gabe tried to mask his own sick apprehension while simultaneously comforting her.

"I don't understand why Max would say those things to you. I suspected a ways back he was queer...not that that matters to me," Gabe said in a whisper, holding Shea's tiny hand in his for comfort. "But I think when you and I started seeing each other...well honestly, I think he became jealous. Not that I'd ever given him reason to think, you know, that he and I ever had a chance."

It was an effective lie because he could see Shea's eyes beginning to soften and the scowl fading.

"Ya know, I figured it was something like that," she said with an approving nod. "He looked kinda gay to me, too, and he did seem like he liked you an *awful lot.*"

Her head tilted slightly, as if retrieving some memory of how Chris had first appeared to her. Those last words she'd uttered hadn't been completely lost on Gabe, who found some security in knowing his lover had at least thought fondly of him as he was tearing down the walls that once protected them both. There was still plenty of concrete to fill into her story. She had to believe this lie because whether she knew it or not, her life depended on it.

"Now I don't know why he made up all that other crap about murders and shit...maybe he was trying to scare you away from being with me," Gabe said with a pained look. His eyes became as big and transparent as he was. He was propping the story up with slight and unsteady timbers, yet making her believe she'd come willingly to the same conclusions he had. She nodded to indicate it all made sense, that she had been afraid of him after Max left. But before Gabe was sure he was in control, he watched a cataract form over Shea's brown eyes—she was perplexed by a stray thought that refused to dissipate.

"He mentioned a bunch of people were killed, and you know they just found a dead body...it popped up at one of our parks. I remember his name it was Carl something or another...it was supposed to be bad. Now that's a strange coincidence, isn't it?"

"Baby, they find dead bodies all the time. It means nothing. If this Whiting dude was murdered, then it had nothing to do with me...*So Relax.*" He gripped her hand gently to show her all was right in her world, but her mystified expression proved he hadn't convinced her near well enough. She looked up in childlike wonder as her mind found the breadcrumbs she'd fortuitously tossed on the ground earlier to find her way home.

"How did you know his name was Carl Whiting? I didn't mention that. I'd plumb forgotten his last name, at least until you said it." She was nervous in that flash but held some faith it was due to her lack of understanding and no one else's.

"I must have heard the same news report on TV you did," Gabe said with a smile that was intended to comfort, yet failing miserably in the attempt.

SHEA HAD BEEN confident her new lover would clear up any confusion. She'd had her suspicions about this Maxwell. And part of her wanted to prove him wrong. But the smile on her lover's face was chilling. It gave him an evil, painted clown appearance. His grin was now longer beckoning and disarming like it had been before. It was plastered across his face like a jagged scar and his whole personality seemed suddenly changed. It was frightening and suspicious and Shea was fast becoming terrified.

"I'm sure you did," she said, trying to smile back. "It's probably been all over the television and radio..."

SHE WAS STALLING for time, he knew, trying to appear undisturbed and relaxed, when it was clear she wasn't. She would surely make idle conversation before offering some lame excuse to leave, or she might just bolt for the door and run screaming into the courtyard. Tense muscles held fast, and the weight of long seconds hovered anxiously in the air between them. For most people, the fight or flight instinct comes natural, but Shea was a diminutive woman and facing impossible odds. Her faint smile barely camouflaged her fear of the massive thing blocking her path.

Gabe recognized the game was over...and that he had lost. Even if he could change her mind, alleviate her fears, there would always be doubts. He couldn't risk her calling the police or informing her friends about him. As much as he was regretting it in that moment, he knew she had to die.

This didn't surprise him as much as he thought it might, because the second Chris knocked at her door, he'd sealed her fate. He may have been the architect of even greater destruction, since he'd singlehandedly ended their relationship and destroyed a trust Gabe thought was rock solid. Moreover, he'd ensured this tiny, innocent woman would never see another morning light. And he may have even done more damage than that.

As if a starting pistol had exploded to indicate the onset of a race, Shea took that second to leap from her chair and run for the door. But she was never intended to be a strong match against Gabe, who extended his arm like the rapid strike of a rattler and grabbed her by the neck, complexly encompassing her throat with a single palm. Her scream was instantly stifled, and Gabe rose from his chair and pulled the woman up with him, her feet dangling two feet above the hardwood.

Shea's hands went out instinctively to break his grip, and even as she struggled, she knew the futility. The big man's expression had never altered. His smile may have faded slightly, but something behind those pale-gray eyes still reeked of pending violence. Tears began streaming down her porcelain cheeks as she hung suspended in his grip, knowing she was breathing in her last bits of oxygen. Images flashed in her mind of the two of them in bed and his gentle embrace after they'd consummated their love. This couldn't be the same figure before her, she thought. But then she remembered the reporter from the radio and visions sparked in her head of a dead body lying in the weeds, one she had never seen but now imagined anyway. She begged silently through her expressions, all while trying to inhale enough air to offer her some strength and a fighting chance, however bare, for her survival. She whimpered through the convulsing sounds of her own tears, trying to convey something to her attacker that might save her life...but he only stood there holding her tightly above the polished wood floor.

In his hands, she felt like a broken-winged bird he'd picked off the ground. One twist of his wrist and he could snap her as simply as a twig. He didn't enjoy having to hurt her, but he did enjoy the power of life and death he possessed over another living person. She was never supposed to die. Without that white-lighter light to guide him, she had only become an accident. Her death was too much like his very first homicide. It, too, was random and for reasons other than his godly mission. That first dead soul and now Shea—neither had been an intentional part of his story. He was killing her because he had to, if only to protect him as well as Chris. That made Shea just as important as the others he'd murdered, just in a totally different way.

His lover was to blame for this death, not him. It had been some jealous response to an insignificant, meaningless event. One he had no control over now. He could have made Shea understand they had no future together. Eventually she'd have moved on, and although it might have created some awkwardness between them whenever he bumped into her in the courtyard holding a bag of groceries or being accompanied by her new beau, she'd still be alive. Chris had upended this chance for them to be together, as much as her chance to meet her next beau. Any sadness he felt for her now was quickly becoming overshadowed by the lack of blame and responsibility for Chris's actions.

With her fingers clutching wildly at Gabe's hands, Shea's face began to change. A dark-blue shade appeared from the lack of air in her lungs. It crept upward from her bruised neck and bubbled to the top of her head while spittle began to form in the corners of her mouth. She'd fought hard, harder than her tiny body would allow, but still she was deteriorating. Without sufficient oxygen or the strength to break his grip, she was going to lose, that much she knew. All she could do was watch while the screaming in her head continued, and the blackness finally took her from being trapped inside her own failing body.

She was a weightless thing, one he could hold nearly all day with her just suspended there. But it wouldn't take that long. She struggled until there was nothing she could do but wither away. When the light behind her eyes faded, she took everything she had with her: any dreams of becoming a great artist, the pain of losing her mother, and that daughterly devotion to a father who had botched it so poorly. Gabe held her for a minute longer to ensure she was gone, before picking her up gently and cradling her body in his arms. He then moved her to the couch and laid her lovingly, faceup, and gingerly closed the lids of both her eyes. He couldn't have her staring up at him and seeing him so sad.

Chapter Thirty

BACK INSIDE THE protection of his condo, Christian should have felt safe and isolated, but it was impossible not to have his conversation with Shea playing over and over in a loop. Sitting on his sofa, his knees pulled up, arms wrapping them like a vice, he looked like a kid who'd just realized he'd done something bad and was surely gonna pay the price when the folks got home. He didn't even want to consider that come-to-Jesus meeting if Gabriel found out what he'd done.

He couldn't believe he'd even built up the nerve to enter Shea's place and tell her all those horrible things. It was out of character, or rather it should've been. He kept telling himself that he'd had his reasons and his little confession wouldn't amount to much and that Shea would simply drop her attraction for Gabriel like a hot-handled skillet. She would just refuse to believe the words he'd told her...quite possibly think the man in her apartment had been insane, envious, bent beyond reason. Maybe she'd decide Gabriel wasn't worth the effort because of the maddening lies and crap that had been thrown her way; a guilty-by-association whisper making her see that he wasn't the man for her.

Either way, he'd fucked up royally. As strange as it sounded in his head, it had never dawned on him that Shea might go to the authorities with what she knew, even though she didn't really know anything. It had never entered his mind that she'd confront Gabriel. He'd just refused to allow himself to see any resulting wreckage he might leave behind, like the flotsam and ugly litter now lining the once beautiful shorelines of the Puget Sound.

But he was seeing it now...as late as that was in the coming. He was feeling that oppressive cloud blowing in and knew it brought thunder. It frightened him to think what Gabriel might do if he ever discovered Christian had tried to warn off his one-time affair. Two things he'd learned about Gabriel were that he was methodic and cautious. Whatever he might've thought about motivations, he was still a murderer, one who was smart enough to still be walking free. If he suspected that Christian had confessed any of this to Shea, it would mean they would both be in danger. He didn't fully understand to what lengths he'd go in an effort to protect himself, but he knew he was capable of killing them both—if only to save his own skin.

This whole thing is unsettling. He felt as if he'd been having a long nervous breakdown that began the day Church first sat down with him at the Cherry Street Grinder. Nothing seemed real in the events since that day. He envisioned himself sitting in an interrogation room again, trying to explain to straight detectives how he'd become attracted to Gabriel Church, and how he'd fallen so deeply that he lost all his rationality when he hadn't run crying to the cops with a sordid story, one even he had trouble believing.

It was becoming more and more evident to him, that there would be no Panama, no San Blas Islands getaway, and no chance that he and Gabriel would remain free together just as their dark past slipped beneath the waves and became gratefully, ultimately forgotten. They couldn't even go forty-eight hours without a major fight these days, and he knew another furious argument was creeping just over the horizon-line. He knew what it was - and feared how'd end, but like a threatening head-on collision you couldn't avoid; he could only tighten his grip on the wheel and steer into the skid. He couldn't help but feel the futility of it all and remember an awful incident from college. A friend he met in class, someone he'd liked a great deal. She was a lovely young thing, though neither of them attempted to date. But they were close. If he ran across her today in the street, he could easily see her as more a fag-hag accessory that was destined to remain at his side. But back then, before his eyes had been forced open, he only saw her as someone he might eventually want to date romantically.

She was an overly dramatic girl from an established family upstate. But she preferred to live her life like some outdated hippy. She hung around other boys who drank too much and smoked too much grass, maybe even danced naked through the poppy fields at some point in their history. The kind of frat boys you could tell had spent too many nights around a makeshift bonfire with their car doors ajar and southern rock music blasting from the speakers. Everyone around Catherine partied too much, and they were all just careless rebels living the unencumbered lives from being the kids of wealthy parents.

Cat was the kind of girl whose eyes were always fixed and dilated all the time, and he firmly believed it was just better to keep her safe until whatever drug she was flying on finally subsided. Theirs was an odd relationship he knew, but Chris genuinely like her. Even despite all the hell she'd put him through in college when he should've been studying.

He remembered one night when Cat rang him around two in the morning. She said she just wanted to talk, but then informed him she'd just taken a half-bottle of Nembutals and had decided to hang with him on the phone. At least until it was all *over*. Frightened and alarmed he recalled jumping out of bed and becoming instantly angry at himself when he wasn't able to get his legs through his jeans fast enough or find a loose pullover he grabbed on his way out the door.

With his phone seemingly surgically implanted to his skull, he was beginning to hear how her words were starting to slur. She was rambling about the futility of life or some bullshit like that, but all he was doing was hoping that his voice wasn't going to end up being the last one she ever heard. Racing across the quad, he immediately burst into her room. He had to wrestle the phone from her hand as she fought the delirium and uttered nonsensical banter. He immediately phoned 911.

He watched the ambulance pull away from a crowd of students drawn outside their dorms from all the commotion. He was transfixed by the blue lights and waling sirens as they faded into the distance. Catherine did survive her feeble attempt and was even back at school within a week or so. But she couldn't forgive Christian for interfering with her plans, that of some glorious exit strategy that would've been the talk of everyone on the campus. They grew apart after that. Even though he made numerous efforts to reconnect, she never again felt the need to allow him back into her good graces.

Before the semester was over, he heard that Cat dropped out of school. He hadn't been around to see her leave or watch whoever picked her up as they disappeared out the gate. Mutual friends assured him that her parents had checked her into some posh rehab facility way up north and t suggested she was probably in good hands and might get help. But by the following year, Chris ran into someone they knew, and he informed him that Cat had actually committed suicide a few months earlier. *"It's all too sad,"* the young man said, shaking his head. But the reality hit hard in that second he first learned of Catherine's passing. He saw clearly in that moment that she hadn't been asking for his assistance to stay alive when she'd called him that morning, she was trying to die and she even more importantly she was saying she wanted his company for those final moments of her wasted existence. Whatever futility she suffered through became an invader into his life after that. Knowing in his heart that he was never meant to be the person who saved her because she was the never the type of person God intended on saving.

He felt that same wash of empty needlessness he felt then as he was sitting on the couch. It seemed many things were predestined and weren't meant to be controlled. Church had been a killer long before they met. And Chris never really had an opportunity of altering that. Knowing him now as he did, he understood how he couldn't control the events that were supposed to be Church's story. Anything less would be an ineffectual, fat-fingered approach if he were to even try.

The rest of the day was spent in jittery anticipation of the fall of that other shoe. Christian moved through his apartment like a ghost caught between planes. His evening wasn't any better. He wrestled inside sweaty sheets half awake, expecting either a knock at his door or for it to be kicked in, and an angry Gabriel to be standing there in the shadows. The lack of contact made him fear that Gabriel had just left town, possibly after finding out Shea had been visited that awful day of their fight.

He bounced from trepidation to anguish, wanting nothing more than to apologize and force his lover to see all the things he'd done never really had a good enough reason. But he was also afraid. He was scared of what Church was capable of and couldn't help wondering if that tiny artist had made matters worse for each of them as individuals. He thought himself capable of filling a novel with all the things he couldn't explain away. He didn't know about Carl Whiting, and he could never have guessed that Church was still committing heinous acts even after their world's first collided. Nor did he know that young Shea Baltimore was presently lying lifeless on her couch or staring frozen at the ceiling with blue lips slightly parted in that scream she was never able to release.

Christian had done the irreversible, the sin that would fell all his angels to earth. It would all come crashing down because of his freaked-out jealousy, and the weight of that was crushing him like heavy stones. It seemed strange to think about other times with Gabriel: being in a club while the multitude of quarter-sized lights raced along the walls from a suspended disco ball, those long walks along Pioneer Square, and the joy of waking up in glorious ecstasy because he was waking with such a beautiful creature. The dichotomy of all the different sides of Gabriel was something he was just barely learning to comprehend, and now he was afraid he was going to witness another personality emerge, and that worried him.

None of those emotions crowned quite as high as they did much later when Christian was lounging in a chair and drinking a glass of wine, trying to calm himself. He heard a knock at his front door, and his heart seized. The vital organ paused its beating just long enough to feel as if it were swelling to five times its size because suddenly he'd forgotten the ability to breathe. Sitting in silence, he tried to gage the intensity of the knocking sound, as if that alone might tell him who to expect.

His hands were trembling as he put his glass on the table, feeling it was all about to be over. He knew it was Gabriel, so few people actually visited him since the two between intertwined. Besides his friendly neighbor, Ruth, was conveniently of out of town at the moment. The rap at the door was strong. It told him Gabe hadn't left Seattle after all. But it couldn't tell him what the man's mood would be, what he knew, and what he didn't. He was shaking when he rose and crossed the floor. Sliding back the lock and allowing the hallway light to force its way in he saw Gabriel standing there. He had an unusual look and a pained appearance in those goddamned lovely eyes.

Neither spoke a word at first, simply stared at each other as both were trying to distinguish whether it had been a mistake to be standing face-to-face. The small fragment of time became destroyed as Gabriel eventually shoved past him and headed inside.

"*We need to talk, baby,*" he said. Christian stood there quietly, still holding the door ajar with a visibly blank and confused expression. His tone seemed calm, but his final word was edgy and uncertain. They hinted with unseen malice. *In for a penny, in for a pound*, thought Christian, as he closed the door on the tail of Gabriel's shadow.

"I know...but you first."

"I had a visitor yesterday. She was really informative..."

Gabriel's timbre, fortunately, remained steady, but a guarded Christian took a step farther away as if prepping for what he figured was a stalwart attack by an angry man. It seemed imminent, and who could blame Gabriel when it finally came? This was his mistake; he had screwed up, and the images of Gabriel and Shea together in bed were forever shoved back into the nether regions. They no longer existed in the face of his criminal confession.

Nervously, he began what he hoped was a road to recovery. "I know what I've done, and I can't begin to apologize. But it's important that you understand what I was feeling when I found out about you and the girl—"

Cutting him off in mid-explanation, Gabriel turned to face him, his countenance the same as cold, polished marble. He didn't seem capable of screaming or showing any anger in that instant. This should have been something which calmed Christian. But he knew the man well enough to understand that his measured responses weren't always representative of anything good about to happen.

"I don't want to talk about your conversation with Shea. I equally don't want to discuss your reasoning behind being the *little bitch* you decided to be. I want to tell you about ramifications and the seeds we sow with our own frustrations."

Christian heard the laced poison in his words, and he backed away unconsciously, just as Gabriel advanced on him, but not to grab him by the collar and throw him around as Christian expected. He was moving forward to make a solid point.

Standing a couple of feet apart allowed him to see Gabriel's three-day growth of beard and the veins in his neck pulsating with every beat from that irregular heart of his. Suddenly he decided to take whatever punishment Gabriel wanted to give, and he planted his feet firmly on his mahogany-stained hardwood floors and expanded his chest, as if he were poised bravely in front of a firing squad. But instead of his expected assault, Gabriel turned away and moved into the living room and the intensity fizzled into nothingness.

"You cost Shea her life, you know."

Even though he'd heard the words, he hadn't understood them. Christian felt that empty void swirling around as he was trying to grasp Gabriel's meaning.

"Shea was never supposed to die. She wasn't one of the ones sent to me for cleansing. You did that, not me."

Christian listened as Gabriel's words spilled into an unsympathetic tone and his knees began to buckle. He was forced to reach for the nearest empty chair for support. *Did he actually hear the words or just think he had?*

He felt disbelief washing over him. Every lie that Shea wanted to hear and maybe everything he fully expected from that first day at the Cherry Street Café. That sense of when everything begins to wobble into abstract shapes and that of falling without anything to hold onto. He was cognizant enough to comprehend that he was about to pass out. He began reaching for any attainable tether he could to yank him back onto his feet. Shaking his head to shove the fog from completely circling his brain, he found that he could stand, he could endure, no matter how difficult the words he'd heard. He stared at Church in astonishment, the man just admitted to killing another innocent person - and this was someone Chris knew personally.

"I had to do it." Gabe began. "You'd told her too much. I suppose you know I have to get the hell outta here now, try to make it as far from the city as possible. But this boy stands at your feet, not mine."

Christian couldn't believe his ears. Hearing Gabriel shift the blame from whatever he'd done to Shea and back onto him was another thing he wasn't able to hold in his head.

"You're saying *I killed her?*" Christian screeched like the sound of fingernails on a chalkboard.

It took only a minute, but when Gabriel finally raised his head, he said, "No...I'm not saying that, not exactly. I'm saying it was because of you! I was never gonna make it out alive. I think I've known that from the beginning. But I couldn't take you down in the process. *I just couldn't.*"

He could see Christian's vacant look and saw that he didn't understand. "If she'd gone to the police, you'd be involved...but now I can just drop outta sight. She'll be found soon enough...and no one ever saw us there together I'm sure. So no one needs to even know about you, or knowing me through Shea. They'll pin it on the stranger who rented a unit under an assumed name, as long as it isn't you."

The clarity of his words was coming into focus. Church had done this horrible act, but he'd done it out of some twisted notion of love. In his own way, he was trying to save Christian from any more damage from his individual destruction or the demons that ruled him.

"You can't say it was for my own good that you murdered Shea!" Christian said loudly as he bravely rose to come within inches of Gabe's body. He wanted to jab his finger into the man's chest to emphasize his anger, but he stopped himself. "There were other choices, you know. The girl was innocent, and she simply didn't know anything...not really. We both could've just left the city together."

"STOP THINKING THIS romance would've ever have had a happy ending," Gabe said, trying to rise his objectivity to place he knew he didn't really believe.

In his mind, as in Chris's, there had always been that smallest bit of hope between them. That insane fantasy of them being able to run away together and the killings to stop and Gabe able to resist the white-light drive he'd always known. It would be nothing more than a bad memory they would lie to themselves...almost as much as they lied to one another. They'd be able to live out whatever days were left, but at least they'd be together. It was something both of wanted more desperately than either could've imagined.

Maybe it had never been more than a hopeful aspiration, but in retrospect, it was written in a book long before the two ever met. The only thing that bothered him more than the harsh reality of everything he learned was wondering now whether he'd been absolutely wrong from the very beginning.

Gabriel Lee Church was a man the thought he understood, even against every fiber that reminded him otherwise. He glimpsed into the darkness and found the face of someone special looking back and he knew his life was never going to be the same again. Maybe if Chris had come along sooner, or maybe if the killing in Texas hadn't occurred...well those were questions without answers and redundant in the face of all he knew then.

Staring out the pane of Chris's high rise window Gabe noticed a beam of light stretching its way across the floor. It was a reminder how late it was getting. Out of all the murders he'd committed over the years he'd only felt remorse by a single one. And it was because of that terrible crime that he needed to leave the city and abandon the only person he thought he'd ever truly love.

AND AS IF his pained expression was revealing everything all at once, Christian stepped closer to Gabe and allowed his guard and his anger to completely fall away. Putting Shea's murder aside, and forgetting all those terrible missteps performed by a sick and deranged man with fucked dogmas he would never fully comprehend, he realized that he had only just enough strength to spin the man around and seize him inside one long lasting final embrace.

Even before he realized it, he felt the dampness against his cheeks. He was crying now, burrowing his head deeply into Church's shoulder. From all those weird and unknowable weeks he'd spent with a serial killer he knew it was finally reaching that boiling point; that undefined place where the pressure and the elevation change every molecule and eventually deliver up something new and unexpected.

"I'm going with you," he said flatly. "But only if you swear it's over with." His words were barely audible, and the wet stain on Gabriel's chest couldn't break the pictures he still had clinging in his head.

"NOT TODAY BOY...this cowboy rides alone," Gabe said quietly, his arms circling his lover for what he knew would be the last time.

Epilogue

THE SEATTLE STREETS felt much lonelier than they had when Gabriel was still around, he mused. But he refused to sit idle in his apartment for even one more day longer. Walking seemed to help, and he found himself strolling around the city streets, regardless of the weather or lateness of the hour. He'd make his way around the University district, and before he knew it, he was staring into the waters of the Puget Sound. Occasionally he'd toss rocks into the waves and finally allow himself to feel all those tiny emotions he'd fought so hard to push aside.

Many times he'd find himself walking around the Elliott Bay Seawall, remembering that time when he'd been there with Church. He was rising from a fog every day, standing on the edges of his own life, still uncertain how he'd made it through so far.

The spray of saltwater off the bay felt reassuring, more now than in those first weeks after his lover disappeared. He knew he'd survive though, he was even considering trying out a new club that had just opened downtown. Maybe he'd risk taking someone home soon, someone to replace that hole what Gabe had effectively created. But in the weeks that followed, he was only lying to himself again and the club became just another place he never visited in the end.

He considered going back to work, but he wasn't sure what he'd even tell his superiors. Since all that time he'd requested to undertake that great American novel had in actually bore no literary success. He didn't relish the idea of having to admit that he had failed. He also thought about sitting down and writing something new, maybe fiction this time. But every time he opened his laptop and stared blindly at the monitor he saw there were no stories left inside to tell. He was more alone than ever now and he possessed a dark secret that he couldn't share and a book he'd never be able to write anyway. The only satisfaction he found; was in knowing his tale was his and his alone. That it would never sit on a dusty shelf somewhere and beg to be disregarded. His friends and family could never know the whole truth, there were never going to be words penned to paper, and that would just have to sufficient enough, he thought. He spent too many days remembering the man and the events which were still currently shaping him. He missed Gabriel deeply but knew he had made the right call by not insisting that they leave together.

Shea was discovered quickly in his apartment, just as Church predicted. Convenient for him since he'd already left town and they never actually had more than the alias he used to rent the rooms. At least she received a decent burial and her story could be concluded. Chris was sure there were warrants for Gabe's arrest, but only in the false names he'd given. Even now Church was racing one step ahead of authorities. He never really worried about a knock on his door by the police. His personal involvement was just as Gabe hoped, was limited after all. Even if the FBI or Washington Police made some kind of connection, he didn't care. He was empty enough, drained to the point of exhaustion, so there was little they could do that he wasn't already doing to himself anyway.

Christian knew it'd be years before the images would fade. But that never stopped him from wondering time to time. He hoped Church was thinking about him as much as he was and eventually he found some peace in something Gabe had said once,

"If you wanna see God laugh—just mention to him about all the plans you have for just how things are going to end up for you."

About the Author

Rodd lives in Dallas, TX and can be reached through his web presence at RoddClark.com.

If you were to ask him, he would say that enjoys M/M mysteries and suspenseful romance mixed in with his thrills. "Give me a good ole spy novel or fantasy to keep me up at night," he might add. When he isn't writing or reading, he claims to be the zookeeper of his menagerie of critters who call his place home. From cats to dogs to friendly raccoons, he enjoys them all.

With a dark and distinctively disturbing voice, his characters are flawed but intriguing; such as the main character of Gabriel Church in his romantic fiction series The Gabriel Church Tales, which begins with *Rubble and the Wreckage.*

Facebook: www.facebook.com/rodd.clark.96

Twitter: @RoddClark

Pinterest: www.pinterest.com/roddclark96

Also Available from NineStar Press

Connect with NineStar Press

www.ninestarpress.com

www.facebook.com/ninestarpress

www.facebook.com/groups/NineStarNiche

www.twitter.com/ninestarpress

www.tumblr.com/blog/ninestarpress

To my fiercest supporters and very first fans,
My Parents.
Without you, this would never have been possible.